Occasional Views, Volume 1

Other Books by the Author

Occasional Views, Volume 1

"More About Writing" and Other Essays

Samuel R. Delany

WESLEYAN UNIVERSITY PRESS
Middletown, Connecticut

Wesleyan University Press
Middletown CT 06459
www.wesleyan.edu/wespress
© 2021 Samuel R. Delany

Manufactured in the United States of America
Typeset in Monotype Baskerville, Mona Lisa Recut,
and Futura Now by Passumpsic Publishing

For acknowledgments of previously published essays, see page 379

Library of Congress Cataloging-in-Publication Data
NAMES: Delany, Samuel R., author.
TITLE: Occasional views / Samuel R. Delany.
DESCRIPTION: Middletown, Connecticut: Wesleyan University
    Press, [2021]– | v. 1: "More about writing" and other
    essays— | Includes bibliographical references and
    index. | Summary: "Gathers the writings of award-
    winning author Samuel R. Delany on a wide array of topics
    related to writing, science fiction, race, sexuality, literature,
    and literary theory"—Provided by publisher.
IDENTIFIERS: LCCN 2021003527 (print) | LCCN 2021003528
    (ebook) | ISBN 9780819579744 (cloth) | ISBN 9780819579751
    (trade paperback) | ISBN 9780819579768 (ebook)
SUBJECTS: LCGFT: Essays.
CLASSIFICATION: LCC PS3554.E437 O33 2021 (print) |
    LCC PS3554.E437 (ebook) | DDC 814/.54—dc23
LC record available at https://lccn.loc.gov/2021003527
LC ebook record available at https://lccn.loc.gov/2021003528

5 4 3 2 1

For
Iva Hacker-Delany
Mischa Adams &
Peggy Delany

Contents

Occasional Views, Volume 1

1

More About Writing

The Life of/and Writing

"The Life of Writing" is a phrase we associate with the eighteenth-century writer, Dr. Samuel Johnson—responsible for compiling the first comprehensive English language dictionary. He also wrote a fantasy, *Rasselas*, that now and again appears from various contemporary paperback houses attempting to add some tone and history to their science fiction and fantasy lines.

When Dr. Johnson used the phrase, the life of writing, it meant, of course, the literary life—and referred to the kinds of things an eighteenth-century writer might be occupied with in the course of an eighteenth-century day, from sharpening goose quills, grinding ink stones, and debating in coffee shops what historical material would or would not make successful subject matter for a profitable poetic tragedy, to negotiating with booksellers (what the eighteenth century had in place of publishers) as to what percentage of the costs you might put up toward printing your most recent profitable poetic tragedy—as all publishing at the time was more or less vanity publishing—though most of your time, money, and energy might be reserved for putting out polemical pamphlets on any subject from the foppery and decadence of women, the nobility, or the young to meditations on taxes, fashions, or God, for which opinions you risked fame, notoriety, or (sometimes) jail.

The life of writing has changed drastically in three hundred years.

But, as the phrase fades into the memory of literary antiquarians, it passes through a strangely luminous moment, when, as its historical meaning verges on the obsolete, it opens up to a host of other possible meanings, comic, surreal, suggestive: in 1970, the poet Judith Johnson Sherwin published a book of experimental short stories with Atheneum, *The Life of Riot*, the title of which clearly takes its resonances from Johnson. And it does not take much for us to read in the original phrase, The Life of Writing, the notion of what, in any piece of writing, makes that writing lively: the life (or liveliness) in writing. And if we look at "life," not as referring to general liveliness, but to the range of everyday life, then, with only a little catachresis, we can read "the life of writing" as meaning the way everyday life is reflected in writing. Thus, as we multiply and survey the possible—if sometimes improbable—interpretations we can unpack from this most unassuming phrase, finally we have to admit that, buried in its text is pretty much every possible relationship that we can conceive as existing between "writing" and "life"—that is, "writing" in any of its meanings and "life" in any of its.

Sometimes I try to suggest that range and multiplicity by taking that weakest of English prepositions, "of," and placing behind it a slash, that, like a slant mirror, reveals that what can be hidden in that loose and lax preposition is the strongest of English conjunctions, "and." Indeed, the "of" and the "and," on either side of that virgule, mirror each other and, I hope, problematize our original phrase out into an infinitude of possible relations between world and text, word and world, action and articulation:

"The life of/and writing . . ."

What are some of these relations?

Teaching at various writers' workshops for more than forty years now, certainly I can remember when some of the complexities of this relational complex were first brought home to me.

A young writer of seventeen or so had handed in a story that struck me at once as both extremely talented and deeply flawed.

In the course of the tale, a young man (of seventeen or so) goes walking along a beach one evening. He comes across a group of some dozen bikers and, there, laughing and being hugged now by one, now by another is . . . his girlfriend!

The young man pauses a moment, then calls to her to come to him. She looks at him scornfully—and laughs. Angrily, he marches in and tries to pull her away, whereupon the bikers proceed to beat the living daylights out of him and, leaving him bloody on the sand, get on their motorcycles. With the young woman on the back of the leader's, they ride away. Painfully, the young man goes to the water, washes his face in the sea, and limps off.

The successes of the story were in the physical evocation of surf and sand and evening light. Its failure was in—how shall I say?—a certain emotional extremity. An intelligent, slender young man of seventeen—with glasses —usually does not throw himself into such an obviously suicidal fray quite so easily, quite so unthinkingly, even under the goad of love. It just wasn't believable.

When, in conference, I pointed this out to young Shakespeare, he pulled his manuscript sharply back into his lap, assuming a position of overtly Freudian self-protection, and declared: "This story is true. And if it's unbelievable, that's just because—I guess—sometimes reality is unbelievable. It all happened. And I put it down just like it was."

What could I say?

As is so often the case, I didn't think of anything to say until three hours after the conference was over. Nor did I get a chance to say it until the young man handed in a second story. This one was an SF tale—and was just as talented, though it still had some problems.

"But I want to go back," I said, "and talk about your first story for a minute. Maybe we can throw a little light on the believability problem in general—that was the one about you, and your girlfriend, and the bikers on the beach. Now this, you say, is your account of something that really happened. I want you to think back to the original incident. And tell me *exactly* what occurred."

"Sure," said unsuspecting Sophocles. "It was on the beach—it's on part of Lake Michigan. I was there last summer. And it was evening. I was walking along, when I saw my girlfriend. She was down the sand, with some guys." Here he fell silent.

So I asked: "How many of them were there?"

After another few moments, he said: "Two."

"Bikers," I said. "With motorcycles."

"Bicycles," he said. Then, after another moment: "One of them was wheeling a bicycle."

"Two," I said, "with one bicycle. What did you do?"

"I didn't do . . . anything. I just stood there."

"Was she laughing and having a good time?"

"She had her back to me—so I couldn't tell. The three of them, they were just walking on the beach . . . like I was."

"What was she wearing?"

"White shorts, I think. And a bathing suit under it. Blue, maybe green. Well, I guess she wasn't *really* my girlfriend—I'd talked to her a couple of times in town . . . so maybe she was just my friend." Then he said: "But I'd *thought* about her being my girlfriend! A lot! And one of the guys had a beer can—or maybe it was a soda. I wasn't too close."

"Did she see you? Did you say anything?"

"No," he said. "I don't think she did. I just turned around, after a couple of seconds, and went the other way. . . . But then I got real upset—like I couldn't breathe, or I was going to cry or something. So I went down and washed my face in the water." After another few moments, he said: "But you see, it's based on the truth, on something that really happened—*basically* it happened."

"Basically," I said, "the twelve bikers, this supposed girlfriend of yours, her scorn, the fight, and her laughter, are a lie. They're a lie you've told yourself to make you feel better about having gotten upset. Now there's nothing wrong with telling lies in fiction. That's what it's all about. I just want to point out that in this case you happened to tell one I didn't believe. And it's often when we're lying to ourselves that we tell the most unbelievable whoppers. You have to watch out for that in your writing. It's possible—though I can't guarantee it—you might have had a better story if you'd told about what you really saw, what the young woman's relationship to you really was, and how that got you upset when you saw her with two of her friends—then how you went and washed your face."

"I thought," he said, "I did . . ."

But of course the language, which is far more truthful than we are, often reflects more things about those of us who use it than we are prepared to show: sometimes it reflects whether we are lying or speaking the truth; or (which I believe is more important than either, because it has not an easy, but a critical, relation to both) whether we are working to put together a rich and rewarding tale.

The notion of language as a mirror has a venerable history in the life of writing (if we may unpack still another meaning from our parent phrase: the life of writing as the history of writing). One of its most famous moments is from Shakespeare's *Hamlet,* Act III, scene ii, when Hamlet exhorts the players who will be speaking his lines, "to hold, as 'twere, the mirror up to nature, to show virtue her own feature, scorn her own image, and the body of the time his form and pressure." It's worth noting here that the Elizabethan audience would have probably heard the word "pressure," in this context, specifically as a printing term, meaning (here) imprint or printed illustration—that is, the term, through typography, comes from the life of writing. Perhaps the second best-known moment is when the French novelist Stendhal borrowed Shakespeare's image and gave back his own reflection on it, his own interpretation of it, when in the 1830s he declared that the task of the novelist was to hold the mirror up to nature as one traveled along the road of life.

Of course, what is missing in both of these moments for us today is that mirrors in the 1830s, and even more so in Shakespeare's day, tended to distort.

What about the mirror's—or the mirroring virgule's—slant?

What kind of distortion is invariably involved with, and inescapable in, the artistic process of reflection, is built in to the very notion of reflection? For even while we sit, giving out our writerly advice to young Balzac to cleave more closely to truth in the tale of his epiphany on the beach, no writer who has examined her or his own process can fail to see something of her- or himself in that very young and very talented liar.

So that even for me to recount the tale of our Clarion conference as I did above is finally to tell a lie to myself—a lie that says, even for the moment of the tale, that in my greater knowledge I am somehow distinct and different from him; I am his opposite, as left is the opposite of right, as a reflection in a mirror is the opposite and the inversion of what is there in life. For it is precisely in the words with which I suggest this that I am obscuring the troubling truth that, again and again and again (indeed all too often), I am, in too many ways, his double.

Certainly one of the finest meditations on the relation of art to life in the last century is the dense and articulate prose-poem, "Caliban to the Audience," the centerpiece of W. H. Auden's *The Sea and the Mirror*, a 1944 poetic meditation on Shakespeare's *Tempest*. In that prose-poem Auden returns, for a moment, to Shakespeare's mirror, Shakespeare's pressure (that is, Shakespeare's illustration), having his audience through the voice of Caliban address the ghost of Shakespeare:

> You yourself, we seem to remember, have spoken of the conjured spectacle as "a mirror held up to nature," a phrase misleading in its aphoristic sweep but indicative at least of one aspect of the relation between the real and the imagined, their mutual reversal of value, for isn't the essential artistic strangeness to which the sinisterly biased image would point just this: that on the far side of the mirror the general will to compose, to form at all costs a felicitous pattern, becomes the necessary cause of any particular effort to live or act or love or triumph or vary, instead of being as, in so far as it emerged at all, it is on this side, their accidental effect?

In the world of art, because pattern and plot, economy and purpose are the method, all incidents are selected (or rejected) with some attention to pattern, order, meaning.

In the world of reality, when pattern or its handmaid insight emerges at all, it is the accident, an excess, mere happenstance.

Thus, because the context of the two worlds is entirely different, the meaning of every incident in an art work is subtly shifted, so that—on the level where it counts—there is finally no possibility of congruence between the meaning of an incident in an art work and its meaning in the world. Art is rich and strange, and we shouldn't even try to deceive ourselves by searching in it for the familiar, much less the truth; in art, truth (in the sense of truth-to-life) is the happenstance, the excess, the accident.

For isn't the world of art, Auden tells us in that same prose poem, "a world of freedom without anxiety, of sincerity without loss of vigor, feeling that loosens rather that ties the tongue"?

After all, the world of art is the world in which a young man calls to his beloved, fights for her (or his own) honor against ludicrous odds, and—chastened by defeat and disillusion—looks out over the water, tears and the sea indistinguishable on his cheeks, with new and ineffable knowledge.

The world of art is—certainly—the world of this essay, where I can dispense writerly advice to young Kafka with all the eloquence of hindsight, but without stuttering, without having to begin half my sentences over, without having to scratch my ear violently in the middle, and without being so concerned with what young Hemingway before me is feeling—about me, about his story—that I lose my train of thought three times and only manage to mumble something to which, out of kindness or terror, he nods, blurts, "Yeah—I see," and hurries off, in a welter of misunderstanding, to nurse his fear and incomprehension at my fear and incomprehension.

Yet, somehow, sometimes, both in life and in writing, ideas emerge that resonate with eloquence and force, even when they are ideas about hesitation, disillusion, and failure.

Picasso said: "Art is the lie that makes the truth bearable." Some years later, science fiction and fantasy writer Ray Bradbury put much the same point into a poem: "We have our arts so we won't die of truth."

Me, I've always found this a shocking idea. Possibly because I'm a writer, and because writing takes place in time, I've preferred to see art as a self-corrective process, a process of self-vigilance, in which we go back and rethink the tale again, even as we tell it. I sometimes think that process, alone as it is reflected in language, is what constitutes the "truth effect" of language. That, along with beauty, is its greatest worth.

Just after the start of the Great War, two very different thinkers in two very different situations came up with remarkably similar statements about the relation of art to life. In his first book, *The Theory of the Novel*, the twenty-five-year-old Hungarian critic Georg Lukács wrote, "The novel is the only art form where ethics *is* the aesthetic problem." And a year later, in 1916, the year *The Theory of the Novel* was published, the twenty-seven-year-old philosopher Ludwig Wittgenstein, while on a vacation trip to Norway, jotted down in his notebook, on the 24th of July, "Ethics and aesthetics are one," a comment he retained two years later, in 1918, for the single book he published in his lifetime, *Tractatus Logico-Philosophicus*, which appeared in 1922, the same year as the greatly publicized discovery of Tutankhamen's tomb, the same year T. S. Eliot published his brooding construction of fragments, *The Waste Land*, the same year James Joyce published his episodic novel of a single day in Dublin, *Ulysses*, all of which helped to usher in the period of High Modernism, with its highly problematic relation to history and the past.

Up till now, the slant of our mirror has generally emphasized a fundamentally playful relation between life and writing. But when we turn to look at statements such as, "The novel is the art form where ethics *is* the aesthetic problem," and

"Ethics and aesthetics are one," we enter a field where it is all but impossible not to begin to overvalue the relation between writing and life.

In Western Europe what is generally considered Lukács's greatest book is *History and Class Consciousness*, comprising essays he had written from 1918 until shortly after, and which in 1930 Lukács was forced by the communist party to disown. And Wittgenstein only wrote for publication one other book, *The Philosophical Investigations*, which by the year of his death, 1951, he'd not yet managed to shape into a form close enough to what he felt was the truth to publish, though he had worked on it diligently and continuously. Clearly these were two men who held the relationship of writing and life to be extremely important—as we might guess from their separate statements, if not from their later experiences.

Till now, we have been playing, however seriously, with an argument that must invariably lead to the impossibility of any ultimate congruence between life and art. But now we turn to an argument which, just as seriously, just as playfully, establishes an inseverable link between them. It does so through another pressure, another imprint, another printing term.

In eighteenth-century France, typesetters who were hand setting type for contemporary newspapers, noticed that writers used certain phrases again and again. Thus, in order to increase their speed, they would set a number of these commonly used words and phrases beforehand, in special clamps or "clutches." Then, when the phrase came up, they would simply reach over for the clutch containing the pre-set phrase, release the clamp, and slide the type into the typeframe. In French, the word for one of these pre-set clamps was "cliché."

If clichés were good for printers, as soon as we pass the 1850s, with writers like Flaubert and Baudelaire, it became the general aesthetic consensus that clichés were bad for readers. Indeed, the cliché soon came to be seen as writing without any life at all.

The argument we are talking about here hinges on a paradox, or seeming contradiction, of aesthetic psychology. On the one hand, what tends to move us the most is that which, over the course of our lives, is most familiar to us: it is the poems our parents recited to us when we were children that, when we re-encounter them as adults—no matter how mawkish or, indeed, cliché they are—will bring tears to our eyes or send chills down our spine. (Can one talk about such effects *without* clichés . . . ?) But at the same time, the phrase or the idea or the plot that has been repeated to us so often, especially recently, which when we see its opening signs we can immediately supply its ending, is what evokes from us the groan—or the dismissal of aesthetic displeasure.

The cliché is the basis for the modernist notion of bad art. The goal of avoiding the cliché joins the idea of quality in art to the idea of originality. Avoidance of the cliché in the quest for clarity is the sign of craft in art; and the avoidance of the cliché, whether or not clarity is achieved, is the sign of talent.

But the cliché has another field of existence, where it is equally important, and that is the field of politics. When we say today that statements such as:

"Blacks are shiftless and lazy."
"Women are lousy drivers."
"Gays are emotionally unstable."

are respectively racist, sexist, and homophobic, what we are saying in effect is that they are political clichés. That they occur in life and work as part of the linguistic stabilizers for complex and oppressive material and economic systems is what makes them ethically abhorrent. That they are repeated so frequently is what makes them aesthetically abhorrent. But they are still easily pre-set lengths of language that can be put aside on the print-shop shelf; and sooner or later some situation will force us to take one down and use it—if only to decry it. But because certain clichés are abhorrent ethically and aesthetically, the cliché (or, rather, its avoidance) is precisely the place where "Ethics and aesthetics are one." And to the extent that certain plot tropes are in themselves clichés, this becomes the field in which the novel (or any other narrative art) is a form in which the ethics of avoiding political clichés is, in fact, one with the aesthetic problem of creating a new, lively, and vigorous—while still moving—tale.

The easy answer so many people, appalled by political clichés, reach for to solve this problem is one style or another of censorship. And while I am all for censuring clichés, wherever we find them—whether they are the uplifting and positive ones, or the demeaning and insulting ones—I am never for censoring them.

There is something fundamentally wrong with the argument: Because I don't want to have certain clichés in the work I write—or in the work I read —then I forbid you to use them in *your* work. First of all, the relation between the cliché and the deeply moving, as we have already seen, is close and complicated. The relationship may be different for every one of us—with those of us who have had the widest exposure to art generally (another paradox) the most critical of, and at the same time the most accepting of, clichés. And while I might emotionally and ethically approve of certain positive sentiments, expressed in the most hackneyed language, in a political speech, I don't want to find them in a poem! Despite Lukács and Wittgenstein, in practical terms, the identity of political ethics and aesthetics only goes so far.

The West really has only two widely accepted models for the way art relates to life. One is Plato's—and it is a depressing model at that. The sole use of art, Plato reasoned, was to provide positive examples of behavior for the people. Plato was as quick to see as anyone else that the artists of his age spent an awful lot of time telling how their heroes called to their loves and fought twelve bikers to win her; even worse were the ones who told the unhappy truth—that nothing was ever really going to work out right: the biker you happened to do in would turn out to be your old man; and your lover was probably your mother anyway; and when you found out, neither she nor you was going to be terribly happy about it.

What kind of example was that?

Artists were, at their best, liars; and when they were any better, they were substantially worse. In his ideal Republic, Plato banished them with an argument not so far very different from the one with which Senator Jesse Helms attacked the Robert Mapplethorpe photography exhibit not so long ago.

When confronted with such an argument, what is there to appeal to except the truth in art? In the same way that we all take for granted that truth is a good in politics, when art is politicized in this way, we have nothing left to fall back on except the truth art may contain. And, as we search for that truth, the argument of Lukács and the suggestions of Wittgenstein suddenly look even more important, as they appear to locate the place where truth, art, and life really connect. And the endless play of value reversals and the problems of representation, or verification, or exhaustiveness that we began with in our Shakespeare-Stendhal-Auden house of mirrors suddenly seem a hopeless embarrassment as they suggest that here, even at this most solid-seeming spot, all is still illusion—and Plato was right.

The next major theory of the relation between art and life came only a generation after Plato from his student Aristotle, who proposed that tragedy, at least, rather than simply setting a bad example, functioned to draw off unhealthy emotions from the audience. Aristotle called it catharsis.

The modernist critic Kenneth Burke called this "the lightning-rod theory of art."

Certain bad examples, then, if they were noble enough, taught us humility —rather than encouraged us to go out and pursue sex, drugs, and rock and roll.

And although our modern examinations of the relation between art and life so often start out with the most modern, if not postmodern, of intentions, it's a little unsettling how often the argument ends up with our liberal critic defending his lightning rod against intransigent old Plato.

My own opinion is that neither Plato's theory of examples, good and bad, nor Aristotle's defense of certain bad examples (noble or not), is to the point. Nor do I think we can find any way out of the house of mirrors that the prison house of language has turned out to be. Rather I seek my answer in the print shop, from which Shakespeare took his "pressure" and which named for us the cliché—and I take just a bit of my answer, as well, from drugs, if not from sex and rock and roll.

Are clichés dangerous?

Yes. They are dangerous to thought, art, and life. But the reason they are not dangerous enough to justify censorship is because, by the time they have become clichés, they have already done their damage.

There are two kinds of drugs. There are drugs like aspirin, called cumulative drugs, which the more you take, the stronger their effects. There is another type of drug, like Darvon, called a titrating drug. Titrating drugs, if you don't take enough of them, don't have any effect at all. At a certain dosage, called the titration level—usually depending on your body weight—they suddenly become effective. After that, if you take more, their effect doesn't really become stronger, at least in terms of pain-killing. Their effect doesn't go up or down. It simply turns on or off.

People who espouse censorship have not necessarily fallen for the Platonic argument (although they may have) so much as they have uncritically assumed that the harm political clichés do, when encountered in art, is cumulative. The more frequently you encounter them, these people feel, the stronger their harmful effects. But I maintain that the danger of clichés, when they arrive in an aesthetic field (even if they start out as political clichés) is titrative. And the proof that the titration point has been reached is precisely that we recognize them as clichés.

The political cliché does its damage during the five or fifty or five hundred times (depending on your "body weight") you encounter it without really recognizing it as a cliché. But once it is recognized, even if it's a cliché you believe in, it cannot do any further harm. Of course sometimes what for one group is a repellant political cliché is for another a deeply moving theme. This is a more unsettling situation, certainly, yet is still a matter of psychic/material economies, rather than semantic content. But I shall come back to this pivotal point in a moment.

I said that I seek my answer in the print shop.

The problem with clichés—with the whole shelf full of pre-set phrases, thousands and thousands of each example, up there in a pile on the shelf—is how much type they use up.

When I gave a version of this argument a couple of years back at the 1987 Sercon in Berkeley, I said that the pathos of clichés was the vast area of silence they imposed around themselves—a silence in which almost nothing else could be said or heard. But here I can say, with another metaphor, if less poetically, the same thing: clichés simply take up too much room on the social print-shop shelf —or too much room in what has come to be called the universe of discourse.

Every time a cliché is said or heard, a live and insightful observation about the world-that-is-the-case is not being said or heard. And while that universe may be relatively infinite for society, for each individual it is limited.

That sense of limitation, along with the incorrect assumption of clichés' cumulative damage (and a sneaking suspicion that perhaps Plato was right), is another reason, if only from the feeling of exhaustion it evokes, why well-intentioned people who otherwise uphold the Constitution finally find themselves condoning censorship.

It's very important to remind people again and again and again—and also to remind the best-intentioned people, because they forget this too—that what makes statements like "Blacks are lazy and shiftless," "Women are lousy drivers," or "Gays are emotionally unstable" racist, sexist, and homophobic is the vast statistical preponderance of these particular statements in the general range of utterances of most people most of the time. That statistical preponderance makes it almost impossible to say anything else about blacks, women, or gays. Again, it's the silences in the discourse such statements enforce around themselves that give them their ideological contour. But this is why you have to correct the statistical imbalance. And it is the titrating aspect of the damage clichés do that makes it futile for people to try to censor such statements in an attempt to right oppressive wrong. You don't right the imbalance—the inequality—by suppressing discourse. What you have to do is allow, to encourage, even more: You must intrude new discourse into the area of silence around these statements and broaden the field of truth. Then such statements just become comments about one or a few observed individuals, statements that are either right or wrong, silly or interesting.

Language, and the political clichés that fill so much of it, whether that language comes in novels or barroom chatter or boardroom discussions, is not the oppressive system itself. Language is merely a stabilizer of those various systems. As language stabilizes, other language de-stabilizes. And that is why, if you are fighting at the level of language, it is best to fight language with more language—more accurate, more logical, more convincing language.

Remember (and here I'm back to what, I suspect, is the most difficult and controversial point in my whole argument): It is not the content of the statements that makes them offensive. Nor is it even the intention of the speakers.

Take the statement, "Blue-eyed people are irresponsibly morose." That's not a racist statement because it's not among the first three things you'll hear about blue-eyed people in any bar or coffee klatch as soon as the topic of blue-eyed people comes up. It's not a racist statement because it's not part of the stabilization system for an economic matrix that assures blue-eyed people will average incomes 30 percent lower than the rest of us. It's not a racist statement because 80 percent of all the artistic representations of blue-eyed people, from folk operas to genre paintings to popular novels, do not automatically portray them as mooning away (irresponsibly) while catastrophes bloom around them; nor do the other 20 percent of the representations—the liberal ones—portray them as overcoming that moroseness with a mindless and wholly unbelievable vigor. It's not a racist statement because it's not part of a system that encourages three-quarters of the blue-eyed population, whenever they feel even vaguely down, to search immediately for possible irresponsibility—who then feel, if they don't find it, that this itself is probably proof they're irresponsible.

What is the statement, "Blue-eyed people are irresponsibly morose" today?

It's a phrase that might appear in a mildly surrealistic poem; a phrase with a vaguely ironic cast; a phrase that may mildly amuse. It's a phrase whose interest is, in short, almost wholly aesthetic. But such a statement could become part of such an oppressive system. And there are many blue-eyed people (many of them rather morose over the past few decades' protests from blacks, women, and gays, as well as over blacks', women's, and gays' changing position in our society) whom one would like to remind just how the process of making such a statement racist works—and whom one would like to see be just a little more responsible in their analysis of what is getting them so down . . .

In terms of you and me, however, whether in the house of mirrors that is art, or in the often equally confusing house of mirrors that is the world, each of us has to seize the cliché down from the shelf, dismantle it to the letters, and, along with the rest of the type in the type box, use those letters to write something else.

After listening to all this, some of you might still want to ask: "Well, what about the other story?"

What other story?

The other story young Heinlein turned in, back at workshop: the science fiction story that you said he handed in after the first one about the guy and the girl and the bikers on the beach. What about the relation between art and life in SF?

I'm sure I don't have to tell you that everything I've said here I feel applies just as strongly to SF.

But what about what makes SF special—what makes it exciting, different, a genre of its own, with its own special delights? Don't those features—the rockets, the ray guns, the imaginative scientific extrapolation—make it less like reality, and therefore more susceptible to the Platonic argument of "bad example" or "no example at all"?

They certainly do; and it's an argument you will hear again and again leveled at science fiction, often by critics who started out proclaiming how sympathetic they were to science fiction.

But there's one more aspect to clichés that we haven't touched on. It's a place where the term "cliché" is probably not the proper one: rather the term "genre convention" is more appropriate—though what we are speaking of bears a strong structural relation to the clichés of language, in the same way that plot tropes do. But it is as hard to distinguish a genre convention from a cliché as it is to distinguish what, from childhood resonance, moves us to tears and chills from what, in light of adult sensibility, bores us to distraction. Why one cliché should become a deep and resonant theme that, when we discern it in works from any number of genres, moves us profoundly, while another, when it slides across the surface of a text, should be a sign of everything that is trite and dull and unthinking, and while still another should become an almost invisible convention that helps hold a given genre stable—this is one of the mysteries of art. The only thing I will hazard here is to suggest that, as is the case with political clichés, it is not the content that controls clichés' meanings or affects, but rather the different larger economies into which each has been drawn.

Although they don't usually sit around in their own clamps, genre conventions are nevertheless real, recognizable, and articulate. It's worth noting, then, some of the things they say.

The overriding convention of sexual excess that characterizes pornography says, for example, that any and every social situation, by just the slightest pressure, can become overtly and rapturously sexual. The overwrought conventions of modern romance, or "bodice buster," says that any and every social situation can, with equally little pressure, become overtly and rapturously romantic. Both are lies. But I'm not sure which lie is the more pernicious.

The conventions of the old-fashioned mystery tell us that crime, however random and violent it looks, is the product of intelligence, cunning, and planning; and that the solution to the crime is therefore always more intelligence, cunning, and planning. The more modern procedural absorbs the intelligence of the detective into a pre-operationalized set of tasks, which, if we follow them mechanically, will get us our man—or woman.

Both tell major lies about crime, for the vast majority of crimes today still go unsolved and are often spontaneous, violent, and all but without motivation of the sort a court might recognize. As a genre, I have no doubt that the range of crime fictions tells far more pernicious lies than does either pornography or romance. But I staunchly oppose censorship for any of them.

Science fiction . . . well, as many have said before: its first message to us is that there will be a future. And the range of possible futures the genre presents suggests that the future is not deterministically predictable. That range also tells us that specific choices we make today will be a factor in determining which of those futures arrives—an interesting comment for writing to make about life.

Now whether or not the promise of a future, or our part in bringing it about, is another generic lie, I don't know. Certainly I hope it's the truth—which is one reason I like science fiction.

Another SF genre convention whose message I have always been drawn to is the one conveyed by the topological convention of the space opera.

The Copernican Revolution succeeded in striking humanity from its place at the center of the universe. With its panoply of worlds a-swirl around a galaxy of suns, those suns all a-swirl around each other in their cloud of galaxies, the space opera goes on to strike the notion of a fixed centrality from the armamentarium of our thinking.

There are only constantly relative, forever moving centers; and everything from our technology to our sociology, from passion to intellect, can potentially be revalued in such a field.

The apprehension of the physical field in which, on a vaster and vaster scale, we are constantly and repeatedly decentered, and the concomitant revaluation of woman, man, and mind that takes place there, we call the sense of wonder. It moved me greatly when I was a child. And I still try to explore those revisions of values with accuracy and insight in such a way that the wonder may still assail. As an adult, I've looked across a great and ragged canyon gap in the sun-glazed noon. A week later, at dawn, I've looked out over the aluminum-colored sea. And a few nights later I've stared up at the precise and distant glimmer of the stars in all that black. Now anyone can see these as three examples of immensity. But what science fiction has done for me is given me an immediate sense of the vastly differing order of immensity each represents—canyon, sea, and stars. There is your sense of wonder; there is your decentering field, within which all that is human is always up for revaluation.

Science fiction of course tells lies too. Like so much art it tends to suggest the world is simpler than we know it to be. But whether we respond to that as a remediable aesthetic problem that may be overcome, at least partially, by the next SF story or novel we read, or a reprehensible political problem fundamental to the SF Weltanschauung, will probably have a lot to do with whether or not we like SF.

The young writer I spoke of in my early anecdote went on to publish two SF novels—one of these two years after he was out of Clarion and one a few years after that. As I said, he was immensely talented. And by the time the first appeared, he was over his believability problems. Then he went off and got a PhD in linguistics and moved to the west coast for a decade and a half to work with vocal data input as a programmer for an electronics company. I really thought he was lost to SF as a writer forever. About five days ago, however, I got a package from him.[1]

(This story is true. It all happened. And I'm putting it down just like it was.)

It contained the MS of a new SF novel.

It's at home on my work table. I haven't read it yet. But getting it in the post, opening up the tan book-mailer, and reading his long accompanying letter—and anticipating reading his novel—is certainly one of the great pleasures of the life of writing.

—1973/2010
New York City

NOTE

1. Jean Mark Gawron, author of *Dream of Glass* (Houghton Mifflin Harcourt, 1993); *Algorithm* (Berkley, 1978); and *An Apology for Rain* (Doubleday, 1974).

WORKS CITED

Auden, W. H. *The Sea and the Mirror*. Edited by Arthur Kirsch. Princeton: Princeton
  University Press, 2003.
Bradbury, Ray. *The Complete Poems of Ray Bradbury*. New York: Ballantine Books, 1982.
Lukács, Georg. *History and Class Consciousness: Studies in Marxist Dialectics*. Translated by
  Rodney Livingstone. Cambridge: MIT Press, 1972.
————. *The Theory of the Novel*. Cambridge: MIT Press, 1974.
Wittgenstein, Ludwig. *Notebooks 1914–1916*. New York: Harper and Row, 1969.

2

Algol Interview

A Conversation with Darrell Schweitzer

Darrell Schweitzer: In some of your essays you've stated that style and content are inseparable, if not identical. Would you expand on this?

Samuel R. Delany: What I meant is that style and content are two *critical* categories. What you've got on paper is a series of words. If the style is what the words are actually doing, you simply cannot cut out the paper between the words and say, "Well, that's the content." You'd have something with no words on it. The actual story itself is a coherent string of words which you cannot slice and have the top half be the style and the bottom half be the content. Almost everything you're willing to talk about in terms of one can be talked about in terms of the other. If you stretch the definition of content you've got the style. If you stretch the definition of style you've got the content. They're two directions on a spectral line, and there's no clear division between them. They're not two things that are sharply bounded.

Schweitzer: Suppose Henry James were alive today, and he were to rewrite one of your books in his style rather than yours. Would this be the same book?

Delany: No, it wouldn't be the same—I assume not! [laughter] No more than if I decided to rewrite one of his.

Schweitzer: I mean if he were to tell exactly the same story, only phrase it differently.

Delany: It just wouldn't work that way. When we read a story we tend to forget that the order we experience it in is the exact opposite of the order in which we remember it. The *last* thing you find out about the story is what it's about. The *first* thing you find out is the nature of the language, because that's what you get after you've read the first paragraph, the first page. Most people will pick up the story and read the first page and decide from that whether they want to read it or not. They're not judging what the story is about. They're judging what the effect of that first burst of language is on them, which sometimes indicates things about the structure of the entire story; but they are not experiencing the entire structure itself. They're experiencing that first burst of language; and again, the same way, the last information you get from the story is the plot—for want of a better word. So when people start to talk about a story they talk about it ass-backwards. They talk as if the first thing you know about the story is what it's about, which it's not, but the last thing, and that somehow the last thing is the language, which is of course the first thing.

Schweitzer: From your essays and from the introductions to the chapters in *The Einstein Intersection*, you seem to be one of the most meticulous writers in the business. Is this why you worry so much over each line?

Delany: One of the reasons I worry is that I was a remedial reader. I didn't learn to read easily. I was dyslectic, and reading was very difficult for me. I've always wanted a lot out of what I read. It wasn't easy. I didn't really learn to read until I was about eight years old. The only way you can get a lot out of a book is, I think, if the writer puts a lot into it. That's actually why I take time, because I assume that whoever is reading my book is somebody vaguely like me and who therefore wants a lot out of it, whoever this bizarre ideal reader is who picks it up and starts reading.

Schweitzer: I find it interesting that you're writing for someone like yourself, a hypothetical friend. You're not writing just to please—

Delany: I'm writing to please that person. It's something that I have said a number of times, that essentially I write books that I would like to read and cannot find. Therefore I must write them myself.

Schweitzer: With your careful revisions, how do you account for the writer who writes everything first draft and it comes out beautifully? Lord Dunsany is a good example. He used to write a short story every morning before breakfast, and novels in three weeks.

Delany: It's a kind of talent. I think there are two ways to account for it. One is a natural talent this kind of person has. The other is the fact that usually anyone who writes his work first draft, like Lord Dunsany or Trollope, is writing in a different *kind* of language. Dunsany, especially, was writing in a very socially formalized language, where the conventions and what have you are much more set than you have with an author who is writing heavy foreground stuff. These people like Dunsany tend to write récit—beautiful conversation. The style is essentially a conversational style where the laws of balance and proportion are the laws that you use in a certain kind of speech. But the person who writes heavy foreground is trying to give you the texture, the *feel* of the experience. They're trying to analyze the front, the absolute, what your psyche is rubbed into when you go through the experience. The one-draft people are writing, in a way, a much more artificial language, a much more literary language. What we *call* literary language is the kind of language that a Dunsany writes, but the more truly literary language is the language that is invented, created for the situation at hand. The language that is practically being re-invented for each sentence.

Schweitzer: Have you ever tried to write in the more formal literary mode?

Delany: From time to time I've played with it, but my approach has been very much as though that's just a different *kind* of foreground that one wants to deal with. That's just because it's easier for me to do it that way. I don't know if that makes sense or not.

Schweitzer: When you write a story, do you then start with the language?

Delany: Like every other writer, it depends on the story. Sometimes it may be a whole idea, sometimes a character, sometimes a setting. Or two settings. I want to use both these settings in the story, and I have to invent a story that will get some people from one to the other. Sometimes it may be a practically didactic theme to pound over people's heads, and then I have to figure out how to write a story which will pound this into the reader without *sounding* like it's pounding.

Schweitzer: Do you plot it all out consciously, or is this a subconscious process?

Delany: A writer has to spend most his time taking care of the conscious part of the story, because the unconscious part will by its very nature take care of itself. That's what it's unconscious for. So there are too many things going on in a story, which you do have to deal with very consciously—or at least I do.

Schweitzer: How much of your work is autobiographical? I notice that most of your novels have the same lead character, and from *The Jewels of Aptor* onward he seems to be getting older. How much of yourself is in this wanderer character?

Delany: Again it's very hard to say. Just sort of anecdotally: I was in a room full of people once, some of whom knew my work, some of whom didn't, and I was asked this question, "How autobiographical are your stories?" And I was about to say what I quite honestly thought: that they're not autobiographical at all. If a story is set two hundred years in the future, how autobiographical can it be? And somebody else said, "Oh, scandalously!" So I thought, well, from one point of view, perhaps they are.

Of course, that was talking about my work up through *Nova*. With *Dhalgren* and *Triton*, I've moved much further away from autobiography. On the one hand, with those books, because the characters were much further away from me, I had to work much harder on their presence; to the extent I was successful, that may be the reason everyone assumes *those* are the autobiographical ones.

On the other hand, you talk about the characters getting older. When I started writing I was rather young. I was nineteen when I first started writing novels that actually sold, and I thought to myself, "This is ridiculous. You can't have a hero of a novel who is nineteen years old. 'No one is serious at seventeen' (*On n'est pas sérieux, quand on a dix-sept ans*: Rimbaud). I'm nineteen, and I've got to have a serious person." So I made a point, for about the first five years I was writing, always to make the character two or three years older than I, because somehow I was convinced when I was nineteen that somebody *twenty-three* was serious. That was grown up, you know. So my characters were traditionally three years older than I was, because I thought that was an age that somebody could take seriously. Then when I started *Dhalgren* the character was somewhere in the vicinity of twenty-seven. I'm now thirty-three, so the character is now younger than I am; so I have grown from younger than the character to older. Their actual progression of chronological age is certainly not on the same slope that my own age is. It was very much a conscious decision when I decided that I wanted the characters older than I. Now is that autobiographical, or is that a conscious decision on the part of the author?

Schweitzer: *Dhalgren* differs from all your other novels in that it is the only one that isn't a rigidly plotted story, and the only one that isn't readily identifiable as science fiction. Do you deliberately set out to write science fiction, or do you just see what comes out?

Delany: You're asking a hard-edged question which has several very spectrally related answers. *Dhalgren* may not be recognizable as science fiction. It is perhaps not rigidly plotted, but it's very rigidly structured. In the same way, if it's got rocket ships in it you know it's science fiction. If it doesn't, you think, "Hm!

Probably somebody is going to wonder whether this is science fiction or not." Again, is that setting out to write science fiction or not?

Schweitzer: A lot of great science fiction doesn't have rocket ships in it.

Delany: And a lot of it does.

Schweitzer: How do you feel about science fiction as a field? Do you think of yourself as a science fiction writer?

Delany: Yes, very much so. Yes. I think of myself as doing that, and I think even the things of mine that least resemble science fiction will be more accessible to someone who has a science fiction background than someone who does not.

Schweitzer: Why were you drawn into this field?

Delany: Somewhat by accident. I liked some of the science fiction that I read very much. Again at that time, writers like Sturgeon and Bester simply sentence by sentence gave me more.

Schweitzer: Do you ever find yourself commercially typed?

Delany: The closest this has come to happening is between *Dhalgren* and my new novel, *Triton*. My original title for the novel was *Trouble on Triton*, and the publisher's absolutely staunch approach was, "Well, your last book was a one-word title, and your next book is going to be a one-word title, and you'd better resign yourself to having one-word titles, young man." So it's *Triton*. Although I'm not unhappy with it, I'm not screamingly jumping for joy either. It doesn't misrepresent the book.

Schweitzer: Also the title "Trouble on Triton" has been used before. I think it was Alan Nourse.

Delany: No it wasn't. I looked this up in the *Day Index*. There is a Simak *Trouble with Tycho*. There is a Henry Kuttner "Trouble on Titan"; there are several with "Trouble on Titan." And there is indeed one "Trouble on Triton," which was a short story that appeared in something like *Startling Stories* in the late 1930s. One of the things I wanted for this particular book was a title that sounded like twenty-seven other science fiction novels. I wanted a title that would evoke a sense of "Haven't I heard of this before?" and the title would sort of slip between your fingers before you actually grasped it. The book is not a funny book, but it has some humorous elements in it. It's a book about people trying to live their lives by clichés. So I wanted this kind of title on the cover. Also, some of the best prose that's ever been written in America is Raymond Chandler's, and it comes out under such titles as *Farewell, My Lovely* and *The Long Goodbye*— which are quite marvelous, the sort of interplay you get in that sort of thing. I wanted to do the same sort of thing there, you know, perfectly clunky. But *Triton* doesn't misrepresent it. It is a science fiction novel, indubitably so.

Schweitzer: Have you ever thought of doing something completely outside of the science fiction field, like a mystery?

Delany: No, I haven't. I think that one of the things you get out of science fiction, one of the ways that science fiction does what it does, is that it uses scientific discourse to literalize and retrieve for the foreground presentation all sorts of sentences that would be nonsense if they appeared in any other mode of discourse. You know, "The door dilated." There's a whole implied scientific discourse about the engineering of large-scale iris apertures. This is what makes this sentence—it's from Heinlein's *Beyond This Horizon*—mean something. Then you get other things that, in other modes of discourse, would just be emotionally muzzy metaphors, like "Her world exploded." That's just a cliché in mundane fiction, but in a science fiction novel it could mean that a planet, belonging to a woman, blew up. Or, "He turned on his left side." That doesn't mean he's tossing and turning. No, in science fiction there's a little switch he can flip to activate his sinistral flank. These sentences are suddenly cast into the foreground by their literal meaning. Or, for example, there's that incredible pyrotechnical scene at the end of *The Stars My Destination*, where the guy is going through synesthesia and he's experiencing smell as sight and taste as touch. And it isn't some sort of metaphorical poetry. This is what's happening. When the taste of lemons raked his skin, that's what happened. Science fiction literalizes the language and casts it into a sort of real mode that you just don't have with any other kind of discourse. There are so many *new sentences*. The actual gallery of sentences is much, much larger than you have in mundane fiction or any other mode of discourse. Once you have been working in this field with this infinitely larger range of possible combinations of words, you can put together and *mean something* with them in a clear, foregrounded mode. To suggest that a writer go back and work in some mundane mode, naturalistic mode is like saying to a twelve-tone composer who's used to working with the entire scale, who has begun to hear his music and the sounds around him in this twelve-tone range with all the notes that are possible to use, that he should go back and write something diatonic. You're saying cut off your right hand and your left hand and leave your foot behind, and now do a dance that way. Nobody is going to want to. What you're asking them to do is work with a much smaller vocabulary. That's one reason why I don't think science fiction writers are too terribly tempted unless they want to do it as some sort of *tour de force*, look-see-I-can-do-it-too. But when they want to say their serious thing, they want to work with a full range of their possible vocabulary. This is one of the reasons I like science fiction, because it gives me that much wider range. I can put more words into more bizarre orders.

Schweitzer: Why do you think it is, then, that until recently science fiction writers have been noticeably limited in their use of language?

Delany: I don't think this is really true. You do have Sturgeon's Law: 90 percent of everything is indeed crap. But the best of Sturgeon's writing is *better* sentence by sentence than anything that was being done contemporaneously with him. When you look at where mundane fiction was in the 1950s, you see it was pretty uninteresting stuff. We hadn't had the sort of thing that you get with Barth and Barthelme, and all the experimentation of Faulkner and Dos Passos was far in the past. Just in terms of Bradbury, Bester, and Sturgeon, you have more exciting language being done in science fiction in the '50s than you have in all of the serious mainstream put together. Yeah, the majority of it was pretty ham-handed stuff, but we don't judge any art by the majority of what is done. We judge it by the best.

Schweitzer: From talking to a lot of people today, it seems to me that readers don't hear language any more. They're really not aware of it.

Delany: In a sense, you don't hear language—you read it. One of the biggest things that I've learned about writing is how different oral language is from written language. They're two entirely different modes. The eye asks for different information in a different order, presented in different intensities, than the way the ear does. The ear wants to hear things repeated again and again and again. It wants things to be reiterated; it wants things to come back in different forms. The eye wants the information once, quickly, precisely, and that's it. It wants to go on to the new thing. You may want to bring up a tone of voice in writing—still, it's a whole different medium.

Schweitzer: They are related in—

Delany: Yeah, they use the same words. But they use different words too. There are a lot of grammatical constructions that are only literary. "The man walking down the street was wearing a red hat." That's purely literary. We don't use the present participle any more in speech adjectivally. You either say, "This guy who I saw," or you'd break it up somehow. You'd say, "you know," and all those noise nodes that we punctuate our speech with.

Schweitzer: The point was that the way to tell if a story is well and smoothly written is to read it aloud to somebody, and if you stumble over a sentence, there's something wrong with it. Would you agree with that?

Delany: No. I've tried too many smoothly written stories out loud. Action —a good action sequence—is meaningless read out loud. Just take anybody who writes good action sequences. First of all, paragraphs tell you an amazing amount of what's going on. In dialogue for instance, you learn the change of speaker by the paragraph. So you don't need to identify the speaker in each sentence, especially if you've just got a dialogue going between two people. You read this out loud in a single voice, and it's complete confusion. One of the most exciting *written* stories that I know of is Roger Zelazny's "The Doors of His Face, the Lamps of His Mouth." I've read that aloud to people. They have no idea what's going on. They cannot follow it. It's pretty much pure action, and I remember when I first read it to a bunch of people, they thought it was experimental writing, the quintessence of the action story, because he's telling us so much with those little indentations for paragraphs—now we're moved over here—and you can't follow that when you hear it out loud. As I said, the ear wants its information presented differently, wants it with reiteration and a lot of repetition and underlining. So stuff that's extremely exciting to read and just reads like greased lightning turns into sort of verbal salad when you read it out loud. It doesn't seem smooth at all. It seems very, very choppy and practically surreal.

Then, of course, sometimes it doesn't.

If there's a tone of voice doing a lot of the real work, that will come across when read out loud. If the tone of voice is not doing all that much work and it's the actual juxtaposition of the words, the images, and what have you that are giving the information, that very possibly is not going to work when read out loud.

Schweitzer: Do you think your own fiction is more printed-page oriented?

Delany: Yes, I do, although from time to time I have given readings, and I know that some things, simply theatrically, work better, and they're not necessarily the ones that are the most popular in terms of general readership.

Schweitzer: When you write, do you build a story from the images and then justify it logically, or do you take the time for the build-a-planet-from-the-gravity-up approach?

Delany: One of the Australians, I think it was John Foyster, said that science fiction should not contradict what is known to be known, which is a nice way of putting it. I can't conceive of myself writing a science fiction story that violated something that I *knew* was a scientific fact, and I've been known to pick up the odd *Scientific American* article and sort of glance at it to make sure I wasn't doing something completely dumb. Although on the other hand, there's something like "The Doors of His Face, the Lamps of His Mouth." I think Roger was once telling me that the thing that inspired writing the story was the fact that one of the Venus probes had come back and said, "No, there is no water on Venus. It's all hydrocarbon gases." And as a sort of a farewell gesture to the science fiction Venus of vast oceans and misty clouds, he wrote this story about hunting sea monsters on Venus. It was sort of a "so long" to that whole set of images which were now rendered obsolete. We now knew that Venus is not ocean. That's the kind impetus that, just by temperament, I'm not inclined to; but I can appreciate it, and I still think the story is science fiction even with that kind of purposeful violation of scientific fact.

Schweitzer: In *Nova*, you have people going through a donut-shaped star. Is that scientifically valid?

Delany: Well something that I didn't realize at the time was that there should have been a Schwarzschild object in the center of the donut, but the donut itself is feasible for a certain kind of nova.

Schweitzer: Did you do a lot of scientific study for that?

Delany: No. Very seldom do I actually sit down and research a story. What happens is that I tend to read popular science articles, and I'm a regular reader of *Scientific American*, and *The New Scientist*, and things like that. And I pick up the odd book. A book that is just a straight mathematical treatise that I've found fascinating in the last couple of years and re-read a couple times is G. Spencer-Brown's *Laws of Form*, which derives the calculus for the Boolean algebras. I'm interested in this kind of thing just as a general reader. Eventually what I have read will just sort of coalesce when I need it. Also, from time to time when I'm sort of stuck, I'll go and check over something, or ask somebody an odd question just to make sure that I'm not doing the wrong thing. There's a section in *Triton*—after the book was written I gave it to a guy named Jack Cohen, who is an embryologist and is also working in birth control, and he suggested a couple of ways of condensing this rather long and rather clumsy expository passage, which was also pseudo-science, with some real science that cut out about a paragraph. But his suggestion was something that was real, that would do the job of my pseudo-science a lot more elegantly. And I was very glad for it, and I used it. But remember that by this time the story had already been written anyway. I didn't go out and research the thing.

Schweitzer: What kind of reading most influences your own writing?

Delany: That which I do [laughs], as opposed to that which I don't. I think science fiction writers tend to be people who are mildly interested in everything, and the same temperament keeps us from ever getting too terribly interested in anything. You want to be interested enough to be able to ask intelligent questions and understand the answers. How interested is that?

Schweitzer: Are you that interested? What intensely interests you?

Delany: Well today it's one thing; tomorrow it's something else. Six months ago, it was René Thom's catastrophe theory. I've got an old copy of a study by Jacques Lacan, the French psychiatrist, on my desk: a reading of "The Purloined Letter" as the archetypal form for the psychoanalytic encounter, which is fascinating. You know, whatever you happen to pick up, if it's interesting. I've just got a new calculator; the instruction manual is fascinating. It's whatever happens to come along. And three weeks later, you might think, "Well, gosh that was nice," and go on to something else. It's sort of a magpie tendency — an intellectual magpie.

Schweitzer: What is your attitude toward science in general? How do you feel about what Alexei Panshin says about science fiction being a sort of subjectivization of science?

Delany: Panshin's ideas are one of the things that, from time to time, I am intensely interested in. One of the things I was hoping he would bring up in his convention talk this afternoon is the fact that there are whole branches of science where the kind of intuitionism that he's talking about, under the name of intersubjectivity, is essential. Without it, for things like psychiatry, sociology — the science wouldn't exist. Any time when the encounter is between two subjects, you cannot use a mechanistic model. The fact that you have two subjects, both of whom have something that the other recognizes as volition, means that you're dealing with an entirely different type of reality. It's only when a field like psychiatry, say, comes to realize that the ontology of its object is different from the ontology of the object in physics or chemistry that it becomes a science at all. It is finally beginning to grow up and take some sort of scientific cognizance of itself. The same thing in sociology. An anthropologist coming to a culture to study it is not like putting a catalyst in a chemistry compound. It's a different thing, and this is why anthropology, psychology, and the other soft sciences are finally beginning to get interesting — because they're beginning to outgrow these mechanistic models and realize what the nature of their object of study is.

Schweitzer: Have you noticed that most people are divorced from the hard science and even pride themselves on their ignorance?

Delany: Most people are divorced from sociology as well. But there is always a sort of fear of hard-edged things, which is sad because we live in a universe that has a lot of hard edges in it. We've made it, so I think it is better to try and understand it than to go around pretending it isn't there. This is the sort of thing that is always with us. It is sad that people are terrified of technology, because by being terrified you simply abnegate your power before it, and that's not the way to deal with the matter. Tools are not what is evil. It's the way they're put to use that makes the problem, and to be terrified of the tool because of the use it's put to gets you nowhere.

—Summer 1976

3

Liner Notes, Anecdotes, and Emails on Theodore Sturgeon

Yes, it was a pretty good day. I could go on making corrections—"novels complete and incomplete"—but I suspect we can stop here, just so we can move forward.

Spent the day with Sturgeon, and still wondering what happened to the last volume in the set.

Using Facebook, I managed to hunt down a little piece I wrote about him, about my second face-to-face meeting with him:

On Jul 17, 2016, at 9:58 PM, Samuel Delany wrote:

Dear Noël [Sturgeon]—

Among some other things, I am getting together a book of essays called *Occasional Views*, and I want to include a few fugitive pieces on Ted, among them some album liner notes that I wrote when I sat in on the recording he made in July of 1976, released as *Sturgeon Reads*. I append them just under this. But I would like to include a footnote about something that happened in the same afternoon, when I was with your dad at the studio. I want to run it past you to make sure you don't object to having it made public. Please let me know if you would rather not have the footnote appear; after all, nothing happened between us. That, at least, I am sure:

NOTES [for Sturgeon Reads] . . .

We gathered at a table (Sturgeon, reader/writer; Roy, producer; Shelley, director; and I, amanuensis), black coffee at one side, iced wine at the other—air conditioner on the blink. Later, at another table, in a Chinese restaurant with non-notable service and exemplary tequila sours (plus pleasantly incongruous Kirin beer), having left engineer Chris back at the studio, we are joined by bookseller Jerry from Boston, who, earlier, in the Strand's rare book room, had located a mint copy of Ted's story collection (British) *Thunder and Roses*, whose cover is a black background on which "a final flower turns a burning head." The line is Zelazny's, but it never would have surfaced, just so, in this genre, without Sturgeon.

Between?

This record: that's ooo (total) takes: one paragraph re-read five times, another sentence re-read seven, still another three-page section re-read—after a dozen stumblings all through it—at such a higher energy, tonal differentiation, and emotional involvement that there is no question it will be the chosen version. (I tell Ted about abandoning forty thousand words of a novel in near suicidal despair. "Nothing gets lost. Your tools just get sharper," which is my writer's voice mauling what he actually said: a pretty poor amanuensis I. But that's why you have the record, no?) To be an artist, says Malraux in his *Anti-Memoirs*, is largely a matter of "slaying certain aspects of the personality." Sturgeon is an artist before whom one (writer or reader) wants to slay all the aspects of personality that move one toward competition, pettiness, meanness. "Chip, we're going to HAVE to have an argument. Do you like salads?"

"Yeah . . . ?" nodding.

"I hate salads. There, that'll do for a while."

I learn: "Waves on waves of agonized ecstasy . . ." Ted deletes "*Waves on waves*" after listening to it back; and all the stops and sibilants in "agonized ecstasy" suddenly stand up and do their phonic best, set up now by the sentence before, buoyed up by the three sentences following it, released to their separate tasks after—how many years? ("Bianca's Hands" was written when Ted was nineteen, and remained unsold for a decade.) Ted points out a paragraph that, after the first two sentences, breaks out into amphibrachs (with the most elegantly placed caesuras this side of Pope), climaxing in two slammed iambs. He discovers a printer's error (transposed lines in the text) that, corrected, retrieves for me (in this story I've read seven times? ten times?) the character's whole emotional development.

There are writers whose works move meticulously inward—low production writers, paying infinite care to the text, to the interface of sensibility (response to the word) and sensitivity (response to the world); there are writers whose works move grandly outward, grasping to get it all in, to encompass the sway and sweep, frequently abandoning poesis/technos (the two forms of fine making that, in art, are finally one) to the urgency of inclusion.

Range *and* precision are what we're talking about.

Sturgeon writes of imbeciles, of geniuses, of ordinary schoolteachers facing the impossible on an impossibly hot day; he writes of the inconceivably affluent, the horrendously poor, of those privileged by politics and technology, of the makers of both, as well as those denied through the abuses of either. He writes over an unbelievable, and sometimes nearly unbearable, range of the precisely real—and sets its prospects and perspectives aright by meticulous and responsible fancy, fantasy, and functional sense. The first dozen-odd Sturgeon characters who come to my mind? A judge, a woman doctor, a Gulf Coast sailor, a psychotic jazz guitarist, an elderly lady recluse, a charming politician, a salesgirl moving into a new boarding house, a crashed astronaut, the richest young woman in the world, a mad scientist, a sane scientist, a janitor . . . and all the sentences are *written*—about, around, and between these people. With that most intelligent of reticences we recognize (almost as we apprehend the words), it forces us to put to the dialogue mainly modes of belief and recognition.

The first three quarters of this century have produced no other American writer of short fiction who does just this, this richly, rich in these ways.*

—*Samuel R. Delany*
July 1976

*I had been hearing about Theodore Sturgeon's alleged bisexuality since I first entered the science fiction community. But it was just that, alleged. I was a known gay father of thirty-four (with a two-year-old daughter). As a writer I had been publicly known to be gay since 1968. For years now I had been publishing stories in a social landscape where to mention anything gay was to confess to the knowledgeable that you were gay yourself.

While our group was walking from the recording studio to the restaurant (or leaving it . . . ?), Ted managed to get me alone on the street and said: "You know, we should get off by ourselves and spend a few days in a motel upstate together, just you and me, Chip—by ourselves. Just the two of us, to see what happens. You know what I mean?"

In 1976, this was a wholly unambiguous request for a sexual tryst. I said, "Um . . . yeah . . . wow . . . yeah, that . . . could be interesting." But because I was completely chicken shit about going up to spend a weekend in bed with someone I felt was the among the greatest living writers in our language, I never followed through or even phoned him about setting it up. The fact that I didn't is among the things I most regret in my life. (Was it performance anxiety? Guilt over what it might mean for his own family? There'd be no problem having Iva stay with my own mother while I went off on a weekend visit . . . I'd done it before.) At any rate, it never happened. But it sealed my own knowledge that Sturgeon was bisexual, in behavior at the very least.

On Mon, Jul 18, 2016 at 5:15 PM, Noël Sturgeon wrote:

Hi Chip:

I appreciate your sensitivity in checking with me, but I am proud to have you include this footnote. I have positive confirmation of Ted's bisexuality from his own self-identification to me, as well as his relationship with a man when he was living in San Diego, but since that was a trio with his female partner at the time, I always wanted to have more evidence. Counter to this was his disavowal of being gay at the end of *Venus Plus X*, but in 1967 perhaps he felt he had to do that.

It does blow my mind to think of the what-ifs . . . if you had an affair with him perhaps you would have been Uncle Chip!

This sounds like an interesting project and I look forward to seeing the results!

I hope you are doing well. Would love to see you sometime. I am still being a Dean in Toronto, so if you are ever up here, do let me know!

Hugs,

Noël

On Jul 18, 2016, at 10:49 PM, Samuel Delany wrote:

Dear Noël—

Thank you so much! I have the warmest of feelings toward you, so I feel just a bit avuncular already!

Best to you and yours.

—Chip

On Fri, Jul 22, 2016 at 11:40 AM, Noël Sturgeon wrote:

Thanks, Chip. Warm feelings are mutual.

A friend passed on that you had a FB post asking to find the liner notes you wrote for "Bianca's Hands." I don't have a copy of the record myself, but you can ask Elspeth Healey, Special Collections librarian at the Spencer Library at University of Kansas if there is a copy in the Sturgeon Papers there. I am pretty sure there isn't a copy of the record, but there may be a copy of the notes. Ted was a real packrat.

You might in fact ask her if there is anything from you or to you from Ted, in case it might help with your present project.

Elspeth is very helpful. Just let her know I suggested you reach out to her. Cheers!

Noël

On Jul 22, 2016, at 1:02 PM, Samuel Delany wrote:

Dear Noël—

What I sent you includes the liner notes (one page) and the footnote (half a page). Again, I was very warmed by your response. It strikes me as very strange that I am now six years older than Ted ever lived to be.

My own daughter is a forty-two-year-old doctor, and my next writing project is a letter to her about all of the things I have gotten from her over the years. Dennis and I lived with her and her husband for eight months at their invitation, and at the end (mostly because of her husband) were invited rather precipitously to leave.

It was a very trying situation, which ended with his not speaking to me at all any more, and my daughter having to run a fair amount of interference between us. And my partner, Dennis, of twenty-seven years, was the most wounded by this of all, I'm afraid.

And I have to store and sell a three-thousand-volume library for my naivete in accepting an invitation that looked too good to be true, and was.

But we are now in our own place, in Philadelphia (rather than in the isolated suburbs of Wynnewood).

All my love to you and yours.

—Chip

On Fri, Jul 22, 2016 at 1:09 PM, Noël Sturgeon wrote:

Hi Chip:

Good to know you have the liner notes you sought.

I share your wonder about Ted's age when he died . . . sixty-seven. The older I get (about to turn sixty) the younger that seems. It is a shame. And yet at the time, he seemed so old . . . years of smoking, poverty and deferred medical care took their toll.

Family conflict like this is so painful. All you can do is express your love and let others deal with their own inadequacies.

And as far as dealing with your library! I sympathize. Dealing with getting Ted's papers and books to UKansas was a painful job that took years. When it was done I felt a huge sense of relief. You will too.

It makes me wonder about what new age we are in when physical books are no longer used or bought as much, letters are all on email or notes on text . . . what kind of material will historians and literary critics have to work with! Sounds like a subject for a SF story ☺

Love,
Noël

—*1976/2016*

4

Star Wars

A Consideration of a Great New SF Film

My first reactions as the final credits rose on the screen? "*Now* what happens?"
—which is to say George (*American Grafitti* and *THX 1138*) Lucas's *Star Wars* is
about the fastest two-hour film I've ever seen: I thought I'd been in the theater
maybe twenty-five minutes.

THX, if you'll recall, looked like it was sired by Godard's *Contempt* out of the
space station sequence in Kubrick's *2001*—i.e., it was basically white, white-on-
white, and then more white. What is the visual texture of *Star Wars*?

Two moons shimmer in the heat above the horizon, and the desert evening
fades to purple rather than blue; into the starry black, huge and/or hopelessly
complex artifacts flicker, flash, spin, turn, or merely progress with ponderous
motion; indoors is all machinery, some old, some new; while plastic storm
troopers and dull grey generals meet and march, circus-putty aliens drink in
a bar where what appears to be an automatic still gleams in the background
with tarnished copper tubing; some of the space ships are new and shiny, some
are old and battered (and you get pretty good at telling the difference between
the two).

Motion: that's the feeling you take away from the film more than any other.
People tramp, run, sprint; sand-skimmers skim; space ships race, chase, or
careen off to hyperspace. One ship explodes—cut to cloaked figure striding
ominously forward, as if out of the explosion itself. The door to a prison cell
falls—cut to a booted foot falling on a light-gridded floor.

Intelligence and invention have been lavished on keeping the background of
this film coherent and logical. (This is perhaps the place to mention that—to

get the film down from two and a quarter hours to a flat two—some sequences have been hacked out: two with young Luke and his friends at the beginning, during which one friend goes off to join the rebel forces, and one at the end where a space pilot tells Luke about his father. In the middle, too, we've lost a few aliens. I hope Lucas is one of those guys who sends a complete copy of his films to the Paris Cinemathique before the distributors et al. start chopping.) The foreground is rather shaky. But in this sort of science fiction, the job of the background is to be *coherent*; the job of the foreground is to be *fast*. In that sense both do their job admirably.

This film is going to do very well, if not phenomenally so, and I can see a lot of the elder statesmen in the SF community intoning: "*That's* because it's got a good, solid story!" *Star Wars*, as far as I can tell, has no story at all—or rather there are so many holes in the one it's got you could explode a planet in some of them (about a third of the way through, one does); but it goes so quickly that the rents and tears and creaking places in it blur out.

You know who the good guys are and who the bad guys are: you get told, in an introductory ribbon of text that diminishes towards the screen top, an homage to the *Flash Gordon* chapter synopses from the twelve-part Saturday afternoon serials of another age. The main good guy is the dissatisfied young farmer, Luke Skywalker, played by an engagingly naive Mark Hamill. Etymologists take note: the relation between Lucas and Luke is obvious. But more, too—the name George comes from the Greek word *georgos*: farmer, i.e., "earth man" or "earth walker." George Lucas/Luke Skywalker, dig? The film is a blatant and self-conscious autobiographical wish fulfillment on the part of its ingenious director.

That Main Good Guy never gets a really direct encounter with Main Bad Guy (the towering and bemasked Lord Darth Vader, played by a sinister and practically invisible David Prowse) is the shakiest part of the plot. Perhaps it's just an oversight. Or maybe material for a sequel. The rumor, at any rate, is that a sequel is under way. Good Show.

The dialogue in *Star Wars* is conscientiously heavy-handed—that kind of humor where what's so funny is the attempt at humor that falls so flat. But sometimes it's just clumsy: when Han Solo, talking about the speed of his ship comments something to the effect, "I made the Kessel run in under three parsecs," the preview audience with whom I saw the film groaned in unison. (A parsec, like a light-year, is a unit of distance, not time, i.e., 3.248 light years.) But despite the groaners—and *Star Wars* has its share (*turbo*-lasers? I assume that's light that's both coherent *and* turbulent at the same time . . . ? Well there're always "wavicles.")—we loved it.

A film is made in tiny, tiny, extremely complicated bits and pieces—and experienced as an almost total gestalt. Very rarely can you locate any element from the gestalt in one and only one of the bits. Nevertheless, some of the

gestalt elements that worked extraordinarily well are worth noting: the particular way the Unadulterated Mysticism of the film interweaves among all the
blasters and space ships and general machinery is very effective. The variation
in locations, planetscapes, starscapes, here desert, there deep space, over here
jungle, over there an urban spaceport, is what makes us believe in the vastness
and the completeness of this universe. And the glorious special effects, which
are the entrance way into each of those varied views, are too effective even to
be described.

Thanks to those special effects, the worlds look big enough to *be* worlds. For
those who haven't seen it yet, some advice: Try to catch this one in a theater
with a fairly big screen where you can sit pretty close. With some films it doesn't
matter much, but on the purely visual level, *Star Wars* is all *about* size—relative
size, variations in size, the way the *very* big can make the ordinary seem *very*
small. And a smaller screen will mute this quality.

Lucas, like his fellow American Bogdanovich and the Italian Bertolucci, is
aware specifically of the history of film. *Last Tango in Paris* had its little recalls
of Vigo and Godard; *What's Up, Doc?* paid its loving tribute to Howard Hawks
and Mack Sennett. Lucas's gestures to the science fiction film as historical
genre may make somebody a PhD some day. Chewie's marvelous head is for
those of you who loved *Planet of the Apes*. The robot c-3po is the "Maria" robot
from Lang's silent *Metropolis*, r2-d2 is first cousin to the little fellow trunding
after Bruce Dern in Trumbell's *Silent Running*. I believe I recall the unextended-
bridge sequence from *Flash Gordon*. Certainly the last time I saw those alien
clarinetists they were taking much more sinister roles in *This Island Earth*; and
the Death Star interior, where Kenobi (played wisely by Alec Guinness) deacti-
vates the Whoseywhatsit, makes a most reverential bow to that shafted city of
Forbidden Planet.

Also, I suspect Lucas rather likes Frank Herbert's novel *Dune* (". . . to the
spice farms!") a lot.

But however many films and other allusions there are, they don't intrude.
They are there for those who enjoy them; those who wouldn't would probably
never know they're there. From beginning to end, the movie is always colorful,
visually energetic, and immediate.

Could it possibly have been any better?

You bet! But to talk about how, we have to talk about the real accomplishment of the film, which we haven't till now touched on; and also show how the
places where it falls short of that accomplishment show a lack of imagination,
a lack of invention, a lack of engagement. For that, we have to delve into a little
theory, and talk about what's been holding the "serious" SF film back till now.

Somewhere around *Brave New World* and *1984* time, the Hollywood picture-
making mentality got fixed in its notoriously unsubtle, collective noggin that science fiction—*all* science fiction—had one message only: In the Future, Things

will be Flat, Uninteresting, Repressive, and Inhumanly Dull. Now there are only so many films you can make about the flat, uninteresting, repressive, and dull. After a while it makes very little difference whether you call it *Alphaville* or *1984*, whether you make it pretty or stark, whether the dull gets overthrown at the end or endures. How many times can you spend ninety to a hundred and twenty minutes where the filmmaker's intention is to show you that things are dull and/or meaningless. (This is not to be confused with the film the *audience* may find dull or meaningless because they can't follow what the *filmmaker* finds interesting. *That* is something else entirely, my friend!)

Lucas's is the first SF film in a long while whose basic assumption—in spite of the flatness of the evil Bad Guys and pure-hearted Good Guys (and tender-tough Good-Bad guys, like Han Solo, played almost antiseptically by Harrison Ford) is that the future will be more interesting than the present. When something is interesting, pretty, or colorful in Lucas's film, we are not (as we are, say, in *Logan's Run* or *Rollerball*) supposed to take it automatically and with no thought as a clear and precise sign for the Superficial, Meaningless, Meretricious, and Tawdry.

In addition to the play Lucas makes on his own name to generate Luke, the very texture and play of the film tells us Lucas would like to live in that future. Whatever the lessons this future has to teach us, about good and evil, about growing up or accepting courage, no matter how painful or unpleasant those lessons, *this* future is seen as a *good* place to learn them, a place where one will have a chance to apply them. It is not the future so many SF films depict, where things are so inhibited that, even if we learn something about life, we will never have a chance to utilize that knowledge short of the place's falling completely to pieces within seventy-two hours of our learning it. And assuming we are lucky enough to survive. In short, there are many ways in which *Star Wars* is a very childlike film. This is to the good.

As frequently, however, it is also childish. And the childishness, whether in the dialogue or in the general conception, *doesn't* work. It is *not* interesting. And it doesn't come *close* to being exciting. Sometime, somewhere, somebody is going to write a review of *Star Wars* that begins: "In Lucas's future, the black races and the yellow races have apparently died out and a sort of Midwestern American (with a few Southwesterners who seem to specialize in being warship pilots) has taken over the universe. By and large, women have also been bred out of the human race and, save for the odd gutsy princess or the isolated and coward aunt, humanity seems to be breeding quite nicely without them. . . ."

When those various reviews surface, somebody will no doubt object (and we'll recognize the voice; it's the same one who said, earlier, ". . . it's got a good, solid story!") with a shout: "But that's not the point. This is entertainment!"

Well, entertainment is a complex business. And we are talking about an aspect of the film that *isn't* particularly entertaining. When you travel across three whole worlds and *all* the humans you see are so scrupulously Caucasian and male, Lucas's future begins to seem a little dull. And the variation and invention suddenly turn out to be only the province of the set director and special effects crew.

How does one put in some variety, some *human* variety? The same way you put in your barrage of allusions to other films, i.e., you just *do* it and don't make a big thing.

To take the tiniest example: wouldn't that future have been more *interesting* if, say, three-quarters of the rebel pilots just happened to have been Oriental women rather than just the guys who didn't make it onto the Minnesota Ag football team. It would even be more interesting to the guys at Minnesota Ag. This *is* science fiction after all.

No more explanation would have been needed for that (They came from a world colonized by Chinese where women were frequently pilots? Possibly they came from a dozen worlds and volunteered because they were all historically interested in the Red Guard? Or maybe it's just because there are, indeed, lots of Chinese women?) than we get for why there just happens to be an Evil, Nasty, Octopoid Thingy in the Death Star garbage dump. (It was busy metabolizing garbage? Maybe it was an alien ambassador who felt more comfortable in that environment? Maybe it just growed?) That kind of off-handed flip is what you can do in science fiction.

In the film world in the present, the token woman, token black, or what have you is clearly propaganda, and even the people who are supposed to like that particular piece of it smile their smiles with rather more tightly pursed lips than is comfortable. In a science fiction film, however, the variety of human types should be as fascinating and luminous in itself as the variety of color in the set designer's paint box. Not to make use of that variety, in all possible combinations, seems an imaginative failure of at least the same order as not coming up with as interesting sets as possible.

In any case, *Star Wars* is a delight. (For those people who like literary parallels, it brings the SF film up to about the *Lensman* stage.) But perhaps the most delightful thing about it is that it brings so forcefully to the imagination the possibility of SF films that are so much better in precisely the terms that *Star Wars* itself has begun to lay out.*

—*May/April 1977*
New York City

*Shortly after my review of *Star Wars* was published in the November 1977 edition of *Cosmos*, I came into the office, where I'd been working as David Hartwell's assistant on the magazine. On the desk was a large pile of mail, which apparently was responses to my review. Indeed, I had never published a piece of nonfiction before or since that so quickly received that much.

I began to open them and read them one after the other and realized, to my astonishment, I had a pile of hate mail in front of me. The only part of my review that anybody chose to respond to were the five paragraphs, out of twenty-nine, that talked about the lack of diversity in the film. By and large, the young, clearly white, mostly male readers had been infuriated. In effect what they said, over and over again, so that I have a clear sense of their response, was "How dare you suggest that there be blacks or Asians or women in *our* film." As one very bright sixteen-year-old analyzed the situation rather insightfully (alas I have to paraphrase): "Whenever we see black characters or characters who don't look like us, it means there is a problem. This was not a film about problems. This was a film about heroic people like us."

By the end of re-reading, today, through the almost three pounds of letters, about the best way I can put it is that I'd had a sudden look through a window at what would largely be Trump supporters or their approving children. It was as startling as any view today of a 1950s Nazi rally in Madison Square Garden, complete with swastikas.

I was rather shaken by the experience, and when, three years later, the next film *The Empire Strikes Back* came out with a black main character, Lando Calrissian, played by Billy Dee Williams, I was pleasantly surprised. If I knew that this was the response to Lucas's fantasia, which I enjoyed and thought was a relatively innocent and fundamentally positive thing in the world, in which there had just been a kind of political oversight, I nevertheless realized it was the source of a great deal of money. Lucas must have known what I knew and had risked alienating a good part of his base by using Calrissian. Indeed, there was only one black character in the film, but it was certainly better than nothing.

When the third film in the initial trilogy appeared in 1987, *Return of the Jedi*, I wrote an overview of the politics of the three films looked at from the point of view of Donna Haraway's *Cyborg Manifesto*. Anyone interested can find that overview as Part II of an essay on Haraway, "Reading at Work," in my collection *Longer Views* (Wesleyan University Press, 1996). It is also an Oedipal reading that starts with the revelation of the relationship between Darth Vader and Luke ("I am your father.") a moment after Vader cuts off Luke's hand, and to escape the dark side, Luke throws himself into "almost certain destruction" until the Millennium Falcon picks him up, and the ritual castration we have just seen precede the fall turns Luke into a hidden cyborg, whose mechanical hand we literally never hear about again in the rest of the series. It is that castration that makes Luke into as much a cyborg figure as Arnold Schwarzenegger in *The Terminator* series.

Over the years, as the franchise grew larger and larger, the diversity quotient grew higher and higher: The most recent leg of the series, now that it has been sold to Disney, turns on a black stormtrooper's—Finn's (played by John Boyega)—disillusionment with the whole military experience, and his friendship with an Asian woman—Rose Tico (played by Kelly Marie Tran). Even if it's Disney, it's somehow warming to see such films take place in a world that produces other successful filmic images such as *Black Panther*'s land of Wakanda and the more pressing realities of Spike Lee's *BlacKkKlansman*.

—November 13, 2018
Philadelphia

5

Samuel Delany, Settling Future Limits

An Interview by Pat Califia

Samuel R. Delany is one of the most widely read writers of modern science
fiction. He is also one of our finest writers, period, of any type. Delany is a
rare gem—a popular writer who does not write down to his audience. The
worst (and bulk) of science fiction (known to fans as SF) utilizes an exotic setting—Mars, a starship, the hive of an alien species—but retains conventional
characters with values and social relations straight out of Twentieth-Century
America. White heterosexual men have all the fun, and their adventures usually include a lot of gratuitous violence and xenophobia. In the background,
buxom blondes simper and plot, and every once in a while they get to hold
the hero's ray gun (or sword) for a few minutes. That's about as sexy as it gets.
There are no queers, no people of color, and no uppity women. Delany is part
of a growing number of fantasy and SF writers (including Elizabeth Lynn,
Joanna Russ, Tanith Lee, Marge Piercy, James Tiptree Jr., and Thomas Disch)
who are changing that. His carefully drawn, three-dimensional characters
come in all colors and ages, both genders, and all sexual preferences.

Some of Delany's more memorable characters include Hawk, the boy
Singer in "Time Considered as a Helix of Semi-Precious Stones," who wan-
ders around clad in filthy black jeans and scars, looking for men who will satisfy
his need for pain; *Dhalgren*'s Tak Loufer, a leatherman with a penchant for
young black men with big dicks, and the Kid, a bisexual man who forms a triad
with a woman and a boy; and Gorgik and Small Sarg, two male lovers who lead
a successful slave rebellion in *Tales of Nevèrÿon* (both of them are ex-slaves, and
one must always wear a slave collar if sex between them is to be satisfactory).

Because the people he writes about are unique and real, Delany can use them to voice social criticism without sounding preachy, academic, or despairing.

In addition to his SF novels, novelettes, and short stories, Delany has written three volumes of SF literary criticism—*The Jewel-Hinged Jaw*, *The American Shore* (a semiotic venture where poststructuralism meets science fiction), and the soon-to-be-published *Starboard Wine*. His book credits also include *The Tides of Lust*. Long out of print but now republished in England by Savoy Books, it is an unabashed and well-crafted porn novel that I can only compare to Georges Bataille's *Story of the Eye*.

Delany was born on April Fool's Day in Harlem. He has traveled and lived in Europe and spent a year or two in San Francisco. In 1961, when he was nineteen and she was eighteen, he married Marilyn Hacker, who in 1975 won the National Book Award for poetry. They had one daughter. After thirteen years they separated and now share custody of the child.

Delany's skill with words is even more amazing if you know that he suffered from dyslexia back in the days when nobody knew what it was, and teachers thought he was playing practical jokes on them when he turned in papers written backwards, which had to be read in a mirror. Today, at the age of forty, Delany lives in New York with his eight-year-old daughter and his lover of five years, Frank.

I've been reading his work ever since 1969, when I was thirteen, so I am really pleased (and also very nervous) when he kindly takes time away from his work to do this interview with me. I've often been disappointed when I've met my favorite authors in the flesh (after all, you can't rewrite and polish first impressions and conversations), but Delany in person is a delight. He is a hefty, deft black man with a good strong laugh that comes easily and often, and he is so articulate that the interview is almost effortless.

I begin by asking why a writer of his caliber would choose to write SF or fantasy—a literary genre that is discounted as being silly, trite, and hackneyed. Delany responds that there was first of all a practical reason, which was that his wife worked as an editorial assistant at Ace Books in 1962 and "used to come home terribly frustrated by the books that she was called upon to edit. Particularly the women characters. Their tendency to be crazed bitches or dottering simps with nothing in between, and the corresponding overmaleness of the heroes, really bothered her." So his first SF novel, *The Jewels of Aptor*, was written "as a kind of in-joke-cum-present for her." But after that first novel, why continue working in that genre?

"You can put together more interesting combinations of words in science fiction than you can in any other kind of writing—and they actually mean something. You can say things like, 'The door dilated.' And it's not just a poetic metaphor. When you say things like, 'Her world exploded,' you are not just giving a muzzy metaphor for a female character's mental state. You reserve the margin for the words to mean that a planet belonged to a woman and it blew up. So SF is sensually very pleasing to work with, just at the level of language. Also, I think what happens with mundane or naturalistic fiction is that you have these characters who succeed or fail in what they try to do, but they succeed or fail against the background of the real world, so that their successes are always some form or way of adjusting to the real world, and their failures are always a matter of being defeated by the real world. So in a funny way, the only thing that mundane fiction can really talk about is either madness or slavery—those people who adjust to the world and therefore are slaves to it, or those people who are defeated by the world and are therefore mad because they shouldn't have tried in the first place. But I do think there's something else to be discussed, other than madness or slavery. In a science fiction story, because success or failure is measured against a fictive world that is itself in dialogue with the real or given world, that dialogue is much more complicated and the resonances are richer for me, and I enjoy working with the harmonies that I can produce. Of course, we all know that there are many things about science fiction that are predictable, too. One of the problems—after having given this glorious and glowing account of all SF's potential—is that for a long time SF has been a kind of marginal writing, a highly conventionalized writing in many ways; so you have a writing situation where you have very many hard and fast conventions. Of course, looked at from another direction, you can do absolutely *anything* in it. But when you can do *absolutely* anything, what you tend to do is fall back on the conventions."

I mention that one of the ways I think he avoids these conventions is to include a broader range of people in his work than most science fiction writers do. I ask him (naively) how many other SF writers routinely use black and Third World characters in their books. He gives me a sharp look. I should already know this.

"Among black science fiction writers there's of course Octavia Butler. She may well be the best of us. And there's Charles Saunders and Steve Barnes; and me. There's always a time as you write in any field where your enthusiasm for it wanes. That's just an occupational hazard. Many, many years ago, one of the things that picked up my enthusiasm for science fiction was Thomas Disch's *Camp Concentration* in which there was a black character, Mordecai. That's the first time I'd seen a black character written by a white writer that just didn't ring entirely hollow. I later asked Disch how he did it and he said, 'By working very hard.' The fact that this happens in science fiction rather than in other areas of writing is probably indicative of something good in the field and in the world. More recently, John Varley has rekindled my interest by the way he integrates science and culture."

However, most science fiction still remains racist, sexist, and homophobic. How come?

Delany lays much of the blame on publishers' and movie producers' "inertia or lethargy: 'This is the way it's been done before; this is the way we will keep on doing it; what's the reason to do it differently?'" But he feels that the audience for SF and fantasy is changing and really doesn't appreciate that anymore. For instance, "I just saw a preview of the movie *Conan the Barbarian* in which there is a really offensive queerbashing scene. The entire preview audience hissed. And in the film's plot, which obviously on some level was designed to be an 'antisexist plot,' there were so many sexist elements that every time one came by, the audience hissed again.

"The other thing probably worth saying is that the bad politics in science fiction come from the same thing that bad politics in most art come from. And it's probably worth noting also that in a number of areas the politics in science fiction are at least a step or two ahead of what's going on in the other arts. I think it's very important to remind people again and again, and also to remind the best-intentioned people, because they forget this—that what makes statements like 'Blacks are lazy and shiftless,' 'Women are lousy drivers,' or 'Homosexuals are emotionally unstable' racist, sexist, or homophobic is not the statements' content, however wrong or ridiculous that content may be. What makes them racist, sexist, and homophobic is the vast statistical preponderance of these particular statements in the general range of utterances of most people most of the time. It's the fact that such statistical preponderance makes it almost impossible to say anything else about blacks, women, or gays. It's the silences in the discourse such statements enforce around themselves that give them their ideological contour. And this is why you have to correct the statistical balance. This is what's wrong with people trying to censor such statements, in an attempt to right oppressive wrongs. You don't right the imbalance—the inequality—by suppressing discourse. What you have to do is allow, *encourage*, even more: intrude new discourse into the area of silence around these statements and broaden the subject. Then such statements just become comments about one or a few observed individuals, statements that are either right or wrong, silly, or interesting."

I compliment Delany on the way he treats women characters. I know I can pick up a book he's written and not be offended by the women in it. How does he do it?

"Well, it had something to do with getting married, even getting married so young. For one thing, I discovered I was married *to* a woman—which was something of an education. I mean, it had never occurred to me, especially in 1961, that men and women live in two entirely different cultures. An incident comes to mind. One day back when we'd been married only a few months, my wife came home from shopping a few minutes after it started raining. When she came into the kitchen door with the groceries, she was sopping wet. So I gave her a pair of my blue jeans to put on. She put her hands in the pockets, and the strangest look came over her face. I said, 'What is it?' And she said, 'Your pockets. They're so big!' Then she showed me the pockets in her girls' jeans. You couldn't get your hand in; you couldn't even get a pack of cigarettes in them! It had never occurred to me before that women's clothing didn't have functional pockets. And I began to think, gee, who would I have been if I had grown up all my life without being able to put my hands in my pockets? I would have been an entirely different person. My whole relationship to my body would be different. Since, as anthropologists do, you define a culture by its costumes, its food, its relationship to money, its relationship to art, its relationship to religion, you have to finally admit that all this is very different for men and women. So men and women live in two very different cultures. It was a problem that I was very unhappy with. The women characters in my early books are fairly strong. They also tend to be superwomen, which is another cop-out and not so new a way of getting around the problem. I also had the feeling at the time that if you only solved the problem once, in one book, it was OK and it was *all* solved . . .

"One of the best ways to portray characters is as a combination of purposeful actions, habitual actions, and gratuitous actions. And somehow the most insignificant male character almost always gets portrayed as a combination of all three. However, the same writers will find it absolutely impossible to portray women characters as exhibiting all three kinds of action. If the woman is an evil woman, she will be all purpose with no habits and nothing gratuitous about her; or if she is a good woman, she will be all gratuitous action, with no habits and no purpose. It's a very strange thing. So when I was writing a set of three books called *The Fall of the Towers*, I sat down and made lists of all three kinds of action for the women characters; then I would get to the end of the chapter and realize I just hadn't put them in. It has all the structure of a psychosis. It really does. When you discover that you are a victim of a psychosis, you realize just how deeply it works into the whole of society."

Delany's work has been controversial because it includes generous dollops of sex. I ask him how he feels about the critics' response to this—especially their characterization of *Dhalgren* as a novel that catered to prurient interest.

"Well, *Dhalgren* is this nine-hundred-page novel of which, by count, I think thirty-six pages could be said to deal with sex explicitly. I *had* to go back and count after all the brouhaha—I'm the kind of person who does things like that, makes lists and counts. What interests me about the specific sex act is the dialogue between what people are thinking at the time and what they are actually doing. That's what makes almost any sexual encounter interesting for me as reading. The most blatant example is the person who, while screwing away madly, is counting the stitches on the mattress. Or the person who is not doing anything at all—you'd think they were counting the stitches on the mattress, but they're actually having a far-out experience. And it's this interplay that makes writing about the specific sexual act interesting. But in a way, that's the same thing that makes any act interesting—the discrepancy between, or the dialogue between, or the distance between how it's being perceived, felt, thought about from inside and what it looks like from the outside. So in that sense I think I like to handle sex as a writer the way I handle everything else. Also, it's beautiful. At its best.

"In science fiction, you can write about sex the way it really happens, whereas in mundane fiction you are more or less restricted, oh, not to the standard missionary position, but at least to the standard missionaries doing it. Sex from time to time happens between more than two people, and sometimes with fewer than two people—which are all good things to deal with. In my new book [*Stars in My Pocket Like Grains of Sand*], I'm writing about a culture in which one of the pieces of folk wisdom, which everybody gets told by the time they are ten, is that in order to have a happy sex life you must have a full masturbatory life, you must have a full life of sex with casual strangers, and a full sex life with one or a few individuals; and none of these three can substitute for any of the others. This is the basic perception of sexuality in this particular world. Which allows people to rebel against *that*: 'Goddammit, I'm going to do *nothing* but masturbate, I don't care what you say! Now, we know that there *are* people who do nothing but masturbate. But the fact that they are doing that in this world, rather than in a world in which the only 'healthy' sex is the sex of standard missionaries, makes it a different kind of rebellion. And since such situations also have resonances with our world, considering *both* worlds—the given one and the SF one—makes the whole thing shimmer a little."

Most of Delany's work takes place in an urban environment. He writes both accurately and poetically about cities, and seems to have little nostalgia for agrarian or hunter-and-gatherer societies. In fact, the much-maligned *Dhalgren* has as much or more to say about the collapse of cities and the anarchic structure of urban subcultures than it does about homosexuality or S/M.

It seems to me that one of his books, *Tales of Nevèrÿon*, is about the formation of the state and the origins of cities, which is pretty heady stuff for "mere" science fiction. Delany talks a little about how *Tales of Nevèrÿon* came to be written.

"I'd been asked to do an introduction to Joanna Russ's sword-and-sorcery-cum-science-fiction series of stories about Alyx the Barbarian [collected in a book: *Alyx* (Greg Press, 1976)]. So I had been doing a lot of thinking about sword-and-sorcery, which is this bizarre subgenre of science fiction that takes place in a distant and completely ahistorical past and that produces things like *Conan the Conquerer*. Sword-and-sorcery tends to be put down in science-fiction circles; you know—science fiction is the *good* stuff! Yet many of the same people like science fiction who like sword-and-sorcery; both genres are published by the same publishers, traditionally; and they're sold from the same bookstore racks. There is this strange give-and-take between the two, and I was wondering what exactly was the connection. One of the things I came up with is the notion that sword-and-sorcery talks about the change from a barter economy to a money economy; it's about this funny transition point—whereas science fiction talks about the change from a money economy to a credit economy. The two of them are doing a similar thing, only one looks backward and the other looks forward. So that's what got me into writing the Nevèrÿon stories. Those stories do tend to be about the interplay between money and barter and the kind of mentalities that go with each one. That book that I've just finished, which is coming out next March from Bantam Books, is the sequel to the Nevèrÿon stories. The title is *Neveryóna*."

We conclude the interview by talking about the difficulties of being a politically aware writer.

"One of my stories that has been most anthologized, 'Time Considered as a Helix of Semi-Precious Stones,' has the ghost of a gay male S/M relationship in it. The story won both a Nebula Award and a Hugo Award for best novelette of its year, but somebody once said to me, 'If most of the readers had picked up on what you were writing about, I don't think you would have gotten the awards.' I've always wondered about that statement. Do I write things so subtle that only a 'knowing few' can get them while the rest think it's all fun and games? Is there something wrong with that, if I do?

"But at this point, I always remember something I heard the novelist and scholar Christine Brooke-Rose say at a Modern Language Association meeting a few years ago, quoting Michel Foucault: 'While we sit discussing the word, power works in silence.' To really change society, you have to go down to the infrastructure—the economics, the demographics, the technology. From there you can see that the upper, verbal level of the discourse—what happens when we sit around talking—has its particular job in the larger scheme. It stabilizes the infrastructure below it. But if it can stabilize, then it can destabilize, which is a great help to the people working for change at the infrastructural level. But to destabilize, you have to start saying really new things, and you have to make the new things said available to people. If all the talk happens in one little room and nobody hears it outside, it's tantamount to its not having been said. But that's what's good about the gay press. That's what's good about science fiction—which, after all, was 16 percent of *all* new fiction published in the United States last year.

"The late French critic Roland Barthes once noted that very few writers fight both ideological repression and libidinal repression. D. H. Lawrence gloried in sexual freedom while abhorring abortion and birth control, in the midst of a bunch of uncritical political notions conservative to the point of fascism. Over the range of his poems, W. H. Auden suggests a psychological and social critique of Western culture that's about as radical as any we've had—but while you read the same poems, you begin to suspect that deep down Auden felt that anything about sex in excess of reproduction, including his own sexuality, was just wrong—however unavoidable.

"The tendency, of course, is to use the repression of political rights or the repression of sexuality as a fixed point from which to launch an attack on the repression of the other. Well, with the work of people like Michel Foucault, Philippe Ariès, and Jacques Donzelot, we're beginning to understand what a self-defeating enterprise *that* one turns out to be! I guess the legacy of the 1960s has allowed us to begin untangling the complex relation between ideology and sexuality.

"Since getting enmeshed in the writing of *Dhalgren*, I've tried to be one of those few writers fighting on both fronts. Since my teens and twenties, I haven't been much of a marcher or a doer, the kind of person who takes real political action. So I'm very glad we have the existing SF platform—not to mention the gay press—where a little of what's truly radical can glimmer, can be seen, and can even, from time to time, cast a shadow beyond our proscribed boundaries."

—April 1982
New York City

6

Introduction to the
Graphic Novel *Empire*

Empire: A Visual Novel, written by Samuel R. Delany and Byron Preiss, illustrated by Howard V. Chaykin.

Have you ever thought how much of our thinking is controlled by gravity? We get a *high* score on an English test; our team gets a *low* score in a volleyball game. Both in anthropology and biology, people will speak of organisms or societies as having evolved to *lower* or *higher* levels—almost everything is measured on this same imaginary scale that runs from *down* to *up*, from *lower* to *higher*. The problem of counting various things by a single measure is one of our major social problems today. How, for example, can we measure time, education, energy, intelligence, usefulness, popularity, attitude, food, shelter, and entertainment all, say, in terms of money? And while we are puzzling over (why not "under"?) this, don't forget that while so many different things are being stuffed, willy-nilly, into the measure of money, money itself is right there on that up-and-down scale: some people are in *upper* income brackets, and some are in *lower* income brackets. The mental pattern that fixes the image of *higher* to the concepts of *larger* and *more valuable* and the image of *lower* to the concepts of *smaller* and *less valuable* frequently leads us to assume that because all things of value are measured on a single scale, all things are valuable or not valuable in the same way.

What has this all got to do with science fiction—with a science fiction story like *Empire,* the story you're about to read? Well, we all know science fiction provides action and adventure, as well as a look at visions of different worlds, different cultures, different values. But it is just that multiplicity of worlds, each careening in its particular orbit about the vast sweep of interstellar night, which may be the subtlest, most pervasive, and finally the most valuable thing in SF (which is what people who *really* like it call science fiction; pronounce it, "Es-ef"[1]). It's a basic image, which, if you left it, can almost totally revise the gravity-bound, upper/lower organization that holds up (or holds down) so much of our thinking. Consider: a rocketship takes off. It goes up, *higher* and *higher*, and still *higher*. At a certain point, after escape velocity is passed, it decreases its acceleration and, inside, suddenly "up" and "down" cease to exist. Everything is in free-fall. The objects that are not tied tight float loosely, unless held by magnets or some other non-gravitic force. Has the direction the ship is flying changed? No. Is it still going "up?" No, because at that velocity, far from a gravitic source, "up" or "higher" simply have no more meaning. But the ship goes on—not necessarily changing its direction, and finally it approaches another world. Suddenly the deceleration rockets cut in. And the ship—*still* without any necessary change in direction—is going *down.*

What's happened?

The whole concept of an endless, linear, vertical measure, ever mounting and with no ceiling, has given way to the concept of relative, unfixed centers, different worlds, different points of view related only by direction, distance, and trajectory. The worlds that provide these centers suggest, by themselves (thanks to their mutual existence and their stellar organization), a very different image of "centeredness" from the kind many people seek today. First off, each world is de-centered, as it were, because it circles around a sun. And every sun —that age-old philosophical image of centrality itself—is de-centered about the revolving galaxy of suns; and the galaxy itself is decentered by the existence of the galaxy of galaxies. And in the most recent star maps and computer-simulation models of the million-plus galaxies so far discovered, though they indeed show many, many clusters (the Virgo Cluster, the Local Supercluster, the Coma Cluster, and m-81, among those that have been named), there is nothing to suggest a real center.

This experience of constant de-centered de-centeredness, each decentering on a vaster and vaster scale, has a venerable name among people who talk about science fiction: "the sense of wonder." And though "sense of wonder" is by no means the last thing to say about SF, enough people read it for precisely that "sense" so that it's not a bad place to start.

Does this mean that linear, *high/low, up/down* thinking is impossible in science fiction? Not at all. It is as prevalent here as it is in any other product of our single world. You'll even find some in *Empire.* But what keeps the whole thing interesting is the way in which the basic SF construct, the worlds to come and the flights between them, suggest, by those de-centerings, ways to *under-*cut that up/down thinking, ways to *over-*come it, ways to surprise it and to subvert it: the SF construct is always suggesting something more—and more exciting.

There's the *real* adventure.

Hold onto your heads.

We're taking off!

—*Winter 1977*
New York City

NOTE

1. For many years, writers and readers of science fiction mockingly pronounced "sci-fi" as if it were "skiffy." It meant mindless, childish, largely thoughtless science fiction. Unfortunately, largely thanks to movies, the term took over anyway and has now become acceptable, similar to the term "nigga" in hip-hop.

7

The Gestation of Genres

Literature, Fiction, Romance, Science Fiction, Fantasy . . .

At the Strasbourg International Colloqium on Genre, in July 1979, French philosopher Jacques Derrida began his essay *"La Loi du genre"* with *"Ne pas mêler les
genres"* (Genres are not to be mixed).[1] The essay proceeds by a series of intellectual feints, turns, and interrogations of its own rhetoric, readings of Gérard
Genette's *L'Absolue littéraire* and of Maurice Blanchot's limpid fable of vision
and blindness, law and the failure of narrativity, crime and the impossibility of
punishment, *"La Folie du jour,"* to suggest that such a law—"Genres are not to
be mixed"—is, for genres, madness.

Derrida goes on to write: "What if there were, lodged within the heart of
the law itself, a law of impurity or a principle of contamination? And suppose
the condition for the possibility of the law were the *a priori* of a counter-law,
an axiom of impossibility that would confound its sense, order, and reason?"

Excerpting synoptic statements, definitive conclusions, or, indeed, any expressed notion that smacks too much of intellectual closure is notoriously difficult with Derrida's writing, which tends to proceed in a style that reminds me
of nothing so much as a white moth in a white cloud, beating its wings against
the mist, only to be repelled by it, again and again, as if its particular luminosity were a species of negative light. But in this essay Derrida comes as close to
an un-self-subverted statement as he does anywhere: "I submit for your consideration the following hypothesis: . . . Every text participates in one or several
genres, there is no genreless text; there is always a genre and genres, yet such
participation never amounts to belonging. And not because of an abundant
overflowing or a free, anarchic, and unclassifiable productivity, but because of

the *trait* of participation itself, because of the effect of the code and of the generic mark." Just before the final movement of his essay, Derrida concludes: "One cannot conceive truth without the madness of the law"—just a paragraph before declaring, "it would be folly to draw any sort of general conclusion here."

What I take Derrida to be saying there and elsewhere in his paper is more or less what Joanna Russ once wrote to me in a letter, after she'd read one or another of my attempts to fix, from the vast gallery of SF rhetorical figures, the specificity of various reading practices and the generality of their organization: "Worrying about the purity of the genres," she wrote, "is like worrying about the purity of the races." I suspect she is right. And I'm afraid I may just be the proof, in both cases, that the horse is already well out of the barn.

But before we leave Derrida's at once dazzling and daunting display of self-subversion and self-interrogation, on the occasion of a consideration of literary genres that has occupied the central spotlight of much recent thinking on genre theory—before we retire to more marginal remarks on generic marks and their problematics within the paraliterary precincts of SF, fantasy, and the like—there is one other passage in this interrogation of *La Loi* that I would like to recall for you:

> Outside of literature or art, if one is bent on classifying, one should consult a set of identifiable and codifiable traits to determine whether this or that, such a thing or such an event belongs to this set or that class. This may seem trivial. Such a distinctive trait *qua* mark is however always *a priori* remarkable. It is always possible that a set—I have compelling reasons for calling this a text, whether it be written or oral—remarks on this distinctive trait within itself. This can occur in texts that do not, at a given moment, assert themselves to be literary or poetic. A defense speech or newspaper editorial can indicate by means of a mark, even if it is not explicitly designated as such: "Voila! I belong, as anyone may remark, to the type of text called a defense speech or an article of the genre newspaper editorial." The possibility is always there. This does not constitute a text *ipso facto* as "literature," even though such a possibility, always left open and therefore eternally remarkable, situates perhaps in every text the possibility of its becoming literature. But this does not interest me at the moment.

Here, in this moment, guided by a gaze cast from the brilliant center of literary and philosophical endeavor beyond the margin to what is "outside of literature and art," I glimpse precisely what interests *me*. Between what "may seem trivial" and what "does not interest" Derrida "at the moment" is what I want to look at with all the interest I am capable of mustering.[2]

Let us re-mark it here:

The generic mark, for Derrida, is a mark that no text escapes, implicitly or explicitly, and is yet a mark always outside the text, not a part of it—such as the designations "science fiction" or "fantasy" on the book spine or cover—a mark that codifies the text on bookstore shelf or under hand, calling into play the codes and reading strategies by which the texts become readable. Readers of Derrida's other works will recognize that this "mark" plays a part similar to a whole host of Derridian terms, running from "supplement" in *De la grammatologie* to "perergon" (or "the framing") in some of his later essays on art.

Well, where do we go to examine these endlessly remarkable marks, outside of literature and art, that lie in that delicate state of in-betweenness, over every text but belonging to none, where, from the point of view of literature, the trivial careens into the uninteresting? I would ask you to consider that odd upper margin in my own text where the title of this paper sits: "Literature, Fiction, Romance, Science Fiction, Fantasy . . ." Where do we go to find this inelegant and ineuphonious set of overlapping marks, some of them clearly on the far side of the literary/paraliterary border? I have simply copied them—re-marked them—from the signs on the edges of the shelves of my local bookstore. And what they mark—what is remarkable about them—is a marginal situation that we who are interested in the workings of genre, especially the interpenetrations and speciation of the paraliterary genres of science fiction and fantasy, might do well to fix, at least momentarily, at the center of our attentions.

These generic marks are the material trace of the inarguable fact that, in the past decade, we have seen the partial mitosis, if not the complete metastasis, of at least three genres. Literature has recently spawned an odd and awkward offspring called "Fiction" (how many bookstores have you been in of late with these two sections clearly marked?) that already threatens to throw off—if it has not already done so—two further subcategories, "Horror" and "Romance" (for a while a term for the novel itself). Certainly all these terms have venerable and staid meanings in the greater history of our language to which all of us, here, certainly have etymological and historical access. Yet, as they emigrate into the workings of our national book production, which contours not only the reading habits of our nation but the millions of dollars and the millions of volumes that bear those marks, not to mention the many more millions of words that are organized by contemporary writers in expectation of the sort of reading those marks have come to call up, meanings change, shift, slip, slide in response to a series of social and economic forces that are, certainly, in their irreducible iterations little different from those that have codified the material reproduction and the critical reduction of all texts over the ages, and thus contoured the protocols by which those texts were read. And Science Fiction, which for many years bore a small, tumorous excrescence, sometimes called "Fantasy" and sometimes "Sword-and-Sorcery," has nearly completed the division into two shelves, "SF" over here and "Fantasy" over there, as distinct as peas and potatoes in adjoining green-grocer stalls, at least in many bookstores around the country.

To examine these generic off-springings even as they spring up around us is to see, as Derrida has told us, that none of these genres are pure, even at birth. ("Every text participates in one or several genres.") We say that "Horror" springs from "Fiction," but clearly the particular Horror genre that Stephen King and Peter Straub have constituted between them—with its fallout among several dozen writers, from V. C. Andrews to Michael Macdowell—owes as much to Science Fiction as it does to Henry or M. R. James, as King himself is the first to acknowledge.

The contemporary "Romance," which we cited, is really two modes: there is the Harlequin and Silhouette Romance, whose origins can be traced back to a sub-genre that fibrillated through the 1960s without ever gaining a mention in *Publishers Weekly*, that is, the "Nurse Novel," which was published at the rate of two a month from one minor paperback house, three a month from another house, their production methods more or less identical to those that Harlequin and Silhouette have now parleyed into the largest single reading experience in the United States, dwarfing on the statistical level the privileged textual canon spotlighted under that more and more beleaguered and ill-bounded category "Literature." The second mode is the historical "Romance," or "bodice buster," which has made Rosemary Rogers the most widely read writer in the American and English languages, her worldwide sales, a few years back, soaring beyond the all-time record of both Shakespeare and the Bible, a position she shares with (in close second place) Stephen King. But how much of interest can be said of either of these two forms of contemporary Romance without citing their immediate predecessor, the contemporary "Gothic,"—the single light in the window and the nightgowned heroine aflight on the rocks or shore or downs—a paperback mode that, a decade ago, seemed destined to reappropriate true generic proportions, but that somehow never got beyond a kind of cult memory of Anne Radcliffe, with a nod to Georgette Heyer.

The current Fantasy genre was spawned in the wake of the J. R. R. Tolkien craze of a few years ago, but it also has resonances with Lord Dunsany, James Branch Cabell, William Morris, and George MacDonald—indeed, a whole marginal literature of the hundred years between the European revolutions of the mid-nineteenth century and World War II—again, an area of writing that has been kept alive by the enthusiasm of SF editors and readers since the 1920s against endlessly changing tides of tastes.

The historical relation between SF and Fantasy, evinced by their current proximity on the shelves carrying both modes in many American bookstores today, is itself a manifestation of the historical coherence of the editorial complex that has overseen both. The relation goes back to the happy accident that *Amazing Stories*, a SF magazine, and *Weird Tales*, a Fantasy outlet, were founded at approximately the same time in the 1920s. Add to this the accident of H. P. Lovecraft's interest in using both SF and Fantasy forms to tell a horror story, and his epistolary energy in conveying his interests and enthusiasms to other writers and, by the middle 1930s, you have a whole range of pulp writers who are now seriously interested in both modes; and there grew up among them an editorial complex to support that interest, an editorial complex that has remained stable and coherent to this day.

This is the light which illuminates the fact that Stephen King assumed that his first published novel, *Carrie*, was an SF novel about a girl with telekinetic powers. It was only because the extra-SF editorial organization at Doubleday, hungry to repeat the commercial success that had attended *Rosemary's Baby* and *The Exorcist*, decided not to place the book in the standard SF line but to publish it as a non-SF-related Horror novel that the artificial ceiling SF at one point imposed on its sales was broken through to begin the Stephen King phenomenon.

It should be clear in the light of these generic developments, that sexual reproduction—syngamy—at least in its usual disexual model, simply does not cover the confused insemination, gestation, and never wholly complete parturition of contemporary genres and subgenres. Indeed, the biological process of syzygy, which Theodore Sturgeon brought to our attention during the "golden age" of SF, is a better explanation of generic speciation. We get a new genre when two old genres, joining, lose their membranous separation, mix and interpenetrate on some intimate genetic level (syzygy), which results in a spurt of growth, multiplication, and the separation of modes, some of which, against an economic and social environment supportive enough, are able to flourish and become genres.

What are the forces that bring this flourishing about? Exposure, advertising, and commercial success—the privileged processes of our specular capitalism —seem to have been necessary to effect this most recent split of the subgenres, "Horror" and "Romance," from capitalism's handmaid and gadfly, "Literature," through the transitory genre of "Fiction." The services the texts themselves seem to supply and stabilize is, in the case of "Horror," a surreal showcase for an endless string of brand names, by which readers recognize the world around them and participate in the commercial success of the text in question; at the same time they are reassured that there is something in that world that is too horrible to deal with, too strange to understand, that will subvert all attempts to change, better, or improve; in the case of "Romance," what seems to have happened is that, in a nation which has been in the midst of one sexual revolution or another at least since the end of England's Edwardian Era, the absolutely safe package for heterosexual carryings-on has once again been found, placing them at just the right historical distance, in just the proper linguistic cloud of aspecific rhetoric and with just the right underlining of emotional and physical violence (read: punishment) to make them palatable to its largely troubled, dissatisfied, and generally underpaid female readership—a job the most literary of genres, the novel, has had to do in one form or another at least since *Pamela*.

Science Fiction, as usual, works differently. First, the coherence of the SF editorial complex created a stabilizing factor absent from these other neogenres.
Ten years ago, the major publishing houses did not have "Horror" editors or
"Romance" editors. Today they do—indeed, a rule of thumb to help us understand what we are reading, what we are buying in the bookstores around us,
might be this: When generic changes become apparent in bookstores, there
have always already been business changes to contour them at the editorial and
distribution levels. Sometimes these changes are causative. Sometimes they are
responsive. But they are there, and the gestation and speciation of contemporary genres are opaque without some understanding of them.

Many publishing houses have had Science Fiction editors for twenty to
thirty-five years, and that editorial complex, now in the dying SF magazines,
now moving its members from publisher to publisher, represents a comparatively stable group, bringing in newcomers slowly, providing a certain training
and even a certain weeding out.

Many people assume today that the Tolkien craze of a few years ago oper-
ated according to the same model that more recently brought King and Rogers
to popularity. They imagine a book discovered by a "literary" editor with a
particularly commercial bent: The text is selected, reproduced, advertised,
published, and becomes exorbitantly popular—and is imitated in a successful
enough manner to establish a genre.

While this was indeed Rogers's situation (and thus gives that phenomenon
a vitality very few in academia are prepared to wrestle with), it is already an
oversimplification of the King phenomenon, and covers the Tolkien phenomenon not at all.

The Tolkien craze could never have occurred without the stability of the SF
editorial complex.[3] Tolkien begins, after an initial appearance as a medieval
scholar turned children's writer, with a set of eccentric volumes, written at the
center of academic Britain, which had a limited but enthusiastic popularity with
—in the 1960s—SF's small, marginal Fantasy audience in the United States
and England, a popularity that endured for nearly seven years, during which
it was observed and remarked by the whole SF community. Only at this point
did an established SF editor decide to make them available in paperback—a
move no general commercial paperback editor would have been likely to make.

The resultant eruption of wide popularity, spilling far beyond the usual SF
audience, not to mention far beyond what were, in those years, its Fantasy margins, makes a situation that is easy to confuse, in its social and economic outlines, with the later situation of Horror and Romance. The difference, however,
is that here what we have was a highly stable, specialized editorial tradition
(in the person of Donald A. Wollheim) that was able to stabilize and organize
the general reproduction, so to speak, of a highly specialized and intellectual
text that would otherwise have been lost to the general readership—rather

than a general fiction editor promoting a commercial find to an explosive and overwhelming popularity.

I think this stable editorial complex—which still oversees jointly Fantasy and SF—is the reason that the Fantasy field today is growing slowly and steadily, by the production of works of comparatively high quality, for example Wangerin's *Book of the Dun Cow* and Ford's *Dragon Waiting*. But I think the same social forces that have created "Horror" and "Romance" as modern genres are at work in the proliferation of contemporary Fantasy in the economic wake of Tolkien, bolstered by the success of Donaldson and Anthony, all of which finally pay for the spread of less commercially successful works that nevertheless serve to educate and stabilize the audience over a given period. We must also note that this editorial stability feeds into an initial reading audience that has its own historically mediated stability of a much greater density and responsiveness than the "Horror" audience (with which it largely overlaps) or the "Romance" audience (from which it is largely distinct, save for a few intriguingly anomalous cases). A genre that explodes onto the social scene with the help of films and television as Horror has exploded can only be stabilized by the audience's lowest common denominator.

The general model that controls the current speciation of "Fantasy" and "Science Fiction" into separate genres is, for better or for worse, the following: the readership of "Science Fiction" is editorially perceived to be about 70 percent male and 30 percent female. The readership of Fantasy is perceived to be about 30 percent male and 70 percent female. In response to this, over the past decade, the SF editorial complex has allowed some editors to specialize in Fantasy—though that same complex, almost without exception, has tended to move such editors slowly but inexorably to a secondary position.

Del Rey Fantasy is the first and certainly strongest attempt to establish a separate Fantasy imprint. The economic reason for this is simply that instead of one lead title every month, Del Rey books can now present two: one Fantasy and one Science Fiction. There is, of course, great pressure from distributors to prevent this: in the larger scheme of things, there are only a limited number of lead slots. And if Fantasy takes one of these over, that it is one less slot for some other publisher, some other genre. Del Rey has only been partially successful. And that, in a word, is why only some bookstores today have separate shelves devoted to Fantasy. But it is also why the SF editorial complex is still on the lookout for texts that will support the notion of a separate and discrete Fantasy genre. And that is doubtless why writers will write them.

It would be silly to predict the outcome of these various generic speciations (and business conflicts); all of them are only more or less complete in their gestations. Ten years hence or twenty years, any one might have vanished, including Science Fiction; and any one might stabilize at a slow and developmental growth, contouring a whole interpretive space around the text toward a range of values we cannot possibly predict today. But there is another possibility: All of them might move toward some homogenized set of unified and codified readings that could easily turn Derrida's assertion, "all texts belong to a genre or to several genres," into a nostalgic memory of a closed historical moment in which there reigned an idealized plurality—though I suspect that the general size of the reading classes sets a lower limit to the homogeneity of generic reading protocols. At least I would hope so. But whatever their futures, I feel safe in predicting that they all will be different; that continuing and developing difference is vouchsafed by the difference of their seeding processes, differences in the varied field through which they have been disseminated, and the innate differences of the dissemination processes themselves.

For many years I have been arguing that Science Fiction is different from Literature. And, like Derrida, I am not all that interested in such marginal texts, such as SF, becoming Literature too quickly—at least before their fascinating and luminous impurities have been studied and stabilized for future readers. And for all its seedings in a marginal practice of imaginative writing, the Fantasy that has been growing under the mark of SF until, recently, it has taken on an organizational mark of its own is, I suspect, worthy of the same respect. For, finally, I *am* speaking of respect. I feel that both SF and Fantasy must be studied in a full awareness of their historical differences as well as their material conflicts and filiations, an awareness of the difference of their discursive organizations, stabilities, opacities, and responsivenesses as they are contoured by everything from their individual interpretive traditions and specific semantic conventions to their hard-edged differences in text production and reproduction.

"Truth is inconceivable without the madness of law." Well, it has been remarked. However great a madness the law of genres ("Genres are not to be mixed.") happens to be, it is strategically indispensable for generic study, even as we admit the staggering impurities, overlaps, and miscegenations that make an appropriate mockery out of any attempt to pin down one text or another in a dead moment of rigorous taxonomy—where, one suspects, death is only inflicted so that the inexorable genre mark may itself now safely be removed.

Those critics who would make SF or Fantasy "Literature," who would deny them their history and nurturance outside the subject-dominated precincts of literature as specific practices of writing with their specific and complex codic responses to the complex object of modern culture—seduced by the nonbelonging of the text to its generic mark—seem to me to be trying to snatch SF and Fantasy out from under their mark to drag them through some genreless, unmarked space in which they will, it is hoped, become "just a text" before relocating them under another mark, which, in its illusory separability from the text, proclaims an innocence, transparency, and purity, free of all history, that no such marking can have.

Within literature, I think the institution of literature itself makes this an impossible crime. Here, in the marginal precinct of paraliterature, where we do not have the protection of a long-established scholarly tradition and a sophisticated critical elaboration, such violence is all too possible, especially when committed in the name of literary authority, even though it entail the greatest and most reprehensible of tortuosities, supressions, and evasions—for the impurities of any text are tenacious. The only thing that will kill them once and for all is concerted historical insensitivity and ignorance.

Genres are not pure. They come to us, always already mixed. But that does not mean they cannot be studied in the specificity of their differences.

To say that Science Fiction (or modern Fantasy) is not the same as literature (or the fantastic) does not mean that what is appropriate to literature is necessarily inappropriate to Science Fiction. ("There is no genreless text, every text belongs one or several genres.") A sophisticated awareness of that difference, of that multiplicity, of those impurities vouchsafe, however, a margin for criticism. It allows us to note when what applies to literature or the fantastic is misapplied to Science Fiction or Fantasy; it preserves a field where critical distinctions can develop in a larger field where too many of the greater social forces militate for an instant and insistent homogenization at the lowest possible denominator.*

—*March–April 1985*
New York

*I have not seen this essay in many years. Looking it over, however, I still abide by what it had to say. I am pleased that the editors consider it worth reprinting after all this time. I no longer remember exactly when the essay was written, but it was published in 1987, so my suspicion is that when it refers to a situation "today," it means a situation that obtained around 1985. Needless to say, though the principles remain in force, the array of genre speciation is notably different today. I do know that when it was submitted, it had a place/date note at the end because all my fiction and nonfiction does, which was—stupidly— removed through some naive notion that something exists in written expression that is universal. Precisely what is worth reprinting thirty, fifty, a hundred years later is worth dating. That is not arrogance. Rather it is necessary humility of the moment.

—*January 2017*
Philadelphia

NOTES

1. Jacques Derrida, "The Law of Genre," trans. Avital Ronell, *Critical Inquiry* 7:1 (Autumn, 1980).

2. I am African-American, but clearly have a lot of European ancestry. Similarly, I am among the earlier mid-twentieth-century SF writers whose work was regularly described, starting in the 1960s, as "literary."

3. By "SF editorial complex" I mean the highly organized readership that goes by the name of "fandom"—with its fanzines and conventions, as many as three or four hundred now across this country, Great Britain, and Europe—and the highly social communication it encourages.

8

Theodore Sturgeon, *In Memoriam*

(February 26, 1918–May 8, 1985)

Sturgeon the writer? I read my first Sturgeon story, in a fat new anthology of science fiction tales, when I was ten or eleven. The story was "Thunder and Roses." Understand, I was a bright, profoundly unimaginative child. (Much of what's called imagination in children is a stark deafness to metaphor coupled with pig-headed literal-mindedness.) Roses didn't have much to do with thunder, so it was a kind of dumb title. The story was mostly about this singer named Starr Anthim, who mostly wasn't there and who sang a kind of anthem, which only made you think about the word itself, its sound and the ways it kept fitting in with other words, instead of just what was happening; and what *was* happening? Well, the tale was full of ordinary guys doing ordinary things like shaving and taking showers, all of which for some reason seemed disturbingly more real than I would have thought anyone could make such things in a story, because there were puddles on the bathroom tiles after the shower, and a crinkled toothpaste tube lying under the mirror. And the only other thing about it was that the world was coming to an end, and everyone felt as powerless as a ten- or eleven-year-old boy to stop it. And when I finished reading it, I was crying . . .

It couldn't have been very good, because that wasn't what stories were supposed to do . . . ?

By the time I was twenty-one, Sturgeon was my favorite writer of any genre. And for all my lack of imagination at ten, Sturgeon's tales taught me as much as any just what a range of incredible things stories, and the language that makes them up, could in fact accomplish.

Sturgeon the man? I met him twenty-five years later. First I got this phone call at the SF Shop on Hudson Street at 12th, where I heard that tenor voice, with its quality like the middle register of an A-flat clarinet and a pacing I start to call drawl—which connotes region or class—while what I heard over the phone that afternoon was a more considered personal rhythm, overlaid on a speech with a geographical variety lingering under the lightness of its L's and R's and over the length of its O's and U's; its articulate U.S. ordinariness put to shame the whole notion of "Midwestern Standard": He was born in Staten Island, N.Y., and raised in a non-Italian neighborhood in Philadelphia.

A few weeks later, in the hotel lobby during a Lunacon, Wina Sturgeon took my arm and said, "Chip, Ted would like to meet you. Why don't you come up in a few minutes. The kids are all there, of course. But if you don't mind them . . . ?" and gave me a room number; and left.

Someone with me made the obligatory comment about the fact that the Sturgeons were (or had been at one time) nudists, with jejune speculations on what an audience with them might be like.

Perhaps my imagination was still underdeveloped; I thought it was sad that precisely the social and personal discomforts nudism, as I understood it, is supposed to defuse seemed to have taken refuge in just that sort of talk circling around it.

Minutes later, I took the elevator up, turned down the hall, knocked on the wood beside the painted metal laundry bin that hung on the door itself, and heard kids laughing.

Someone said, "Come in." Then someone opened the lock.

Yes, the room was filled with Sturgeon children, Tandy, Noël, Robin, Adam . . . and Wina; and a couple of more friends.

Sturgeon was sitting on the bed, back against the headboard, wearing some handmade embroidered pants—maybe sandals, I don't remember. A medium-height man and deeply tanned, he was on the upper side of middle age, with gray hair grizzled on the thinning chest. The only picture I'd ever seen of him was the Ed Emsh portrait in the fantasia cover for the special Sturgeon issue of *F&SF* for September, 1962. What I saw there in the hotel room was that same face, with its beard and fine bones—described in one or another article I'd read as "Puckish" or "pixie-ish." But it was that face aged by a decade. Sturgeon gave out a measured calm that was glimmering through the confusion of children's questions and visitors' comments, very natural and very winning. An impossible situation for conversation?

No, not at all.

It was a pleasant, friendly evening, with lots of mutual good feeling; but all that saying it makes me want to do is take the cliché "pleasant and friendly" and figure out some way to retrieve the meanings that I've worn off the words from overuse. Because that pleasant evening started like a warmth behind the knees and rose through the body until it reached the shoulders, letting loose—

now at the amused chuckle from Ted, now with someone's observation about some situation two thousand miles away, then a stern word to a child and a hug to the same child a moment later—all the tensions, one by one, that comprise the opposite of "pleasant" without reaching pain, so that the expectation of nervousness and all I brought with me could settle into the simpler and more intense feeling of friendliness.

A pleasant, friendly evening . . .

Sadly, it seemed a long time before I saw Ted again.

One of the things I thought going up to that room, and I thought it again as I left: Sturgeon's stories had starred the whole of my reading life. And now I have met him. And I felt terribly proud and privileged.

If I may strain a metaphor: Language is the sky we all live under. It's pretty much a total surround, both to thought and to action. "For poetry makes nothing happen," remarked Auden on Yeats. But once in a while, by luck or by skill, in poetry or in prose, a writer can put words together so that, if they don't make things happen, they make us for a moment see things happening. The range of Sturgeon's work is an immense and astonishing galaxy of such dazzling and precise lights against the night of ordinary speech.

I have written before, and I stand by it: "The corpus of science fiction written by Theodore Sturgeon is the single most important body of science fiction by an American today." But that is because, held up against American writing of its time Sturgeon's is simply among the best writing, period.

Our acquaintanceship—and I know Ted would have let me call it friendship—was limited to the last decade of his life, during which I met him only four or five times.

The second of those meetings was most of the day I spent with him when he was recording "Bianca's Hands," "The Hurkle Is a Happy Beast," and the "Britt Svenglund" section from his then-unpublished novel, *Godbody*. The record (*Theodore Sturgeon Reads*, 1976) was done for Roy Torgeson's Alternate World Recordings. My overly compressed account of the meeting at Roy's, our Chinese lunch, and the recording session itself make up the album's liner notes (see pages 27–31 in this collection). The next time I saw him was maybe five or six years later after that, with his new life-companion Jayne and, again, daughter Tandy, who instead of being fifteen or sixteen as she had been in that hotel room was now a new published poet in her twenties with a wonderfully proud and happy father, for all his natural modesty.

Pride? Modesty? Like pleasure and friendship, their nuances sat so neatly and easily in Ted that afternoon, while we ate sandwiches in a beige SF convention meeting room with Jayne and Ted and Tandy and Judy Merril and Art Saha and half a dozen other people moving around it and through it, that I just wish somehow I could fix the delicacy of their angle and interface for you. But

I can't. Which is frustrating. Because Ted himself was a writer who could make just such delicate emotional conjunctions as real as the change in texture from cast face to broken face as you run your thumb over the corner of a cracked brick, or the combination of smooth and rough when you grasp a camshaft sticking from a flange leaking grainy oil.

A few times in our meetings, Ted and I made plans to get together and really sit down and talk—even going as far, the last time I saw him in Vancouver in June 1984, as to fix a summer date. But somehow summer came and went. So did winter. And Ted is dead.

So I must be content—once more—with reading him once more.

But the shock shakes up the sky and sets the stars to shiver.

We have lost our writer.

—May 1985

9

Note on Le Guin

The Kesh in Song and Story

Ursula K. Le Guin, *Always Coming Home*, with illustrations by Margaret Chodos and music by Todd Barton (New York: Harper & Row, 1985); boxed set: book and cassette.

With high invention and deep intelligence, *Always Coming Home* presents, in alternating narratives, poems, and expositions, Ursula K. Le Guin's most consistently lyric and luminous book in a career adorned with some of the most precise and passionate prose in the service of a major imaginative vision.

Mrs. Le Guin has created an entire ethnography of the far future in her new book. It's called a novel. But even to glance at it is to suspect it's more than, or other than, that: the oversized trade paperback is boxed with a cassette tape of delicate songs, poems, and haunting dance pieces, purportedly recorded on site. Liner notes are included. Are they by the composer, Todd Barton, or by Ursula Le Guin? It's not indicated. I would like to know, since each entry, with its song or poem, is a small story in itself. Margaret Chodos's fine line drawings portray animals, birds, sacred implements and symbols, tools, mountains, and houses (but no people); and we have charts, maps, alphabets, and a glossary. The book contains a short novel, *Stone Telling*, spaced out in three parts, narrated by a woman called Stone Telling; and "Chapter Two" from another novel, *Dangerous People*, by Wordriver. Along with Marsh, Cowardly Dog, and Mote, Wordriver is among the great novelists of the Kesh, the people of the Valley, the subjects of Mrs. Le Guin's pastoral vision. In addition there are poems, children's stories, adult folk tales, verse dramas, recipes, essays, and a host of

Kesh documents. Though the word "Indian" does not appear from one end of the book to the other, the reader is likely to feel after only a few pages that much Native American culture has become a part of this dark, wise, stocky people's way of life. Mrs. Le Guin has given us the imaginary companion volume of "Readings" that might accompany a formal anthropological study.

When did the Kesh live? They haven't, yet. The Kesh have access to a daunting computer system. But they live five hundred years or more in our future, on the northwestern coast of what's left of a United States gone low-tech and depopulated by toxic wastes and radioactive contamination. The Kesh are an attractive people. One noun serves them for both gift and wealth. To be rich and to give are, for them, one verb. They do not share the West's present passion for origins and outcomes: their pivotal cultural concept is the hinge, the connecting principle that allows things both to hold together and to move in relation to each other. Their year is marked off by elaborate seasonal dances. Their lives and work are organized in a complicated system of Houses, Lodges, Arts, and Societies.

A minor tribal war occurs between some thirty-odd young men of Sinshan, the Kesh village, and a few of the neighboring Pig People. There is a much larger and longer one between the Condor Men and the Valley people that occupies the periphery of *Stone Telling*. In the end both wars are shown to share the same small-scale tribal form, for all their real deaths, real suffering, and real shame. But they are very different from the technological mega-wars of our century.

The emotional high point, for me, was the transcription of a Kesh play, "Chandi," a retelling of the biblical tale of Job. A society in which such a tale is important cannot be a simple utopian construct: a Job (or a Chandi)—that most anti-utopian of myths—reminds us too strongly that as long as culture is pitted against nature, along whatever complex curve, the best of us may slip into the crack to be crushed by unhappy chance. The Chandi play is followed by a luminous meditation on a scrub-oak ridge by Mrs. Le Guin's ironic alter ego Pandora—giver of all gifts, mother of all afflictions, guardian of hope —who, throughout the book, "worries about what she is doing," to the reader's delight and enlightenment.

Mrs. Le Guin has put some expository pieces in a hundred-plus-page section called "The Back of the Book." These are among the most interesting, the most beautiful. I suggest going straight to them and reading "What They Wore," "What They Ate," and "The World Dance" before beginning the book proper. They will enhance Stone Telling's tale of her childhood considerably. (By the same token, don't read "The Train," or you will spoil a pleasant narrative surprise earlier on.) Grouped between the prose pieces, the seventy-odd poems slow up a straight-through reading. Not particularly difficult or particularly bad. But a contemporary reader, for whom poetry is still a high art, and for whom the poet is at once on the margins of society while oriented toward the center of culture, simply finds it hard going through the Kesh's overwhelming poetic saturation. And while we understand the poems as simple surface utterances, at a deeper level, where we expect poems to be meaningful, they don't make much sense. I only wish Mrs. Le Guin had written more prose about the practice of poetry in the Valley with, say, the same energy and vividness she employed to write about the cosmogenic Dance of the World or the Saturnalian Dance of the Moon—two of the book's most spectacular set pieces.

Mrs. Le Guin is among the half-dozen most respected American writers who regularly set their narrative in the future to force a dialogue with the here and now, a dialogue generally called science fiction. She is also a much loved writer. And *Always Coming Home* is a slow, rich read, full of what one loves most in her work: a liberal utopian vision, rendered far more complex than the term "utopian" usually allows for by a sense of human suffering. This is her most satisfying text among a set of texts that have provided much imaginative pleasure in her twenty-three years as an author.

—September 1985

10

Eden, Eden, Eden

Genesis 2:4–22

A small park—really a square—sits between some buildings on 48th Street, just beyond 8th Avenue. Before a tan brick wall along the western edge or at a few spots between the three rows of benches, trees stand in built-up brick planting areas. I call it Social Security Park: New York City's Social Security Offices are about two doors further east. For the last year, I've often gone there to write—sometimes to read. I read most of Paul Ree's *Heidegger* volume there. The place houses a shifting population of a dozen or so homeless people, four women—one Asian, two whites, one Hispanic—and at least eight men, mostly Hispanic or black. A few have been there for two years or more. Most are crackheads. All drink.

At any given time, on opened-out cardboard cartons, under blankets or sleeping bags, or stretched on the benches' unpainted gray planks, two to six will be asleep—day or night. The soap-opera component is high. They're always swiping things from one another (IDs, birth certificates, money), especially when a stranger comes to sleep on one of the benches. A bizarre undercurrent of sex inheres there. Twice now I've caught guys in the corner masturbating while they watch one or another homeless woman, whose clothes are coming apart, asleep on some cardboard.

Because so rarely is anyone there whom you could call sober, people make endless (and often wildly inaccurate) calls on who stole what from whom.

At one time or other, I've had half-hour to three-hour conversations with pretty much everyone who stays there.

The women have all been, or are still, occasional prostitutes. Even the most beat-up and dilapidated of them plays a constant game with the various men: How long can she hold out and for how much, whether it's a swallow from a bottle of beer or wine, a hit from a stem of crack, a bite of food, the distribution of clothes, or what have you before this man or that one grabs a feel, hug, or fondle.

I'm tempted to give portraits of its several individual denizens. This summer Darrell Deckard (of my book *Times Square Red, Times Square Blue*) has been sleeping there regularly, with his current partner, a good-looking young Hispanic. The last time I ran into them, I gave them change toward a quart a milk, as they'd gotten hold of some cookies. Both were going on about how good cookies and milk were.

But I'll turn from this node of degradation, misery, and excrement—the toilet is the corner drain: three square yards of pavement stay contagiously foul with urine turning to ammonia, shit, and flies darting off or spiraling down—along with heroic attempts to wring some enjoyment from life (cookies and milk!) despite crack, homelessness, and material forces like the cops' visits (every two days or three, to throw out blankets, cardboard, any belongings and junk), which shatter what passes here for happiness—for another park to the east.

Here's my promised reading of the Garden of Eden story, as the J-Writer's version (those biblical texts presumably written in the late period of the Court of David, shortly after 722 BCE) has been separated out from that of the later P-Writer (the Priestly Writer, as he is called; or often the *Elhoist*, since this writer uses the word Elohim, which James's translators rendered "God," instead of the J-Writer's YHWH, which they translated as "the Lord God") and the D-Writer (the Deuteronomist).

It might help to consult the Friedman translation, the Rosenberg translation, and the King James (this last with the later-written P-Writer's material still attached to the front: the traditional seven days' creation). The best way to appreciate what follows is to read all three, then my exegesis—then to read the translations again.

A trope repeats twice in the tale of the Garden of Eden, more or less clearly, in all three translations. To retrieve that trope's narrative force, however—along with its narrative playfulness—we must look at two contextual aspects and two translational fine points.

The first contextual element is YHWH's humanity, remarked on many times by generations of commentators. The J-Writer's YHWH has a very different feel and affect from the P-Writer's Elohim in the opening chapter (along with the first three verses of the second chapter) of Genesis. Elohim is a Spirit that moves on the water and on the land and speaks and creates the world in seven days—making man on the sixth in His own image—and rests on the seventh day, which he blesses and sanctifies. But the J-Writer's YHWH is far more embodied. He dirties His hands in mud, blows on clay figures, calls, speaks, grows angry, mutters to Himself, and walks and searches among the trees of the garden.

As noted, today, the general scholarly consensus is that the P-Writer (author of Genesis 1) wrote about five hundred years after the J-Writer, and (believes Friedman, correctly by my lights) that a later editor (possibly the Deuteron-omist [D], or the Redactor [R]) cut the J-Writer's text up and "filled out the story, for and aft, with the more recently written pieces.

YHWH fashions man, however, from wet mud. After putting Adam (Hebrew: Of Red Earth; Of Red Clay; Of Red Mud) to sleep, YHWH pulls a rib loose from his creation, from which, by the time Of Red Earth wakes, YHWH has made a woman. YHWH walks in the garden during the afternoon breeze. YHWH makes garments of skins for the naked Adam and the woman. But over and above the human scale of YHWH in the works of the J-Writer (who, now and again, as we shall see, rivals a nineteenth-century realist in her delineation of human idiosyncrasies[1]), there is a repeated playfulness to the narration itself, which we shall examine in this second but chronologically earlier of the two creation stories that open Genesis, the first book in the Bible.

At the start of that earlier story, after a rising mist wets the earth and creates a garden, YHWH places two trees therein, the tree of life and the tree of the knowledge of good and evil. He forbids eating from the second tree, with a threat of death ("for on the day that thou eatest of that tree you shall surely die")—and eating only from the second tree. Though J does not specifically say so, all the others are allowed, including the first. But the subtle serpent beguiles the woman in a conversation back and forth that is made up almost entirely of quotes and paraphrases of what God has already said (presumably as recounted to her by Of Red Earth), with the serpent adding a bit of what God knows, in order to explain and interpret the words:

> The woman: "God hath said, Ye shall not eat of it, neither shall ye touch it, lest ye die."
> And the serpent said unto the woman, "Ye shall not surely die; for God doth know that in the day that ye eat thereof, then your eyes shall be opened, and ye shall be as gods, knowing good from evil."

This conversation is, I believe, the playful core of the story. I call it playful because it suggests a contradiction that the text itself must resolve, a resolution that can only be carried out through the closest reading of the text's rhetorical play. Indeed, to stray too far from the specific language that tells this tale is to obscure the resolution which marks *both* the original text as literature *and* the King James translation as the best of the three I have here included. Any such straying begins to make the tale noticeably less interesting. For if what God says is true, then the serpent is a liar and the truth is not in him. But if what the serpent says is true, then God is a liar and the truth is not in *Him*. From a superficial reading of the text, at least, it would seem that the serpent's words are the literal truth. The woman and Adam eat the apple, and on that day they are cursed and expelled from the garden—but both Adam and Eve have many years of life and childrearing left them. This seems to contravene everything we know of "the word of God." One seriously doubts that, if the reigning interpretation of the tale had been "God speaks falsely," the redactors who assembled the texts that made up the *Bible* would have even included it, much less put it first.

A careful reading of the text, I maintain, shows, however, that *both* speak versions of the truth; God's truth appears simple but, we shall see, is in reality complex. The serpent's truth at first appears more complex than God's (it takes more words to say). Finally, however, it is revealed to be only partial—indeed, tragically incomplete: what today we might call "a lie of omission."

God is right.

The serpent is wrong.

But we cannot understand the nature of the resolution of the apparent textual aporia unless we start with exactly what it means to be "as gods." Is it *just* a matter of knowing good from bad? (That is the translation Friedman prefers, and we shall adopt it.) Or is it more complex?

I maintain that it is more complex, but that we only find out what the complexity is in the last sentences of this opening story from the J-Writer (she provided many tales in the Pentateuch, including the story of Abraham and Isaac, identified by *vocabulary, grammatical form*, and *syntactical usage* [i.e., specific rhetoric], these latter modes being two that St. Jerome, the Bible's earliest "modern" editor, does *not* take into account when assigning various texts to various authors[2])—and, what's more, that complexity is set up by the previous employment of the same trope earlier on in the story.

The other contextual knowledge that we need is knowledge of gardens, deserts, snakes, and the realities of the birth of human beings.

Now, having highlighted the core, we can go back and read the story from the beginning. It was written down sometime toward the end of the reign of the Court of David (possibly, suggests Harold Bloom, as one of a set of teaching tales for children; and surely, suggests Friedman, as the opening symbolic movement for a prose history of brilliant construction).

Once again, from the beginning:

The story starts, before there was a man to till the ground, on the day of the misting that saw YHWH's creation of earth and sky. When the fog retreats, there is a pleasant garden—of the sort that often blooms after such alluvial floods, as are common around Middle Eastern rivers once, indeed, the river returns to its bed. Now two trees are mentioned that YHWH caused to grow, the tree of life and the tree of the knowledge of good and bad.

Next we survey the four rivers and four lands of the area, before the tale continues.

This paragraph may also be an interpolation from a later written text. (Cush is an old name that covered an indistinct region including some of Egypt and stretching south into Ethiopia.) But the passage is small enough so that it can be absorbed by the tale, by the text.

YHWH models the first man from wet clay, into whose nostrils He blows life and sets the man in the garden to work it and to watch over it. With that responsibility goes the command: "You *may eat* from every tree of the garden. But from the tree of the knowledge of good and bad: you shall not eat from it, because in the day you eat from it: you'll *die!*" (Translation modified.)

Now, we must look more closely at those italics, *may eat* and *die*. Friedman tells us that, in Hebrew, these represent what he calls infinitival intensifiers. Literally: "you to eat in order to eat from every tree" and "you will to die in order to die." In English the literal translation is almost without meaning. (But not quite—and on that not quite hinges the truth of YHWH's assertion.)

In a number of languages infinitives and participles do similar work. Translations far closer to the literal meaning of the Hebrew are: "you in eating may eat from every tree" and "you will in dying die." (This substitutes English participles for Hebrew infinitives.) Friedman points out that the intensifiers are sometimes translated, as the King James translators do, as "may certainly (or 'of course') eat" or "surely die." But we must remember the other, literal meaning: "You may, in order to eat, eat" and "You will, in order to die, die." That is to say, there is a complex and nuanced literal meaning as well as the more colloquial meaning, signaling simple intensity.

In my reading, both meanings of both phrases are appealed to in the story. Those phrases will, by the end of the tale, be re-read to take on the literal sense: especially "you will, in dying, actually die"—as opposed to *not* actually dying when you die. Or, as I would interpret it, not actually dying when you know the real significance of dying. (Not *truly* dying when you learn the real meaning of death.)

But we shall get back to this in due time.

The other translation point has to do with the words "good" and "bad." Friedman tells us he uses these words rather than the more austere, abstract pair "good" and "evil" that King James's translators employed, because, in fact, in Hebrew the words (*tov* [good] and *ra* [bad]) are the most ordinary words for what's good and what's bad—often in the sense of what's good for you and what's bad for you. The connotation of evil and goodness are secondary, not primary, but rather a bit of historical transcendentalizing the postmodern reader should easily be able to bracket.

Very well: The tree of "knowing what's good and what's ill" (another possible translation) has, in that sense, a suggestion of prophecy in it: Knowing the good to come and the ill to come.

This might be seen as a primitive, but also a practical notion of wisdom itself: the foreknowing of the good outcomes of things and the bad outcomes of things. This is, of course, one of the ways gods and men differ: presumably gods have a greater—even an absolute—foreknowledge of how things are going to work out that mortals lack. Indeed, part of the great historical importance of this story is that it is the earliest text with any popular dissemination that recounts humanity's learning of its own mortality, its philosophically defining characteristic.

Now we come to the creation of woman. Though there are many things to say about this mini-story inserted into the larger story, we mention only three: First, overtly it contravenes common sense and adult experience, putting us directly into the world of folktale and myth. Second, the story is used to explain the reason man dominates women (it tells us that this *is* a patriarchal society) and also—third—that this is (for all the society's patriarchal structure) also a *matrilocal* society: Man parts from his father and mother to go live where his wife lives, as was the custom in most Middle Eastern tribes at the time.

Now . . . The serpent tempts the woman by offering her the possibility of being "like God"—by opening her eyes to the knowledge of good and bad. So the woman, then Adam, eats the apple: "And the eyes of the two of them were opened, and they knew that they were naked."

Here we have to ask: What precisely does this mean? What *exactly* did they know? And is that *all* they knew? Or did they know something else as well?

Here again, one question must be: *Has* the serpent spoken the truth—or has he lied?

Looking ahead, the answer is clearly: He speaks the truth as far as he goes. He simply does not speak the *whole* truth. "Eat of the forbidden fruit, and you will be like God *in one aspect*"—but, the serpent has failed to say, "You will not be like God, in another."

What *is* this distinguishing aspect?

Well, here, when God comes walking in the garden and confronts first Adam, the woman, then the Serpent, the text would seem to play a little joke on us.

As we said, the first knowledge that Adam and the woman appear to have taken on is that they are naked—that they are without clothes against the elements, that they are unprotected, both from the contingencies of the world and from the ebb and flow of their own sexuality. Some control over this last is what covering the genitals presumably affords them. That done, they can now choose when to have and when not to have sex. Do you think they now know also what the outcome of sex is likely to be (i.e., children)? Probably—though the J-Writer skirts that issue with the indirection of the fig-leaf tale: The fig leaf is the leaf that accompanies and often hangs down to cover the incredibly sweet and luscious fruit of the fig itself.

But, again, what *other* knowledge have their eyes opened to?

Is the narrator telling us all his or her archetypal humans know, or only some it—the way the serpent told Adam and Eve only the way in which they would be like God (but, again, not mentioning an all-important way in which they would *not* be)?

Any attempt to control sex is to put oneself in a matrix of shame and embarrassment. To *cover* the genitals is—practically by definition—to court shame and embarrassment when they are *uncovered*, or uncovered at the wrong time; or, indeed, even when they are uncovered at the right times! What starts as simple conscious logic, soon becomes social habit—and the violation of the social, even for so necessary a process as procreation, is always anxiety ridden. Fortunately the urge for pleasure seems to be stronger than that all-powerful superego that is the primitive motivation for the story itself. The question is: Is the story a mythical expression *of that superego*, or is it a sophisticated literary dialogue *with/against (a playful engagement with) that superego*? I maintain it is the second—and that the sign that it is the second is the permanent undecidability as to whether it is the second or the first, an ambiguity literature has to maintain in order to survive. ("Literature survives by fertile ambiguity.") The J-Writer would seem to have had a sophisticated understanding of the move from sexual innocence ("they were naked and they were not ashamed") to the trammels of, dare we call it, "adult sexuality," in which some responsibility is assumed ("they saw that they were naked and they were ashamed"). The insight is worthy of Freud.

The text conveys the anxiety of Adam and the woman's explanations to YHWH by other reduplicated intensifiers that Hebrew can muster (rather like present-day Swahili), "the snake that snake" (reduplicated nouns) and "she that she" (reduplicated pronouns) and "tricked in tricking me" (this last, another infinitival), which Friedman and the King James's translators again convey by italics—and which Rosenberg ignores:

> (8) And they heard the voice of the Lord God walking in the garden in the cool of day: and Adam and his wife hid themselves from the presence of the Lord God amongst the trees of the garden.
>
> (9) And the Lord God called unto Adam, and said unto him, Where *art* thou? ["Hey, where *are* you?" "Where have you gotten off to?" "Where are you that you are?"]
>
> (10) And he [Adam/Of Red Earth] said, I heard thy voice in the garden, and I was afraid, because I *was* naked ["After all, I was naked." "I was that I was naked."]; and I hid myself.
>
> (11) And He [the Lord God] said, "Who told thee that thou *was* naked?" ["Who

told you that you were actually naked?"] "Has thou eaten of the tree, whereof I commanded thee that thou shouldst not eat?"

(12) And the man said, The woman whom thou gavest *to be* with me ["whom you gave to be with me that she be with me," "whom you really gave to me," "whom you gave to me to be mine," "the woman you *gave* me, after all"], she gave me of the tree, and I did eat. ["The woman whom *you* gave me yourself, she *gave* me the fruit, and so I ate."]

(13) And the Lord God said unto the woman, What *is* this *that* thou has done? "Did you *really* do *that?*" And the woman said, The serpent beguiled me.

But we can hear the raised voices, the stressed words (the reason we use italics for stressed words today is because that's how King James's anonymous translators dealt with them), the intensity of their utterances, as Adam offers his anxious explanation to YHWH, and the woman gives Him her timid excuse. . . . Though we might lose some colloquial details, we can recognize an auctorial attempt to register not a heated exchange, but an extremely emotionally invested dialogue, across translation and three thousand years! That's *quite* a piece of literary ventriloquism.

YHWH's response is to curse the snake (verses 14 through 19), before turning to extend that curse to the woman and Adam. Like a Celtic *flyting*, here the text reverts to poetry. In the course of that curse suddenly we, the hearers, learn something about the serpent that we could not have known before. Declares YHWH to the snake:

(14) . . . "Because you did this . . . you'll go on your belly, and you'll eat dust all the days of your life."

Suddenly we have to revise our whole picture of the past of this story. We all know that in folktales animals talk. But *we* thought that the snake was crawling around all the time, just the way snakes do today. Now, subtly, the J-Writer has told us that our picture of the snake up till the present has simply been wrong. The snake has been *walking* upright till now, even in this very story just as God walked in the Garden, just as Adam and the woman walked, or indeed the other domestic animals walked—walked upon legs.

Adam, the woman, and YHWH certainly all knew this before the apple. Only the ideal first-time hearers of the tale (the children that the tale may have been intended to instruct, gathered together on the floor, as surely their parents lingered in the background of the palace chamber) do not.

The J-Writer has used her account of some overheard words, spoken by YHWH in anger, to open their eyes to a bit of folk history.

What has happened is that, in effect, by having overheard a few words uttered by the angry YHWH, we have taken on knowledge that the history of the world, especially of snakes, is different from what we thought it was only a word or two before YHWH spoke. We have had to revise our picture of what the world was like before we learned this—even the very part of the story we have just read.

Such an effect can only be done with words. It cannot be done—with the same results—in pictures or theater. This is one of the supreme moments of the tale that makes it literary.

In a moment's irony and humor, I believe, this is also the story's controlling trope: for, shortly, at an entirely different level, the tale will surprise us with the same trope once again. Only then the story will use it to effect the narrative's *major* point. The double usage of this trope, among many other skillful effects, again, makes the story literature—and, yes, great literature.

The snake is cursed—and with that curse we gain our knowledge of its upright (or, at any rate, four-legged) history prior to the curse.

The question of sex (specifically the attempt to control sex, and therefore procreation, which the nakedness/shame/fig-leaves allegorize) returns us to the story of the creation of the woman from Adam's rib. The mode of this sub-tale (verses 18–25) is in the same mode, we should note, as that of the revelation of the serpent's ambulatory history: which is to say, it told us that—as counterfactual as it may seem—years closer to the origin, even so fundamental a process as birth itself, under the hand of YHWH, could occur entirely otherwise from the way we now know and experience it. Unlike the revelation of the serpent's walking, however, it is not accomplished by a verbal trick. Rather it was told to us relatively directly—perhaps to prepare us for the later revelation of a formerly upright serpent: If you'll accept this, you'll accept anything it says, with its somewhat knowing tone, even as it evokes what the Romantics will eventually dub "the suspension of disbelief." But just see *how* knowing that tone is. Certainly rumors of farmers and husbandmen with their flocks and herds—the tales of feral children (c.f., the childhood of the beast-man Enkidu, the secondary hero in the Epic of Gilgamesh: surely the result of an unnatural union)—were as common then as now, if not more so.

> (18) And the Lord God said, *It is* not good that the man should be alone; I will make him a help meet for him.
> (19) And out of the ground the Lord God formed every beast of the field, and every fowl of the air, and brought them unto Adam to see what he would call them; and whatsoever Adam called every living creature, that *was* the name thereof.

(Sometimes the verb *to be* and certain pronouns are simply understood in the Hebrew. These added words are also indicated with italics by the scrupulous translators.) Adam names them all, but they are apparently not help meets (i.e., help-mates, i.e., helpful companions/powers) enough. At least one sign of their insufficiency of help to him is that—certainly known to the more knowing among the audience—congress with them (re)produces neither their kind nor his nor any other. Thus YHWH causes a deep sleep to fall on Adam. YHWH tugs free a rib from Adam's side, from which he fashions a notably more helpful mate, presumably for sex and everything else.

Surely, this is the place to note that, even so far along in the story, the woman has not yet received her name from Of Red Earth. It is easy to imagine a patriarchal discourse in which each of God's creatures is brought before Of Red Earth so that he may know this creature (and we may read "knowing" in as knowing a tone as the tale-teller might use to tell the tale)—whereupon the mark of his knowledge is the name he gives. This, then, would be the dramatic incident in which Adam comes to know (in both senses) the woman. This explains why his naming of her only comes at the far side of the curse of Edenic expulsion.

The pleasure and joy of sex is, in brief, what they knew before the apple.

The results of sex and the responsibilities those result in is part of the knowledge that comes with eating the apple itself.

But the very complexity of such knowledge should re-prompt the question we have already asked once: Have they learned anything else?

Before we leave this tale within a tale, however, we note that at this time the conventions of dialogue are not as fixed, at least in the precinct of narrative, as they will be even five hundred years later when the P-Writer will remake God (Elohim)—from a body that speaks and even mutters, and in whom such speech can result from an excess of emotion—into a spirit (a breath) and a voice (that moves over the waters) alone; or, as Erich Auerbach notes in *Mimesis*, a few hundred miles across the Aegean *The Odyssey*, with rhetorical figures such as Odysseus's scar, will construct more intricately mimetic modes of narrative. There are two places in the tale where we are not sure who is speaking, character or author:

(23) And Adam said, This is now bone of my bone, and flesh of my flesh: she shall be called Woman, because she was taken out of man.

(24) Therefore shall a man leave his father and his mother, and shall cleave unto his wife: and they shall be one flesh.

(25) And they were both naked, the man and his wife, and were not ashamed.

Clearly Adam speaks the indicated words that conclude verse 23. As clearly, the teller speaks the whole of verse 25. But where, today, should the concluding quotation mark fall?

At the end of 23? At the end of 24—or even somewhere in the middle of it? The most probable answer is certainly the first (at the end of 23). But the content of 24 is knowledge that all men and women and Adam are presumed, by the narrative, to share with the narrator, so that she might, in the all-knowingness of the folk tale, speak it.

After YHWH lays his eloquent three-part curse upon the serpent, upon the woman (who is still without a name), and upon Adam—spoken actually as a poem (again: somewhat akin to a Celtic *flyting*, a poetic denigration, curse, or insult)—Adam names the woman Chava (Hebrew: Living) "the mother of all livings" (anglicized: Eve), and YHWH now clothes them in skins. Just after he does so, we hear him speak again:

> (22) And the Lord God said, Behold, the man is become as one of us, to know good and evil: and now, lest he put forth his hand, and take also of the tree of life, and eat, and live forever:
>
> (23) therefore the lord God sent him forth from the garden of Eden, to till the ground from when he was taken.
>
> (24) So he drove out the man: and he placed at the east of the garden of Eden cherubim, and a flaming sword . . .

Again, the question is where the concluding quotation mark falls. Again I suspect we are to read this as an early narrative version of realist mutterings. But of the three translations, the one that best preserves the rhetorical sign of a historical discourse is the King James (perhaps because the English novel with all its vast invention of rhetorical techniques to specify time, place, perception, incident, and specific sequence did not yet exist).

And the Lord God said, "Behold, the man is become as one of us, to know good and bad: and now, lest he put forth his hand and take also of the tree of life, and eat, and live forever . . . and from this moment the Lord God sent him forth from the Garden . . . ," etc.

Adam and the woman have put on fig leaves so that they may know/control/protect themselves from their own uncontrolled sexuality. (Knowing and sexuality will be associated all through the J-Writer's texts.) Now YHWH continues what they started by giving Eve and Adam garments of skins (and thus, through the offstage killing and flaying of beasts, the so-human YHWH—and not Earth or Chava—brings death into the garden, as more than one commentator has noticed) to protect them from the physical effects of the weather outside the garden.

Next a conflicted God, both angry and concerned, readies himself for his next act, while muttering: And YHWH said, "Here the human has become like one of us, to know good and bad."

While the infinitive carries the meaning it would in English, "in order to know good and bad," it also carries the meaning we have used before: "Here the human being has become as one of us, in (or by) knowing good and bad." And now, in case he'll put out his hand to take from the tree of life as well, and eat and live forever . . ." YHWH's words trail off, as he puts Of Red Earth out of the garden of Eden, to work the ground from which he was taken. But, in the same way that YHWH's overheard words once let us know, before, about the history of the serpent, here the overheard words of YHWH let us know the answers to a set of questions that we have been asking up till now—or, more accurately, let us know the answers to questions that we should have been asking, but may have been too ignorant to have posed (in the same sense that we were too ignorant to have questioned the Serpent's means of movement about the garden):

[First: What is the significance of the tree of life?

[Its fruit grants eternal life.

[Second: In what way did the serpent deceive Adam and Eve by his partial truth?

[He did not tell them to eat of the tree of life. Had he told them to do that *before* they ate of the tree of knowledge of good and bad, then, indeed, they would have been "as God" in the aspect which actually counted.

[Third: What ways are God and human beings different?

[God knows good and bad and lives forever. Human beings know some good and bad, but we die. And we know it.

[(And) Fourth: What is the significance/truth of God's Prophecy, "You may in eating, eat from every tree of the garden. But from the tree of the knowledge of good and bad: you shall not eat from it, because in the day you eat from it: you shall, in dying, die." With the intensifiers restored, and in light of the tale's end—

And He expelled the human, and He had the cherubs and the flame of a revolving sword reside at the east of the Garden of Eden to watch over the way to the tree of life.

Indeed, it is the combination of His muttered words before the expulsion and his subsequent action afterward—the setting of a guard to keep the way back to the tree of life—that actually open, as it were, our eyes. Suddenly we understand that YHWH was speaking above with the same signifiers of anxiety that Adam and Eve spoke with in their protests and excuses to Him, the anxiety that comes from too much knowledge: You may, in eating, eat of any tree —and, indeed, you should have . . . that is, you should have eaten of the tree of life. But what the hearer knows, now—and we learn it only on overhearing God's last words to himself as he expels Eve and Adam from the garden—is the remainder of the knowledge Adam and the woman actually took on when they ate the apple: "We should have eaten from the tree of life, first! Because we have all these other things to take care of, we will be caught short. And because we disobeyed instead of doing what we might have done, we shall—now we know it—die. Though we disobeyed innocently, as children disobey when tempted by evils they do not fully understand, we incurred God's anger and now we know truly why disobeying is bad for us."

We have already noted the serpent's partial truth. Now we can understand the truth in YHWH's prophecy: "On that day: You shall in dying, die." The story has already made clear that, no, they are not actually killed on that day, but go on to live for a substantial number of years, in sweat and toil outside the garden. A superficial reading would suggest that the serpent was right. ("You will not die in dying die, on that day!" the serpent told the woman.) Thus, the way in which the serpent was again right is clear. But now, we must ask, in what way was God also right—so that, indeed, we can say again that the serpent was only partly right?

Again, I think we have to reread—and specifically reread that infinitival intensifier—in light of the new knowledge we have gained of the knowledge Adam and the woman gained, through our overhearing YHWH's final angrily muttered words. By the same token that Adam and Eve now realize they have not eaten of the tree of life (but have eaten of the tree of knowledge instead), now they know they will surely die—and that dying is bad and frightening. Before, unless they happened to have eaten from the tree of life (which, in the story, specifically they know not to do), they still would have died, but they would not have realized the significance of dying. (As Freidman points out, no-where in the extent of the J-Writer's words is there any mention of an after-life. The idea does not seem to come in till several hundred years later.) What God's words actually were, "On that day (and thus from that day on): you shall (when-ever it is that you shall, and you will) in dying die (you will really die: you will know the significance of dying, the terror of extinction, the meaning of death: On that day you will become a cognizant mortal. On that day, you will become someone who shall in dying—whenever it happens—die). Presumably, before the woman and Of Red Earth ate the apple, and their eyes were opened to the problems of living and reproduction, they could not even understand the words of YHWH in this sense. (What the woman presumably hears is, "On that day you shall certainly die," as do most readers of the text today; she hears that because she only knows enough to hear that; and the subtle serpent beguiles her by saying, in effect, and quite rightly, no, that's not what it means.) Thus, in dying, they would not, as it were, really have had to die with the terror and fear of death. They would not have known death. It would not have meant to them what it means to us—and what it would subsequently mean to them.

On that day, however, along with the knowledge of sexual control (not sex), they also took on the knowledge of death's terror and inevitability. To the ex-tent that on that day they know the terror of death, in effect they now can understand death in the same way that they will at the moment of its actual arrival (know death's meaning).

That knowledge of death's terror is, of course, the loss of the garden just as the knowledge that procreation/generation can ameliorate some of that fear, however provisionally, is the possibility of at least its provisional and interim recreation. But the moment we try to control generation, however (i.e., to know it), either to make it happen or to hope for it to happen or to guide its happening or to work to make the world a better place in which it might happen, immediately the garden vanishes once more in the web of guilt, shame, worries, and civilized anxieties, which attend the knowledge of how to effect any of this. And we are always already expelled. That is what prevents our return.

The story of the Garden of Eden is the West's earliest tragedy of knowledge. It says, most simply: An unavoidable fallout from taking on knowledge is that one must also take on with it the knowledge of how ignorant you were before you learned whatever it was you learned; as well, you must learn, along with any knowledge, the irrevocable and tragic mistakes you made before you took that knowledge on: the fatal errors you made in the very process of pursuing the knowledge, before you actually gained it.

Those errors can have tragic consequences. Because you have gained the knowledge of good and bad, you know as well that it would have been good for you to have eaten of the tree of life, and that it is bad—at least terrifying—to have to die. But now God has set out some cherubim (the Hebrew plural[3]) with a flaming sword (I suspect those cherubim are an avatar of the Greek Chronos, or rather, not Time so much as the Irreversibility of time) whirling about, to prevent your going back and getting its fruit—and, with the apple, you took on the fear and knowledge of dying, which you must live with and around, until you die, a fear that can make of any day in your life a death itself.

It says as well that during your pursuit of knowledge, you will learn things, in passing, that are contrary to common sense: that snakes once walked on their feet or that, while today baby boys and baby girls come out of the womb of laboring, screaming, protesting women, once a woman came quietly out of the side of a sleeping man.

But the price of knowledge is knowing your own ignorance, as well as the effort you must expend to put that knowledge to work in the world as it has become, now that you are expelled from the garden—the easier world of childhood and the ignorance that went along with not knowing.

By the particular narrative trope of the overheard words of YHWH (in both cases, words attendant on a curse: indeed, in the second case/curse, the words are the mutterings that follow it, a further example of the human-scale portrait of YHWH), the narrator makes us twice return to revise our picture of the story —first our knowledge of the way in which serpents once walked, and second our knowledge of what Of Red Earth and the woman knew when they ate the apple. It is interesting to compare the J-Writer's Story of God's overheard words and what they reveal to us with the story of the hearing of the words of Prajapati, God of Thunder, in the second Brahmana of the fifth lesson of the Bhradáranyaka Upanishad (see my *Shorter Views*, 156).

But its astonishing how many other stories—most famously Goethe's *Faust*

—tell fragments (or even versions) of this same story. Many others, from Conrad's *Heart of Darkness* and James's *The Turn of the Screw* to Wells's *The Time Machine* and Joyce's *The Dead*, from Cather's *My Mortal Enemy* to Kafka's *Metamorphosis* and Wescott's *The Pilgrim Hawk*, from D. H. Lawrence's *Odour of Chrysanthemums* and Disch's *The Asian Shore* to Davenport's *Robot* and Russ's *Souls* tell it, or tell parts of it, with extraordinary beauty and artistry. But any accurate story of the taking on of knowledge must, in some of its aspects, retell it. Few tell the whole story, however, and none tells it with such clarity, irony, concision, and power.

* * *

Two years—almost three—beyond 9/11, Social Security Park has been closed up, remodelled, and opened once more. The benches have been removed and replaced with metal seats and tables. Today, in the center, is a monument to the firemen from the firehouse around the corner on Eighth who died in that September 2001 catastrophe. At night, great gates are pulled across the front and locked, so that it is no longer so hospitable to the homeless, who have been exiled off in Central Park, to the north. Though it is far more pleasant, because one October afternoon as I was sitting there writing I watched while the police arrived to drive out those who had lived there a year or more, tearing up their papers, confiscating their clothing and blankets, while some begged and cried to have them back, I do not find myself returning all that often.

—1985–2003
New York

NOTES

1. For a number of provocative reasons, both Friedman and Bloom assume the J-Writer is a sophisticated noble woman in the later days of King David's court.

2. q.v., Michel Foucault, "What Is an Author?," in *Aesthetics, Method, and Epistemology: Essential Works of Foucault, 1954–1984*, vol 2, ed. James D. Faubion, series ed. Paul Rabinou, (New York: New Press, 1999). Such an omission has endless ramifications for criticism today, as Foucault's great essay suggests. It is what supports the notion that any criticism worthy of the name "modern" or "postmodern" must take grammar and rhetoric (i.e., style) into account. Style is not only "l'homme lui-méme" (Buffon), but is as well both history and the major technique by which the writer steps ahead through history: it is the repository of signs for the shift of discourses. Not to acknowledge this is to obliterate these two aspects of the historical from any possibility of sophisticated critical understanding.

3. The cherubim of Solomon's time were not pudgy wingéd putti but rather giant, terrifying winged sphinxes with the bodies of lions and the heads of humans. (Such a "cherub" riddled Oedipus at the Theben gates. This shared image between Greece, Egypt, and Mesopotamia is a major sign of the living dialogue between the cultures.) The plural may be a plural of respect, like the royal "we," or the editorial "we," especially since "sword" is in the singular. But the King James translators preserved it. Also, the Throne of David and the Ark of the Covenant each sat on a platform held on the backs of a pair of such cherubim—which suggests that cherubim came in pairs. Possibly the pair guarding the way back into the garden tossed a single sword back and forth between them, so that it "turned and flashed or flamed or burned every which way."

11

How Not to Teach Science Fiction

Thoughts on Sturgeon's "Hurricane Trio"

A lyrically written, brilliantly observed, and deeply moving tale appeared in *Galaxy Science Fiction* in 1955: Theodore Sturgeon's "Hurricane Trio."[1] Later the same year Groff Conklin anthologized it in that astonishing collection of Sturgeon fantasy and science fiction entertainments, *A Way Home*.

"Hurricane Trio" provides an interesting critical laboratory in which to explore some of the things science fiction does—because Paul Williams, who interviewed Sturgeon extensively in the 1970s, mentioned in his story notes that Sturgeon did not originally write the story as science fiction.[2] For some months or more, presumably, a manuscript of that title by Sturgeon made its way around among the various mid-century slick magazines. Since his first SF appearance in 1939 with "Ether Breather," Sturgeon had created quite an astonishing name for himself in the SF field: there he was the writers' writer, the poet of the genre, the man whom even that far more popular but far less subtle writer, Ray Bradbury, had paid homage to; he was, in James Blish's words, "the most consummate artist science fiction has yet produced."

Some of the events in science fiction of the early 1950s?

Due to an eccentric review by Christopher Isherwood in *The Saturday Review of Literature*, Ray Bradbury had come to the attention of a far wider and more discerning circle of readers than he'd commanded during the 1940s. In the late '40s, Robert Heinlein and Murray Leinster (under his real name, "Will Jenkins") had begun to place stories in *The Saturday Evening Post*, and from the attention that had accrued to him he had become one of the prime creative forces on the film *Destination Moon*. And while Heinlein and Bradbury were indubitably interesting and important in the field (both, thanks to the attention they received, were to become even more so), both were markedly inferior to Sturgeon as writers. And one can be fairly sure Sturgeon knew it. The question could well have been, then: Could the most consummate artist SF had yet produced sell a story to *Harper's*, *The Saturday Evening Post*, *The Atlantic*?

If this was indeed the case, here is a reasonable reconstruction of the opening of a non-SF version of "Hurricane Trio," as best we can manage without the original manuscript to go by:

> Yancey lay very still with his arm flung across the pillow, and watched the moonlight play with the color of Beverly's hair. Her hair was spilled over his shoulder and chest and her body pressed against him, warm. He wondered if she was asleep. He wondered if she could sleep, with that moonswept riot of surf going on outside the hotel. The waves blundered into the cliff below, hooting through the sea-carved boulders, frightening great silver ghosts of spray out and up into the torn and noisy air. He wondered if she could sleep with her round, gentle face so near his thumping heart. He wished the heart would quiet itself—subside at least to the level of the storm outside, so that she might mistake it for the same storm. He wished he could sleep; it might quiet his heart.
>
> Beverly, Beverly, he cried silently, you don't deserve this! He wished the bed were larger, so that he might ease away from her and be but a shriek among shrieks, melting into the hiss and smash and ugly grumble of the sea's insanity.
>
> In the other bed, Lois shifted restlessly under the crisp sheet. . . .[3]

If the story did make the rounds as a mundane tale, it did not place. What is "Hurricane Trio" about? A bright and rising engineer, Yancey Bowman, and his very ordinary wife, Beverly, go on a vacation to a lodge; arriving in the pouring rain, soaked and miserable, they are taken in by Lois, the lodge's manager. Lois is beautiful, efficient, self-possessed—everything that Beverly is not. When Yancey invites Lois for a drink and Beverly runs out to get some ice from the vacationers in the cabin next door, there is an electric moment, full of sexuality, between Yancey and Lois. But instead of doing anything about it, Yancey decides to cut short the vacation by a day. And Beverly, who basically does everything she possibly can for her adored, brilliant husband, goes along with it.

For two years, Yancey, with Beverly in tow, has rising successes in his job; Beverly supports him in every way; and the two grow together in the manner of married couples; then, off on another vacation, Beverly and Yancey again run into Lois. No longer a lodge manager, now Lois is merely another tourist, like Yance and Bev—and this time there's a hurricane and deluge.

No rooms are to be had at any of the hotels on the highway. Beverly insists that Lois come with them and, remembering Lois's kindnesses to them two years before, invites Lois to sleep in their room with them. This is, of course, where our story starts; the rest is told in flashbacks.) Shortly, Bev gets up and leaves the room with her watch and a copy of *Anna Karenina*. ("The silver light made everything in the room look like an over-exposed photograph, but Beverly's flesh seemed pink—the only thing in the whole mad, pulsing world that had any color but grey or black or silver.") She goes off to read in the bathroom, and as he lies there in the dark Yancey realizes that his wife has understood the electricity between him and Lois all along. She is actually contriving to give the beautiful, elegant Lois (who is so much more than Beverly) to him—because she knows he wants her. And Beverly has always given him everything he wants: this has been the entire strategy and *raison* of her marriage—and is responsible for all the good things that have happened to them over the years. On realizing this, he realizes as well that he cannot accept the gift and calls his wife back to bed. ("'Beverly!' he bellowed.") Inside the bathroom he hears her drop the book to the tiles.

And the story concludes:

> She switched off the light and came in. A moonbeam swept across her face as she approached. She was looking across him at Lois, her lips trembling. She got into bed. He put his arms around her, gently, humbly. She turned to him and suddenly held him so tight that he almost cried out.

One assumes that such a marriage would have been destroyed by this final self-sacrifice on Beverly's part; but because of Yancey's insight, it is saved.

"Hurricane Trio" is a paean to marital fidelity, to self-sacrificing wives, to the value of monogamy, and to every myth of the "quiet inner strength" of women vs. the "overt brilliance" of men. As well, it reinforces the idea that the basic goodness and morality of such womanly sacrifices must bring out the good in the most egotistical and lustful of men. Had the story been accepted and printed in a non-SF publication, and had it gained the least little literary attention, one can easily see it having gone on to have become the benchmark of its decade, the 1950s.

But the story is by Sturgeon.

The eye it casts on all three characters, the kind of understanding it requests of the reader, the sharpness of the pains it delineates, the astonishing strength it tells us that such a sacrifice requires, and the simple sensitivity to the physical and emotional world it demands make the story begin to unsettle precisely the values it appeals to. And its honesty and accuracy of observation make it clear, by the end of the tale, that these are three quite extraordinary people after all and that, indeed, only extraordinary people might actually behave this way. Even today the tale has an element of shock on the emotional level that has little or nothing to do with sex per se.

If Sturgeon had let an earlier, mundane version of the story continue to circulate, who knows what might have happened. But in a situation where financial pressure was on him, presumably, at a certain point he decided to rewrite it as a science fiction story—and sell it in the markets where he and his work were already valued commodities. Indeed, the rewriting recalls nothing so much as the opening movement of his first story ("Ether Breather," 1939) and its irate writer hero who re-wrote his "Seashell" first as a short story, then a novelet, then a novel, then as a three-line gag, and finally as a television play—as if the picture of genre-jumping with which Sturgeon opened his SF career were somehow predictive of the situation he was to find himself in sixteen years on.

The factors that turned 1955's "Hurricane Trio" from the most sensitive of mundane fiction stories into a beautifully written—but finally rather ordinary—SF story would be almost entirely in the form of additions. (I know few people who would list the tale among their top twenty-five Sturgeon stories—though, in its mundane version I might well put it in my top twenty-five stories by all American writers for that decade.)

The plot of the SF version differs only by one element. Between the first meeting with Lois and the second . . .

But before we discuss plot, let's look at the language. The opening few lines of the SF version differs only by one phrase from the mundane version: "Yancey, who had once been killed, lay very still with his arm flung across the pillow, and watched the moonlight play with the color of Beverly's hair. . . ."[4]

Before we turn to the plot of the published, SF version of this story, a more immediate and possibly richer question at the textual level is: What is the significance of this wholly non-normal—even jarring—intrusion of death into the opening sentence of this tale? Certainly, it suggests to the average, competent SF reader, that this is, indeed, an SF story. It is what allows us to name the situation "non-normal" in the first place. People who have "once been killed" don't usually lie about watching much of anything.

Our hurricane trio—Yancey, Beverly, and Lois—will plot out almost the identical path as did the mundane version of themselves; but the intrusion of death into the opening sentence will function as a semiotic marker for the intrusion of death into the center of the diegesis itself:

What happens differently in the SF version?

After Yance and Beverly's first meeting with Lois, and before their second encounter, Yance's speeding car crashes into an alien space ship that happens to have landed on the road—and Yancey is killed. The alien ship takes the mangled car and its dead occupants into itself; the aliens put them back together, now making them a little bit better and more efficient than they were before; then they are set out on the road again, returned to a new life and an even greater health than they had, to continue the old story—which, save a phrase here and a brief paragraph there, remains the same.

The somewhat tepid denouement (also an addition of a single brief paragraph) is that Yancey realizes, in the end, that he was not the only one who had died in the crash against the space ship; Beverly had died, too, and been brought to life again as well. The strength to make her gesture had been given her by the aliens—as, indeed, had his strength to refuse it. What he first thought only a gift to him turns out to have been a gift to them both.

Indeed, what the SF version does is throw into question precisely that set of '50s values that the mundane version of the story so supports. In the mundane version, both Yancey's and Beverly's strength simply comes from two years of living and growing ever closer in what, to all outside appearances, seems a very ordinary marriage. The SF version says, in effect: "Come on. Who are you kidding? I don't care how wonderful a wife she was, this is just not the way a normal woman—or a normal man—would act in this situation, unless there was non-normal interference." And it is precisely because the original tale had the moral and psychological interstices built into it that were later filled up with the SF rationale of the benevolent aliens that—doubtless—the original story was unsettling enough to keep it out of the general fiction outlets where Sturgeon had originally hoped the tale might go.

But despite all my speculations, this troubling death still hangs there, pendent in the first clause of the first sentence, still somehow in excess of my particular ideological reading. "Yancey, who had once been killed . . ."

If the tension between its syntactic propriety and its semantic contradictions render this phrase a signifier of science fiction, what happens when we follow that signifier to the web of signifiers that make up its signified in the text of "Hurricane Trio"?

Certainly the major set of them gather almost twelve pages after the opening, in a scene almost three pages long—the major science fictional interpolation in the original tale that produces the ideological skewing I spoke of.

If only for its precision and science fictional poetry, it is worth reading, even if I make various abridgments. Yance and Bev Bowman are speeding away from the lodge, speeding away from the electric encounter between Yance and Lois, the encounter that, at this point, Bev has all but (pretended?) not to have noticed, with Yancey driving faster and faster, growing angrier and angrier at what he takes to be Beverly's obtuseness:

> . . . He sent the car howling through a deep cut in the crest of a hill, and around the blind turn on the other side, which is where he collided with the space ship and was killed.[5]

Here there is another page back in the hotel room, where Yancey is recalling all this; then the scene goes on:

As the space ship lifted, it retracted its berthing feet; it was one of these which Bowman's sedan struck. The car continued under the ship, and the edge of the flat berthing foot sliced it down to the belt line, leaving a carmine horror holding the wheel. The ship hovered momentarily, then drifted over to the side of the road where the mangled automobile had come to rest. Directly above the car, it stopped. An opening appeared in the bottom of the ship and dilated like a camera iris. There was a slight swirl of dust and leaves, and then what was left of the car rose from the ground and disappeared into the ship . . .

Exactly what was done to him, Yancey could not know.

He was made aware of the end results, of course. He knew that what had been injured had been repaired, and that in addition certain changes had been made to improve the original. For example, his jaw hinges had been redesigned to elim-inate a tendency to dislocation, and a process was started which would, in time, eliminate the sebaceous cysts which kept forming and occasionally inflaming ever since he was an adolescent. His vermiform appendix was gone—not excised, but removed in some way which would indicate, in the event of an autopsy, that it had never formed in the first place. His tonsils had been replaced for reasons which he could not understand except that they were good ones. On the other hand, such anomalies as his left little toe, which since birth had been bent and lay diagonally across its neighbor, and a right eye which wandered slightly to the right when he was fatigued—these were left as they had originally been. . . . In sum, he had been altered only in ways which would not show.

He did know, however, why these things had been done. There was inside that ship an aura of sympathy mixed with remorse unlike anything he had ever felt. Another component was respect, an all-embracing respect for living things. Somewhere near where he lay in the ship's laboratory was a small covered shelf containing a cicada, two grasshoppers, four summer moths, and an earthworm, all casualties of his accident. Their cell structure, organic functions, and diges-tive and reproductive processes were under study as meticulous as that which was being lavished on him. For them restitution was to be made also, and they would be released in as good condition as this unthinkably advanced science could make them . . .

He was to find out later that they had done the same things with his car as they had done with him. He had not the slightest doubt that if they had wished they could have rebuilt the old sedan into a gleaming miracle, capable of flight and operable forever on a teacup-full of fuel. He found it looking as it had always looked, even to rust spots and a crinkling around the windshield where moisture had penetrated the laminations of the safety glass. Yet there was a little more pickup, a little more economy; the brakes were no longer grabby in wet weather; and the cigarette lighter heated up in fewer seconds than before. . . .

Most miraculous, of course, was the lowered impulse-resistance of his nervous system, including the total brain. He needed no longer run over and over a thought sequence, like a wheel making a rut, to establish a synapse and therefore retain knowledge. He had superfast physical reactions. He had total recall (from the time of his release from the ship) and complete access to his previous memory banks. . . .

So it was that after death had struck one Friday morning, that same morning hour on Sunday revealed a strange sight (but only to some birds and a frightened chipmunk). Slipping out of the earth itself, the ship spread topsoil where it had lain, covered it with a little snow of early-fallen leaves, and shouldered into the sky. It wheeled and for a moment paralleled the deserted highway below. The opening on its belly appeared, and down through the shining air swept an aging two-door sedan, its wheels spinning and its motor humming. When it touched the roadway there was not so much as a puff of dust, so perfectly were wheels and forward motion synchronized.

The car hurtled through a cut in a hilltop and around the blind turn on the other side, and continued on its way, with Yancey Bowman at the wheel, seething inwardly at the unreachable stupidities of his wife. . . .

So he drove too fast and was too quiet, and his anger bubbled away until at length it concentrated into something quieter and rather uglier. As it formed, he drove more sensibly, and Beverly relaxed and leaned back, turning now and again to inspect the shutters or the curtains in a house they passed, watching the sky up ahead while she thought her own thoughts.[6]

The particular combination of the lyrical and the precise is one of the elements that makes this scene uniquely Sturgeon's. You will find it neither in Heinlein, Asimov, nor Clarke. And when Alfred Bester approaches it, he does so in an entirely different voice and timbre. For we suspect deeply that the "aura of sympathy" and the "all-embracing respect for living things" that Sturgeon imputes to his unknowable aliens (if not the "remorse") is, indeed, at the core of the Sturgeon enterprise, and as such is the source of both the lyricism and the precision as well as the marvelous voice we associate with him.

Yet if momentarily we can bracket all these elements—acuteness, music, and timbre—and if we can look at the text above with a critical squint that reduces it simply to a collection of semantic nodes, a collection of signs in a web of signs, a collection of signifiers of those signs, we find ourselves with an interesting, even paradoxical, pattern.

The signifier that led us to this scene as it meaning—"Yancey, who had once been killed . . . ," the first indication of science fiction in this tale's text—is a signifier of SF through virtue of its misplacement of death. And the signified it points to—the scene we have just quoted—is, paradoxically, a profligate intermixture of signifiers associated as much with death as with life. Possibly even more with life. And also with knowledge.

The images are of reparation, restitution, correction, and cure. From the initial homonymous paradox of the "berthing"/birthing foot (Sturgeon spells it with the nautical "e," but who does not hear in it the obstetric "i"?) that accomplishes the actual slaughter, however, death and life, under the aegis of knowledge (the "unthinkably advanced science"), compete and interweave through the text.

All one has to do is go through the scene and construct the most cursory of semantic clumps, and one finds on one side, "rut, casualties, injure, eliminate, excise, dislocation, sebaceous cysts, bent, remorse," while on the other we get, "lavish, restitution, miraculous, repair, result, improve, redesign, altered, sympathy, synchronized." Through all of them weave "know, aware, knew, know [again], find out, knowledge, thinking, thoughts," until indeed a restitution of the text itself takes place, and the sentence that introduces the scene and locks it to the story's first sentence ("He sent the car howling through a deep cut in the crest of a hill, and around the blind turn on the other side, which is where he collided with the space ship and was killed") is restored to the text in a slightly improved version—a way that almost, unless one reads them one after another, does not show: "The car hurtled through a cut in a hilltop and around the blind turn on the other side and continued on its way, with Yancey Bowman at the wheel, seething inwardly at the unreachable stupidities of his wife."

(I only note one further paradox: Sturgeon tried to improve the salability of his story by making it science fiction. In the story itself, the movement of the text is clearly toward improving a sentence by allowing it, in its restored form, to drop the signifier of science fiction—that misplaced death—from among its very words. Is this enough to justify my attempt to restore the text, for the sake of critical comparisons, to its pre–science fictional form?)

What this particular play of life, death, and epistemology was a sign of— what it signified, what further complex web of signifiers it might lead us to, within the SF genre—was a question I could not have begun to answer until eleven years after the story was published.

In the winter of 1966/1967, I spent three weeks in London (my second visit[7]), during which time Langdon Jones, then assistant editor of *New Worlds Magazine*, under the auspices of editor Michael Moorcock, called a meeting at his home of as many *New Worlds* writers as he could get together. As a visiting American SF writer who'd written a guest editorial for the magazine the previous summer, I was invited—but circumstances contrived against my actual attendance. Nevertheless, the proceedings were reported to me by Tom Disch, Pamela Zoline, John Sladek, and others.

At the meeting Jones located three "conventions" of traditional science fiction.

The first was the Generous SF Universe: In a world where no one survives an ordinary jet plane crash, in a solar system with only one oxygenated planet, science fiction nevertheless went on blithely writing about crash-landings of space ships on other worlds from which everyone walks away, more or less unscathed, into a landscape of breathable atmosphere, amenable flora and fauna, and often civilized beings. . . . But this only begins to sketch out the generosity science fiction attributes to the universe. I'm sure each of you can add your own examples.

The second convention was the Linearity of SF Intelligence: In a world where the reigning math genius at any given university is eighty pounds over- (or under-)weight and can't keep his shirt buttons in their right holes, science fiction insistently presents scientific geniuses who just happen to have black belts in karate and are able to negotiate with total suavity any social situation whatsoever. Indeed, the SF genius/hero is invariably a genius not only in his own field but in everybody else's as well. At a certain point, one realizes that it is the concept of what intelligence is, how it forms, and its function in the human condition that classical SF presents in a distorted manner.

The third convention was that of Individual as Historically Effective: In a world where no socially meaningful progress seems possible unless groups of people work long and hard together, science fiction constantly presents tales in which a single individual is capable of changing the entire path of human history.[8]

These were, of course, three conventions of science fiction that Moorcock and Jones were *not* interested in promoting in *New Worlds*—the publishing spearhead of the 1960s "New Wave."

What they published from the end of 1966 on must be read in light of this conscientious aesthetic program, but it basically was out of sympathy with the kind of fiction I was writing, which included *Nova* (1967), if not *Triton* (1976) and *Stars in My Pocket Like Grains of Sand* (1984). They still make their points in a "generous universe."

Recently, however, I've become interested (first) in the often subtle interrelationship of these three conventions and (second) in their astonishing tenacity in the SF field. Along with them is the astonishing number of SF stories and novels that evoke one or more of these conventions precisely to criticize the others—or, in a number of fascinating limit cases, in order to critique the very convention they evoke.

Let us bracket the last two conventions and look at the first in a bit more detail—the generous universe; for that generosity is rampant among all the paraliterary genres, even as it manifests itself in different ways in the different genres. Consider the generosity of the universe of the classical mystery novel, where crime is always the manifestation of logic and thus always accessible to a greater knowledge (certainly not a very realistic view of the "crime," say, that plagues the nation's greater cities, high or low, today); or the generosity of the world of the "cliff-hanger" film (such as the latest Spielberg offering, *Indiana*

Jones and the Last Crusade), where simply to touch the hand of whoever hangs from cliff or cornice is to rescue him or her[9]—in a world where the government reports that more than eighty-five percent of the males and females of this country over the age of sixteen cannot raise their own bodyweight a full eighteen inches, much less pull themselves (or a friend) to safety when dangling by his or her fingertips.

Or consider the endless sexual generosity of pornography.

Looked at in context of the paraliterary genres, one begins to notice alongside that generosity that the profligacy of death—the incredible number of lives that cowboy and espionage and mystery films have been wasting for years —is actually the disturbing underbelly of that same generosity. When the universe is so unrealistically, so insistently, so unrelentingly generous, death simply cannot have the same meaning. One thinks of nature—where an abundance of life means, finally, that life itself becomes ridiculously cheap. It is almost as if, to highlight the astonishing abundance of unbelievable coincidences, strengths, and skills with which these genres glut the pages of a paperback novel and lavish over the screen, they must provide a background of innumerable deaths to foreground the heroic in these tales. In this light, then, we might even say (once more with a hint of paradox) that the meaningless death becomes a symptom of the generosity of the paraliterary universe, especially when we turn to action film.

And if we again approach Sturgeon's tale, taking up its initial science fictional sentence ("Yancy, who had once been killed, lay very still with his arm flung across the pillow, and watched the moonlight play with the color of Beverly's hair"), certainly it is not difficult, at this rereading, to see it not only as a sign of science fiction but as a symptom of the generosity that we will find, later on, precisely in the specifically SF scene to which, as signifier, it will lead us.

For that is certainly what this precise and lyric scene, with its redesigned jaw-hinges and banished cysts, is all about: a marvelously generous universe in which, as if this particular story were in itself a limit case, an accidental and meaningless death can, through the generosity of a universe replete with aliens of an "unthinkably advanced science," be restored not only to a living, but to a living that is even finer than life without it, or than living before it—in much the way that the science fictional scene allows the restoration of the new, improved non–science fictional version of its own signifying sentence.

But unlike mysteries and espionage fiction and (*pace*) pornography, science fiction—the best science fiction—as it clings tenaciously to its conventions, indulges an articulate critique of precisely those convention. Asimov's Foundation series, as it set itself up to dramatize the entire materialist infrastructure of history, turned (in 1945) under the example of Hitler and Stalin (when it took on the character of the Mule) to ask, yes, precisely what is required for one man to change the course of history? And John Brunner's *The Whole Man* (1964), following in the footsteps of Stapledon's *Odd John* (1935) and Weinbaum's *The New Adam* (1939, 1943), took up the challenge of what, precisely, is this thing: intelligence, genius, or its constituents; and left it teased apart so that Disch, in his own astonishing novel *Camp Concentration* (1966), could once again—in perhaps the most generous universe of all—ally it to pain, death, and disfiguration—certainly one of the high points in the publication career of *New Worlds*, under which these conventions were first articulated.

What does Sturgeon's story, in the double version, finally tell us? "Hurricane Trio"—by being science fiction—tells us that no ordinary man and woman could actually cleave successfully to such monogamous values without the intervention of an "unthinkably advanced science" in an unthinkably generous universe capable of triumphing over death itself—a message that then, and now, could not possibly be acceptable to a general readership magazine.

"The meaningless death is a symptom of the universe's generosity."

But think how differently that diagnostic sentence reads when applied to the shoot-'em-up adventure film or when applied to written science fiction—when applied to this science fiction text. In the shoot-'em-up, it is the sheer number of deaths "without funerals or burials" (as I once heard it put) that renders these deaths meaningless, even while the filmic apparatus, now through slow motion, now with the cut at the sound of impact, continually insists that, somehow, there is a meaning here—though often the only meaning we can lift out of it is the obliteration of meaning itself. An important point to be sure, even if that meaning is one whose structure is identical to the repetition of the endlessly iterated neurotic symptom—an action repeated in a futile attempt to master a meaning it is now cut off from, but which at one time the neurotic subject vaguely suspects or suspected that he or she might once have wholly possessed. In the shoot-'em-up, these deaths are pure effect (that is, they always depend on misplaced effect), pure pretense (no matter how skilled), and the very insistence with which the genre repeats them, in its yearning for meaningful closure, is the signature of their meaninglessness.

In "Hurricane Trio," no repetition compulsion renders Yancey's death in the first sentence "meaningless." It would be more accurate to say that the syntax of the clause "who had just been killed" displaces death from its traditional position as a termination of life. Rather, that semantic/syntactic/generic economy fixes death in the midst of a life that exists on both sides of it. Meaning has been displaced, but not obliterated.

In the shoot-'em-up, the generosity lavished on the hero—the hair's-breadth escapes, the extraordinary combination of skill, luck, and courage—invariably originate outside the text. More accurately, in the realistic tradition to which these films and stories overwhelmingly appeal, and to which the notion of a textual inside and outside is pivotal, the only location for this generosity is extratextual unless we are prepared to indulge a great deal of mental double-think and self-reflexive bracketing, which, indeed, the general audience for these tales is trained to do from the age of eight onward.

With the audience's consent, this generosity is always mystified by the text—that is, the movement of these texts is always toward normalizing these deaths, toward hiding their origin, toward making them seem the most natural thing in the world—at the same time as it never lets them close with the profligate generosity they symptomatize.

Thus, in the shoot-'em-up, both symptom and cause operate in the area of the inarticulate, the repressed, and the pathological—that area traditionally labeled the "immature."

But this is not what is going on in "Hurricane Trio." Here the generosity of the universe associated with science fiction intrudes precisely to demystify a heroic literary assumption hidden and inarticulate in the mundane text: Yance and Bev are not engaging in normal behavior.

Death's intrusion is precisely articulated, with lyricism and precision. That generosity is spelled out in the scene we read. And it is that generosity which—articulately and in the narrative foreground—displaces the death it brings symptomatically with it and rescinds its effect. Cause and symptom are, so to speak, one. The generosity is the displaced meaning. This displacement of the meaning is the generous act. And where does the excess, if there is any, of that generosity fail?

On "a cicada, two grasshoppers, four summer moths, and an earthworm."

Thanks to that "respect for all living things" (and this respect is precisely what is pathologically absent in the shoot-'em-up), deaths that would have ordinarily been meaningless are given, within the story, a meaning.

"The meaningless death is a symptom of the universe's generosity."

Rereading our diagnostic sentence, we notice that (in the context of science fiction) it is only the pathological connotations hovering about the word "symptom" that are, in the case of Sturgeon, out of place.

A more accurate articulation here might be: "In SF, the displaced meaning of death is a sign of the true universe's generosity."

Having committed this revision, we can see: In much the same way as the text of "Hurricane Trio," by becoming science fiction, moved to restore Yancey to life and greater health, as it moved to restore (by a science fictional move) a science fictional sentence to greater precision and congruence to the mundane, it also moved to take our very diagnosis of it and articulate that diagnosis's repressions, strip it of its pathology, restore it to a semiotic purity, and redesign it at an order of strength and precision that, without the science fictional critique, we simply would not have had access to.

But this brings us, by commodious recirculation as it were, back to the title of our talk: How not to teach science fiction. Is the sort of reading I have outlined here, for Sturgeon's tale, the way I wish science fiction not be taught?

Clearly this represents the kind of reading I'd wish, rather, to encourage. Indeed, among the first texts my SF class will read, next term, at the University of Massachusetts at Amherst, is my reconstructed mundane version of "Hurricane Trio" *en face* with the SF version. And my first lecture on these paired texts will make many of the points I have made here.

But I must conclude by saying that I don't believe science fiction can be taught in the way I have been exploring it here unless we agree not to do certain things.

In the very first lecture to my science fiction classes, I usually perform the following move. I ask the class to tell me what they think the traditional "themes" of science fiction are. And I ask those people who are regular readers of SF not to participate in the discussion. I explain that I want only those who view SF largely from outside to give me their impressions. Within five minutes, from even the most comatose freshmen, I can usually generate the following list of half a dozen SF themes:

Time.
Space.
Technology.
Exploring New Worlds.
Aliens.
Utopia/Dystopia.

I ask those in the class who are SF readers if this list doesn't, when all is said and done, cover what most of the criticism of SF they've encountered more or less cleaves to? And, usually, they agree. Then I make the point, at whatever degree of sophistication I think the class can handle, that it seems somewhat odd to me that people who don't even read the genre can so quickly and easily come up with these apparent SF "fundamentals." Perhaps, I suggest, the ease with which these can be pointed to by people wholly illiterate in the genre suggest they are not so fundamental after all, but only blatant and obvious. (For a more critically sophisticated class, I may, at this point, give the historical provenance for these "themes" to show that each of them originates outside of science fiction, at various places in the eighteenth-, nineteenth-, and early twentieth-century criticism of, respectively, European and American literature, and that, indeed, most of them have been sloughed off, or even imposed, on science fiction because in the larger field of literary criticism, nobody really wants them anymore.) Then I suggest that, because these ideas are so self-evident that anyone who has even glanced at a SF comic book can probably come up with them, perhaps they are not the most interesting things about science fiction—that perhaps they are not the things that we, in a science fiction class, should be spending our time with.

Then I start to talk about patterns, about conventions, about dispositions, about moods of science fiction that can only be teased out from actually read-ing science fiction texts—and reading them carefully and alertly. Often, here I begin with the three conventions that the "New Wave" initially launched its aesthetic program against.

Then we read some of the New Wave stories and examine how subtly the stories cling to those conventions in spite of the writers' (and the editors') clear attempts to get away from them.

But there are many, many more such SF conventions—or apparatuses, or *dispositifs*, or dispositions—than the three I have mentioned or the one I have traced out in Sturgeon's story of sacrifice and restoration. (I shun the word "theme" because it suggests, as do "Time," "Space," and "Technology," that once one has located it, mapped it out through the text, and traced its edges, you have somehow done your critical job and the theme's location has some-how disposed of the text in some meaningful way; and I don't think this is ever what the critic—or the teacher—should ever let happen.) In short, I think the way *not* to teach SF is to glance at the SF text and say the first thing that presents itself to mind.

For what presents at such a glance is always something that has been im-posed on the text.

I think the way to teach science fiction is to read the text, to read it carefully, to impose oneself as a reader on the text, and to listen with the most alert of critical ears, to look with the most alert of critical eyes at what the text does in terms of the genre—even to the point of exploring how the text subverts the very dispositions, generic or otherwise, it taught us to be alert to in the first place.

—Spring 1989
New York City and Amherst

1. Originally presented on Saturday afternoon, June 3, 1989, at the Eastern Con-necticut Library Association Conference on The Literature of Science Fiction; then published in *The New York Review of Science Fiction* 13 (September 1989).

2. Theodore Sturgeon, *Thunder and Roses: The Collected Stories of Theodore Sturgeon, Volume IV*, ed. Paul Williams (Berkeley: North Atlantic Books, 1997). Sturgeon to his mother, January 2, 1948: "Margaret Cousins of *Good Housekeeping*, which pays a mini-mum of $750 per story, has been profoundly impressed by my work. "The Professor's Teddy-Bear," a horror story, which my agent sent to her for fun, scared the hell out of

her; it was followed immediately by a slick story [a story with no SF elements] called "Hurricane Trio," which had three characters, two women and a man, and the entire action takes place in bed . . . all in the best of taste, of course, and very lushly written." [Ellipsis in the original.] "She wanted to meet me after that and did; I had a nice long chat with her; she gave me a collection of 25 *Good Housekeeping* stories and begged me to write something for her." The story never sold, however.

In his introduction to Sturgeon's first story collection, *A Way Home* (Funk & Wagnall, 1955), editor Groff Conklin wrote: "The author has said that, in its original form, this story ['Hurricane Trio'] contained no element of science fiction, and perhaps some will consider that it should have been written that way. Mr. Sturgeon's point, however, is not that he used an alien *deus ex*—or rather, *in*—*machina* to resolve his plot, but rather to highlight the basic human reality with which the story is concerned and its slow solution by the three people involved."

The editor of the volume, Paul Williams, goes on to write in his story notes: "Poet Ree Dragonette, a childhood friend of Sturgeon's who lived with him in New York in 1946, told me in an interview in 1976 that a difficult moment in their relationship occurred when they were visiting Cape Cod in the summer of 1946 and found themselves confined indoors by the wind and rain of a nearby hurricane" (355–56).

3. The quoted passage is from Sturgeon's *Thunder and Roses*, 214; slightly revised.

4. *Thunder and Roses*, 214.

5. *Thunder and Roses*, 229.

6. *Thunder and Roses*, 230–33.

7. The first tabloid-size issue of *New Worlds* had appeared shortly before I flew from New York to London; it contained the first section of Thomas Disch's *Camp Concentration* (1966), which had excited everyone who read it and literally made it an international sensation. I was staying at John and Margorie Brunner's and had been planning to turn up for dinner at Michael and Hillary's at 4 Ladbroke Grove (Judith Merril lived around the corner at the time, in Blenheim Crescent) in fulfillment of an invitation I had gotten back in New York. On my first phone call to Hillary to let her know I was planning to come, I learned, somewhat to my surprise, that the relation between the Moorcocks and the Brunners was not the easy one I had envisioned on my first trip to their home back in April of 1966, and that, to quote Hillary, if I "brought the Brunners with me to Christmas dinner, Michael would probably commit Hara-kiri at the dinner table." So I ended up bringing a shopping bag full of Christmas presents on the day before Christmas Eve, where I actually met for the first time Tom Disch, who was babysitting at the moment for the Moorcock's two daughters, Sophie and Katherine.

8. The sort depicted in the Indiana Jones films (1981–2022), which harken back to a celebration of pulp-style storytelling.

9. As in the climactic scene of Hitchcock's *North by Northwest* (1959), where this convention is parodied by cutting between the two sequences of Cary Grant and Eva Marie Saint at Mount Rushmore and the top-bunk of the railroad sleeping car.

12

Letter to *Science Fiction Eye*

Some Impertinent Rebuttals

Samuel R. Delany's alter ego "K. Leslie Steiner of Ann Arbor, MI" responds to "Some Impertinent Remarks," Elizabeth Hand's review in *Science Fiction Eye* of his Return to Nevèrÿon series: *Tales of Nevèrÿon, Neveryóna, Flight from Nevèrÿon,* and *Return to Nevèrÿon*.

I was very pleased to see Elizabeth Hand's overview of Samuel R. Delany's Return to Nevèrÿon series in the last *EYE* (#4). (Anyone who has read my preface to Delany's sword-and-sorcery tales published in this country as an appendix to the last volume, *The Bridge of Lost Desire*, but, in the current English edition [Grafton Books] actually heading volume one, *Tales of Nevèrÿon*, knows I'm nobody's unbiased, or even disinterested, commentator.) Hand calls the tales "brilliant, funny, erotic, and beautiful," so that anyone who appreciates them should be pleased—yet, well . . . something in her article troubles me.

It's *not* that she also calls them "dull, pedantic, academic, and rhetorical." They are. But some inaccuracies in her piece make me wonder at certain other of her judgments, whether the positive ones or the much more fully detailed negative ones.

When I finished reading Hand's "Some Impertinent Remarks," in something of a state I fired off a postcard to Delany in Amherst, where I'd heard he was now teaching, my comments cramping the address and menacing the little square where the stamp goes. (I still haven't met him, and, from what I gather, I'm the only one in the Western world he's never invited to call him "Chip"!)

Those cramped notes covered what I took to be the most pointed among Ms. Hand's remarks; along my bottom margin I vowed to rescue Delany from those points in the letter column of the next *EYE.*

A week on I received a card back, more succinct (and certainly wiser) than mine. I quote it in toto: "Answering critics is a thankless task. I have too much to thank you for already. It really isn't necessary. Best wishes, Samuel R. Delany."

Well, it did make me wait a bit before sitting down to write you. But here I am, nevertheless, with my defense.

I don't know what Delany will make of what I write here, when and if he sees it. Probably he'll sigh and wonder whether, with friends like me. . . . But while many in the SF world know him *personally* much better than I, I try to read his work attentively. So, save the postcard which I've transcribed, these ideas are mine—not his. The writer I picture him to be would probably send you no response, save thanks, at all.

Hand seems to have missed the meaning of "paraliterary" entirely. "Paraliterature" is the academic term in Popular Culture studies for comic books, pornography, sword-and-sorcery, westerns, mysteries, romances, and, of course, science fiction—as well as popular song lyrics, commercials, and the instructions on the back of the box. In spite of some heavy arguing by people both positively and negatively disposed toward his book, Delany has insisted that no matter how highfalutin' it all sounds, his work is not literature but paraliterature, and should be analyzed, however seriously, as such.

I'm one of the people who disagrees with him. But his arguments are worth looking at. Mainly they circle around the fact that sword-and-sorcery (the most paraliterary of paraliterary genres?) is the product of very specific historical forces, quite different from those that produced "literature," and that these are the same forces that have both produced his work and are, at once, the topic of it. But whether you agree with him or not, his assertion renders questionable at least three of Hand's contentions: "Delany terms the four volumes a work . . . of paraliterature, which catapults it from the backyard barbecue of conventional SF into that literary garden party where the names of Foucault and Lévi-Strauss and Calvino are more likely to be uttered than those of Heinlein or Gene Wolfe or even Gabriel Garcia Marquez." By insisting that his work is paraliterature, he has staked out a far more limited area. Unless you discuss his work in terms of Robert E. Howard and his mighty thewed spawn, claims Delany, you cannot discuss it seriously.

In effect, Delany has chosen to shun both barbecue and garden party and hang out here with us. (See his lengthy interviews in *Alive and Writing* (edited by McCaffery/Gregory, University of Illinois Press, 1987); in *Diacritics* (Fall 1986); and in *Science Fiction Studies* (42, vol. 14, part 2, July 1987.) Whether or not we want him here is another matter.

Later on, Ms. Hand refers to "other works of paraliterature" and goes on to list "Nabokov's *Ada*; John Barth's *Chimera*, Flann O'Brien's *The Third Policeman*." Here she must mean something like "metafiction" or "surfiction." But whatever else they are, these are centrally literary works—not paraliterary in any way, at least not in the way Delany (and most others who write about SF) use the term.

Hand begins the last section of her article: "Delany makes it clear that his work is to be taken very much on its own terms . . . our conventional criteria for evaluating a novel or a traditional sword-and-sorcery tale à lá Moorcock or Howard can't be applied to these stories." Had she a better grasp of Delany's critical context, she might have made the more interesting point that neither can that criteria be applied to Howard or Moorcock. Specifically under attack in Delany's criticism (and, by extension, what is given so little quarter in his work) is the critical convention of appealing to a hopelessly inflated and wholly unrealistic "entertainment value" as the basis for analysis. This critical convention pollutes genre criticism in exactly the same manner—as Delany has argued: see his interview in *Cottonwood* 38/39 (Summer/Fall 1986), or his essay "Science Fiction in Literature: The Conscience of the King" in *Starboard Wine* (1984)—that the equally inflated and unrealistic notion of "literary value" has polluted literary studies.

Now, I suppose, we must wait for a letter from Delany himself saying I've got it all wrong . . .

Well, then, to more minor points. On the second page of her article, Hand writes that the "four volumes that comprise the Nevèrÿon series . . . encompass twenty-three tales and six appendices." By my count the four volumes contain eleven tales (twelve, if you take the reprint of the opening tale of volume one at the close of the terminal volume as a separate story). The sixth tale is the complete novel, *Neveryóna*. The ninth is another novel-length work, "The Tale of Plagues and Carnivals," and is also an appendix in the American edition (though I gather Delany has demoted its status to that of "just another story" in the English edition soon to see print) of *Flight from Nevèrÿon*. Could Hand have counted *Neveryóna*'s thirteen *chapters* as thirteen individual tales? Whatever the answer, it makes one wonder how careful her reading was.

There are other, smaller inaccuracies all through her piece. In the first sentence, she refers to "the empire once known as Neveryóna." No, the city of Kolhari was once known as Neveryóna. (It turns out, in the novel of that title, so was another, smaller city in the south.) But it's pretty clear from the series that the empire was always called Nevèrÿon.

She cites quotes from both Madame Keyne and the Earl Jue-Grutin as coming from *Tales of Nevèrÿon*. But both come from *Neveryóna*.

In order to clarify the out-of-context quote from the Earl, she inserts a phrase in brackets:

. . . All instinct tells us: one of [the reasons for speaking the truth as opposed to lying] must be art, the one that demonstrates a clear concern for the detail of what it represents that is finally one with the concern for the details of its own material construction, so that either concern, whether for representation or just skill in the maneuvering of its own material, might replace the other as justification for our contemplation without the object's abnegating its claim to a realism including and transcending either accuracy or craft . . . (336)

It's a daunting passage, certainly, in or out of context! But it would have been at least comprehensible if Hand had put into her brackets something closer to Delany's text, say: ". . . one of [three samples of writing] must be art, the one that demonstrates a clear concern . . ." She might even have explained that the particular writing sample discussed was in the form of small painted statues of fruit trees, cattle, grain heaps, and field laborers, representing the produce accounts from a prehistoric brewery. (The other two samples were two other versions of the same brewery accounts, one done in pictures of the same trees, cattle, grain, and workers inked on parchment; the third consisting of crude suggestions of still the same figures, this time burned onto what was taken to be the skin of a slave.)

But perhaps her point is that Delany is such a murky writer she cannot be sure . . . ?

Hand is uneasy with Delany's AIDS exegesis, "The Tales of Plagues and Carnivals." So am I. But I'd just mention that this novel, finished in June 1984 and published in April 1985 (in the collection of three short novels, *Flight from Nevèrÿon*) was the first novel in the United States from a major publisher to deal with the AIDS situation at all. (Daniel *Things You Do in the Dark* Curzon published *Facing It* a few months earlier; but, if I'm correctly informed, it was written marginally later.) And this "ill-conceived" (Hand, 39) intrusion of an allegory of "the strategies people use to avoid thinking about the illness" (Delany, *Flight*, 188) into his carnivaleque progression of sword-and-sorcery tales both before and after it may be what Delany's "attempt to allegorize the disease" (Hand) is all about.

The point is: suspect (see section 22 of Delany's novel) that terms such as "ill-conceived" (or "well-put") already allegorize disease ("*ill*-conceived") just as the word "disease" allegorizes the notion of disease/discomfort, uneasiness, trouble, bother, or upset; the metaphorical process (you'll find all this suggested in sections 2.4, 2.5, 3.0, 3.1, and 3.2 of "The Tale of Plagues and Carnivals") is, as such, inescapable. Meaning X is always a metaphorical displacement of meaning Y, which is in turn a metaphorical displacement of . . . Thus we inadvertently use such disease metaphors and allegories in the very sentences with which we are saying we don't approve of them, such as Hand's: "I feel that with all the best intentions and up-to-date medical information in the world, this attempt to allegorize the disease is simply ill-conceived" (Hand, p. 39).

The intrusion of disease allegories and metaphors into the otherwise happy progression of our sentences (or even the intrusion of whole tales into the progression of our narratives) is a matter of language and our level of awareness of it. The choice seems to be between analyzing or "avoiding thinking." Delany's allegorical analysis of the intricate ways the two processes are always inter-subversive makes up almost half his novel (sections 5.21, 5.22, 9.81, and 9.83), a stretch in which—Hand ought to approve—AIDS does not intrude at all and there is no mention of any other disease save a bad cold. I, for one, would have been curious to read how she read it.

For all her pertinent discussion of metafiction and deconstruction, I believe Hand has missed one point and has possibly only brushed one even more important,

I don't think it's letting any literary cats from their bag to mention the model for (most of) Delany's Nevèrÿon stories is the story type of Isak Dinesen's *Seven Gothic Tales* and *Anecdotes of Destiny*—or perhaps Marguerite Yourcenar's *Hadrian's Memoirs* or *The Abyss*. (I don't know if Dinesen and Yourcenar were actually in Delany's mind when he was writing his stories. But they could helpfully serve as models for us when we read them.) Really, there's no more author comment or analysis in Delany than in either of these two European writers—both of whom have, from time to time, been remarkably favored by good old American readers; both have been bestsellers more than once.

But there have always been fictions of analysis—Proust's, Musil's, and our own Henry James's—that simply have no existence without their constantly modulated commentary stream (from which the events in the story must, finally, be inferred). Whether Delany is as good as any of these others, or whether he has fitted the form of the analytical tale to his often sensational subject matter, is for each of us to judge. (One of my favorite comments by an impressed reader: "Henry James would have loved these stories—once he got over the culture shock.") But the suggestion that the form of the stories themselves represents either some huge, unassimilated clumsinesses—or that what might be perceived as clumsinesses are somehow willed metafictions—sidesteps the fact that these are simply stories ("The Tale of Plagues and Carnivals" excepted) in an old-fashioned, and largely continental, tradition. They are not related in any very interesting manner either to Joyce or to Raymond Chandler. They are rather tales by a writer who more likely values *The Recognitions*, *The Good Soldier*, and *Parade's End*, and likely the writings of Thomas Mann and Harry Mathews. Certainly it might be useful to criticize the separate tales' successes or failures with some of this in mind.

The second point is more important—at least I feel it is. Though the suggestion is fairly muted in Hand's piece, others have certainly claimed that

Delany is trying to appeal to the "ordinary reader" but has wholly and tragically forgotten how, while others declare he is purposefully trying to alienate the "ordinary reader," both by his subject matter and his discursive, digressionary manner. Myself, I feel he is trying neither to appeal to nor to alienate the "ordinary reader." Rather, he writes—as was once said of Robert Musil—in total disregard of the ordinary. And I think it's fair to say to anyone: "If you are looking for an ordinary read, don't even bother." But is it the ordinary we are searching for when we move, on finishing one novel, to the next not yet begun?

Why this question is important, and important for science fiction, is just this:

Here, in our SF precinct, so uncomfortably poised between populism and elitism, where Delany insists on locating himself (even though a fair number of people seem to have been waiting a decade or more now for him to flee the ghetto, à la Vonnegut or Ballard), we have always considered ourselves out of the ordinary. (What else is the whole "mundanes" vs. "fans are stans" hooey about?) But when we get a writer who takes us at our word, it is deeply troubling.

Specifically, I don't think it's Delany's sexual subject matter that shocks. It's rather that he is willing to analyze, to dissect, and even—yes—to bore about what other writers will only use for shock effects (which for most of us, let's face it, are not shocking at all); and that is, in itself, shocking—and specifically shocking to us who value the paraliterary, i.e., to those of us who think SF, sword-and-sorcery, comic books, or even pornography can yield, through their art and intelligence, major, positive cultural insights. It would have been interesting to see, through some direct analysis, what Hand made of just this troubling quality.

From the various critical quotes gathered in it to the general thrust of its argument, Hand's piece seems informed by a generalized terror of boredom. But Hand could just as easily have assembled a gallery of quotes from critics maintaining that all great art has its necessarily boring passages . . . which is merely to raise the question: What does such an argument as Hand's mean when presented here, in the context of paraliterary, rather than literary, criticism?

Writing now for this fanzine, now for that one, I've often wondered over the years if it isn't the fear of boredom that infantilizes so much SF. (The fear of boredom in art is, I fear, one with the fear of death.) It's an unrealistic fear since so much SF is inescapably boring—and I'd rather be bored by Delany than by another Jack Chalker (yawn!) adventure. But though there may be something elitist in my expression of it, I don't think there's anything elitist about the feeling. It's just a preference for one sort of reading experience over another—at one particular time. I certainly don't begrudge Chalker his readers. There are times when I am among them. But at that point, I don't find Chalker boring, though what interests me about him may not be what the "packaging" of his texts (Chalker's internal packing material of his publisher's external package) claims those texts are doing—which is, I suspect, Delany's point about the interest of paraliterature in general, Delany's own included. At any rate, Delany and our responses to his sword-and-sorcery tales make a fascinating laboratory in which to observe some really interesting things about our genre(s).

—*From* Science Fiction Eye *1, no. 5
(July 1989), eds. Stephen P. Brown
and Daniel J. Steffan.*

13

An Antiphon

> I made this longer than usual, only because I have not the time to
> make it shorter.   —Blaise Pascal

The essay that follows was a response to a piece by a young woman writing as
Hazel D. Schuler, which was published along with with my answer in *The New York
Review of Science Fiction* 29, January 1991.

I agree with most of what Ms. Schuler says. One of the problems that comes
with age, however, is that we have had time to see the extraordinarily effective
methods sexism, racism, and homophobia have for healing themselves over a
period of a decade or twenty years, when, indeed, we once saw them suffer
such staggering attacks that we were sure that they could never, at least in certain circles, be notable problems again.

Such experiences can even drive us to theory. And I wouldn't be surprised
if there were aspects of the problem, having to do with the self-reparation
potential of conservative conceptual schemas, that I think are worse than
Ms. Schuler does. There are three places where I feel Schuler's argument might
be stronger. First, Dr. Johnson's famous kicking of the rock to prove that the
real was the real (what I assume to be "Johnson's deeply misguided premise
that Schuler accuses me of clinging to") was, of course, posed as an argument
against Idealism, a metaphysical position holding that what was most important about matter was fundamentally outside the human conceptual schema
and that the conceptual schema that we move through as the world was itself
illusion. This, as Boswell notes in his discussion with Johnson, is a metaphysical

position. And metaphysical positions cannot be reasoned about without recourse to "first truths" or "original principles," be they of Bouffier, Reid, Beattie, or whoever—principles that function as do axioms in mathematics, i.e., they posit given (i.e., non-provable) elements or processes that are taken to exist outside our conceptual schema/world/reality.

It doesn't matter what is posited as the ontological bedrock outside that conceptual schema/world/reality: idea, Godhead, energy, or the soul (a subject)—the metaphysical choices which ground various forms of Idealism; or provability, relationship, time, energy, or matter (an object)—the metaphysical choices which ground various forms of materialism. Regardless of which we believe exists over and above any access to it by means of the conceptual schema of the world we actually and socially have, it (or they) force the conceptual schema to become, against that choice, only a more or less inaccurate, fallen, or illusory limitation/account of the metaphysical sub-(super-) structure. The various metaphysics implied by these choices produce everything from Platonism to positivism to scientism. But metaphysical arguments, because they take as their objects of inquiry what is outside our conceptual schema, what grounds that schema, can't be argued with from within the conceptual schema—as Boswell and Johnson both knew. And it is no accident that Boswell specifically states that it was Johnson's interest in "politicks" that had turned Dr. J. aside from such unresolvable metaphysical arguments.

Now the principles that Schuler appeals to in her opening paragraph seem to move toward the position of the poststructuralist

After we came out of the church, we stood talking for some time together of Bishop Berkeley's ingenious sophistry to prove the non-existence of matter, and that every thing in the universe is merely ideal. I observed that though we are satisfied his doctrine is not true, it is impossible to refute it. I never shall forget the alacrity with which Johnson answered, striking his foot with mighty force against a large stone, till he rebounded from it, "I refute it *thus*." This was a stout exemplification of the *first truths* of *Père Bouffier*, or the *original principles* of Reid and of Beattie; without admitting which, we can no more argue in metaphysicks, than we can argue in mathematicks without axioms. To me it is not conceivable how Berkeley can be answered by pure reasoning; but know that the nice and difficult task was to have been undertaken by one of the most luminous minds of the present age, had not politicks "turned him from calm philosophy aside." What an admirable display of subtlety, united with brilliance, might his contending with Berkeley have afforded us! How must we, when we reflect on the loss of such an intellectual feast, regret that he should be characterized as the man,

'Who born for the universe
narrow'd his mind,
And to party gave up what
was meant for mankind?'

My revered friend walked down with me to the beach, where we embraced and parted with tenderness, and engaged to correspond by letters. I said, "I hope, Sir, you will not forget me in my absence." Johnson: "Nay, Sir, it it is more likely you should forget me, than that I should forget you." As the vessel put out to sea, I kept my eyes upon him for a considerable time, while he remained rolling his majestick frame in his usual manner: and at last perceived him walk back into the town, and he disappeared.

—From *Saturday, 6 August 1763* entry in *Life of Johnson* by James Boswell.[1]

notion, associated with Derrida, that language is arbitrary and that anything we assume to exist outside the arbitrarily constituted conceptual schema that is language forms our metaphysics/transcendentals/religion—an idea I concur with. Derrida, at any rate, says we all have a metaphysics, and precisely at the points where we think we are most free of it, we are most deeply mired in it and are most critically blind to it. (The only pointed difference between Derrida and Boswell at this philosophical moment is that Derrida has identified the conceptual schema with language, in its particular Saussurean version: language is the arbitrary conceptual schema.) Derrida's famous catchphrase anent all this is: "We are never outside metaphysics"—an idea without which the often iterated assertion that all we can ever see, know, or experience is the arbitrary conceptual schema of language makes little sense. But that poststructuralist idea also presupposes an anti-idealist position just as much as Johnson's kick—since, in that argument, language has its conceptual priority precisely because it is social/cultural/political. Thus, it seems to me, unless we suspect transcendentals outside of language-in-this-sense are somehow being appealed to, arguments about whether language is representational or presentational, or whether texts are gestural or realistic, are largely arguments about metaphors (since, as Schuler states, all language is metaphor—no less true for the metaphors of presentation and gesture); but while I think the metaphor of language as a transparent and unmediating window opening on to the real is currently all but useless, the metaphor of language as a mirror—especially when that metaphor is used, as I was using it in "More About Writing," to highlight the mirror's reversals and distortions, and to bring out, by use of the mirror, elements of linguistic mediation likely to be overlooked—doesn't particularly bother me.

As Rodolphe Gasché might put it, my topic was the mirror's glass, tain (the silvery backing that allows the mirror to take part in the illusion of reproduction), and mathematics, not what we presume the mirror to show.[2]

The more radical of the poststructuralist positions say that in transcendental terms there is neither a self nor a real—that is, the self and the real are only a language (i.e., a socio-political) effect. But to say that we have access to no transcendental or ideal reality outside of language and its political dispositions is very different from saying that there exists only an ideal reality (and, thus, the socio-political has no priority at all because all we experience as reality is only an illusion)—the latter being an idealist position both Johnson and Derrida, in their different ways, are arguing against. (The conclusions of the older Wittgenstein is a discussion I have to bow out of, through lack of familiarity with his late work. But I note that the younger Wittgenstein of the *Tractatus* was quite content with "the picture theory of language"—although I have argued with that position; see "Shadows," §21–§29, in *Longer Views*, an argument with which I still concur.) But if I can so wildly reread, misread, and rewrite Johnson's phrase "The Life of Writing" as I did in my essay (with its subtitle "The Life of/and Writing," on page 1 in this volume), I can't very well argue with Schuler for doing with Johnson's rock what I take to be the same.

The point is, in terms of the argument at hand:

To say that what we so often take for a "rock" hard, invariable, and finally transcendental real is actually a manifestation of malleable, provisional, changeable, and arbitrary language means that when a fictive work asks by certain signs (such as, in the anecdote I recounted in my essay, the young male writer's claim that his story was "true") to be judged against the world, we are judging language against language—not judging language against something transcendental, even if we think we are. To judge a story well observed or badly observed or to judge a story sexist, say, because the male characters are well observed when the female characters are not observed at all (or, even more common, are just not there) is still a matter of codes, of judging language against language. These are situations for which the alternative metaphor "reflection"—alternative to the metaphor "observe," i.e., to attend at a distance, as a good servant does (not only is all language metaphorical, it is also all political)—might still, to some profit, be used. Schuler could have put her argument about what the exclusionary list of Great White Males in my essay "reflects" of the socio-politics of patriarchy, or what she had "observed" in it and of it, and it would—at least for me—have been just as powerful an argument. Also, it probably would be clearer for most of our readers. But such dialogues as Schuler's and mine often progress in terms of contaminated/uncontaminated terms. And for Schuler, right now, "reflection" is a contaminated term because it suggests purity, transparency, and lack of mediation, often used in the context of a sexist metaphor, whereas for me—because I was discussing the impurities, the distortions, and the mediations constitutive of all mirroring (even though the mirror can sometimes fool you into thinking it's a window)—it isn't.

That the statistical preponderance of male writers named in "More About Writing" makes the piece an all-but-perfect example of what, in its latter half, it purports to decry is also identified through codes. No argument there. But those names, when they appear in my text, no more reflect some transcendental reality than they do when they appear in Schuler's. Because they can (and do) refer only to a social code that is itself constituted in its arbitrariness by language (e.g., if the term "female" included not only, as it does, all humans with internal genitalia, but also, just as arbitrarily, all humans who wore glasses, then the code would be different and Schuler's critique could not be articulated in the same way: because my selection would then contain "some" females) is precisely *why* the exclusion is, as Schuler points out, so reprehensible. But this also means I don't think that's where I have broken faith with the presuppositions she cites in her first paragraph, or that I have gone over to sit on Dr. J.'s rock (as Schuler reads it), nursing my sore toe. Even when I wrote that I told the young male writer "you might have a better story if you'd told about what you really saw, what the young woman's relationship to you really was, and how you got upset when you saw her with her two friends," those *really*s are pretty informal. They don't refer to any transcendental reality that somehow escapes the highly arbitrary (in the Saussurean sense) conceptual schema that is our perception of the world-that-is-one-with language (and which, true, we sometimes refer to as "the real"). They only refer to the verbally negotiable part of that conceptual schema that the young writer had *already* negotiated with his own words by means of codes (i.e., by means of language) he had already shown *himself* to have had access to.

Second, I don't read Karen Joy Fowler's comments in the fine *Science Fiction Eye* piece, with Wendy Counsil, Lisa Goldstein, and Pat Murphy, as having quite the vector that Schuler takes them to have. But I suspect the main problem is that myriad instructor/student relations exist at Clarion.[3] Fowler's et al. were comments about *one* Clarion. And the particular sort of "sponsoring" spoken of (sending letters or phoning to editors or agents on behalf of students, say) is very rare. Many, many Clarions go by where no such thing happens at all. It's so rare, I think it would even be reasonable to ask if such letters or calls were actually sent or made by any instructor, male or female, in the Clarion under discussion.

If there was only one case of it, it presents real problems in terms of any generalizations that might be drawn from it.

In the twenty-two-odd years I've been teaching (on and off) at Clarion, I've never done it. Nor do I think it should be done. The closest I've ever come to it is (once) when, some years after, a Clarion (male) ex-student showed me a novel manuscript, which I encouraged him to submit—and I did, indeed, next time by chance I saw the editor, mention that I thought it was a good book. But, of course, other sorts of help are offered at Clarion.

Several times at Clarion, I've encouraged both female and male writing students to submit work to editors. But while I was at the workshop (or shortly afterward) I certainly wouldn't write such a note or make such a phone call. A writer who does is showing off to his (or her) students. And I should think it's much better for a young writer to know that a story was accepted on its own merit than for that young writer (and that young writer's peers!) forever to wonder if the story wasn't finally accepted as a favor to the instructor. If such notes or phone calls get made at Clarion, all the students have a right to resent them—especially if the story gets taken. The doubt those notes and calls must cast over the story's quality just isn't the best way to launch anyone's career—especially that of a talented writer. But I'm sure many other Clarion instructors, male and female, feel as I do, which is probably one reason why such notes and calls are as rare as they are.

This is not, incidentally, at all the same as an editor/instructor (who, indeed, may also be a writer) who buys a story at Clarion, first, because she or he likes it, and, second, for the pedagogic shock of pointing out to the students that what they're doing is serious. That writer/editor is, unlike the phoner/ letter-writer, putting her or his own reputation on the line: if enough people decide that the editor is only playing games by purchasing poor-quality student stories, that editor is not going to be asked to edit again. And though showing off or playing games is not ruled out in such a situation, economic pressure still militates for the editor's putting first things first. And such an editor is, at least, not playing with the student's life any more than she or he is playing with her or his own—or with the lives of the other writers s/he buys from.

The pedagogic shock, of course, only dramatizes a point. But whether the point is or isn't dramatized—or dramatized in that particular way—the se- riousness is still there. And other instructors have other ways, of course, of making the same point.

Schuler's point and the discussion in the *SF Eye* tetralogue do, however, highlight another problem. Because there are so many ways in which instruc- tors can help students, or become special to a younger writing student, student/ instructor relations become very difficult to generalize about and still retain any precision. Schuler uses the terms "mentor" and "protégé," for instance, which Counsil, Fowler, Goldstein, and Murphy do not.

I'll only mention that when, personally, I think of a mentor/protégé relation from Clarion, the one that comes most strongly to my mind is twenty-three- year-old Octavia Butler, who came, worked, and went on from Clarion as Harlan Ellison's discovery and protégé. The complexities of the problem begin because, especially when the protégé is of a different gender from mentor, the term "protégé" often carries sexual suggestions that it should not—as it cer- tainly shouldn't in the case of Ellison and Butler. These sexual suggestions, however, are likely to make most uncomfortable precisely the people who know sex was not involved, because they observed the particular mentor/protégé relation; but that is why, two or three years later, when, say, Butler's reputa- tion began its well-deserved blossoming on its own, this relation was no longer referred to in mentor/protégé terms. Indeed, it tended not to be talked of at all, though Butler herself is certainly generous in acknowledging it. Because of this general feeling that the language available is loaded and inadequate to portray accurately the situation, mentoring relations between male writers and female writing students, between female writers and male writing students, and between writers of either sex known to be gay (like myself or Russ) and writing students of the same sex do not persist in the overt and positive Clar- ion "mythology; while, very often, relations where sex either is known to have been involved, or has been suspected, do persist in the covert Clarion "folk- lore" (as vaguely uncomfortable jokes). Because of the discomfort factor, only male/male mentor/protégé relations, where both males are perceived as safely heterosexual, form a linguistically stable unit—i.e., a relationship that can be spoken of, without the informed speaker having to resort to endless, anxiety-producing qualifications—over any length of time. But this means that neither myths nor folklore do justice—especially over a period of years—to the range of mentoring relations of many sorts and orders that most definitely form and flower and—sometimes—go rotten at Clarion.

So many women SF writers have taught at Clarion, however, (e.g., Judith Merril, Kate Wilhelm, Joanna Russ, Ursula Le Guin, Rebecca Goldstein, Nancy Kress, Karen Joy Fowler, Joan Vinge, Elizabeth Lynn, Marta Randall, Chelsea Quinn Yarbro, Patricia Murphy, Vonda McIntyre, Octavia E. Butler, Susie McGee Charnas, Patricia McKillip . . . and let me end my non-exhaustive list by mentioning that Clarion West has had a policy, in effect a number of years now, that at least three of its six instructors are *always* women; have they ever had more than three? It certainly wouldn't hurt), that I must believe at least some of these women have done *some* mentoring—and that they have mentored women students.

I've certainly done so. And so have other male instructors.

The problem of talking about these mentorings, of analyzing them, of making known their very real (i.e., culture-formed and culture-changing—not transcendental, but political) existences, of critiquing their advantages and dis-advantages, as well as the discomforts and difficulties of both the relations and the articulation of the relations, is a real (again, read "political" if you prefer) writerly problem: but I can think of no better group of writers and aspiring writers to tackle it than the Clarion instructors and students.

The general problem with a critique such as Schuler's, which tries to in-terpret everything in terms of the dominant ideology, is that such a critique, short of active research and concerted seeking out of evidence, is not likely to discover its true object: the way in which subdominant, oppositional, and resis-tant ideologies function, preserve themselves, protect themselves, and transmit themselves across various social spaces where they work—as they often do at Clarion. (I assume this to be a major lesson of feminist praxis: What women have written is far more important than what they haven't written because of men, and far more important than men's devaluing what women have written because they were women. Similarly, the mentoring relations involving women at Clarion are far more important than the reasons why so many people, men and women, find them uncomfortable or difficult to talk about. Thus a discus-sion of the latter is only useful if it can lead to a discussion of the former.) And I probably don't need to tell Schuler that it is the multiplicity of codes and their overdetermination (as well as their always-already arbitrary malleability) that allows us to write about things that haven't been written of before—or to con-sider new evidence in an argument—and still leave Johnson's rock to Johnson.

But back to Clarion:

If not *enough* female mentoring or female "protégéing" goes on at Clarion, that may well be because the articulation of those relations is not high enough to stabilize them as a Clarion institution; thus, every time a woman enters such a situation at Clarion, either as a student or teacher, she may at times feel as if she has to reinvent the wheel, as it were. By my own observation, however, four times out of five in a mentor/protégé relation, whether the protégé be male or female, it is the protégé who has sought out the mentor—often overcoming great resistance on the mentor's part against forming such a relationship. A mentor is rarely a *reward* a young writer gets for being talented; rather it's a *job* certain young writers can occasionally coerce older writers into doing by being likeable first, teachable second, persistent third, and then talented—four traits, any one of which can easily preclude the other three. The fundamental incompatibility of the four is why it takes so much energy for the prospective protégé to juggle them in her or his own personality—more energy, perhaps, than it's worth! And because talent is the last thing a prospective protégé needs, many who achieve protégédom—the vast majority who manage to elicit it in any notable way—usually amount to very little. Still, the lack of discourse about female protégés (and certainly there was none in "More About Writing") can discourage a young woman who might get something out of the protégé/mentor relationship from putting out the very great effort that is needed to establish such a relation with the Clarion mentor of her choice, female or male.

Far more important than instructor/student mentorships at Clarion (i.e., a relation between a particular student and a particular instructor that becomes an unusually strong two-way intellectual and/or emotional bond) and far more frequent are the strong relations that develop between students, which often have mentoring (or mutually mentoring) aspects to them. These relationships, possibly more often between women than between men or between men and women, are stabilized by the informal Clarion discourse. But they might certainly benefit by some further articulation that puts them in some relation with the range of student/instructor relationships—though I still feel, when all is said and done, a special mentorship, unless it develops outside of Clarion, is one of the least important factors to a writer's career.

Some of the things that militate against instructors' mentoring at Clarion are: (1) Save for the most unusual circumstances (e.g., Knight and Wilhelm as a married couple coming for two weeks), instructors are only at Clarion eight to ten days and are usually working very hard all through them—whereas students, working even harder, are nevertheless there six weeks. (2) Clarion instructors take our job seriously, and that usually involves conscious attention paid to not playing favorites once you get there. (3) Part of the Clarion process is that on the day two instructors overlap, there is a conference between them where the previous instructor runs over her or his impressions of the class for the newcomer—both in terms of talent and in terms of personality. A standard trope in this conference is: "So-and-so is very shy (or very socially awkward) but very talented. See what you can do to bring her/him and her/his work forward into the group." One I've never heard or said, though I've occasionally felt it, is: "So-and-so is great to hang out with but can't write for beans." But since such personal likes vary so much, person to person, one makes the gesture, at least, of letting the new instructor find how that falls out for her or him on his or her own. The process both of articulation and reticence is, of course, fallible; there is always bias, always mistakes, always disagreement, always oversight. Because there are six instructors, however, there's a lot of margin for correction. But, in general, the networking of instructors pushes for a general equalizing of instructor attention. Still, specific student/instructor friendships (that may or may not involve much intellectual content) do develop.

There is also always racism, sexism, and homophobia—manifested in the writing of the twenty or so students that attend. But there are also always between three and a dozen students who are ready to tackle, loudly and articulately, these problems in the workshop sessions—and there are always a handful of instructors who are willing to support, guide, and mentor such critiques. If there weren't, Clarion would not have interested me nearly as much as it has over the past two decades.

But what about racism, sexism, or homophobia manifested by instructors? Again, having six highly varied instructors is one way to mitigate some of that, as it is certainly there.

I can only start to answer this by mentioning that the two cases where I developed strong friendships at Clarion with students I met there involve one woman (white) and one (white) man. (Several such friendships developed with ex-Clarion students who sought me out months after the workshop; but we will proceed to other examples.) In the case of the woman, Lee Wood, I was all but lame that year and had to be driven distances of more than a block—and she drove a truck. She volunteered to ferry me about, when needed (dorm and classrooms that year were about half a mile apart); we became friends. In the case of the young man, Jake Tully, he was lame—leg in a hip-to-ankle cast. Two days before I was to leave, he broke rather drunkenly into my room through a window at two o'clock in the morning, and there was some fumbling sex, followed by a rather interesting conversation till after sun-up.[4] When Clarion was over, I became good friends with him and his young wife. They came to stay with me in New York for a week sometime later.

The young man has not published anything professionally nor pursued his writing in recent years, as far as I know.

In three cases, I've known young women's work before Clarion and have actively urged them to attend. All three did. Two have gone on to professional writing careers. But you would have to ask the women involved, or the other students of their years, whether they perceived my friendship as one between protégé and mentor. It's probably not the term I'd choose to characterize those particular friendships—which continue, by the bye. But while I'll give anyone who asks information about Clarion, and will try supportively to reflect the enthusiasm level of anyone who lets me know he or she wants to go, I don't believe I've ever actively encouraged a man whose writing I knew to attend who hadn't made it perfectly clear he already wanted to go.

The question must be, does this pattern correlate with all Clarion instructors? Or all male Clarion instructors? Or all gay Clarion instructors? Or all black Clarion instructors? Or all black gay Clarion instructors? Or all black gay male Clarion instructors? But though one might speculate, this could only be ascertained by active, investigative research—and the findings could be explained only by some pretty sensitive (sociological) theory. The lack of that research ultimately hides the workings of what, ideologically, goes on at Clarion, oppositional or otherwise.

Until such research is done, however, any generalization about "what goes on at Clarion" ideologically is all guesswork, all subjective account—certainly material that can raise questions and suggest research; but it cannot predict the answers.

This is probably the place to point out that theory's purpose is not to replace evidence, but rather to alert us to the ways evidence is always being used to support foregone theories: the ways in which evidence is assumed to be transcendental rather than provisional.

When I think of my own mentors, during the pre-women's liberation 1950s and early '60s through which I passed between the ages of sixteen and twenty-three, I think of three men and two women. The men, Jesse Jackson, Bernard Kay, and Dick Entin—writers and roving minds, all three—tended to be laid-back, non-confrontational, emotionally supportive, ready to discuss pretty much anything I wanted to. The women, Marie Ponsot and Bobbs Pinkerton—one a fine poet, one a fine editor—were far more intellectually astringent than the men, in the best sense.

The men let me browse in their bookshelves and take home what interested me.

The women picked books I'd never heard of off the shelves and told me, "Take this home and read it"—Djuna Barnes in the case of Marie, Naomi Mitchison in the case of Bobbs.

The men were ready to feed me if I needed food, or pick up the pieces after whatever emotional disaster I might have just gone careening through.

The women exerted effort on my behalf and changed my life: Marie was personally responsible for my getting a work-study scholarship to the Bread Loaf Writers' Conference when I was eighteen. Bobbs first put me in touch with the man who remains my agent today, back when I was twenty-three.

The men, if I adopted an absurd position, would take the time to tease out, carefully, jokingly, gently, what I was probably trying to say—leaving me to contemplate my own idiocy in the gentlest way. Thus the men I could relax with.

Without being precisely confrontational, the women were always ready to argue if I said something stupid. The women I had to live up to.

And I believe I sought out the company of both equally.

Reading this over, it suggests some sort of yin/yang equipoise that James Tiptree Jr., at the 1975 "Women in Science Fiction Symposium," was one of the first to call sharply into question for me. Such seemingly innocent opposi- tions are always hidden hierarchies; someone always comes out notably on the short end of the stick.

But who?

It occurs to me that, today, when I meet bright young men, I tend to act toward them like the male mentors I had when I was a youngster acted toward me. (I seem to cook for them a lot.) When I meet a bright young woman, I tend to act more like the women who mentored me: We don't eat much, but the conversation is a lot more sparky. And I'm far more likely to take control and suggest firmly: Do this, do that, and I'll go do this for you, and you respond to it thus.

Is this a "genderal" pattern? And, if so, of what sort? What are its political ramifications? What are its sociological explanations?

Perhaps, finally, the ones who lose out are the bright young women who don't get the laid-back, emotionally supportive mentoring from either men or other women—which is where I see the section from the *SF Eye* tetralogue moving toward but not quite getting to the point of articulating.

My final point is that at least one section of Schuler's argument hinges on the assumption that a paragraph of mine is "*not* [italics Schuler's] ironic":

"After all, the world of art is the world in which a young man calls to his beloved, fights for her (or his own) honor against ludicrous odds, and—chas- tened by defeat and disillusion—looks out over the waters, tears and the sea indistinguishable on his face, with new and ineffable knowledge."

What can I say? "More About Writing" began as a talk at ConDiego,[5] and when I spoke this paragraph, the audience laughed as they did at my mention in the talk of most of the names on my/Schuler's list of Great White Males. I'd hoped and expected they would, since the point of the central anecdote was to poke fun at the absurd masculinist cliché the young man's story was based on—a cliché which, up till that age (seventeen), he had never ques- tioned the adequacy of to represent the truth about him as a male, much less questioned the adequacy of the wholly sexist trope it turned on to represent anything at all about a young woman he happened to have had some feeling for, even if he didn't know her very well. I can't say "ineffable knowledge" with a straight face—much less "beloved." I certainly smiled when I said them in San Diego.

Schuler goes on to suggest some variations here: "Imagine if the protagonist were female, and the object of desire male, flirting with other females. . . . Or better yet, if the protagonist were female, the object of desire also female and the competition either male or female. . . . Hmm: the latter almost works for me. Still: 'A young woman calls to her beloved, fights for her/his (or her own) honor against ludicrous odds, and—chastened by defeat and disillusion —looks out over the water, tears and the sea indistinguishable on her face, with new and ineffable knowledge.' So suppose a young female Clarion student presented Delany . . . with such a story. Would he be likely to read it as anything but a trivial case of (hysterical—or frustrated) female fantasizing, fit only for trashy working class magazines, unworthy of Great Art?"

I should say here, for the record, that I believe in very good art, running all the way down to very bad art, with many sorts of interesting art at all levels. But I don't believe Great Art exists; and to start speaking of it is to begin traipsing around with the transcendental again. Along with the ineffable, I believe too there's always an element of self-deception when you uncritically accept any of the three notions—at least until you've made a pretty concerted effort to "eff." But it's the "effing," the raid on the inarticulate, the attempt to write what does not fit into the ordinary modes of discourse, that produces the necessity for self-correction, the oppositional pressure, the energy needed to effect the alterations, micro-element by micro-element, in the overall literary trope—to transform it into the equally tropic form that the writer can codically identify somewhat more (it is not a completable task, as anyone who has tried it has to realize) as the trope of truth, and thus achieve some of the "truth-effect" I wrote of. (I don't believe ethics is aesthetics, either, by the bye; that's what the young Wittgenstein of the *Tractatus* believed—but not, for better or for worse, Delany.) But this may be to mute Schuler's considerable irony in her own passage the way, I fear, she may have been monovocalizing mine—and that isn't going to accomplish much.

But if a young Clarion student presented me with any of Schuler's variations (or, indeed, with any version of my own revision of it that I urged the writer to), she (or he) would get a lot more from me than the time of day, as I think she would get from almost any Clarion instructor. Such reversals and revisions are very easy to come up with in fun—and very hard actually to think through as stories. Yet such reversals, now gross ones, now subtle ones, are the only way to start telling new stories at all. (Not finish; start.) Any writing worth the time to read it must begin with some form of the fundamental reversal: "I'm not going to write what the literary hero does; I'm going to write instead about what I do, or Jane does, or Susan does, or Fred does, or Lerlene does, or my mother does, or my father does, or my friend does, or the stranger I saw with her shopping cart in the supermarket does . . ." I get hoarse at Clarion urging students to break out of the clichés they are boxed into by seriously considering just such reversals, larger or smaller. (Forget the ineffable knowledge. Try having your protagonist learn something statable—whether she actually states it or not.) Such reversals were the first writerly moves I ever made in my first published writing, and I still believe they're a good place to get going. But other such reversals were the places where Russ, Heinlein, Le Guin, Brunner, Merril started. . . . The paradox, however, is that such reversals still belong to art: that's what makes art a house of mirrors, rather than a transparent and unmediating window onto some transcendentally grounded real. Such a text—such a tale—is a gesture, a gesture against the masculinist and sexist plot cliché of the young male writer's "true" tale. And that's why, all else being equal, I would praise the one—and why I chose, however gently, to criticize the other. (With the young—or the sincere of any age—simply to say "Your piece is sexist/ racist/homophobic claptrap and you ought to go home and take up some intellectually non-taxing job" does not teach much. But I have used equally gentle teaching strategies when presented with racist and homophobic stories, both by women and men.) And while I might, at a particular Clarion, with a particular student, be more interested in one revision than another, that's not because I feel that one is more transcendentally or necessarily true than the other, or that it somehow escapes its provisional status of the moment and achieves "Greatness," "Transcendence," "Truth." That is also why, when you're busy looking at one problem, at one set of provisions, someone can come up behind you and say, "Look, these over here are a lot more important"—which is what, fairly and necessarily, Schuler appears to me to be doing. Finally, however, I think it's precisely the fact that such reversals, some of them anyway, can say things about the (socially constructed, linguistically constituted) world which the clichés they are parasitic upon cannot say that confirms my argument that it is context, not content, that controls the ideological reading of a given string of language—a context that has to include how frequently and in what situations an iteration of the same language string shows up. Otherwise, such reversals could not even begin to set anything in motion, could not free anything toward greater meaning.

But the reversals have to be multiple, as well as partial, as well as critically and energetically (dis)placed, to keep things in motion, which is another "truth-effect" affect. "Truth" outside of a set of codic, provisional, however urgent-seeming choices, like the "Real," I don't believe I've appealed to in anything other than an ironic mode.

Does this mean that "truth" is relative? Not in the least. Does it explain why people *argue* about what is or isn't true? All the time.

I'll wind this up with an anecdote about the same (young, male) writer I wrote of in "More About Writing." While it has nothing directly to do with Schuler's argument, it may amuse, if not instruct. When, at nineteen, this young man published his first science fiction novel, *An Apology for Rain* (Doubleday, 1974), because the book centered on a late-adolescent female protagonist (who was tall, gangly, white-haired, and smoked lots of cigarettes), and because the young man's first name was of an ambiguous gender (Lee, Carol, Vivian, Pat . . . you know the litany: in his case Jean), when Theodore Sturgeon reviewed the book most favorably in the *New York Times Book Review*, Sturgeon wrote throughout of ". . . the writer, she . . ." Not notable in itself; still, eventually, in this same review, Sturgeon began to explain that certain books, such as this one, could *only* be written by women. Certain effects could only be achieved by women writers, for example (Sturgeon went on), a certain presentation of precise and intense anger. The book under his consideration, Sturgeon held, portrayed such quintessentially female anger superbly—as did the work (Sturgeon cited) of Joanna Russ and Josephine Saxton—in a way that *only* a woman could. Male writers, Sturgeon suggested, were constitutionally incapable of writing about such anger and could only write about blunt rage, a quintessentially male trait—even when they occasionally, clumsily, and obviously attributed it to their women characters.

The same week that Sturgeon's review appeared, James Tiptree Jr. was re-vealed to the SF community as Alice Sheldon—and Robert Silverberg's claim, in his introduction to *Warm Worlds and Otherwise*, that Tiptree's stories could only have been written by a man, entered the realm of up-front SF mythology.

In the fifteen-odd years since, whenever I have referred to the one, I have always discussed the other as well. The two are marvelously and mutually illu-minative pieces of idiocy.

But I must also note that while the Silverberg shuffle is today as well known as any "fact" about science fiction, the Sturgeon slip over Jean M. Gawron has been all but forgotten. Consider, however: when women succeed, however briefly, in masquerading as men—George Eliot, George Sand, James Tiptree Jr.—the deception must be marked and remembered. A woman has, however briefly, crossed the power border and made out on the other side. That's dan-gerous, and threatens the border in such a way that patriarchal culture is always ready to put up a marker and note: Here the enemy breached the lines and, for a moment, got in. But by the same move, those markers and memories of male pseudonyms confirm, above all else, that a certain male power (marked by that border) exists. After all, by effort, intentions, and deception, certain women were able to mimic it (who was the '50s male critic who wrote, "George Eliot mounts to greatness, but with laboring breath"—or do we need to remember him here?) or, in a liberal reading, even achieve it.

The Sturgeon slip is, however, far *more* dangerous to the existing power struc-ture. And because it is *more* dangerous, it *must* be forgotten—or repressed—to facilitate the same ends for which the marker must be set in place and stabilized in memory when and where women breach the power line. The Sturgeon slip says that without effort, without intention, without deception on the part of a writer (and there was certainly no intent to deceive: Jean's book jacket bore a photograph of the lanky young writer—but Sturgeon reviewed the book in galleys), a male critic, presumably working at the height of his observational powers, has misread the power structure. That male power, which men and women both, feminists and feminist sympathizers as well as non-sympathizers and committed sexists, all agree is there, was, for a moment, simply not seen. It was not in evidence around a man—even for someone who was presumably looking very hard. The border itself became, for a moment, invisible. Could it possibly be, then, that this male power is not even a social construct, but worse, a social accident, a phenomenon that can actually be dismantled, a phenomenon that, on any level that we might call "real" (transcendental, or when the contradictions of all the various social codes such as this slip itself represents are resolved into a more elegant, pragmatic, and acceptable code) simply does not exist . . . ?

The slip suggests that because the battle has to take place in codic terms, rather than against transcendental powers, there's a good chance of making headway, of making changes. That's what the Sturgeon slip suggests—and that's why I think it is so important to remember it along with the Silverberg shuffle.

Schuler's reading list of women writers was warming. (I might add Donna Haraway to it, in her "pleasure in the confusion of boundaries," which organizes much of the argument above.) The only one whose work I could say I'm not familiar with was Christine de Pizan—and I shall try to remedy that. I'm happy for the suggestion. Simply for my personal reading pleasure (*jouissance,* if you will), I'd likely turn to almost anyone on that list before I would turn to anyone on Schuler's and my joint GWM roster, I'm particularly pleased with Schuler's inclusion of Gayatri Chakravorty Spivak, which iterates my recommendation of Spivak in the appendix to *Flight from Nevèrÿon* and at the end of the third part of my three-part article on theory in *New York Review of Science Fiction* 8 (April 1989). Spivak's *In Other Worlds* essays and her interviews in *The Post-Colonial Critic* are wonderfully exciting in the ways they open up the problem of Johnson's rock (the problem of the sore toe, its ability to change your mind about things, and by extension of bodily pain in political torture or, indeed, anything citable as lived experience, in a world constituted by language; see Spivak's translation of Mahasweta Devi's "Draupadi," included in *In Other Worlds,* for openers) with far greater insight, acuity, and energy than I have been able to write here.

—January 1991

NOTES

1. See James Boswell, *Life of Johnson* (New York: Oxford University Press, 1953), 333–34.

2. See Rodolph Gasché, *The Tain of the Mirror: Derrida and the Philosophy of Reflection* (Cambridge: Harvard University Press, 1986).

3. The Clarion Writers' Workshop, which specializes in imaginative writing, fantasy, and science fiction, has been held annually since 1967. It runs for six weeks during the summer, June through July, and takes place in two locations during the same period, with one branch held at Michigan State University and the other, Clarion West, in Seattle, Washington, with a different professional writer in attendance as instructor each week. Since 2004, Clarion South has been held in Brisbane, Australia; for one summer, Clarion South was held at Tulane University in New Orleans. Clarion graduates include such nationally known writers as Octavia Butler, George R. R. Martin, Gustav Hasford, Nalo Hopkinson, and Kelly Link.

4. I learned that my encounter with Jake Tully had been preceded by a drunken boast that he would fuck anything, and someone had suggested that he try his rough-and-tumble charms on me. So—cast and all—he broke in the window.

5. ConDiego was the fifth North American Science Fiction Convention, held at the Omni Hotel in San Diego, California, on August 30 through September 3, 1990.

14

Atlantis Rose . . .

Some Notes on Hart Crane

> He is a great average man; one who, to the best thinking, adds a proportion and equality in his faculties, so that men see in him their own dreams and glimpses made available and made to pass for what they are. A great common-sense is his warrant and qualification to be the world's interpreter. He has reason, as all the philosophic and poetic class have: but he has also what they have not—this strong, solving sense to reconcile his poetry with the appearances of the world, and build a bridge from the streets of the cities to the Atlantis. . . . He never writes in ecstasy, or catches us up into poetic raptures.
>
> —Emerson, "Plato"

I.

A reading at once sophisticated and rich—of a poem as complex as *The Bridge* —must start with details and distinctions: the realization, perhaps, that, in Crane's case, even if they started off as one, by the end of his poem Cathay and Atlantis do not allegorize the same notion. Cathay was the mistaken goal from which Columbus, on his first voyage to the New World, returned, and, after three more, one of which was a major colonization push with seventeen ships and fifteen hundred colonists, died unaware he had not found.

Atlantis was the goal of Crane's own vision.

In 1922 Harold Hart Crane first read Eliot's *The Waste Land* in that November's *Dial* and conceived his own poem as an answer to Eliot's that would offer—without any particular jingoistic pretensions—a specifically American affirmation to counter Eliot's presumably international despair. Crane worked in spurts, on *The Bridge*'s "Finale" and other poems, that year and the next, around his job at J. Walter Thompson's Advertising Agency, where his accounts included Pine Tar Honey, Sloan's Liniment, and, yes, Naugahyde. Possibly after an incident in which the hungover Crane threw a lot of perfume out the office window, he quit Thompson's in October 1923 to spend November and December with sculptor Gaston Lachaise's stepson Edward Nagle and writer William Slater Brown at the Rector house in Woodstock, New York.

There, while visiting one evening, Woodstock resident and art critic William Murrell Fisher told Crane about the Viennese-born poet Samuel Bernhard Greenberg (December 13, 1893–August 16, 1917), sixth of eight children and youngest son to Jacob and Hannah Greenberg.

An embroiderer specializing in gold and silver, largely for religious purposes, Jacob Greenberg had brought his family to New York's Lower East Side when Samuel was four or five. The family moved frequently about the city's Jewish neighborhood, while during the week Samuel attended Public School 166 at Rivington Street and Suffolk, and on Saturdays Hebrew school. Hannah died on February 19, 1908, and was buried in a Brooklyn cemetery. On the chill funeral day, the family rode back home in a wagon—across the Brooklyn Bridge. Between 1909 and 1911 Samuel lived with his older brother Daniel. In 1910, through his older brother Morris (Morris and Daniel were both serious piano students), Samuel met a circle of musicians and artists, including art critic Fisher, who worked at or were connected with the Metropolitan Museum of Art.

From 1911 on, Samuel lived with Morris—when not hospitalized. Between spring and autumn of 1912, while working in his older brother Adolf's leather bag shop, Samuel was diagnosed with tuberculosis. Three days after the first of the year in 1913, Jacob died. For six or seven weeks starting in May that year, Samuel was hospitalized at the Montefiore Home, after which he stayed a month or so with his sister's family in Westerly, Rhode Island, convalescing and working for his brother-in-law in a horse-drawn wagon, selling piece goods in Rhode Island and Connecticut. Back in New York, he pursued his writing, painting, and music when not working at Adolf's, visiting his friends at the Metropolitan, or going with them to concerts or coffee shops. After seven hospitalizations over four years, early on a muggy summer's evening in mid-August, 1917, Samuel died, age twenty-three, in the paupers' hospital on Ward's Island.

After Samuel's death, older brother Morris Greenberg gave Fisher five of his younger brother's notebooks. Morris entrusted them to Fisher in hopes that their art critic friend might get his brother's poems published—which Fisher did, after a fashion. A year after Greenberg's death, he printed Greenberg's poem "The Charming Maiden" in a magazine edited out of Woodstock by Hervy White, *The Plowshare* of June 1918.

Two and a half years later, in the January 1920 issue, writing under his professional name, William Murrell, Fisher wrote and published an eight-page appreciation and memoir of the young poet, "Fragments of a Broken Lyre," followed by a selection of ten of Greenberg's poems.

Three years later in 1923, on that winter evening in Woodstock, fascinated by Fisher's account of Greenberg and his poetry, Crane arranged to borrow the five Greenberg notebooks in Fischer's possession—at least one of which was a leather-bound, book-sized album with marbled endpapers (which had belonged to someone named Sidney in 1898, for that is the name and date written in pencil and later erased from the first page, though legible even today), and which Greenberg had half-filled with neat fair copies of his poems for 1913 and 1914. On nineteen sheets of yellow foolscap, Crane typed out forty-two of Greenberg's poems. (Unbeknownst to Fisher or Crane at the time, Daniel Greenberg had preserved another thirty-five pocket notebooks, memorandum pads, and sketchbooks, as well as fugitive papers belonging to his younger brother: these contained, among more memorable items, drafts of a letter from a hospital, more poems, miniature portraits of Fisher and Halprin as well as of various Jewish men seated on benches about the Lower East Side, a stunning view north through the crossed cables of the Brooklyn Bridge, and a sketch of the Judson Church tower done from Washington Square in summer.) Slater Brown recalls Crane actually taking Greenberg's manuscripts back to New York City on the train with them a little after Christmas; but, as Fisher remembers Crane's returning them just before leaving Woodstock, Brown is probably confusing Crane's own typescripts with the originals.

We'll digress for a few more pages, because, even though they never met, Samuel Greenberg is still an important and poignant figure in the Hart Crane story.

After a page-and-a-half divagation on the differences between the romantic view and the realistic view of the relation between poverty and the artist, "Fragments of a Broken Lyre" goes on:

> The case of Samuel Bernhard Greenberg is exceptionally affecting, both in the sudden flowering of his gift and in the pathos of his end: for it is indeed remarkable that a boy of no education or advantages should write such beautiful lyrics as he has done, and it is a sad reflection on our appreciation and hospitality that he died in a public institute for destitute consumptives. . . . Greenberg's brief story is interesting; born in Vienna of Austrian-Jewish parentage, he was brought to New York when a child, and after a few months in the public schools was put to work in a leather goods factory. At the age of seventeen his inherited tendency

to consumption had been so fostered by the dust and confinement of the leather shop that he was told he was too weak to be of any further service there. Then began what he pathetically referred to later as his "freedom" and his "education."

It was at that time I first heard of Sammy, as we all called him, through a friend [George Halprin] who was giving music lessons to some other member of the Greenberg family [i.e., Daniel Greenberg, Samuel's oldest brother]. Arriving at the flat on Delancey Street one evening, my friend was much surprised to hear fragments of Chopin's 2nd Ballad imperfectly yet sensitively played by someone in the inner room. Knowing his pupil had no such delicacy, either of feeling or of touch, my friend inquired who was at the piano, and he was told it was "only Sammy." My friend entered the twilight room, and distinguished a tall thin figure upon the stool. The boy seemed dull, could not or would not say anything, except, in answer to questions, that he could not read music, that he played by ear only. Upon this my friend offered to teach him, and tried to do so, but made little progress, as the boy found difficulty in focusing his attention, and seemed unable to grasp the more conscious mathematics involved. Nevertheless my friend was much impressed by the boy, and came to tell me about him, and said he would bring him to see me, adding: "He is uncanny and inarticulate, but there is something wonderful about him."

And so it proved. When Sammy came to see me he volunteered nothing except that Mr. George Halprin had sent him. But he used his eyes well—took in everything, and waited. I examined him curiously: tall and thin of figure, with a small face framed in wavy, gold-brown hair, a high forehead, two wonderfully nice brown eyes, a rather large wide nose, and a full red mouth which made his chin seem smaller than it actually was. His manner was quiet and his voice gentle. I tried to converse with him, but to no purpose. I then asked if I could help him in any way. His glance immediately fell upon my table.

"You have books?" he questioned.

"Yes," I replied, "would you like some?"

"You have good books—classics? I have only a little time."

At that moment. I did not realize the significance of his saying he "had only a little time," but I humored his demand for classics and gave him Carlyle's *Heroes and Hero-Worship*, Emerson's Essays, and an anthology of English verse. I inquired what he had been reading, and was astonished to hear him say: "The Dictionary."

And a few months later he brought me a handful of poems—some of which are among the best he has done. I encouraged him to write, and from that time on (until his breakdown some two and a half years later) I saw much of him. His gentle, ingenuous personality exercised a great charm over all who met him, and his early diffident silence gave way to an elliptical, rather epigrammatic style of conversation which was continually surprising his friends by reason of its direct and simple wisdom.

After a further pair of paragraphs on art, the average man, and the civilization that obtrudes between them—and the rare individuals, like Greenberg, who see "both beyond and through" them—Fisher concludes:

> Samuel Bernhard Greenberg is of this company, is as frank and mysterious as a child. He is much younger than his years, and much wiser than his knowledge —for he is of the few rare, child-like spirits which never become sophisticated, yet through mystic penetration surprise our deepest truths with simple ease. Born with a look of Wonder in his eyes, he has never lost sight of the Beauty of the world, nor of the Divinity of its inhabitants: though painfully aware that they themselves have.
>
> Seated one evening in the house of a friend, where a few had gathered to speak of Music, Art, and Song, he exclaimed (after one present had read a poem exemplifying the freeing of poetry from the trammels of versification): "Ah! Delancy [*sic*] Street needs that!"
>
> Now, although we knew he lived down there, we did not at once see the connection. But his next remark was quietly eloquent of his whole attitude: "I should like to walk nude with a girl through Delancey Street."
>
> And we who knew him immediately understood that he craved to feel the presence in all the world (of which Delancey Street was but a symbol) of a guilelessness which could see nakedness and be unashamed, of a simplicity of thought and action which should be pure, artless, and brotherly.
>
> For such he is: and yet, as I have suggested, possessed of a mystic wisdom which quite disarms and sets as naught our dear-bought worldly Knowledge.

In this account there are a few inaccuracies—young Greenberg attended school for quite a bit more than the "few months" Fisher allots to him. Similarly, he worked in his brother Adolf's leather bag shop a good deal longer than Fisher suggests—on and off from his tenth year through his eighteenth. But the young man's general affect is certainly there in Fisher's recollections.

Back in 1915, Greenberg, who had been making fair copies of his poems for some months now, approached Fisher about the possibility of publication. On April 22 of that year, Fisher wrote to Greenberg:

> I am happy to hear that you propose to publish some of your poems, and I shall be glad to aid you in any manner possible. But first, as I have your best interests at heart, I feel I should warn you that a careful selection should be made, and that some of the poems will have to be slightly changed—a word or an expression.

Publication did not come, however, till after Greenberg's death.

Here is the text of "Serenade in Grey," the fourth of the poems Fisher printed after his appreciation—first as I transcribed it (line numbers are added)

from Greenberg's fair copy, now in the Fales Collection at New York University,
followed by Fisher's *Plowshare* version.

Serenade in Grey[1]

Folding eyelid of the dew doth set
The cover remains in the air,
And it rains, the street one color set,
Like a huge grey cat held bare
5   The shadows of light—shadows in shade
Are evenly felt—though parted thus
Mine eyes feel dim and scorched from grey
The neighboring lamps throw grey-stained gold
Houses in the distance like mountains seen
10   The bridge lost in the mist
The essence of life remains a screen
Life itself in many grey spots
That trickle the blood until it rots
A good sized box with windows set
15   Seems like a tufted grey creature alive
Smoothly sails o'er the ground
Like the earth invisible in change doth strive
Black spots, that rove here and there
Scurry off—float into the cover
20   Spot of grey—were close together
When color mixes its choice, a lover.

—SBG 1914

Now, Fisher's *Plowshare* version—with Fisher's "slight" changes of "a word
or an expression":

IV Serenade in Grey

The soft eyelid of the dew doth set,
Yet the cover remains in the air,
And it rains; the street one color set,
Like a huge grey cat, out there.
5   The shadows in light, the shadows in shade,
Are evenly felt, though parted thus.
My eyes feel dim and weak from the grey,
And the nearby lamps throw gold-stained dust.
Houses in the distance like mountains seem,
10   The Bridge is lost in the mist,

And life itself is a warm grey dream
Whose meaning no one knows, I wist!
A long black box within a window bound
Seems like a furry creature alive,
15   And is, as it smoothly glides o'er the ground,
Like the earth which in viewless change doth strive.
Black spots, that flit here and there,
Scurry off—disappear in the cover.
Two spots of grey—were close together,
20   When color mixes to choice—behold a lover!

(The McManis and Holden version of 1947 is somewhere in between my transcription and Fisher's emendation, though it does not alter any of Greenberg's actual words—only punctuation marks.) The sort of "fix-up" Fisher imposes (if not McManis and Holden) is out of favor today—though Emily Dickinson suffered similar "corrections" practically until the three-volume variorum edition of her complete poems in 1955. What is notable about Fisher's emendations is that while here and there a comma may, indeed, clarify Greenberg's initial intentions, the general thrust of his changes is to take the highlight off the word as rhetorical object and to foreground, rather, coherent meaning.

All poetry—good and bad—tends to exist within the tensional field created by two historic propositions:

As Michael Riffaterre expresses the one, on the first page of his 1978 study *The Semiotics of Poetry*: "The language of poetry differs from common linguistic usage—this much the most unsophisticated reader senses instinctively . . . poetry often employs words excluded from common usage and has its own special grammar, even a grammar not valid beyond the narrow compass of a given poem . . ."

The opposing principle for poetry has seldom been better put than by Wordsworth, writing of his own project in the "Preface to Lyrical Ballads, Pastoral, and Other Poems" in the 1802 edition of *Lyrical Ballads*: ". . . to choose incidents and situations from common life, and to relate or describe them, throughout, as far as possible, in a selection of language really used by men . . ."

Now, in the very same sentence in which he upholds the difference between poetic and ordinary language, Riffaterre goes on to remind us that ". . . it may also happen that poetry uses the same words and the same grammar as everyday language." And on the other side of a semicolon, in the same sentence in which he extols the "language really used by men," Wordsworth reminds us that poetry tries, for its goal, "at the same time, to throw over them a certain coloring of imagination, whereby ordinary things should be presented to the mind in an unusual way . . ." Presumably this secondary task is accomplished by unusual language.

The question then is not which is right and which is wrong, but which is primary and which is secondary—and how primary and how secondary. At various times over the past two hundred years the perceived relation between them has changed. The ministrations of a Fisher (in the case of Greenberg) during the late teens of the century currently ending, or of a Higginson (an early editor of Dickinson) during the '90s of the previous century, merely document where the tensions between them had stabilized at a given moment.

The archaic forms, the inversions, as well as the specialized vocabulary were, in the first third of the twentieth century, simply part of poetry's *specialized* language. And although they would be almost wholly abandoned by poets during the twentieth century's second half, even a high modernist such as Pound was using them as late as *The Pisan Cantos* (1948)—"What thou lovest well remains." "Pull down thy vanity!"—though, after that, even in the *Cantos*, they pretty much vanish.

Once past the almost certainly Whistler-inspired title, Greenberg's "Serenade" gives the effect of an observation so exact that, now and again, because of his strict fidelity to the observation process, *we* cannot tell *what* is being observed; this effect is as much a result of the poem's incoherencies where we cannot follow the word to its referent, as it is of those places where the conjunction of word *with* referent seems striking. In Fisher's revision, things run much more smoothly—and, I suspect for most modern readers, much less interestingly. Violences at both the level of the signifier (e.g., "mine eyes feel dim and scorched from grey") and of the signified (e.g., the rotting blood) are repressed, and with them, the sense of rigor cleaving to whatever writing process produced the poem. Both Fisher and Holden/McManis strive to clear up the ambiguity of the antecedent of "though parted thus"—though, under sway of Empson (*Seven Types of Ambiguity*, 1935), the modern reader is likely to count that ambiguity among the poem's precise pleasures. Is it the shadows of light and shadows in shade that are parted . . . or the eyes? (Or even the *lids* of the eyes?) Greenberg's undoctored text (or *less* doctored text: even letter-by-letter, point-by-point transcription involves judgments; and who can say what doctoring Greenberg himself would have approved had he been able to see his poems through the ordinary channels of copy editing and galley correction usually preceding print) generates a sense that, for all the strained rhymes and inversions, that process is one of intense energy, rigor, and commitment. This vanishes—or at least becomes much less forceful—after Fisher's changes.

When, after their conversation that winter night in Woodstock, Crane came to make his own transcriptions of Greenberg's poems, what's important to remember is that Crane went back to Greenberg's actual notebooks, the ones loaned him by Fisher, and thus to Greenberg's exacting and difficult originals —not to Fisher's *Plowshare* revisions. Given the development of Crane's own poetics, as well as Crane's influence on the poetic development of the times to come after him, this is meaningful.

Like most young writers—like many young readers—Crane had already encountered a number of writerly enthusiasms: Nietzsche, Wilde, Rimbaud . . . all of whom had left their marks on his poetry, all of whom had raised questions for the young poet that set his work in interesting tension with theirs. But Greenberg was particularly important because in many ways he seemed Crane's own discovery, and because the fact that he had been ignored by the greater literary world despite his undeniable verbal energy and poetic vigor made it easy for the then all but unknown Crane to sympathize and identify.

Back in New York City in 1924, after a precarious January and February between 45 Grove Street, 15 Van Nest Place (now Charles Street), and the Albert Hotel on University Place and 10th Street, all in Greenwich Village, Crane finally got another job as a copywriter at Sweet's Catalogue Service, where he worked with Malcolm Cowley.

At the end of the second week of April, Crane moved into 110 Columbia Heights in Brooklyn, into a room on the third floor—and, in the course of it, consummated a recently begun affair with a Danish sailor, three years his senior, Emil Opffer (April 26, 1897–[?]), a sometimes communications officer and sometimes ship's printer. Goldilocks was Crane's sometimes nickname for him (and sometimes Phoebus Apollo); Crane's own sexual *nom d'amour* was occasionally Mike Drayton.[2] Number 110 was Emil's father's building. A one-time seaman like his son, and now editor of Brooklyn's Danish-American paper *Nordlyset*, Emil Sr. lived there too.

The relationship began in blissful happiness for both men. Probably during the first two weeks of September 1924, while Emil Jr. was away on a voyage, Emil Sr. went into the hospital for an operation, during which—or just after which—he died. On Emil's return from sea, Hart and Emil's brother Ivan met Emil at the dock, broke the news, and took the disconsolate young man home. Now Hart and Emil took over the father's old room, Hart again working on his poetry. Emil went back to sea on another voyage . . .

Eventually the relationship devolved into jealousies, finally to break up and resettle into a more or less distant friendship (according to Crane's close friend Sam Loveman), which continued until 1930, the last time the two men saw one another. I quote at some length from Loveman, who in his seventies wrote an account of the relationship (two years before Stonewall, by the bye) in his introduction to the young critic Hunce Voelcker's impressionistic 1967 study, *The Hart Crane Voyages*:

> [Crane] urged me to come to New York. "I want you to live near me," he said. "Brooklyn Heights is one of the loveliest places in the whole world. Imagine, the

panorama incessantly before one's eyes—a glorification of beauty with the New York skyline always before one, Brooklyn Bridge, ships that come and go by day and night—and sailors. You will never care to live elsewhere, and wherever I may be I shall always return to you."

He continued to disclose his happiness. "I have met a young man, a seaman, at Fitzi's [Eleanor Fitzgerald, director of the Provincetown], and I realize for the first time what love must have meant to Greeks when one reads Plato. He's a Scandinavian and extremely handsome, yellow-haired and blue-eyed—a real human being. I believe my love is returned. He's at sea now; you must meet him when his voyage is over. I'll never come back to Cleveland. If mother wants to see me let her visit me in New York. For the first time in my life I'm utterly free from the ghastly family bondage and the internal squabbles between Mother and Father. Their divorce seems to have made no difference. Money and me seem to be the sole crux of their dissension. I'll be out of it for good."

I met Hart's "Greek" ideal on his return from the voyage, and he answered his description—an extremely well-coordinated and attractive youngster, certainly prepossessing but outwardly unemotional, and since Hart was inwardly a veritable cauldron of conflict, I felt that this balance in friendship was sufficiently warranted. I continued to see him day after day; his later acceleration in drinking was not then present and his promiscuity apparently absent. He had acquired what he claimed to be the first copy of *Ulysses* ever to reach America, smuggled in by a friend (Gorham Munson), and bored me interminably by his insistence on reading it to me aloud. Spirited and certainly assertive on occasions of ordinary conversation, Hart's recitals abutted into a kind of clerical drone. He, on his part, assailed my own way of reading.

Then, the inevitable happened. His friend, returning unexpectedly one evening to their apartment at 110 Columbia Heights, encountered Hart's stupid betrayal. There was no explosion, except Hart's ineffectual hammering protestations and attempt at an explanation—then silence. The friendship was resumed; their love never.

Yet in this fulmination of love and disaster, there emerged the creation of Hart's *Voyages*—poetry as passionate and authentic as any love-poetry in literature. Whether it be addressed to normal or abnormal sexuality matters little. There is nothing to be compared with it, excepting possibly in the pitifully extant fragments of Sappho, the Sonnets of Shakespeare, John Donne's love poems, or Emily Brontë's burning exhortations to an unknown lover. Compared with it, Mrs. Browning's much-belauded saccharine and over-burdened "Portuguese" sonnets are sentimental valentines. In his *Voyages*, stripped of the verbiage that emphasized so much of Hart's poetry at its weakest, and which is transparently present in many passages of *The Bridge*, the poet of *Voyages* becomes blazingly clairvoyant and achieves astonishing profundity. *Voyages* is a classic in English literature.

After the breakup recounted above, Hart returned to Cleveland over Christmas of 1924 to visit his mother—after which he again took up a peripatetic existence.

The eldest of the three young men by a handful of years, Loveman had first met Crane more than half a dozen years before in a Cleveland bookstore. An aspiring poet himself, he had just been released from the army, and the teenaged Crane was enthusiastically looking for books. Whether they were lovers, even briefly, is hard to say. But their friendship continued on and off throughout Crane's life: Loveman claimed to have received a letter from Crane only two weeks before the poet's suicide in April of 1933.

Most of us today will recognize that Loveman was writing out of a tradition within which the term "American Literature" was much rarer than it is today. Because Americans wrote in English, their works—especially if important— were considered, at least by Americans of a certain aesthetic leaning, to be part of "English Literature." The three other things that the contemporary reader is likely to find somewhat anomalous in Loveman's account—things that the reader may wonder how to fit into the narrative—are, first, the extraordinary passion with which Crane entreats this gay friend—who is, after all, not (at least then) his lover—to be with him; second, the seemingly gratuitous sexism of the swipe at Elizabeth Barrett Browning; and third, that "verbiage" which characterizes "Hart's poetry at its weakest" and which Loveman says must be stripped away to reveal the achievement and clairvoyance of the great love lyrics. Bear all three in mind: all three will be contextualized, in their place, as we proceed through these notes.

Crane's enthusiasm over the then-illegal *Ulysses* suggests an elucidation of an allusion in "Voyages II," the next to the last completed poem in the lyric series, that he would have been working on during the time Loveman writes of, or a few months after. (Though the series is clearly a love series, they seem to project—in critic R. W. Butterfield's words—an air of "searing loneliness," while the poet's seafaring lover is away.) "Voyages II," which opens with that extraordinarily scalar inversion, in which the sea is referred to as "—And yet this great wink of eternity . . ." (That "—And yet," functions much like the Greek "*Autar epie*" at the beginning of *The Odyssey*'s Book Lambda, which, translated, became the "And then" opening the first of Pound's *Cantos*) has sustained the most concerted exegesis of all the *Voyages*. A. Alvarez claims Crane's poem to be all affect and devoid of referential meaning—which, to the extent it's true, only seems to spur the exegetes on. Critics Butterfield and Brunner have suggested that Greenberg's sea images in poems like "Love" ("Ah ye mighty caves of the sea, there pushed onward, / In windful waves, of volumes flow / Through Rhines—there Bacchus, Venus in lust cherished / Its swell of perfect ease, repeated awe—ne'er quenched," is the sonnet's first quatrain, as transcribed by Crane in his manuscript copy; returning to Greenberg's manuscript, Holden and McManis read the punctuation notably otherwise) possibly nudged Crane to connect the idea of love and the sea in a poetic series—not withstanding the fact that Crane's current love was a sailor, or the fact of Crane's general fascination with "seafood," or his recent reading of Melville. The first stanza of "Voyages II" employs the idiosyncratic word "wrapt"—which also appears in "Atlantis"—suggesting a kind of Greenbergian term halfway between "wrapped" and "rapt." In earlier drafts of the poem, Crane used the phrase "varnished lily grove" from Greenberg's sonnet, "Life," though he eventually revised it out. Philip Horton has told us, in his biography of Crane, that the "bells off San Salvador" in the third stanza ("And onward, as bells off San Salvador / Salute the crocus lustres of the stars / In those poinsetta meadows of her tides,— / Adagios of islands, O My Prodigal, / Complete the dark confessions her veins spell") refer to a Caribbean myth Opffer had recounted to Crane about a sunken city whose drowned church towers, during storms, sounded their bells from beneath the waters to warn passing ships.

Earlier versions of the poem were much more directly erotic: that third stanza once read, "Bells ringing off San Salvador / To see you smiling scrolls of silver, ivory sentences / brimming confessions, O prodigal, / in which your tongue slips mine— / the perfect diapason dancing left / wherein minstrel mansions shine."

Crane himself later used the phrase "Adagios of islands" to explain what he called his "indirect mentions," in this case the indirect mention of "the motion of a boat through islands clustered thickly, the rhythm of the motion, *etc.*" ("General Aims and Theories"). Crane was also reading Melville, and both "leewardings" in the second line and "spindrift" in the last have their source —if indirectly—in that novelist of the sea: "The Lee Shore," chapter 23 of *Moby-Dick*, praises "landlessness" as the residence of "the highest truth." And Crane had first used Melville's term "findrinny" in an earlier draft but, unable to find it in any dictionary, finally settled on "spindrift," which means the foamy spray swept from the waves by a strong wind and driven along the sea's surface.

In stanza four Crane's use of the biblical word "superscription" (that which is written on a coin; an exergue) recalls Jesus's dialogue from the Gospel: "Show me a penny. Whose image and superscription hath it? They answered and said, Caesar's. . . ."

But to review all this is to wander quite a ways from Joyce. Today's reader forgets that a good deal of the controversy over *Ulysses*'s supposed obscenity (which is why Crane had to have a smuggled copy) centered on the terminal paragraph of the flower-laden fifth section of Joyce's novel, which Stuart Gilbert designated "The Lotus Eaters" in his famous book *James Joyce's "Ulysses"* (1930), one of "those passages of which," Judge Woolsey would write, nine years later in his decision of December 6, 1933, "the Government particularly complains." (The other point of controversy was Bloom's erotic musings during his stroll along the strand in the eleventh episode, "The Sirens.") In that passage, Bloom (whose *nom d'amour* is Henry Flower, Esq.) imagines himself bathing and, in his mind's eye, regards his own pubic hair and genitals breaking the surface of the tub's soapy water: ". . . he saw his trunk riprippled over and sustained, buoyed lightly upward, lemonyellow: his navel, bud of flesh; and saw the dark tangled curls of his bush floating, floating hair of the stream around the limp father of thousands, a languid, floating flower." (Writes Gilbert, somewhat disingenuously: "The lotus-eaters appear under many aspects in this episode: the cabhorses drooping at the cabrank . . . , doped communicants at All Hallows . . . , the watchers of cricket . . . and, finally, Mr. Bloom himself, flowerlike, buoyed lightly upward in the bath" [Gilbert, 155].)

Joyce's "floating flower," as a metaphor for the limp male genitalia (". . . father of thousands . . ."), suggests a possible unraveling of another one of Crane's "indirect mentions" in the penultimate stanza of the second *Voyages* poem ("her," here, refers to the sea):

> Mark how her turning shoulders wind the hours,
> And hasten while her penniless rich palms
> Pass superscription of bent foam and wave,—
> Hasten, while they are true,—sleep, death, desire
> Close round one instant in one floating flower.

Indeed, one "generic" way of indicating a forbidden sexual reference is through the use of a classical metaphor or figure taken from an age or culture less restrictive and repressive. It's possible, of course, that the congruence of phrases—"floating flower"—between Joyce and Crane was an accident; or at any rate an unconscious borrowing by Crane. But, given Crane's enthusiasm for the volume at this time, as Loveman recounts it (and biographer Unterecker also attests to Crane's enthusiasm: Crane arranged for more "smuggled" copies to go to Allen Tate and others, all before 1924; Unterecker calls *Ulysses* a "Bible" for Crane, and tells us, in his essay "The Architecture of *The Bridge*," that Crane prepared a gloss on the novel, copying out long passages from it for still another friend who could not obtain a copy), it's far more likely to represent a conscientious bit of intertextuality.

If the "floating flower" does stand for the genitals, it's possible that, in Crane's poem, we should read it as female genitals, since Crane has already personified the sea as a woman with, first, shoulders, then palms, and then a "floating flower"; such a reading would simply continue her embodiment. But if the allusion to Joyce is really there, it opens up other possible readings: Crane may be critiquing Joyce's use of the "floating flower" figure for the genitals —saying, in effect, it should be used for female genitals, rather than for male. But, by the same token, he could be using the relation to Joyce covertly to bisexualize his own personification of the ocean—evoking a "floating flower" so recently and famously used to figure the male genitalia.

*   *   *

Crane's poem "Emblems of Conduct," written shortly after his discovery of Greenberg, is an amalgam of stanzas and lines from Greenberg's poems, mostly Greenberg's "Conduct." But words, phrases, and lines from Greenberg ("gate" and "script" are two words and, finally, two concepts all but donated to Crane by Greenberg) turn up in both Voyages and *The Bridge*. Some years later, after he had almost finished *The Bridge*'s final section, and very possibly while pursuing Greenberg's readings in Emerson, Crane opened Emerson's "Plato" and, coming upon the paragraph that heads these notes, decided, in a kind of challenge to Emerson's praise of Plato's lack of poetic ecstasy, to rename "Finale," *The Bridge*'s ecstatic conclusion, "Atlantis."

For if there is one poet who is not described by the motto heading these notes—a common-sensical, super-average man—it is Crane!

But this might also be the place to look back, six years before, to Crane's 1918 meditation on Nietzsche—a defense of the philosopher against those who, with the Great War, would dismiss him along with everything German. In the second paragraph of that astute, brief essay (misleadingly titled "The Case Against Nietzsche"; a more apropos, if clumsier, title would have been "The Case *Against* the Case Against Nietzsche"), Crane mentions that Schopenhauer was (along with Goethe) one of the few Germans whom Nietzsche had any use for at all. It's possible then that the nineteen-year-old Crane had read through Nietzsche's essay, "On Schopenhauer as Teacher"; the following passage from it may have been—then—one of the earlier texts, if not the earliest, to begin sedimenting some of the ideas, images, and terms that, in development, would become Crane's major poetic work half a dozen or more years on:

> Nobody can build you the bridge over which you must cross the river of life, nobody but you alone. True, there are countless paths and bridges and demigods that would like to carry you across the river, but only at the price of your self; you would pledge your self, and lose it. In this world there is one unique path which no one but you may walk. Where does it lead? Do not ask; take it.

Indeed, to examine how Crane's *Bridge* critiques the specifics of this passage is to begin to trace what, in Crane, is specific to his own view and enterprise.

For Nietzsche the bridge is the instrumentality with which one negotiates the river of life. For Crane the bridge *is* life. In her 1978 interview with Opffer, Helge Normann Nilsen records Opffer as saying that Crane often told him, "All of life is a bridge" or "The whole world is a bridge." The bridge for Nietzsche is the unique and optimal path by which the brave subject can, in crossing it, avoid losing his proper self. One suspects that for Crane a multiplicity of selves can all be supported by the bridge's encompassing curveship—that, somehow, authenticity of self, above and beyond that of authentic poetry, is not in question.

In the Nilsen interview with Opffer, Opffer tells a tale about his own father, also a sailor, "who once jumped from a ship in Denmark just to see how long it would take for them to pick him up." Crane lived in the building with both father and son, and before his death Emil Senior may have amused both Crane and Emil Junior with tales of this early jape. It stuck in Opffer's mind till he was over eighty; it may well have stayed in Crane's too . . .

When one reads through Crane's letters to his literary friends, his family, his theoretical statements, and his various defenses of his own work, one has the impression that, above all things, Crane wanted to be taken as an intellectual poet. He was as fiercely a self-taught intellectual as a writer could be. Certainly he was aware that only reading strategies that could make sense of the high modernist works of Eliot and Pound could negotiate his own energetic, vivid, but densely packed and insistently connotative lines.

The argument often used to impugn Crane's intellect—that Crane took the epigraph from Strachy's early seventeenth-century journals for *Powhatan's Daughter* (Part II of *The Bridge*) from a review by Elizabeth Bowen of William Carlos Williams's *In the American Grain*, where Bowen had quoted and abridged the same lines, rather than taking it from Williams's book directly or from the edition of Strachy's journals that Williams himself consulted—is simply jejune. (From other passages in *The Bridge*, as well as reports from Williams of a letter from Crane (now lost), in which Crane wrote Williams of the use he had made both of *In the American Grain* and also of Williams's poem "The Wanderer" in structuring *The Bridge*, we know Crane read Williams's book all the way through.) Crane took the idea for "Virginia," in "Three Songs," from a popular 1923 tune by Irving Caesar, "What Do You Do Sunday, Mary"; and he took the Latin lines at the end of the second act chorus of Seneca's *Medea* for the motto to "Ave Maria" (*The Bridge*, Part I) from a scholarly article in a 1918 issue of a recondite classics journal, *Mnemosne*. What, by the same silly argument, do *these* sources say about Crane's intellect—save that, like many intellectuals, he read lots, and at lots of levels? The point is the use he made of those textual allusions and their resonances in his poem—not their provenance or the purity of their sources!

Besides being an intellectual, however, Crane was also a volatile eccentric, often loud and impulsive. A homosexual who, by several reports, struck most people as unremittingly masculine, at the same time he was disconcertingly open about his deviancy with any number of straight friends at a time when homosexuality was assumed a pathology in itself.

Crane was also—more and more as his brief life rolled on—a drunk.

The last three or four years of Crane's life were largely the debacle of any number of literary alcoholics who died from drink: read Henry S. Salt's biography of James Thomson (B.V.); read Kevin Killian's and Lewis Ellingham's account of Jack Spicer; read Douglas Day on Malcolm Lowry—or anybody on Dylan Thomas. But the resultant biographemes that have sedimented in the collective literary imagination about Crane, from the typewriters thrown out windows, the poems composed with the Victrola blaring jazz, and Crane's own laughter spilling over the music and the racket of his own typewriter keys (but Cowley has told us how meticulously Crane revised those same poems) to the explosive break between Crane and Allen Tate and Caroline Gordon —with whom Crane had been living for a summer in Patterson, New York, when, unable to take him any longer, they precipitously put him out—and his midnight pursuits of sailors around the Navy Yards of Cleveland, Washington, D.C., and Brooklyn, to the more and more frequent encounters—both in New York and Paris—with the police, as well as in his last years various drunken suicide attempts. And above them all are the murky surroundings of his final hours, traveling on the steamer *Orizaba* back to the States from Mexico—with his "fiancée" Peggy Baird (Mrs. Malcolm Cowley, waiting for her divorce papers to come through)—from which the thirty-three-year-old Crane was being deported for still *another* drunken suicide try with a bottle of iodine. After several days of drinking and making a general nuisance of himself, on shipboard a few hours after sailing from Havana (where he'd written two cheery postcards, one to a Spanish professor friend of his in Mexico and one to the woman caretaker of his mother's property on the Isle of Pines, both by a bit of linguistic contingent propinquity named Simpson), on the evening of April 26th—Emil Opffer's birthday—a drunken Crane descended into the *Orizaba*'s sailors' quarters. He tried to read the sailors his poems—that's one version. He tried to make one of the sailors and was badly beaten—that's another. He was also—probably—robbed; at any rate, the next morning his money and his ring were gone. A sedated Baird had been confined to her room with a burned arm from an accident the day before, when a box of Cuban matches had caught fire. Now, sometime after eleven, in his pajamas and a light topcoat, a disconsolate Crane went to Baird's cabin. Baird said: "Get dressed, darling. You'll feel better."

As mentioned, it was the day after Emil's birthday. Was Crane perhaps thinking of the tale Emil's father had told . . . ?

"At about two minutes before noon," wrote Gertrude E. Vogt, a passenger on the ship, many years later to Crane's biographer John Unterecker, "a number of us were gathered on deck, waiting to hear the results of the ship's pool —always announced at noon. Just then we saw Crane come on deck, dressed, as you noted, in pajamas and topcoat; he had a black eye and looked generally battered. He walked to the railing, took off his coat, folded it neatly over the railing (not dropping it on deck), raised himself on his toes, then dropped back again. We all fell silent and watched him, wondering what in the world he was up to. Then, suddenly, he vaulted over the railing and jumped into the sea. For what seemed five minutes, but was more like five seconds, no one was able to move; then cries of "man overboard" went up. Just once I saw Crane, swimming strongly. But never again. It is a scene I am unable to forget, even after all these years."

After Crane's leap from the ship's stern, the *Orizaba* came to a stop, but the Captain figured either the ship's propellers, sharks, or both had finished the poet. The *Orizaba* trolled for him a full hour; the body, however, was not found. But all these images have displaced the less sensational—and earlier—images called up by the compulsive and omnivorous reader of Frazer, Doughty, Villard, the Elizabethans, Nietzsche, Emerson, Whitman, Dante, Melville, Joyce, LaForgue, Rimbaud, Ouspensky, Eliot, Pound, Frank, and Williams—to cite only a handful of the writers with whose work Crane was deeply familiar by the time he was thirty. Crane was not a reader of formal philosophy—and was quick to say so, when necessary. (From a letter to Yvor Winters in 1927: "I . . . have never read Kant, Descartes or the other doctors . . ." But he *had* read his Donne, Blake, and Vaughan.) His languages were French and nominal Latin; he used both.

The productive Crane was a young man: all but a handful of the poems we remember him for were written before he had completed his twenty-eighth year. But *by* twenty-eight, he had read and thought more about what he'd read than most twenty-eight-year-olds have, even twenty-eight-year-olds headed toward the academy.

The French have their concept of the *poète maudit* for such fellows (many of whom—though not all—were gay). Nineteen-twenties America had only Flaming Youth and the stodgy old professor—but no template for those between, much less one that encompassed the extremes of both. But those were the extremes Crane's life bridged.

II.

Beginning with his contemporaries Allen Tate and Yvor Winters, the traditional view of Crane is that as a poet he was an interesting, monumentally talented, yet "splendid failure" (the words come from the final line of a frequently reprinted essay, "Notes on a Text of Hart Crane" by R. P. Blackmur): a view that began with the uncomfortable perception by Winters and Tate of correspondences between Crane's homosexuality, his drunkenness, his suicide, and his ideas—especially his appreciation of Whitman—along with his work's resistance to easy elucidation. This view carries through the majority of Crane criticism to this day. It is perhaps presented in its clearest current form in Edward Brunner's *Splendid Failure: The Making of* The Bridge (1985). Still, I suspect, Crane's contemporaries could not quite grasp that Crane was often writing a kind of poem that simply did not undertake the task of argumentative (the word they often used was "structural") clarity, narrative or otherwise, then expected of the well-formed poem. But the primary sign of Crane's ultimate success is the crushing lack of critical attention we now pay to all those poems written at the time that dutifully undertook that task and performed it quite successfully. Among critical works on Crane that have directly taken up this point are Lee Edelman's rhetorically rigorous *Transmemberment of Song* (1987) and Paul Giles's paronomasially delirious *Contexts of* The Bridge (1986). Indeed, after the three major biographies (Horton, Weber, and Unterecker), which give the context of Crane in his times, Brunner's, Edelman's, and Giles's studies of the poems are probably the most informative recent books on Crane's work *per se*.

As Edelman suggests, perhaps the most careful account of Crane's "failure" is first laid out in Yvor Winters's quite extraordinary essay, "The Significance of *The Bridge* by Hart Crane, Or What Are We to Think of Professor X," reprinted in Winters's 1943 collection, *On Modern Poets*. There Winters relates Crane's enterprise to the pernicious and maniagenic ideas of Ralph Waldo Emerson via the irreligious pantheism of Whitman (read: relativism—in "Passage to India" Whitman blasphemes by claiming the poet is "the true son of God") and the glossolomania of Mallarmé. (At least that's how Winters saw them.) Winters had begun as one of Crane's most enthusiastic advocates. The two had an extensive correspondence as well as one warm and productive meeting. But, on the publication of *The Bridge* in 1930, a growing doubt about Crane's achievement finally erupted in Winters's review. Over it, the two men broke. But it is important to realize that the rejection—or at least the condemnation—of Crane, for Winters as well as for many of Crane's critics, was the rejection and condemnation of an entire romantic current in American literary production, a current that included Whitman and Emerson, with Crane only as its latest cracked and misguided voice. Those who shared Winters's judgments, like Brom Weber and R. P. Blackmur, also felt T. S. Eliot was as much of a failure as, or more of a failure than, Crane, and for the same reasons!

It is also worth noting that Winters's piece, while it is far more illuminative of what was going on—because it is more articulate about its anti-Emerson, anti-Whitman, and finally anti-American position (as well as those European currents, like Mallarmé, that Winters saw as supporting it) than many others— was also practically without influence, because it was all but unavailable from the time Winters wrote it until the 1960s.

But Blackmur's "New Thresholds, New Anatomies: Notes on a Text of Hart Crane," an essay that, despite its criticism, is probably as responsible as any other for Crane's endurance, basically takes the same tack and was widely

available from the time of its publication in 1935 through Blackmur's arrival
at Princeton in 1940, given his vast popularity as a critic ever since. (It is still
available today in Blackmur's *Form and Value in Modern Poetry*.) That essay begins:

> It is a striking and disheartening fact that the three most ambitious poems of our
> time should all have failed in similar ways: in composition, in independent objec-
> tive existence, and in intelligibility of language. *The Waste Land*, the *Cantos*, and *The
> Bridge* all fail to hang together structurally in the sense that "Prufrock," "Envoi,"
> and "Praise for an Urn"—lesser works in every other respect—do hang together.

Today, the general consensus on T. S. Eliot and Ezra Pound has wholly
reversed; since studies of Eliot and Pound by critics such as Elizabeth Drew
and Hugh Kenner, Blackmur's Pronouncement tinkles like a quaint bell, a bit
out of tune, from the past. The consensus on Crane however, has not. But, as
Edelman has argued, we best go back to the early critics of Crane in order to
commence whatever rehabilitation we might wish to undertake.

Winters accused Crane of following linguistic impulses, rather than in-
tentionally creating his ideas—of automatic writing rather than careful articulation of meanings—unaware that all writing (even the most logical and
articulate) is, in some sense, automatic. But the fact is, what Winters says of
Crane is perfectly true. Where Winters is wrong is in his assumption that there
is another, intention-centered, consciousness-bound, teleographical approach
to the creation of poetry in particular and writing in general that is, somehow,
actually available to the poet/writer other than as a metaphor or as a provisional construct dictated by the political moment. The teleology Winters could
not find in Whitman's pantheism is ultimately not to be had anywhere.

All sentences move toward logic and coherence—or, indeed toward whatever their final form—by a kind of chance and natural selection. The sentence
moves toward other qualities of the poetic in the same manner. Intention, consciousness, and reason are not a triumvirate that impels or creates language.
Rather they sit in judgment of the performance after the fact, somewhere
between mind and mouth, thought and paper, accepting or rejecting the language offered up; and—when they reject it—they are only able to wait for
new language they find more fitting for the tasks to hand. But while intention,
consciousness, and reason can halt speech (sometimes), there is some other,
ill-understood faculty of mind which fountains up "that virtual train of fires
upon jewels" (Mallarmé, translated and quoted by the disapproving Winters)
that *is* poetic language as much as it is analytical prose. It is something associ-
ative, rhetorical, dictational—and always almost opaque to analysis. Intention,
consciousness, and reason can only make a request of it, humbly and hesi-
tantly—a request to which that faculty may or may not respond, as if it were
possessed of an intention wholly apart from ours; or, more accurately, as if it

functioned at the behest of other, ill-understood aspects of mind apart from will or intention or anything like them. One can only hear the resonances of a word *after* it has been uttered, read its associations *after* it has been written; and, judging such associations and resonances, intention, consciousness, and reason can at best allow language to pass or not to pass. And from what we know of Crane, he was as much at pains to guide his poetic output as any writer in the language. But I also believe that a writer who thinks he or she can do anything else is likely to brutalize, if not stifle, his or her output—likely, at any rate, to restrict it to something less than it might be.

When, in his 1919 essay "Tradition and the Individual Talent" Eliot made his famous call for "depersonalization" in poetry—

> What is to be insisted upon is that the poet must develop or procure the conscious-ness of the past and that he should continue to develop this consciousness through his career.
>
> What happens is a continual surrender of himself as he is at the moment to something which is more valuable. The progress of an artist is a continual self-sacrifice, and continual extinction of personality.
>
> There remains to define this process of depersonalization and its relation to the sense of tradition . . .

—to the extent that the process of the poet is one with the poet's progress through the sentences that make up her or his poem, I suspect Eliot was refer-ring to the identical process I spoke of above, involving at least the provisional suspension of intention, consciousness, and reason, i.e., person-ality. Moreover I suspect Winters recognized it as such. And on the strength of that recogni-tion, he condemned the author.

In his book *Hart Crane and the Homosexual Text*, the late Thomas Yingling cites a passage from Crane's 1925 essay "General Aims and Theories" as expressing the very opposite of what Eliot, above, was calling for. Crane put together these notes for Eugene O'Neill when O'Neill was contemplating writing an introduction to Crane's first collection, *White Buildings*: "It seems to me that the poet will accidentally define his times well enough simply by reacting honestly and to the full extent of his sensibilities to the states of passion, experience and rumination that fate forces on him, first hand."

I think, however, that the notion of an *accidental* definition, the idea of an *honest* reaction to the states of passion, experience, and rumination to the full extent of his sensibilities is a poet speaking of, yet again, the *identical* creative experience in which intention (or whatever produces the "intention" effect), consciousness, and reason must not be employed too early—before there is material for them to accept or reject—and are signs that Crane and Eliot are speaking of the same phenomenon. The *difference* in how they speak about it has to do with what, as it were, each sees as fueling what I have called that "ill-understood faculty of mind" that first produces language. In 1919, Eliot saw it as literature. In 1925, Crane saw it as passion, experience, and rumination.

To ruminate is, of course, what ruminants do. Its metaphorical extension is not so much thinking, but thinking "over and over," as the *OED* reminds us. Repetition is inchoate in the metaphor. If there is a margin for intellection in Crane's model, it comes under the rubric of "rumination." And because that model suggests not so much "reading" as "rereading" (as well as the political margins for experience and passion), it is likely to appeal to the modern sensibility more than Eliot's.

Yingling's book points up how much of Crane's "failure" is intricately entailed with the homophobia of his critics—till finally Crane comes to represent more than anything else the most damning case of bad faith among the New Critics, who claimed above all to believe in the separation of the text from the man. But faced with Crane's homosexuality, as Yingling shows, they simply couldn't do it. This part of Yingling's argument one does not in the least begrudge him. Still, his overall thesis would have been stronger if he had been able to historify his discussion, relating (and distinguishing) Crane's case specifically to (and from) the extraordinarily similar marginalization (and persistence in spite of it) of Poe (1809–1849) as well as, say, James Thomson (B.V.) (1834–1882), Ernest Dowson (1867–1900), and Lionel Johnson (1867–1902), this last, one of Crane's adolescent passions. A book of Johnson's is recorded as part of Crane's adolescent library—doubtless the 1915 edition with the introduction by Ezra Pound. Alcoholism was a huge factor in all these poets' lives—and deaths. Perversion—in the form of pedophilia—haunted both the case of Poe and, only a trifle less so, of Thomson and Dawson. Homosexuality was certainly a factor in Johnson's life, and may or may not have been involved with the others. And in all cases major attempts were launched after their deaths to establish them as canonical; in all cases the arguments more or less triumphant against them were finally and fundamentally moral. Arguably this was outside Yingling's interest; still, had Yingling been able to extend his study even to the process by which poets of major canonical interest during their lives—like Edna St. Vincent Millay, a woman, or Paul Lawrence Dunbar, a black man—were, in the years after their deaths, systematically removed from the critical center (finally by the same process that has elevated Crane), he would have given us a major political analysis of canon-formation. But for all the insight he gives us into Crane's critical treatment, finally the process of establishing a poet or an artist's reputation is just more complex than Yingling presents it.

> O Thou steeled Cognizance whose leap commits
> The agile precinct of the lark's return;

Within whose lariat sweep encinctured sing
In single chrysalis the many twain,—

In a chapter called "Words" from her wonderfully wide-ranging 1959 study *Poetry: A Modern Guide to Its Understanding and Enjoyment*, critic Elizabeth Drew's terse judgment on Crane's address to the bridge is that it is an example of rhetoric "out of place" (73). Briefly she compares it to James Thomson's (not B.V.) (1700–1748) inflated address to a pineapple in *The Seasons* (1726–30):

> But O thou blest Anana, thou the pride
> Of vegetable life . . .

For Drew the simple juxtaposition is enough to damn both poets. Both, for her, are inflated and preposterous. One wonders, however, if Drew isn't —possibly unconsciously—following Poe's critique of the young American poet Joseph Rodman Drake (1795–1820), a near contemporary of Keats, who died at age twenty-five and whose poems his friend the poet Fitzgreen Halleck published in 1836, sixteen years after Rodman's death. In his famous review of the two poets' work, Poe calls the invocation to Drake's poem "Niagara" ("Roar, raging torrent! And thou, mighty river, / Pour thy white foam on the valley below. / Frown, ye dark mountains," etc.), "ludicrous—and nothing more. In general, all such invocations have an air of the burlesque." But finally one wonders, with all three poems, if it is not the fact that all three examples are apostrophes (rather than the elaborateness of the language in which the apostrophes are couched) that controls the "out of place"-ness—or ludicrous-ness—of the figures. Wouldn't the most colloquial—"You, waterfall," "Hey, pineapple!" or "Yo, Bridge!"—strike us as equally ludicrous or out of place?

Critic Harold Bloom has recounted (in his 1982 study *Agon: Towards a Theory of Revisionism*, 270) how, at age ten (revised down from eleven in an earlier version of the essay, published in Alan Trachtenberg's collection of essays on Crane) he first read, "crouched over Crane's book in a Bronx library" sometime in the 1930s, the same lines Drew denigrates. For Bloom (and, he explains, many others in that decade) they were what "cathected" him onto poetry. Like's Marlowe's rhetoric, Bloom argues, Crane's was both "a psychology and a knowing, rather than a knowledge." Begged as a present from his sister when he was twelve, Crane's poems were the first book Bloom owned.

I recall my first reading of those lines too—as a teenager in the late 1950s. (Crane's poems were one of the first trade paperbacks I purchased for myself.) I suspect that, like Bloom, I was not too sure what the lines actually meant; but in dazzling me—for dazzle me they did—they established the existence of a gorgeous meta-language that held my judgment on it in suspension precisely because I could not judge the meaning, even as it was clear this meta-language, as it welcomed glorious and sensual words into itself from as far afield as the Bible, the cowboy film, and the dictionary's most unthumbed pages ("thou," "cognizance," "lariat," "encinctured" . . .) welcomed equally such figures as the apostrophe—even more out of favor in the 1950s and '60s than it is today. What this language was in the process of knowing—the psychology it proffered—was that of an animate object world, a world where meaning and mystery were one, inseverable and ubiquitous, but at the same time a world where everything spoke (or sang or whispered or shouted) to everything else—and thus the apostrophe (the means by which the poet joined in with this mysterious dialogue and antiphon) was, in that sense, at its center.

I also remember, even more forcefully, the lines that for me—at sixteen —sent chills racing over me and a moment later struck me across the bridge of my nose with a pain sharp enough to make my eyes water. It came with the lines from "Harbor Dawn" that Crane the lyricist of unspeakable love had just managed to speak:

> And you beside me, blessèd now while sirens
> Sing to us, stealthily weave us into day—
> . . . *a forest shudders in your hair*

For suddenly I realized that "you" was another man!

One should also note, however, I had all but the same bodily reaction to my first encounter—at about the same age—with Ernest Dowson's "*Non Sum Qualis Eram Bonae Sub Regno Cynarae*," though the object there was clearly heterosexual: a female prostitute.

The point with Crane, however, was that there was a critical dialogue already in place around him that could sustain the resonances of that response in the growing reader—whether that reader was Harold Bloom or I.

But while nearly everyone seems to have ravaged Dowson's poems for titles[3] (*Gone with the Wind, The Night Is Thine, Days of Wine and Roses, Love and Sleep* . . .), no dialogue about the significance of Dowson, no argument over the meaning of the tradition he inhabited and developed, remains in place, save a few wistful comments by Yeats and the bittersweet memoir by J. Arthur Symons that introduces at least one edition of Dowson's poems. What's there is a monologue, not a dialogue. And it is all too brief.

Dowson took his Latin title from the first Ode in Horace's Book IV, in which the poet, near fifty, entreats Venus/Cynara not to visit him with love: love is for the young, such as Paulus Maximus. ("But why," he asks in the last two stanzas, "is there a tear on my face? I still remember thee in dreams, where I chase after thee, across the green, among the waves . . .") Horace describes Venus in the Ode as a "cruel mother," as a goddess "hard of heart"—so that there is a good deal of irony in the line Dowson has chosen for a title, signaled by the placement of *"Bonae"* as far away from its noun, *"Cynarae,"* as it can get: *"Non Sum Qualis Eram Bonae Sub Regno Cynarae"* ("I am not such as I was under the reign of the kindly Cynara." The "kindly Cynara" (*bonae Cynarae*) is very much *"Venus tout entière à sa prois attaché"*—kindly in the sense that the Eumenides are "the kindly ones." To praise Dowson's poem for its insight into the realities of love among the worldly, contrasted with the romantic memories of love among the innocent, is to revivify part of the dialogue about him. But though there was once a dialogue about Dowson, it is nearly impossible to reconstruct it from, say, the stacks of the twenty-one-story library at the University of Massachusetts, whereas the volumes debating the reputation of Crane, by comparison, practically leap from the shelves.

Another aspect of the dialogue over Crane is that at first it seems, at least to the sixteen-year-old if not to the ten-year-old, that its questions are transparently easy to resolve. But later, we begin to notice that, even as we, like Yingling, begin to demystify some of these questions, others are revealed to be even more complex. And those questions—What are these poems about? How do they signify and continue to signify today?—invariably take us *to* the poems, not away from them.

But finally it is the dialogue created between the critically enlivened concept of "Crane-the-failure" and the elusive meaning of the poems themselves that sets critics listening intensely—in a way that almost no one today is prompted to listen to Winters or Ridge or Wheelright or Bodenheim, to name a handful of poets whom we turn to, if at all, because we are in pursuit of some insight Crane had while reviewing them, or because he mentioned something they wrote in a letter.

This is the dialogue that sustains the new readers of Crane. This is the dialogue that makes old readers go back and reread him.

A reader of Yingling's book with a sense of this, gay or straight, will, after a while, be compelled to observe that however much Crane was marginalized because of his homosexuality, he's a good deal less marginal today than any number of straight male poets of his time—certainly less so than Tate or Winters. Indeed, after Eliot, Pound, and Yeats, the only poet of his era who precedes Crane in reputation is Wallace Stevens—another male homosexual poet.

As it is now, however, that part of Yingling's argument about Crane's reception is open to the counterargument that if Crane had not been the "failure" he was, he might all too easily have been nothing at all!

And that is not a good argument—which is to say it only points up the weakness in Yingling's.

Certainly it's ironic that in 1927 Winters wrote his own poetic series, *The Bare Hills* (which Crane once offered to review), all but unread today, which —though it has its delicate, minor-key beauties—performs with none of the force of Crane's work, possibly because it strives after poetry through a method insistently deaf to the processes and poetic product Winters had excoriated so in Crane. Though Crane did not review it, the reviewers of the day found *The Bare Hills* "austere." The modern judgment would be, I suspect, if such a judgment could be said even to exist: thin.

*   *   *

In a letter to Winters, responding to Winters's exhortation that the poet be a "complete man," Crane ends with a warning Winters might well have heeded: "I have neglected to say," Crane wrote, "that I admire your general attitude, including your distrust of metaphysical or other patent methods. Watch out, though, that you don't strangulate yourself with some counter-method of your own!" For the morality of a text has to do with its use, not its intent—or, even more frequently, its lack of intent to espouse a position that a later time (sometimes only months on) has decided is more ethical than the unquestioned commonplace of an earlier moment. Would that Winters had been able to distinguish a description of a state of affairs—how language works—from a posed poetic methodology.

In a strange near-reversal at the end of his essay "The Significance of *The Bridge* by Hart Crane, Or What Are We to Think of Professor X?" Winters finally claims for Crane a superiority, both of intellect and poetic apperception, over a generalized "Professor X," who is cozily in love with Whitman and the American Transcendentalists and simply blind to the dangers in their romantic program—dangers that polluted Crane's poetic enterprise and drove him through (in Winters's judgment) obscure poetry to madness and suicide. (Only a strict New England background, reasoned Winters, plus the fact that he had far less poetic talent than Crane in the first place, kept Emerson from the same disastrous ends.) Claims Winters: Crane understood these ideas in all respects except their mortal flaws and consciously pursued them as such, at least having the courage of his convictions to follow them to the end—which (says Winters) Professor X, who professes to approve them, has not.

The irony of Crane's reputation, however, is that many academic critics —descendants of Winters's Professor X—who, today, have now read their Emerson, Eliot, and Mallarmé pretty carefully and would argue hotly against Winters's reading of them, if not against his reading of Whitman, are still comfortable with the notion of Crane-as-poetic-failure: what they are blind to now is the realization that Crane's "structural failure" is—just like Eliot's—his modernism; as it is his continuity with the outgrowth of the romantic tradition high modernism represents.

But how did meaning and mystery work together to communicate the existence, now and again in Crane's poems, of a same-sex bed partner—as it did to me that afternoon in 1958?

One cannot make too much more headway in such a discussion of Crane without some comment on "homosexual genres." While "genre" may well be too strong a term for them, these are nevertheless forms that, in various ages, various works have taken—forms that have been readable as gay or homosexual by gay or homosexual men and women in their particular times. In various ages these genres change their form. (Indeed, to discuss them fully in historical terms is beyond the scope of such notes as these. To quote Crane: ". . . the whole topic is something of a myth anyway, and is consequently modified by the characteristics of the image by each age in each civilization.") Most recently however—say, since the nineteenth century—the aspect that might be cited as most characteristic of this genre or genres is that they are structured so that straight, gay, male, or female readers and critics can read the homosexuality *out* of them, for whatever reason, whenever it becomes necessary or convenient.

One particular poetic form of this genre (of which *Voyages* is an example) includes treatments of love in which the object of desire is specifically left ambiguous as to gender. This allows critics of one persuasion to read it: "Of course it's speaking of heterosexual desire—since the vast majority of desire is, and the writer has left no positive sign that this portrait of desire is any different from most." Meanwhile critics of another persuasion may read it: "Of course it's speaking of homosexual desire. The rhetorical lengths to which the author has gone not to specify the gender is its positive sign." Another example of this form is, as I suggested, Crane's "Harbor Dawn" in *The Bridge*.

After the aubade of the first five stanzas, the poem, with its next line, locates itself directly with the lovers in their bed: "And you beside me, blessèd now while sirens / Sing to us, stealthily weave us into day— / Serenely now, before day claims our eyes / your cool arms murmurously about me lay. . . ." For a total of eleven lines, the poet goes on about his beloved without once mentioning "breasts" or "tresses," or any other explicit sign of the feminine. About the room we do not even see any of the "stockings, slippers, camisoles, and stays" that were so famously piled on the divan in the typist's bedsit before "the young man carbuncular" arrived in *The Waste Land*'s (once notorious because of it) "Fire Sermon." In the pre-Stonewall late 1950s, when "homophobia" was indeed a universal, pervasive, if silent, fear, even this much explicit lack of feminization was as articulate to an urban sixteen-year-old boy as any Gay Rights flier or Act-Up poster today.

My first response was to weep.

Given the tears I swallowed (in order that no one else in the house hear them), that explicit lack may well have had an order of power that, in these post-Stonewall times, has no current analogue.

The rubric Crane added to (the right of) the poem after the first printing works to heterosexualize our reading—or, more accurately, to bisexualize it: ". . . or is / it from the / soundless shore / of sleep that / time /// recalls you to / your love, / there in a / waking dream / to merge your seed // —with whom?"

("Merge your seed," followed by the daring "—with whom?," certainly suggests two men coming together) "Who is the / woman with / us (possibly with the poet and the reader, but equally possibly with the poet and the poet's lover) in the / dawn? . . . / Whose is the / flesh our feet / have moved / upon?" The woman is so clearly a spiritualized presence, even a spiritual ground, and the columnar text of the poem is so clearly of the "ambiguous" form mentioned above, that when I first read the poem as a sixteen-year-old in 1958, it never occurred to me that it was anything other than a description of homosexual love, with a few suggestions of heterosexuality artfully placed about for those who preferred to read it that way—which, after all, is what it is.

Even today, when I read over Winters's heterosexual reading of the poem, I find myself balking when he refers to the loved-one as "she" or "her," having to remind myself this is not a misreading, but is rather an *alternate* reading the poet has left, carefully set up *by* the text of the poem, precisely *for* heterosexual readers like Winters—or, indeed, for any critic, gay or straight, who had to discuss or write about the poem in public—to take advantage of.

But while a heterosexual reading may find the poem just as beautiful and just as lyrical (that's after all, what the poet wanted) it will not find the poem anywhere near as poignant as the homosexual reading does, because the heterosexual reading specifically erases all reference to the silence surrounding homosexuality for which the heterosexual reading's existence, within the homosexual reading, is the positive sign. That is one reason the homosexual reading seems to me marginally the richer.

While more common in fiction than in poetry, another homosexual form is the narrative that takes place in a world where homosexuality is never mentioned and is presumed not to exist—but where the incidents that occur have no other satisfying explanation. (To use another phrase made famous by Eliot, they have no other "objective correlative" save homosexual desire.) This is Wilde's *The Picture of Dorian Gray*, Gide's *L'Immoralist*, and Mann's *Tod im Vennidig*. This is Alfred Hitchcock's *Rope*. Again, because homosexuality is implied in such works, not stated, a literalist reading of such texts can always more or less erase it. Such a text, also, is Crane's "Cutty Sark." That's one I didn't get at sixteen.

But by the time, at twenty-five, I'd stayed up all night in half a dozen similar situations, yes, I got it!

Still a third homosexual form is the light-hearted, good-natured, innocent presentation of rampant male (heterosexual) promiscuity: the sort of young man who'd "go to bed with anything!" The assumption here, of course, is that the young man does—only the writer has opted not to specify the homosexual occurrences. (The classic example, despite Yingling's italics and multiple punctuation marks of surprise is, yes, *Tom Jones: The History of a Foundling* [1749].) Often in such works the heterosexual conquests are accompanied by extraordinarily complacent husbands—presumed to be getting some from the young man off stage and on the side. Sometimes a wise or silly older woman, especially if a widow (the nickname for one of the most popular gay bartenders in New York City's heavy hustling strip along Eighth Avenue is "Jimmy the Widow," who has worked there more than twenty years now) is read as a satiric, coded portrait of an old queen, who briefly has the young man's sexual favors.

The classical homosexual reading that replaces Proust's "Albertine" (the heroine of À la recherche du temps perdu) with "Albert" (Proust's own young male driver) is a prime example of the same homosexual reading trope where women substitute in the text for men: generations of gay readers have pointed out to each other, with a smile, that Marcel's kidnapping and detention of Albertine for weeks is lunatic if she is *actually* an upper-class young woman—and only comprehensible if she is a working-class young man.

The male narrator to whom Willa Cather goes to such pains, in the frame story of *My Ántonia*, to ascribe the text recounting the narrator's chaste, life-long love of a wonderfully alive Czech immigrant woman is another, easily readable (and wholly erasable by a literalist reading) example of a (in this case lesbian) homosexual trope.

One of the most famous—and, at the same time, most invisible—examples of such a form is presented in the closing moments of Wagner's prologue-plus-trilogy of operas, *Der Ring des Nibelungen*. The sixteen-odd hours of music (usually heard over four nights) comprising the work are intricately interwoven from motifs that take on great resonances, both psychological and symbolic: this motif associated with the completion of Valhalla, that one associated with the Ring of Power, another with the Spear on which the Law is inscribed, while another represents the Sword given by the gods to mortals to free themselves, and still another stands for the renunciation of love necessary for any great human undertaking in the material world. These motifs have been traced in their multiple appearances throughout the *Ring* and explicated in literally hun-dreds of volumes. At the closing of the fourth and final opera, *Götterdämmerung*, when the castle of earthly power lies toppled, the castle of the gods has burned down, and the awed populace gazes over a land swept clean by the flooding and receding of the Rhine, the tetralogy ends with a sumptuous melody that registers to most hearers as wholly new—a fitting close for this image of a new world, awaiting rebirth at the hands of man and history.

But, as many commentators have now noticed and pointed out to each other so that others would hear, that closing melody is not *completely* new. Clearly it's based on some five or six seconds—no more—of what, in *The Perfect Wagnerite* (1896), George Bernard Shaw called "some inconsequential love music" that first sounded toward the middle of *Die Walküre*'s Act III. What makes it "incon-sequential" is, of course, that it is not music from any of the passionate, incestu-ous, heterosexual loves that shake the quadrature of operas and—often—the audience unto the foundations. The music Wagner uses for *Götterdämmerung*'s terminal D-flat melody are not some moments from the searing, sun-drenched love of Siegfried and Brunhilda (or, indeed, the possibly more searing, moon-drenched love of Sigmund and Siglinda). Rather, this music accompanies Siglinda's profession of love to Brunhilda, who, after Sigmund's death, protects Siglinda (and the as-yet-unborn Siegfried) by sending them into the uncivilized wood where Wotan will not follow. A nineteenth-century tradition holds that the love of two women is the single purest love, a tradition going back at least as far as the biblical tale of Ruth and Naomi. This purity is certainly part of what Wagner wished to evoke in his closing. Still, he chose this clearly Sapphic moment when, because a daughter defies her father for love of another woman, the other woman declares her love in return.

No critic overtly mentioned this sapphism during Wagner's lifetime. Possibly that emboldened him to write his next opera, *Parsifal*, surely and famously—it has been so called repeatedly throughout our century—the most blatantly homoerotic of operas in the repertoire.

Some commentators (e.g., Shaw) have gone so far as to claim that the recall of those few moments of melody from *Die Walküre* at the close of *Götterdämmerung* is an oversight on Wagner's part. It's the single "motif" that appears only twice in the work: surely Wagner must have forgotten his first use of it, or at least assumed no one would recognize it. But, besides the fact that such recognitions, blatant and hidden, comprise the entire structure of the *Ring*, critics who claim such have simply never composed an opera. Such things are *not* forgotten; endings are much too important; and the single previous appearance makes it that much more certain it was a considered and conscientious decision.

More recent critics have taken to calling it the "praise Brunhilda" motif —which, yes, covers the situation: when in *Die Walküre*'s Act III mortal Siglinda sings those moments of melody, she is, indeed, "praising" Brunhilda, her then still immortal half-sister. Nevertheless it sidesteps the yearning, the desiring, the straining for the other that inform that wondrous melody almost as powerfully as they do the "Liebestod" of *Tristan und Isolde*.

They are not subtle, the tropes characterizing the "homosexual genres." Often, they are based on the most stereotypical heterosexist assumptions about homosexuality as an inversion of the masculine or of the feminine, or of homosexuality as the replacement of one by the other, or of homosexuality as a third, neuter (i.e., unspecified) sex. Because they are generic (or very close to it), they represent the gross forms of the particular work. But that's why they are as recognizable as they are, by isolated adolescents with only the most fleeting and hearsay knowledge of a homosexual community—and, I'm sure, were quite accessible to straight readers who were interested enough to pursue them. But, at the same time, their coding is always in an erasable mode: They register as an absence, an oversight, a formal arrangement in which the homosexual reading can always be dismissed as an over-reading. That's what makes them, as it were, safe in a profoundly homophobic society—in which even to mention homosexuality is to risk contaminating oneself with it.

One could go so far as to argue that these forms were only visible to those (of whatever sexual persuasion) in the work's audience who saw form itself as an articulating element in art—and that, by the same token, they remained invisible to those who saw only manifest content as defining what a given work of art was "about"; as such, they are part of a code whose complexities are certainly not exhausted by the simple signaling of a possible sexual preference. They have, rather, to do with the figuration of a formalist conception of art itself.

Even Loveman's characterization of *Voyages* ("Whether it be addressed to normal or abnormal sexuality matters little") is simply an articulate characterization of the erasability of the homosexuality built into the form of the six individual poems in the sequence, just as Loveman's subsequent citing of Sappho and Shakespeare as his first two writers for comparison—two writers in whom homosexuality may be read in or read out at will and according to a long tradition—implicates his statement within the very genre he is, with the quoted phrase, articulating.

But seldom, of course, are these genre forms or their tropes as pure as I have presented them here. Seldom, indeed, are they as clear as the ones I've already located in Crane. The problem with trying to read these texts in the light of current "gay" politics is, however, that they are already figures of an older "homosexual" politics, which, as they metaphorize the silence and the yearning behind the social silence once enforced around homosexuality, are (if read "literally" and not "figuratively") precisely limited, by their writers' most carefully crafted presentation of the formal conventions, to an articulate statement of homosexuality's existence—but often of almost nothing more.

What I've described is not the particular form of Whitman's poems or Melville's novel, of Shakespeare's sonnets or Sappho's fragments. These are not the form of Musil's *Young Törless*, of Baldwin's *Giovanni's Room*, of Vidal's *The City and the Pillar*. These are all works in which the content is manifestly homosexual—though, in the case of the older works, the same erasural reading of homosexuality contingently links them, as it were, to the ones described; and in the 1950s, occasionally critics tried to dismiss the more recent ones as cautionary case histories, rather than accept them as rich and moving statements, which may well have been the start of a similar dismissive move. But these genre forms do cover, say, Thomas Beer's 1923 biography *Stephen Crane: A Study in American Letters*.

We have gone into this genre (again, if that is what it should be called) in so much detail because Crane from time to time employed it: again, *Voyages*, "Harbor Dawn," and "Cutty Sark"—not to mention "This Way Where

November . . ." ("White Buildings") and "Thou Canst Read Nothing . . ." ("Reply")—are all examples.

Paradoxically, the existence of such a homosexual genre and its forms as I have described (gay is the last thing one should call them), as well as their problematic, even mythic, status (they could not be talked about for what they were and remain effective in any way; whether or not they actually existed had to be kept in a state of undecidability), may represent one of the largest obstacles in the development of a historically sensitive gay studies faced with the task of diligently teasing out what, in specific examples of such genres, is in excess of their simplistic conventions.

But today—if only because they are unsubtle and generic—there is no reason for the heterosexual critic, male or female, not to have access to the homosexual reading of the work of a poet such as Crane. If anything, it behooves us, in our enthusiasm as gay critics, occasionally to recall just how much rhetorical energy such writers expended in the employment of these forms to ensure that a heterosexual reading was available for their texts.

III.

From some thirty years ago I can recall a conversation in which a young poet explained to me how practically every rhetorical aspect of then-contemporary experimental poetry—it was c. 1963—had been foreshadowed forty to forty-five-odd years earlier by T. S. Eliot, either in "The Love Song of J. Alfred Prufrock" or in *The Waste Land*. With much page turning and flipping through volumes, it was very impressive.

If any factor contributed most to the image of Crane the lyricist-sometimes-too-ambitious, it was his prosody. Eliot—and Pound, of the quintessentially experimental *Cantos*—was half in and half out of the traditional English language iambic pentameter measure. And when they were in it, they were often working mightily to make it vanish under the hyper-rhythms of the most ordinary speech. ("What thou lovest well remains . . . ," that most famous passage (in Canto 81) of *The Pisan Cantos*, though written in classical hexameters, strives to rewrite itself in blank tetrameter.) Crane often used a loose pentameter, however, to flail himself as far away from the syntax and diction of common speech as he could get and not have comprehension crumble entirely beneath him.

At that time, probably few would have called Crane's poetry "experimental." By the late 1950s or early '60s (after the 1958 reprinting of his poems), Crane seemed a vivid, intense lyricist, whose poems, a little more frequently than was comfortable, lapsed over into the incomprehensible. Gertrude Stein's considerable effect was felt almost entirely within the realm of prose. Pound and Eliot were still the models for poetic experimentation among the young.

And one suspected that any experiment whose rhetorical model could not be found within them was an experiment that had failed—by definition.

Once Eliot first published them in 1917's "Prufrock," for the next fifty years couplets like

> In the room the women come and go
> Talking of Michelangelo.

and

> I grow old . . . I grow old . . .
> I shall wear the bottoms of my trousers rolled

astonished young writers again and again with their LaForguian bathos. Like many poets of the 1920s, Crane had followed Eliot back to LaForgue; he'd early-on translated "Three Locutions des Pierrots" from LaForgue's French.

One of the first poems where Crane thought about responding to Eliot —one of the first to which he committed the whole of his poetic abilities and in which he first began to create lines that regularly arrived at the a-referential form we now think of as characteristic of him—was "For the Marriage of Faustus and Helen." But if this poem sounds like anything to the modern ear, it sounds more like a pastiche of Eliot's "Prufrock" than a critique of it.

Crane's feminine iambic couplets, such as

> The stenographic smiles and stock quotations
> Smutty Wings flash out equivocations.

and

> Three winged and gold-shod prophesies of heaven,
> The lavish heart shall always have to leaven

must recall to the sensitive reader Eliot's near-signature feminine rhymes:

> And time yet for a hundred indecisions,
> For a hundred visions and revisions.

and

> Oh, do not ask "What is it?"
> Let us go and make our visit.

As well, Crane's generalized apostrophes—

O, I have known metallic paradises
Where cuckoos clucked to finches

—recall not only the apostrophe above it but recall equally Prufrock's general claims to knowledge:

And I have known them all already, known them all . . .
And I have known the eyes already, known them all . . .
And I have known the arms already, known them all . . .

Further comparison of the two poems, however, reveals a far greater metric regularity in Crane's verse than in Eliot's (or, if you prefer, a greater metrical variety in Eliot's verse than in Crane's): Eliot often pairs tetrameters with hexameters, now in trochaics, now in iambics (which the ear then tries to re-render into more traditional paired pentameters), where Crane generally relies on blank or rhymed couplets.

With a full seventy years, however, Eliot's variety has finally been normalized and absorbed into the general range of free verse, so that it is almost hard to see his variation today as formal. As Eliot's idiosyncrasies have become one with the baseline of American poetic diction, Crane the occasionally-over-the-top lyricist has metamorphosed into Crane the rhetorical revolutionary.

The study of eccentric figures on the poetic landscape tends to blind us, with the passage of time, to the mainstream that made the eccentric signify as it did. What was the scope of mainstream poetry during the '20s—Crane's decade?

In 1921 Edwin Arlington Robinson's *Collected Poems*, with the award of the Pulitzer Prize for Poetry, made the fifty-year-old poet—till then all but unknown, though he had been publishing books of verse since the 1880s—into a famous man. Eliot's *The Waste Land* (along with Joyce's *Ulysses*) appeared in 1922, but it was a success de scandal, not a popular triumph: the talk alone of people who talked of poetry. Then, that same year, so was Amy Lowell's *A Critical Fable*—a humorous survey of the poetic scene since the War, whose title was taken from her forebear James Russell Lowell's *A Fable for Critics* (1848), both with their tour de force introductions in rhymed prose. (That same November in Paris, Marcel Proust died, leaving unpublished the last three sections of his great novel.) The year 1923 saw Edna St. Vincent Millay's *The Harp-Weaver and Other Poems* receive the Pulitzer; 1924 saw it go to Robert Frost for his third book-length collection, *New Hampshire*. That same year, Robinson Jeffers's *Roan Stallion, Tamar, and Other Poems* was an extraordinary popular success with the reading public, setting off a controversy over Jeffers's poetic merit that has not abated. In France that year, a poem touching on many of the same political concerns as Crane's *The Bridge* appeared, a poem that makes an informative contrast with it: St-John Perse's *Anabase*. (Perse's *Amitié du Prince* appeared the same year.) And in America in

1924, Wallace Stevens wrote what was to become one of his most famous poems, "Sea Surface Full of Clouds," before entering half a dozen years of comparative poetic inactivity. And in 1925 twelve-year-old poet Nathalia Crane's *The Janitor's Boy* appeared, with introductory statements by both Nunnally Johnson and William Rose Benét (citing other poetic prodigies of merit such as the Scottish Marjorie Flemming, Hilda Conkling, and Scottish-born Helen Douglas Adam), and went through a dozen-plus printings in no time. Robinson's next book, *The Man Who Died Twice* (1925), won him another Pulitzer; the 1926 Pulitzer went, posthumously, to Amy Lowell for *What's O'Clock* (published the same year—also posthumously—as her two-volume biography, *John Keats*). And the following year Robinson received his third Pulitzer for his book-length poem *Tristram* (1927), which became a bona fide bestseller. Poetry bestsellers were certainly not common in those years, but they were more common than in ours. In the same year, Millay's verse drama *The King's Henchman*, on which Deems Taylor based his successful opera of the same title, went through twelve printings between February and September (while in Germany, also in 1927, Martin Heidegger's *Being and Time* appeared, a work whose enterprise can be read as the cornerstone of his earliest attempts to poeticize the contemporary world, against a rigorous critique of metaphysics). That year American scholar John Livingston Lowe first published exhaustive and illuminating findings from his researches into the early readings of Samuel Taylor Coleridge, *The Road to Xanadu: A Study in the Ways of the Imagination*. In 1928, Stephen Vincent Benét's novel in verse *John Brown's Body* captivated the general reading public. And through it all, the various volumes of Millay, for critics like Edmund Wilson, marked the true height of American poetic achievement.

What characterizes this range of American poetry is its extraordinary referential and argumentative clarity (argument used here in terms both of narrative and of logic)—often to the detriment of all musicality (as well as rhetorical ornamentation) not completely controlled by the regularity of meter and end-rhyme.

This was the mainstream of American poetry that Eliot, Pound, H. D., and William Carlos Williams—as well as Crane (and Lowell, while she was alive)—saw themselves, one way or the other, at odds with. And this is the context that explains Loveman's seemingly gratuitous swipe at Mrs. Browning. First, the simple sexism that it represents is certainly at work in the comment—as it was against Amy Lowell, who worked as hard as any poet to ally her work and her enthusiasms with the new. To deny it would be as absurd as denying the homophobia Yingling found at work in the structure of the reputation of Crane. But, we must also remember, as a traditional poet, Elizabeth Browning was popular, even in the 1920s. She was accessible. Thus she was seen to be on the side of referential clarity that those associated with the avant-garde felt called upon to denigrate. But, as is the case with the homophobia directed toward

Crane, we must remember that it works not to obliterate the reputation, but rather to hold the reputation at a particular point—which was and is, finally, higher than that of many male poets of the time.

Today, it's the L=A=N=G=U=A=G=E poets whose works wrench Crane out of his position as a lyricist-too-extreme and force us to reread him as a rhetorical revolutionary. Precisely what has been marginalized in the early readings of Crane—or, at any rate, pointed at with wagging finger as indicative of some essential failure—is now brought to the critical center and made the positive node of attention.

For what is now made the center of our rhetorical concern with Crane is precisely that "verbiage" Loveman would have stripped from the work—those moments where referentiality fails and language is loosed to work on us in its most immediate materiality.

Again and again through Crane's most varied, most exciting poems, phrases and sentences begin which promise to lead us to some referentially satisfying conclusion, through the form of some poetic figure. And again and again what Crane presents us with to conclude those figures is simply a word—a word that resists any and all save the most catachrestic of referential interpretations, so that readers are left with nothing to contemplate save what Language poet Ron Silliman has called the pure "materiality of the signifier." It is easy to see (and to say) that Crane's poetry foregrounds language, making readers revel in its sensuousness and richness. But one of the rhetorical strategies by which he accomplishes this in line after line is simply to shut down the semantic, referential instrumentality of language all but completely:

> Time's rendings, time's blendings they construe
> As final reckonings of fire and snow.

Or:

> The Cross, a phantom, buckled—dropped below the dawn.
> Light drowned the lithic trillions of your spawn.

The final words—"spawn," "fire and snow"—arrive in swirling atmospheres of connotation, to which they even contribute; but reference plays little part in the resolution of these poetic figures. Reading only begins with such lines as one turns to clarify how they resist reference, resist interpretation, even as their syntax seems to court them. But to find examples we can look in any of Crane's mature work.

In 1963—the same year I was having the conversation about T. S. Eliot with the aforementioned poet—in France, Michel Foucault was writing, in an essay on contemporary fiction, that the problem was not that "language is a certain distance from things. Language is the distance."

Thirty years before, Crane's suicide had put an end to a body of work that
—not till twice thirty years later—would be generally acknowledged as among
the earlier texts to inhabit that distance directly and, in so inhabiting it, shift an
entire current of poetic sensibility in a new direction.

*   *   *

We like to tell tales of how confident our heroes are in their revolutionary
pursuits. But it is more honest, in Crane's case at any rate, to talk about how
paralyzingly unsure he was—at least at times—about precisely this aspect of
his work; though, frankly, in the twenties, how could he have felt otherwise?
    In a 1963 interview, Loveman recounted:

Once—I don't know whether I ever told you—he tried to commit suicide in my
presence.

    We had been out having dinner; he got raffishly high and we went to a lovely
restaurant in the Village. No one was there but Didley Digges, the actor, in one
corner, Hart waltzed me over to him with a low bow. Then he began to dance ma-
zurkas on the floor. He loved to dance. It was a big room, and we had an excellent
dinner. He got a little higher, and when he went out, as usual, he bargained with a
taxi driver. He would never pay more than two dollars fare to Brooklyn. And then,
usually, because he always forgot that he hadn't money with him, the person with
him had to pay it. Through some mishap, we landed at the Williamsburg Bridge,
I think there is a monument or a column there and Hart went up and as a matter
of rite or sacrilege pissed against it. Then we started across to Columbia Heights.
He lived at Number 110. When we got to Henry Street, it was around eleven or
eleven-thirty. In one of the doorways we saw four legs sticking out and a sign, "We
are not bums." They were going to an early market and their wagon was parked in
the street. Hart became hysterical with laughter. Well, when we got to Columbia
Heights, the mood changed. The entire situation changed. He broke away from
me and ran straight up the three flights of stairs, then up the ladder to the roof,
and I followed him. I was capable of doing that then. As he got to the top, he
threw himself over the roof and I grabbed his leg, one leg, and, oh, I was scared to
death. And I said, "You son of a bitch! Don't you *ever* try that on me again." So he
picked himself up and said, "I might as well, I'm only writing rhetoric."

Here the interviewer comments: "That's what was bothering him."
And Loveman continues:

He could no longer write without the aid of music or of liquor. It was impossible.
He had reached the horrible impasse. So, we went downstairs to his room, I lived
a couple of doors away, I worried myself sick about him. He poured himself some
Dago Red, turned on the Victrola, and I left him.

How important this incident might have been for Crane is hard to tell. Was it a drunken jape, forgotten the next morning? Or does it represent the deep and abiding *veritas* classically presumed to reside *in vino*? Again, none of the three major biographers utilizes it . . .

Unterecker characterizes Crane as a "serious drinker" from the summer of 1924 on. But drunkenness figures in Crane's letters—and in the apocryphal tales about him—from well before. And as so many people have pointed out (to repeat), in trying to explain the context of prohibition in cities like New York and Chicago to people who did not live through it, even though alcohol was outside the law, it was so widely available the problem was not how to get it but rather how to stay sober enough to conduct the business of ordinary life!

It was a problem many in that decade failed to solve—Crane among them.

Let me attempt here, however, what I will be the first to admit is likely an over-reading of the evening Loveman has described with Crane—with all its a-specific vagaries.

The night begins in a Village restaurant, with an actor, a speaker of other writers' words. Directly following, a cab driver mangles Crane's (or possibly Loveman's) verbal instructions home: "Take us across the Bridge to Brooklyn . . ."

But instead of taking them to the Brooklyn Bridge, the driver takes them to the Williamsburg Bridge at Delancey Street, where, realizing how far off they are, they get out.

At the time, the nighttime plaza before the Williamsburg walkway had to be approached by steps. Crane urinates on one of the stone columns leading to the raised entrance yard. Such a public monument makes a certain kind of public statement. To urinate on such a raised architectural monument is, at the very least, to express one's contempt in the most bodily way possible (short of smearing it with shit) for its sententiousness, its pomposity, its civic pretension —those enunciational aspects traditionally designated by the phrase "empty rhetoric."

But to recount the above in this way is to point out that we have begun an evening where every event, as narrated by Loveman, one way or another foregrounds a more and more problematic relation with language—specifically with something about its rhetoricity.

Having given up the errant cab, Crane and Loveman decide to walk home, down through the Lower East Side, presumably to the Brooklyn Bridge, to cross over to 110 Columbia Heights by foot. (Loveman—a published poet in his own right, as well as, later, an editor of some reputation—tells us further on in the interview that at the time John Dos Passos lived in the apartment below Crane's.) Crossing Henry Street, around the corner from the great daily markets of Orchard and Hester, just up from the Fulton Fish Market, they find two men sleeping together in a doorway, legs sticking out. There is the identifying cardboard, "We are not bums," which reduces Crane to hysteria —as he perceives the comedy of rhetoric at its most referential, stating what the speaker/writer hopes to make obvious in fear of the very misreading the writing presumes to obviate, participating through it in the same pretentious inflation on which, fifteen minutes before, Crane had just emptied his bladder: the entrance to a suspension bridge of the same order as the one which was to be the focus for his major marshaling of rhetorical forces.

It intrigues me that this night's walk across the Brooklyn Bridge, usually such a positive symbol for Crane, and across which he had walked before, holding hands with Emil, is elided from Loveman's account. Does the elision suggest that—that night—the Bridge did not have the usual uplifting effect on Crane that, often in the past, it had had? Is there anything that we can retrieve from the elision? What, on any late night's stroll across the Brooklyn Bridge in the 1920s, were two gay men likely to see, regardless of their mood?

The nighttime walkways of the city's downtown bridges have traditionally been heavy homosexual cruising areas, practically since their opening—one of the reasons that, indeed, after dark, Crane and Emil had been able to wander across it, holding hands, with minimal fear of recriminations. They certainly could not have walked so during the day.

But perhaps that evening, with his old friend Loveman, on the Bridge's cruisy boardwalk, Crane might have heard the rich and pointed banter of a group of dishy queens lounging against the rail, or, perhaps, even the taunts leveled at them from a passing gaggle of sailors, who often crossed the Bridge back to the Navy Yard, in their uneasy yet finally symbiotic relationship with the bridge's more usual nighttime pedestrians. But even if the bridge were deserted that night, even if we do not evoke the memory of language to fulfill the place of living language, we can still assume without much strain that the conversation of the two men, at least now and again, touched on those subjects which it would have been impossible for such as they to cross the bridge at such an hour and not think of. Something in the human speech that occurred in that elided journey, whether the received public banter of cross-dressers or simply the speculation of Crane and Loveman to one another, is likely to have broached those sexual areas so easily and usually characterized as residing outside of language—at least outside that language represented by the municipal monument, outside that language which claims rhetorical density by only stating the true, the obvious, the inarguable—even as the very act of stating them throws such truths and inarguables into hysterical question. (To indulge in gay gossip, or indeed in any socially private sub-language, unto the language of poetry itself, is at once to take up and to invest with meaning an order of rhetoric the straight world—especially in the 1920s—claims is empty, meaningless, and at the same time always suspected of pathology . . .) This, at any rate, is the place we can perhaps also best contextualize the urgency behind

Crane's operatically passionate addresses to Loveman in his letter. One begins with the obvious statement that this was pre-Stonewall. But one must follow it with the observation that it was also pre-Matachine Society—which is to say, this rhetoric is from the homosexual tradition that the Matachine Society was both to spring from and (after its radical opening years under Harry Haye) to set itself against. The Matachines, recall, would eventually seek equal rights for homosexuals under the program that claimed homosexual males could be just like other men if they tried; and that they did not have to live their lives at such an intense level of passion in their relationships with their love objects and their friends, of the sort represented by Crane's exhortations to his friend Loveman, is the situation that defined, at the time, a distinct, homosexual male community.

In the first of his *Voyages*, Crane—in that most referential of introductions to this transreferential cascade of poetic rhetoric—had exhorted the young boys frisking with sand and stick and shell:

> . . . there is a line
> You must not cross nor ever trust beyond it
> Spry cordage of your bodies to caresses
> Too lichen-faithful from too wide a breast.

The traditional reading certainly takes that line to refer to the boundary between innocence and sexual knowledge—and, for readers who know of Crane's love for Opffer, specifically homosexual knowledge. Here we are not beyond referentiality but only into the simple foothills of metaphor. The caresses not to be trusted are those that are too "lichen-faithful," i.e., clinging, that originate from a breast "too wide," i.e., from a breast wider than a child's, i.e., a grown man's (or a grown woman's).

But it is also a line of rhetorical referentiality, of referential clarity, a line Crane had to cross specifically to write his love poems, a line beyond which all was music, affect, connotative brilliance—but without reference, a poetic land where the intended topic was always instantly erasable: "nothing but rhetoric." As a poet working in America, Crane had broached this verbal area all but alone. Wilde, the early hero of Crane's juvenile effort "c33," had doubtless first taught him the form to use in dealing with sex. ("c33" was Wilde's cell number when he was imprisoned at Reading Gaol for sodomy. The reader aware of this fact is, as it were, welcomed into Crane's poem; the reader who is not, is excluded from it and finds its subject opaque.) "c33" was Crane's first attempt to separate his readers into two camps before the topic of homosexuality, in this case by means of homosexual folklore and erudition. But eventually Crane seems to have glimpsed within such practices an entire apparatus for articulating the inarticulable. And since Dada and surrealism were European movements to which he had no real and immediate access, it's no wonder that, from time to time (on such rhetorically problematic nights, when language and the machinery of the night as we have described it had, perhaps too quickly, escorted him there, arm in arm, like Loveman himself), that rhetorical area looked to Crane like a verbal waste land.

How much of this was behind Crane's drunken attempt, maybe half an hour later, to leap from the roof—well, we must answer Loveman's interviewer's rhetorical question ("That's what was bothering him") in the same manner as Loveman: Silence—before turning to another topic.

IV.

The Bridge is a poem whose *"Proem"* and eight sections fall into two astonishing halves. The first half—*"Proem"* and Part I, "Ave Maria," through Part III, "Cutty Sark"—ranges over themes roughly connected by the concept of Time: history, the present, tradition, youth, age. The second half—Part IV, "Cape Hatteras" through Part VIII, "Atlantis"—recomplicates many of the same themes by considering them in the light of Space: territory, landscape, the city of lust and love, transportation. The idea of love—sometimes spoken, sometimes unspeakable—is the Bridge among them all.

The Brooklyn Bridge makes three appearances in the poem, two of them spectacular, one almost invisible. The spectacular appearances are in the introduction (*"Proem"*) and the coda ("Atlantis"). The near invisible one falls at the poem's virtual center, just before the closing movement of "Cutty Sark," when a veiled account of an unsuccessful homosexual pick-up of an aging, drunken sailor concludes with the line, "I started walking home across the Bridge . . ." But a controlling irony of the poem would seem to be that images of the Bridge are, themselves, bridged by images from the land either side of it.

For me, this suggests the two great stanchions at either side of the bridge, and the way, at the center, the cable all but vanishes below the raised walkway.

On at least one level, Crane's enterprise in *The Bridge* is majestically lucid. God—or the Absolute—as an abstract idea is too vast for the mind of man and woman to comprehend directly. Such an idea can only manifest itself— and then only partially—through myths. Living in the rectilinear architecture of the modern city, for Crane the curve, the broken arc, most visibly suggested the vastness and transcendence of deity. It is part of the curve that holds the planets around the sun, the suns around the galaxies' centers. That curve was, one suspects, the same Ouspensky-generated curve-of-binding-energy that Crane's friend, black writer Jean Toomer, was so insistent about having represented in the book design—before "Karintha," "Seventh Street," and "Kabnis"—of *Cane* (1923). But the curve of gull wing or bird flight, of wave crest or sea swell, was too impermanent. So Crane turned to the man-made curve of the Brooklyn Bridge "to lend a myth to God." (It was Melville's method in *Moby-Dick*, in his rewrite of *Paradise Lost*, where the white whale is the stand-in for God/Nature to Ahab's Satan.) Numerous other curves, some enduring, some momentary—from the mazy river's, the railroad's steel, and the movement of Indian dancers to that of a burlesque queen's pearl strings shaking at her hip—inform the Bridge's curve with meaning, just as the multiple uses of a word in language determine its meaning in any individual occurrence.

And an early reading of *The Bridge* in which we pay attention to curved things that vanish and curved things that remain, in contrast with straight and angular things, equally stable or fleeting, is as good an entrance strategy as any into the further complexities of the poem.

As far as the source of that symbolic/mystic curve in the Ouspensky/Gurdjieff teachings, it's fair to suppose that Crane had what most of us would regard as a healthy skepticism toward the practical realities of the Gurdjieff movement. In an often-reprinted letter of May 29, 1927, that we have already referred to, Crane wrote to Yvor Winters, who had urged him that poems should reflect a picture of "the complete man" (which completeness, for Winters, seems somehow to have included being heterosexual):

> The image of "the complete man" is a good idealistic antidote for the horrid hysteria for specialization that inhabits the modern world. And I strongly second your wish for some definite ethical order. Munson, however, and a number of my other friends, not so long ago, being stricken with the same urge, and feeling that something must be done about it—rushed into the portals of the famous Gurdjieff Institute and have since put themselves through all sorts of Hindu antics, songs, dances, incantations, psychic sessions, etc. so that now, presumably the left lobes of their brains and their right lobes function (M's favorite word) in perfect unison. I spent hours at the typewriter trying to explain to certain of these urgent people why I could not enthuse about their methods; it was all to no avail, as I was told that the "complete man" had a different logic than mine, and further that there was no way of understanding this logic without first submitting yourself to the necessary training. . . . Some of them, having found a good substitute for their former interest in writing by means of more complete formulas of expression have ceased writing now altogether, which is probably just as well. At any rate, they have become hermetically sealed souls to my eyesight, and I am really not able to offer judgment.

But while Crane could frown at their methods, he had read and been impressed with Ouspensky's *Tertium Organum*, and he had gone to the lectures and dance demonstrations—and had taken in a good many of the ideas. Would that Toomer (likely the referent of that unhappy "probably just as well") had been as able as Crane to maintain a similar distance. Finally, in the letter Crane gets to homosexuality (Winters had apparently compared Crane positively to Valéry and Marlowe—possibly without realizing Marlowe was gay—but warned that Crane might end up like the asexual Leonardo, who started endless projects of genius but finished less than two dozen):

> Your fumigation of the Leonardo legend is a healthy enough reaction, but I don't think your reasons for doubting his intelligence and scope very potent—I've never closely studied the man's attainments or biography, but your argument is certainly weakly enough sustained on the sole prop of his sex—or lack of such. One doesn't have to turn to homosexuals to find instances of missing sensibilities. Of course I'm sick of all this talk about balls and cunts in criticism. It's obvious that balls are needed, and that Leonardo had 'em—at least the records of the Florentine prisons, I'm told, say so. You don't seem to realize that the whole topic is something of a myth anyway, and is consequently modified in the characteristics of the image by each age in each civilization. Tom Jones, a character for whom I have the utmost affection, represented the model in 18th Century England, at least so far as the stated requirements of your letter would suggest, and for an Anglo-Saxon model he is still pretty good aside from calculus, the Darwinian theory, and a few other mental additions.

Quoting this letter at even greater length, Thomas E. Yingling in his *Hart Crane and the Homosexual Text*, a book rich in political insight, is astonished, possibly even bewildered, at the *Tom Jones* (1749) reference. But I can certainly remember being a teenager, when gay men of letters assumed that the good-natured foundling's light-hearted promiscuity was a self-evidently coded representation of bisexuality, or even homosexuality.

Here may be the place to mention that a reader taking his or her first dozen or so trips through *The Bridge* is likely—as were most of its early critics—to see its interest and energy centering in the lyricism and scene painting of *"Proem,"* "Ave Maria," and the various sections of "Powhatan's Daughter"—that is, *The Bridge*'s first half.

But a reader who has lived with the poem over years is more likely to appreciate the stately, greatly reflective, and meditative beauties and insights—as well as the austere and lucid structure—of the second half.

"Cutty Sark," with which the first half ends, leaves us, as we have said, with the poet walking home over the Bridge at dawn, as Crane must have walked home many times to 110 Columbia Heights, contemplating the voyages of the great steamers, and probably remembering returning home—if we are to trust the restored epigraph that follows—to Emil. At this point, *The Bridge* begins its final, ascending curve.

"Cape Hatteras" looks to the sky . . .

After the divigation of "Three Songs"—where the theme of sexual longing is heterosexualized for straight male readers (the Sestos and Abydos of the epigraph are two cities on opposite sides of the Hellespont, separated by water, whose literary import is precisely that they are not connected by a bridge, a separation that precipitates the tragedy of Hero, Priestess of Hesperus)—"Quaker Hill" (most cynical of the poem's sections) looks out level with the earth . . .

With the epigraph from Blake's "Morning," "The Tunnel" plunges us beneath the ground for an infernal recapitulation of the impressionistic techniques of the poem's first half (the fall of Atlantis proper), in which the poet glimpses Whitman's—and his own—chthonic predecessor, Poe . . .

. . . to leave us, once more, in "Atlantis," on the Bridge, flooded by the moon.

* * *

As a kind of progress report on *The Bridge*, on March 18, 1926, Crane wrote a letter to philanthropist Otto Kahn, who, a year before, had subsidized him with a thousand dollars.

> *Dear Mr. Kahn:*
>
> You were so kind as to express a desire to know from time to time how the Bridge was progressing, so I'm flashing in a signal from the foremast, as it were. Right now I'm supposed to be Don Christobal Colon returning from "Cathay," first voyage. For mid-ocean is where the poem begins.
>
> It concludes at midnight—at the center of Brooklyn Bridge. Strangely enough that final section of the poem has been the first to be completed—yet there's a logic to it, after all; it is the mystic consummation toward which all the other sections of the poem converge. Their contents are implicit in its summary.

"Cutty Sark" was composed shortly after "Ave Maria," the opening Columbus section; and though it's possible that, at first, Crane was not planning to include it in *The Bridge*, it is almost impossible to read it, right after the earlier poem, without seeing the aging, incoherent, inebriated sailor of the second poem as an older, ironized version—three hundred years later on—of the Christopher Columbus figure who narrates the earlier transatlantic meditation. (Try reading "Cutty Sark" against Whitman's poem, "Prayer of Columbus," the poem in *Leaves of Grass* that follows "Passage to India"—a poem whose importance in *The Bridge* we will shortly come to.) The five sections of Part II, "Powhatan's Daughter," which, in *The Bridge*'s final version, intervene, dilute that identification somewhat. But the suggestion of the individual's persistence through history, associated, say, with "Van Winkle," still holds it open.

In his letter to Kahn, Crane included a plan for the whole *Bridge* that may well have been growing in his mind for years:

  I. Columbus—Conquest of space, chaos.
 II. Pokahantus—The natural body of America—fertility, etc.
III. Whitman—The Spiritual body of America.
     (A dialogue between Whitman and a dying soldier in a Washington
     hospital; the infraction of physical death, disunity, on the concept of
     immortality.)
 IV. John Brown (Negro Porter on Calgary Express making up births and
     singing to himself (a jazz form for this) of his sweetheart and the death
     of John Brown, alternately.)
  V. Subway—The encroachment of machinery on humanity; a kind of
     purgatory in relation to the open sky of last section.
 VI. The Bridge—A sweeping dithyramb in which the Bridge becomes
     the symbol of consciousness spanning time and space.

Soon Crane wrote even longer outlines of the parenthetical narratives in Part
III and Part IV, including the following, recalling Whitman's poem "To One
Shortly to Die" and scenes from *Specimen Days*:

"Cape Hatteras" section (the forge)
     Whitman approaches the bed of a dying (southern) soldier—scene is in a
Washington hospital. Allusion is made to this during the dialogue. The soldier,
conscious of his dying condition, at the end of the dialogue asks Whitman to call
a priest, for absolution. Whitman leaves the scene—deliriously the soldier calls
him back. The part ends before Whitman's return, of course. The irony is, of
course, in the complete absolution which Whitman's words have already given
the dying man, before the priest is called for. This, alternated with the eloquence
of the dying man, is the substance of the dialogue—the emphasis being on the
symbolism of the soldier's body having been used as a *forge* toward a state of Unity.
His hands are purified of the death they have previously dealt by the principles
Whitman hints at or enunciates (without talking up-stage, I hope) and here the 'religious gunman' motive returns much more explicitly than in F & H. [A reference
to Crane's poem "For the Marriage of Faustus and Helen."] The agency of death
is exercised in obscure ways as the agency of life. Whitman knew this and accepted
it. The appeal of the scene must be made as much as possible independent of the
historical 'character' of Walt.

And a still later outline for "Cape Hatteras," much closer to the poem as
written, reads:

(1) Cape—land—combination

conceive as a giant turning
(2) Powerhouse

(3) Offshoot—Kitty Hawk
Take off
(4) War—in general
(5) Resolution (Whitman)

Cape Hatteras is a narrow, sandy strip comprising North Carolina's east-ward, bog-sequestered coast and the site of Kitty Hawk, where Wilbur Wright's plane, piloted by Wilbur's brother Orville, made the first motorized heavier-than-air flight (59 seconds), December 17, 1903. By October 5, 1905, Wilbur was flying as much as 38 minutes over a range of 24 miles. In 1908, he took his airship to France, giving demonstrations at Le Mans, Pau, and Rome. Along with Benjamin Franklin, Thomas Edison, and George Washington Carver, the Wright brothers came to represent a particular image of American ingenuity and inventiveness, the meeting ground of science (the Wrights had achieved that first 59-second flight through data gathered from tests in an early wind-tunnel of their own devising), technology, and practical inventiveness that, for many, during the first half of the twentieth century, was one with science itself.

Crane wrote a substantial portion of "Cape Hatteras" in France, while a guest of the Crosbys, starting in February, 1929, in a burst of energy that may have been directed, if not inspired, by the twenty-fifth anniversary celebration, only two months before, of the Wrights' 1903 achievement—a celebration that, though centered at Kitty Hawk, was national, even international, head-line news. In Crane's poem, however, the triumph at Kitty Hawk is darkened by the Great War's flying lessons.

Lines on Crane's worksheets not used in the final version of the poem, possi-bly because they state a problem or a focus of the poem in terms too reductive ("talking up-stage"), include, after the fourth stanza:

> Lead me past logic and beyond the graceful carp of wit.

And:

> What if we falter sometimes in our faith?

The epigraph for "Cape Hatteras" is from Whitman's "Passage to India" (which contains this parenthetical triplet, harking back to "Ave Maria": "Ah Genoese, thy dream! thy dream! / Centuries after thou art laid in thy grave / The shore thou foundest verifies thy dream"). As do most of the epigraphs in the poem, it functions as a bridge between the preceding section, in this case "Cutty Sark" (which, with its account of the unsuccessful pick-up, is the true center of unspoken homosexual longing, the yearning for communication, in *The Bridge*), and the succeeding "Cape Hatteras." With one line fore and three lines aft restored (lines, critic Robert Martin first pointed out, Crane probably expected the sagacious reader to be able to supply for himself), here is the Whitman passage from which the epigraph is actually taken:

> Reckoning ahead O soul, when thou, the time achiev'd,
> The seas all cross'd, weather'd the capes, the voyage done,
> Surrounded, copest, frontest God, yieldest, the aim attain'd,
> As fill'd with friendship, love complete, the Elder Brother found,
> The Younger melts in fondness in his arms.

It's arguable that the elided homosexual (and incestuous) resolution of the epigraphic passage confirms the homosexual subtext of the previous section, "Cutty Sark," as it makes a bridge between "Cutty Sark" and "Cape Hatteras."

The "Sanskrit charge" in the Falcon Ace's wrist (again in "Cape Hatteras"), critic L. S. Dembo opined, is another reference to the Absolute, via the passage following the epigraphic lines in Whitman's poem:

> Passage to more than India!
> Are thy wings plumed indeed for such far flights?
> O soul, voyagest thou indeed on voyages like those?
> Disportest thou on waters such as those?
> Soundest below the Sanscrit and the Vedas?
> Then have thy bent unleash'd.

Note the development of "Cape Hatteras" from Crane's initial narrative outline to the poem as written. In Crane's poem as outlined, it's a dying southern *soldier* who calls to Whitman for aid and absolution. The poem is conceived as a narrated *dialogue* between them. At the end, deliriously the *soldier* calls out to the departed Whitman . . .

In Crane's poem as realized, it's a very pensive *poet* (who has, yes, lived through the Great War; there is reference to the Somme—as Whitman lived through the Civil War—and Appomattox), who calls to Whitman. And instead of a death-bed dialogue, the poem is now the poet's reflective *monologue*, with only the plane crashes at its center providing a specific thanatopsis. At its end, however, deliriously, the *poet* calls to Whitman . . .

"[T]he eloquence of the dying man . . . is the substance of the dialogue," Crane wrote in his outline; in the monologue as written, Crane has expanded that "substance" into the entire poem. Its ironies are still in place, or even further recomplicated: the reason that the yearned-for cleaving of hands cannot ultimately take place at the end of the poem as we have it is because Whitman, rather than the soldier, is dead. What remains of Whitman is the eloquence his language and vision have given to the poet/narrator.[4]

* * *

In 1923 Crane had read and been impressed by *Nation* editor Oswald Garrison Villard's recent biography of John Brown. And, in the outline, under the title "Calgary Express," he wrote:

> Well don't you know it's mornin' time?
>   Wheel in middle of wheel;
> He'll hear yo' prayers an' sanctify,
>   Wheel in middle of wheel.

The "scene" is a Pullman sleeper, Chicago to Calgary. The main theme is the story of John Brown, which predominates over the interwoven "personal, biographical details" as it runs through the mind of a Negro porter, shining shoes and humming to himself. In a way it takes in the whole racial history of the Negro in America. The form will be highly original, and I shall use dialect. I hope to achieve a word-rhythm of pure jazz movement which will suggest not only the dance of the Negro but also the speed-dance of the engine over the rails.

And from the time of the briefer outline for "Cape Hatteras" he left this interesting sketch for "Ave Maria," *The Bridge*'s opening section:

> Columbus' will—knowledge
> Isabella's will—Christ
> Fernando's will—gold
> —3 ships
> —2 destroyed
> 1 remaining will, Columbus

Over the next year when the bulk of the poems comprising *The Bridge* were written, Crane veered from, expanded on, broke, crossed, bridged, and abridged much of this template. A year later, in the early months of 1927, he sent Yvor Winters another, typewritten outline of the poem, this one in ten parts:

Projected Plan of the Poem

Dedication—to Brooklyn Bridge
1—Ave Maria
2—Powhatan's Daughter
  # (1) The Harbor Dawn
  # (2) Van Winkle
  (3) The River

(4) The Dance
   (5) Indiana
3—Cape Hatteras
4—Cutty Sark
5—The Mango Tree
6—Three Songs
   7—The Calgary Express
   8—1920 Whistles
9—The Tunnel
10—Atlantis

Beside "The Mango Tree" Crane jotted a note to Winters by hand: "—may not use this" and beside "1920 Whistles": "—ditto." Crane's final handwritten comment across the page's bottom: "Those marked # are completed."

"The Mango Tree," a prose poem was, yes, dropped. (That he was planning to mix prose poetry in with his poetic series is the first suggestion, however faint, that at one point or another Crane might have had Novalis in mind.[5]) "1920 Whistles" never became a separate poem; and eight stanzas of what he'd done on "The Calgary Express" Crane now appended to the closing section of "The River"—and abandoned the railroad poem. (Today it looks like rather astute poetic tact. Clearly Crane felt that his American poem should contain "the whole racial history of the Negro in America" but, as clearly, he felt he was not the one to write it.[6] Still, from the earlier outline, I. Columbus, II. Pokahantus, V. Subway, and VI. The Bridge are what we have today as I. Ave Maria, II. Powhatan's Daughter, VII. The Tunnel, and VIII. Atlantis, so that the initial template is highly informative about what Crane ultimately and actually decided on.

The order of composition—which reveals its own internal logic—is "Atlantis," "*Proem: To Brooklyn Bridge*," "Ave Maria," "Cutty Sark," "Van Winkle," "The Tunnel," "Harbor Dawn," "Southern Cross," "National Winter Garden," and "Virginia." After that, things become a bit murky. From then on the probable order is: "The Dance," "The River," "Calgary Express" (abandoned and cannibalized for "The Dance"), "Quaker Hill," "Cape Hatteras."

At the end of 1927, Stephen Vincent Benét—younger brother of critic William Rose Benét (who'd been notably hostile to Crane's first, 1926 volume, *White Buildings*)—published his book-length poem *John Brown's Body*; over the next year it became a major, even enduring, middlebrow success. In it, Whitman is a minor figure and John Brown a major presence. Though hardly any critic mentions it, surely Benét's poem was a good reason for Crane to have dropped the John Brown narrative, if it was not simply a confirmation of the rightness of his earlier tendency to abandon the heavily foregrounded narratives he had once planned for the parts of *The Bridge* concerning Brown and Whitman.

* * *

Though we have already cited the Emerson passage that prompted Crane, sometime in 1926 or '27, to change the title of his final (if first written) section of *The Bridge* from "Finale" to "Atlantis," we are still left with a problem: What is the phenomenal effect of the new title of the poem's closing section on the reader? What—or better, how—does it signify?

The problem of poetic sources (at whose rim we now totter) makes a vertiginous whirlpool directly beneath all serious attempts at poetic elucidation, now supporting them, now overturning them. For a most arbitrarily chosen example, take Gonzolo's famous utopian expostulation in Shakespeare's final play, *The Tempest*, II, i, 148–73 (the play is usually dated in its writing as just before its 1611 performance), on how he would run an ideal commonwealth set up on his isolate island:

> I' th' commonwealth I would by contraries
> Execute all things. For no kind of traffic
> Would I admit; no name of magistrate;
> Letters should not be known; riches, poverty,
> And use of service, none; contract, succession,
> Bourn, bound of land, tilth, vineyard, none;
> No use of metal, corn, or wine, or oil;
> No occupation; all men idle, all;
> And women too, but innocent pure;
> No sovereignty . . .
> All things in common nature should produce
> Without sweat or endeavor. Treason, felony,
> Sword, pike, knife, gun, or need of any engine
> Would I not have; but nature should bring forth,
> Of it own kind, all foison, all abundance,
> To feed my innocent people.

Once we've ransacked our Elizabethan glossaries to ascertain that "contraries" here means "contrary to what is commonly expected," that "traffic" means trade, "Letters" are not just literacy but secret messages of condemnation, that "service" means servants, "succession" inheritance, "tilth" tillage, "bourn" boundary, "engine" weapon, and "foison" abundance, we turn to Michel de Montaigne's (1533–1593) essay, "Of the Cannibals," in which Montaigne praises the American Indian nations for their savage innocence—an essay widely read in Elizabethan England—to discover (after a quote from Plato: "All things," saith Plato, "are produced by nature, by fortune, or by art. The greatest and fairest by one or other of the first two, the least and imperfect by the last.") the following passage (in John Florio's 1603 translation) on an imagined ideal nation, suggested by the far-off lands of the American Indians:

> It is a nation, I would answer Plato, that hath no kind of traffic, no knowledge of letters, no intelligence of numbers, no name of magistrate, nor of politic superiority; no use of service, of riches, or of poverty; no contracts, no successions, no partitions, no occupations but idle; no respect of kindred but common, no apparel but natural, no manuring of land, no use of wine, corn, or metal. The very words that import lying, falsehood, treason, dissimulation, covetousness, envy, detraction, and pardon, were never heard amongst them. How dissonant would he [Plato] find this imaginary commonwealth from this perfection?

It is not just the ideas—which here and there, in fact, differ—that seem to have been ceded from Montaigne to the bard; rather it is impossible to imagine Shakespeare's passage written without a copy of Montaigne to hand, if not underscored on the page then loosely in memory.

But even as we declare the above example arbitrary *vis-à-vis* Crane, the careful reader will remember that, at the close of "Cutty Sark," among the great boats that Crane/the poet sees from the Bridge, their names in traditional italics, with all their suggestions of travel, the last one we find is, with a question mark, concluding the section, "Ariel?"—named after the airy sprite Shakespeare gives us in that same play, first as an androgynous fey, then (after line 316 of the play's second scene), on next entrance, as a "water nymph" for the play's remainder.

There is as little question that Crane's interrogative "Ariel?" has its source in Shakespeare as there is that Shakespeare's "metal, corn, or wine" (not to mention traffic, magistrate, letters, service, or commonwealth itself) has its source in Montaigne's (*via* Florio's) "wine, corn, or metal."

But what about the utopian concerns that Shakespeare (at least for the length of Gonzalo's speech) and Montaigne share? Crane's use of Atlantis, of Cathay, within the American tradition, leans toward similar concern. Is the singular question of the single shared term "Ariel?" enough on which to ground an intertextual bridge between an Elizabethan England and a contemporaneous France and Crane's vision in the American 1920s? If so, what is its status? Historically, the "commonwealth" on which Montaigne literarily—and Shakespeare metaphorically—grounded a utopian vision is the same one that Strachy's journals, quoted in William Carlos Williams's *In the American Grain*, presents: the journals from which Crane took (*via* Elizabeth Bowen's review of Williams's book) his epigraph for "Powhatan's Daughter." Here, perched on the most tenuous intertextual filaments, we are gazing down directly into the very maelstrom we began with, whose chaos casts its spume obscuring intention and origin, conscious choice and writerly history, source and filiation, where the signifieds accessible to the individual poet become hopelessly confounded with and blurred by the signifieds at large in what is called "culture," all of them a-slip beneath the rhetorical storm, even as all greater poetic possibilities must rise over such turbulence to produce an effect of order, and in the name of such order soar above it.

Atlantis is traditionally the name for an island, or frequently a city, which had reached a pinnacle both of military might and of culture; it was swallowed up by the sea over a cataclysmic day and night's tempest of torrential rains and earthquakes.

But, in *The Bridge*, after we read Crane's title—"Atlantis"—we find, following it, not a description of an island city (however utopian or no), but, rather, a glorious evocation of the Brooklyn Bridge drenched by the moonlight. As such, then, the title does not caption the poem in the usual way of titles; the relation is rather, perhaps, sequential, suggesting another of Crane's indirect mentions: *first* Atlantis, *then* the topic of the poem—the bridge, leading perhaps from, or to, that city. But is there anything else we can say about the still somewhat mysterious title, as it functions in the poem?

To answer this, we undertake what will surely seem our most eccentric digression, bridging centuries and seas and poetic history, though we hope to move only over fairly reasonable textual bridges . . .

* * *

Almost certainly (in a comparatively late decision), Crane took the title for *The Bridge*'s introductory section—"Proem"—from the poetic introduction of James Thomson's (1834–1882) *The City of Dreadful Night* (1874). Certainly it's the most likely, if not the only, place for him to have encountered the archaic word. (He might well have called the opening "Invocation," "Prologue," or any number of other possible titles; as late as 1927, he was calling it "Dedication.") Thomson's "Proem" contains the lines:

> Yes, here and there some weary wanderer
> In that same city of tremendous night
> Will understand the speech, and feel a stir
> Of fellowship in all-disastrous fight;
> 'I suffer mute and lonely, yet another
> Uplifts his voice to let me know a brother
> Travels the same wild paths though out of sight.'

Many poets and readers over the years have felt themselves a "brother" to Thomson; and *The City of Dreadful Night* retains a certain extracanonical fascination to this day. Much of Thomson's poem (The "Proem" and sections 1, 3, 7, 9, 11, 13, 17, 19, and 21) falls, ironically enough, into the seven-line rhyme scheme of the usually light and happy French rondolet, though without the line-length variations (i.e., the traditionally defective first, third, and seventh lines) ordinarily found in that form; rather, for his purposes, Thomson used the more stately iambic pentameter for his moody monody. Thomson's series has been popular with poets, eccentrics, and night lovers since its first publication over two issues of the *National Reformer* in 1874. George Meredith and George Eliot were among its earliest enthusiasts. But there is a good deal more shared between the two poetic series than simply the title of their opening sections. Both *The Bridge* and *The City of Dreadful Night* are largely urban poems, yet both have powerful extra-urban moments. As well, the variation in tone among *The Bridge*'s fifteen separate sections is very close to the sort of variation we find among the twenty-one sections of Thomson's nocturnal meditation on hopelessness and isolation.

Indeed, it's arguable that—granted the dialogue between them we've already mentioned—one purpose behind both *The Waste Land* and *The Bridge* was to write a poem, or poem series, of the sort for which Thomson's *City of Dreadful Night* was the prototype;[7] if, indeed, that was among the generating complexities of both poems, then certainly, on that front, Crane's is the more successful.

Today, Thomson experts will sometimes talk of his poems "In the Room," "Insomnia," "Sunday at Hampstead," and even his narrative "Waddah and Om-El-Bonain." But to the vast majority of readers of English poetry, Thomson is (he is even so styled in many card catalogues,[8] to distinguish him from his eighteenth-century ancestor of the same name, author of *The Seasons* [mentioned already] and *The Castle of Indolence*) the "author of *The City of Dreadful Night*."

James Thomson was born at Port Glasgow in Renfrewshire, a day or two more than a month before Christmas in 1834. His mother was a deeply, almost fanatically religious Irvingite. During a week of dreadful storms, his father, chief officer aboard the *Eliza Stewart*, suffered a paralytic stroke and was returned to his family an invalid—immobile on his right side, as well as mentally unsound—when James was six. Two years later, James's mother enrolled her eight-year-old son in a boarding school, the Caladonian Asylum, and died a month or so later. His father was far too ill to care for his sons. (James had, by now, a two-year-old brother, and had already lost a two-year-old sister a couple of years before.) So James began the life of a scholarship/charity student at one or another boarding school or military academy over the next handful of years.

An extremely bright young man, by seventeen James was virtually a schoolmaster himself at the Chelsea Military Academy. His nickname from the Barnes family with whom he now lived was "Co"—for "precocious." At sixteen he'd begun to read Shelley and, shortly after, the early German romantic Novalis. Soon he was publishing poems regularly in London under the pseudonym "Bysshe Vanolis" (or, more usually, under the initials "B.V."). Bysshe was, of course, Shelley's middle name and the name he was called by his friends; "Vanolis" was an anagram of Thomson's new Germanic enthusiasm.

At eighteen, Thomson became officially an assistant army school master —that is, a uniformed soldier who taught the children associated with Camp Curragh in the mornings and the younger soldiers in the afternoon.

Novalis—the Latin term for a newly plowed field—was the penname of Friedrich von Hardenberg (1772–1801), remembered for *Heinrich von Ofterdingen*, a mystical novel about a poet's pursuit of a "blue flower" first seen in a dream, and an intriguing set of notes and fragments, among them the famous "Monologue," and the even more famous pronouncement, "Character is Fate"—as well, of course, as for such wonderful observations as these (in Carlyle's fine translations from his 1829 essay on the young German poet):

> To become properly acquainted with a truth we must first have disbelieved it, and disputed against it . . .
>
>   Philosophy is properly Home-sickness; the wish to be everywhere at home . . .
>
>   The division of Philosopher and Poet is only apparent, and to the disadvantage of both. It is a sign of disease, and of a sickly constitution . . .
>
>   There is but one Temple in the World; and that is the Body of Man. Nothing is holier than this high form. Bending before men is a reverence done to this Revelation in the Flesh. We touch Heaven, when we lay our hand on a human body.
>
>   . . . We are near awakening when we dream that we dream . . .

—and the disturbingly prescient observation, quoted by Guy Debord in *The Society of the Spectacle*, "Writings are the thoughts of the State; archives are its memory."

As well, Novalis wrote a series of poems, *Hymnen an die Nacht* (*Hymns to the Night*), one of the most influential series of poems from the exciting ferment of Early German Romanticism.

Trained as an engineer, the twenty-three-year-old von Hardenberg was working as an assayer in the salt mines where his father had worked before him. In the small Saxon mining town, he met and fell in love with a thirteen-year-old girl, Sophie von Kühn. He sued her family for her hand, and was finally accepted—though the marriage was not to take place until she was older. Hardenberg was devoted to his young fiancée. Two and a half years later, on March 17 of 1797, Sophie turned fifteen. But two days later, on the 19th, after two operations on her liver, she died. Not a full month later, on April 14, Hardenberg's younger brother Erasmus passed away. Now Hardenberg wrote a friend in a letter:

> It has grown Evening around me, while I was looking into the red of Morning. My grief is boundless as my love. For three years she has been my hourly thought. She

alone bound me to life, to the country, to my occupation. With her I am parted from all; for now I scarcely have myself any more. But it has grown Evening . . .

And in another letter, from May 3:

> Yesterday I was twenty-five years old. I was in Grünigen and stood beside her grave. It is a friendly spot; enclosed with simple white railing; lies apart, and high. There is still room in it. The village, with its blooming gardens, leans up around the hill; and it is at this point that the eye loses itself in blue distances. I know you would have liked to stand by me, and stick the flowers, my birthday gifts, one by one into her hillock. This time two years, she made me a gay present, with a flag and national cockade on it. To-day her parents gave me the little things which she, still joyfully, had received on her last birthday. Friend,—it continues Evening, and will soon be Night.

Soon after that, Hardenberg composed both his fragments and his *Hymns*. An early manuscript shows us that Novalis first wrote all six of his hymns as verse. But later he reworked and condensed the first four (and much of the fifth) into a hard, glittering, quintessentially modern German prose poetry. It was only the final hymn, the sixth, "Sensucht nach dem Tode" ("Yearning for Death"), that Novalis let stand as traditional poetry. The prose-poetry version was the one published by the brothers August Wilhelm and Friedrich Schlegel in their magazine *Athenaeum* 3, number 2, in 1800.

By inverting a traditional metaphor, the *Hymnen* (a series quite as notable in its ways as *The City of Dreadful Night*, *The Waste Land*, and *The Bridge*, though it lacks the two modern series' urban specificity) introduce an astonishing trope into the galaxy of European—and ultimately Western—rhetoric: To those of a certain sensibility (often those in deep grief, or those with a secret sorrow not to be named before the public), the day, sunlight, and the images of air and light that usually signify pleasure are actually hateful and abhorrent. Night alone is the time such souls can breathe freely, be their true selves, and come into their own. For them, night is the beautiful, wondrous, and magical time —not the day.

In the second half of that extraordinary fifth Hymn, in which both prose and verse finally combine, Hardenberg even goes so far as to Christianize his "*Nachtbegeisterung*" ("Enthusiasm for the night"): Night, not day, is where the gods dwell as constellations. It was through the night the three kings traveled under their star seeking Jesus, and it was in the night they found Him. Similarly it was during the night that the stone was rolled away from the tomb and, thus, it was in the night that the Resurrection occurred.

Writers who were to take up this trope of the inversion of the traditional values of night and day and make it their own include Poe and Baudelaire—in both cases, directly from Novalis. And the great second act of Wagner's *Tristan und Isolde* has been called simply "Novalis set to music." Certainly Thomson's *The City of Dreadful Night* is the poetic moment through which it erupted into the forefront of English poetic awareness. The Christianizing moment makes the trope Novalis's own, but writers were to seize that basic night/day inversion —Byron for Childe Harold and Manfred, Poe for C. August Dupin—till we can almost think of it as *the* romantic emblem.

By comparison to Novalis (or Thomson), Crane's *The Bridge* is overwhelmingly a poem of the day—yet it has its crepuscular moments, where one is about to enter into night.

From Crane's opening "*Proem*," addressing the Bridge:

> And we have seen night lifted in thine arms.
>
> Under thy shadow by the piers I waited;
> Only in darkness is thy shadow clear.
> The City's fiery parcels all undone,
> Already snow submerges an iron year . . .

Though Crane is the author, this is Novalis (does Crane's capital "C" in "City" consciously link it to Thomson's?)—and Novalis by way of Thomson, at that!

As well, in *The Bridge*, there is the pair of aubades, "The Harbor Dawn" and "Cutty Sark," when night is being left behind.

But let us linger on the Thomson/Novalis connection a little longer. Eventually it will lead us back to Crane, and by an interesting circumlocution: Thomson not only took Novalis's pen name and Novalis's famous poetic night/day inversion for his own. Working with another friend, he taught himself German and translated Novalis's *Hymns*; though his translation has never been published in its entirety, the sections reprinted by various biographers are quite lovely;[9] the manuscript has been at the Bodley Head since 1953. Thomson also appropriated, however, a bit of Novalis's biography.

When he was eighteen and an assistant army schoolmaster in Ballincollig near Cork, Thomson met the not quite fourteen-year-old daughter of his friend Charles Bradlaugh's armourer-sergeant, Mathilda Weller, with whom he was quite taken. They danced together at a young people's party; presumably they had a handful of deep and intense conversations. Two years later, before she reached her sixteenth year, Mathilda died.

In later years, Thomson claimed that her death wholly blighted the remainder of his life. (Mathilda just happened to be the name Novalis had given to the character inspired by Sophie in his novel of the mystical quest for the blue amaranthus in *Heinrich von Osterdingen*.) On his own death from dipsomania, at age forty-seven in 1882, Thomson was buried with a lock of Mathilda's hair in the coffin with him. But it's quite possible Thomson used this suspiciously

Novalis-like fable to excuse the fact that he did not marry, also to excuse his increasing drunkenness, and quite possibly as a cover for promiscuous homosexuality in the alleys and back streets of London, where he eventually finished his life. While Friedrich von Hardenberg survived Sophie von Kühn by only four years—tuberculosis killed him shortly before he turned twenty-nine (as it would kill the twenty-three-year-old Greenberg)—James Thomson survived Mathilda Weller by nearly thirty years. An incident in Thomson's young life that may have come far closer to blighting the remainder of it than Mathilda's death occurred in 1862, however, when Thomson was twenty-seven and still teaching in the army. Thomson and some other schoolmasters were at a pond. Though it was a private lake and no bathing was allowed, someone dared one among them to swim out to a boat in the middle. Thomson was recognized but, when questioned about the incident later, refused to give the names of his companions. For this, he was demoted to schoolmaster 4th Class, then dismissed from the army.

Whether any of the other schoolmasters involved were dismissed has not been recorded.

Thomson's earliest biographer, Henry Salt, makes little of the incident and claims Thomson was not guilty of any personal misconduct but was simply unlucky enough to be part of "the incriminated party."

But Thomson's 1965 biographer, William David Schaefer, feels the explanation is wildly improbable, detecting about it some sort of Victorian cover-up —possibly involving alcoholism. Thomson's drinking had already established itself as a problem as far back as 1855. Perhaps the young men at the pond were both rowdy and soused. I would go Schaefer one further, however, and suggest there was some sort of sexual misconduct involved as well, for which the swimming incident was, indeed, used as the official excuse to expel the group of possibly embarrassing fellows. But we do not know for sure.[10]

What we do know is that Thomson now went to London and began a career of writing scathingly radical articles for the various political journals of the times; often living off his friends, and drinking more and more. And it was only now that (some of) his poems began to refer to a secret sorrow—presumably Mathilda Weller's death. In London, Thomson lived with his friend Charles Bradlaugh (and Bradlaugh's wife and two daughters) on and off for more than twelve years—as a kind of tolerated, even fondly approved of, if occasionally drunken, uncle—until a year or so after *The City of Dreadful Night* was published in the March and May issues of Bradlaugh's magazine, *The National Reformer*. (Bradlaugh skipped the April issue because of objections from readers, but still other readers, among them Bertram Dobell, wrote to ask when the poem would continue; and publication resumed.) But with Thomson's newfound fame, the poet-journalist's drinking escalated violently—and he and Bradlaugh finally broke over it.

The City of Dreadful Night begins with two Italian epigraphs, one by Dante, one by Leopardi. The Dante says, *"Per me si va nella citta dolente"* ("Through me you enter into the sorrowful city"). But this is not the all too familiar motto over the Gate of Hell. Rather, from Thomson's poem, we realize this is Thomson's motto for the gate of birth, and that the city of life itself is, for Thomson, the sorrowful city, the city without hope or love or faith. And Leopardi is, after all, the poet who wrote to his sister Paolina about the grandeur that was Rome: "These huge buildings and interminable streets are just so many spaces thrown between men, instead of being spaces that contain men." *The City of Dreadful Night* is a blunt and powerful, if not the most artful, presentation of the condition of humanity bereft of all the consolations of Christianity as well as the community of small rural settlements—next to which *The Waste Land*, with its incursions of medieval myth, occultism, and Eastern religions to provide a possible code of meaning and conduct, looks positively optimistic!

Back in his twenty-second year, however, in 1857, while still stationed at Ballincollig, Thomson wrote what, today, we must read as a "dry run" for the more famous series (which he would go on to write between 1871 and '73, with trips to both the U.S.A. and Spain coming to interrupt its composition). Called *The Doom of a City*, its four parts ("The Voyage," "The City," "The Judgment," and "The Return") run to some forty-three pages in my edition—fifteen pages longer than the twenty-eight-page *City of Dreadful Night*. Although Plato's mythic island is never mentioned by name, clearly this is the young Thomson's attempt to tell his own version of the story of Atlantis.

Again, the basic idea may have come from his idol: On a shipboard journey in chapter III of Novalis's *Ofterdingen*, merchants regale Heinrich and his mother with a tale of Atlantis, in which Atlantis's king is enamored of poetry, and his daughter, who rides off and meets a young scholar in the woods, loses a ruby from her necklace which the young man finds; she returns for it the next day, stays to fall in love, retreats to a cave with the young man in a storm, and lives with him and his father for a year before returning to court with her child and the lute-playing young man, for a glorious reunion with the king. This is a fairy tale whose overwhelming affect is its reliance on time's ability to absorb all intergenerational, or generally Oedipal, tensions, so that the reference to its destruction in the closing line, *"Nur in Sagen heisst es, dass Atlantis von machtigen Fluten den Augen entzogen worden sie"* ("Only in legends are we told that mighty floods took Atlantis from the sight of man"), falls like a veil between us and a vision of paradise.

In Part I of *Doom of a City*, "The Voyage," the despairing poet rises in the middle of the night and, leaving his own city, takes a skiff that brings him over the lightless water—after a brief, but harmless, confrontation with a sea monster—to dawn and the shore of a great and mysterious City. The day, however, grows stormy.

After waiting out the day on shore, here is the City the poet finally finds at
sunset:

> . . . Dead or dumb,
> That mighty City through the breathless air
> Thrilled forth no pulse of sound, no faintest hum
> Of congregated life in street and square:
> Becalmed beyond all calm those galleons lay,
> As still and lifeless as their shadows there,
> Fixed in the magic mirror of the bay
> As in a rose-flushed crystal weirdly fair,
> A strange, sad dream: and like a fiery ball,
> Blazoned with death, that sky hung overall.

Night descends; and the poet enters the darkened City's gates:

> The moon hung golden, large and round,
> Soothing its beauty up the quiet sky
> In swanlike slow pulsations, while I wound
> Through dewy meads and gardens of rich flowers,
> Whose fragrance like a subtle harmony
> Was fascination to the languid hours.

In the moonlight, he finds a garden of cypress, a funeral come to a halt, and
a market. But all the inhabitants are frozen stone instead of living people. He
moves on into the City:

> My limbs were shuddering while my veins ran fire,
> And hounded on by dread
> No less than by desire,
> I plunged into the City of the Dead,
> And pierced its mausolean loneliness
> Between the self-sufficing palaces,
> Broad fronts of azure, fire and gold, which shone
> Spectrally valid in the moonlight wan,
> Adown great streets; through spacious sylvan squares,
> Whose fountains plashing lone
> Fretted the silence with perpetual moan;
> Past range on range of marts which spread their wares
> Weirdly unlighted to the eye of heaven,
> Jewels and silks and golden ornaments,
> Rich perfumes, soul-in-soul of all rare scents.
> Viols and timbrels: O wild mockery!
> Where are the living shrines for these adornings?

The poet explores on, but instead of a populace in the City—

> What found I? Dead stone sentries stony-eyed,
> Erect, steel-sworded, brass-defended all,
> Guarding the sombrous gateway deep and wide
> Hewn like a cavern through the mighty wall;
> Stone statues all throughout the streets and squares.
> Grouped as in social converse or alone;
> Dim stony merchants holding forth rich wares
> To catch the choice of purchasers in stone;
> Fair statues leaning over balconies,
> Whose bosoms made the bronze and marble chill;
> Statues about the lawns, beneath the trees
> Firm sculptured horsemen on stone horses still;
> Statues fixed gazing on the flowing river
> Over the bridge's sculpted parapet;
> Statues in boats, amidst its sway and quiver
> Immovable as if in ice-waves set:—
> The whole vast sea of life about me lay,
> The passionate, the heaving, restless, sounding life,
> With all its side and billows, foam and spray,
> Attested in full tumult of its strife
> Frozen into a nightmare's ghastly death,
> Struck silent by its laughter and its moan.
> The vigorous heart and brain and blood and breath
> Stark, strangled, confined in eternal stone.

The poet continues to regard the urban landscape around him with its stony populace—

> Look away there to the right—How the bay lies broad and bright,
> All athrob with murmurous rapture in the glory of the moon!
> See in front the palace stand, halls and columns nobly planned;
> Marble home for marble dwellers is it not full fair and boon?
> See the myriads gathered there on that green and wooded square,
> In mysterious congregation,—they are statues every one:
> All are clothed in rich array; it is some high festal day;
> The solemnity is perfect with the pallid moon for sun.

As he finally sees the stony autarch of the city (beside whom crouches the skeleton of Death), the whole, frozen vision, with all its populace turned to stone, lit with a full moon, a series of towering gods appear (Part III, "The Judgment"), and a booming Voice proceeds to judge wanting one aspect of the

City after another; and, on each judgment, that section of the City falls into the sea or is toppled by an earthquake, to be swallowed up.

The judgment on the City begins with—

> A multitudinous roaring of the ocean!
> Voices of sudden and earth-quaking thunder
> From the invisible mountains!
> The heavens are broken up and rent asunder
> By curbless lightning fountains,
> Swarming and darting through that black commotion,
> In which the moon and stars are swallowed with the sky,

Finally, only the young poet is spared by the Voice, as one who has sought after truth. The day dawns; what remains of the city is only the good and the pure—which, indeed, isn't very much. The poet regains his boat and returns whence he came over the blue waters and under the brilliant sun.

The city to which the poet in his boat returns in the evening is, however, sordid and lurid. (In the two stanzas describing it—II and III of Part IV, "The Return"—we have the first intimations of what Thomson will publish eighteen years on, in the more powerful, but less Atlantian, *City of Dreadful Night.*) So once more the poet takes to his boat and returns to the ruined site of the mythic City, to hear the Voice again deliver a jeremiad against the greed and evil of urban corruption.

With this sermon threatening the fall of the real city, *The Doom of a City* ends.

The question is: Did Crane at some point encounter the two volumes of *The Poetical Works of James Thomson,* edited and published after Thomson's death by Bertram Dobell in 1895—where, indeed, he might have found *The Doom of a City?* As we have said, Crane's *"Proem"* at the start of *The Bridge* makes it almost certain that he knew *The City of Dreadful Night.* But would his curiosity have drawn him to pursue Thomson back to this Ur-version of that paean to urban psychic disaster: Thomson's own twenty-three-year-old's retelling of the destruction of Atlantis?

Periodically, starting with his death, there were attempts to establish Thomson as an important canonical poet. But everything from Thomson's militant atheism and radical politics to his dipsomania and dreadfully sordid final years militated against it—especially during the first-wave attempt, spearheaded by Dobell, in the 1880s and '90s. (That both Poe and Thomson, in the manner of Novalis before them, were associated with tragic affairs with much younger women is not, as it works toward the moral marginalization of both, without its meaning.) Thomson is a poet a full understanding of whose work hinges not only on Novalis (and Shelley), but also on Heine and Leopardi: he translated significant amounts of both. (Indeed, Thomson's literary tastes were quite advanced:

he championed Whitman, Emerson, and William Blake when all three were majorly controversial figures in England.) But two World Wars, with Germany as the villain (and Italy not far behind), have made English writers with leanings in those national directions less sympathetic to us than they might otherwise be.

Crane's essay "The Case Against Nietzsche" (1918) was his own attempt to fight that particular sort of jingoism, which, after the Great War, often seemed a tidal wave of pure anti-intellectualism. But certainly Thomson, with his secret sorrow and tragic life, could have been a poet that Crane in his later years, drinking himself into a poetic silence, as did Thomson, might well have sympathized, if not identified, with. The brilliant moonlit evocations of the City that litter Thomson's earlier poem all through its second quarter certainly put one in mind of the moonlight-flooded structure that is the vision behind Crane's "Atlantis"—the terminal section of his own major poetic series—as if all that was needed between Thomson's vision of London and the moon-drenched vision of his own Atlantis was, somehow, a bridge . . .

An early *Encyclopedia Britannica* article on Thomson that Crane might well have read—I first looked him up the same year I first read Crane, in 1958, the same year I came across a powerful fragment from *The City of Dreadful Night* in an old Oscar Williams paperback anthology ("As I came through the desert, thus it was / As I came through the desert . . .")—while generally praising Thomson, closes by chiding him for "the not infrequent use of mere rhetoric and verbiage," terms we have already heard in our pursuit of Crane.

In 1927, Henry Holt and Company published a 251-page selection of *Poems of James Thomson, "B. V.,"* edited by Gordon Hall Gerauld. After an elegiac sonnet written in memory of Thomson by Philip Bourke Marston (the blind poet in whose rooms the destitute Thomson suffered his final, fatal collapse), this collection commences with still another "Proem" Thomson had written—Dobell's two-volume, complete *Poetical Works* includes three poems by Thomson of that title—and concludes with both *The City of Dreadful Night* and *The Doom of the City*. In his 1927 introduction, Gerauld spends a few sentences of his praiseful introduction retrieving *Doom* from the juvenillia to which Dobell had consigned it in the second volume of his 1895 compilation. Gerauld writes:

> *The Doom of a City*, as he [Thomson] called his magnificent if not wholly achieved and sometimes incoherent poem, is a work of youth, but it could have been written only by a youth of genius. [Shelley's] *Alastor*, let us recall, is by no means without faults of construction, and [Keats's] *Endymion*, as Keats was the first to discover, did not fulfill the hopes with which it had been conceived. Like *Alastor* and *Endymion*, *The Doom of a City* is a precious and beautiful work of the human imagination, which no lover of poetry can afford to ignore. . . . The same austere but melodic dignity [that one finds in *The City of Dreadful Night*] is to be found as early as *The Doom of a City* and as late as *A Voice from the Nile*.

Thus, and even bearing this critical pointer, the poem would have been available to Crane if, as poets do, he had wandered into a bookstore sometime during 1927 and looked through the new volumes of verse—for that was the year in which Crane put the most concerted work into organizing and revising his own poem. In 1926 in a flurry of creative activity on the Isle of Pines, Crane had first drafted "Dedication to Brooklyn Bridge"—a flurry that also yielded drafts of "Ave Maria," "Cutty Sark," and "The Tunnel"—as well as "Eternity." (His stay was ended by the hurricane the aftermath of which that poem so vividly details.) But when the "Dedication" received the title "*Proem*," I've been unable as yet to ascertain. In 1927, when the Gerauld volume of Thomson's poems appeared, Crane was living (through to the start of '28) in Patterson, New York, with frequent and extended trips to New York City specifically to buy books. While in Patterson, a reading of Spengler's *Decline of the West* (what young American writer, exposed to those paired volumes, seductive as any Ayn Rand novel, has not at least been shaken by their *en passant* arguments, even if not convinced of their major thesis) inspired another bout of writing and revision on *The Bridge*. Thus Crane could have easily seen Thomson's poems. More important, he could have seen them at a time when we know him to have been particularly receptive and actively at work on his own poem.

While the 1927 publication date is not a smoking gun, in terms of the possible influence of Thomson on Crane—it's not a note or journal entry of course—certainly it's a warm one.

But even if there was no direct influence (though there may well have been an intentional dialogue), certainly there's no *harm* in holding the young Thomson's moonlit Atlantis up to provide the missing city for Crane's.

V.

Like Brom Weber's before it, Marc Simon's 1986 edition of *The Poems of Hart Crane*—with an introduction by John Unterecker, author of the National Book Award–winning Crane biography *Voyager* (1969)—is designated by the editor a "reader's edition." (Weber promised a variorum edition, but it has yet to appear.) Simon expands the corpus of Weber's 1966 edition, *The Complete Poems and Selected Letters and Prose of Hart Crane*, by a hefty handful of fragments and incomplete poems, as well as more early and uncollected poems. Simon's omission of the word "Complete" quietly suggests there may even be other poems to come—possibly some of currently dubious attribution. (In 1993 the Simon volume was reissued as *Complete Poems of Hart Crane*.)

Weber's 1966 edition had replaced the hasty 1933 edition, *The Collected Poems of Hart Crane*, which Waldo Frank had put together (reprinted in 1958 as *Complete Poems*), which contained Crane's only two published books, *White Buildings* and *The Bridge*, along with a third volume, unpublished at Crane's death, *Key West: An Island Sheaf*. The Simon volume is longer than the Frank by more than sixty poems. The problem, however, is that the general poetry reader today is a very different person from the general poetry reader of circa World War I, when the academization of literature began to divide significant writers' works into specialist and non-specialist editions—the non-specialist edition free of extensive notes and usually printed fairly inexpensively. But—today—the reader who is wholly unconcerned with biography and devoid of interest in or even knowledge of the times in which Crane wrote, and who aims to get all her or his pleasure only from an encounter with the bare and unadorned text, is simply an artificial construct.

Certainly one would like to see *The Bridge* accorded the textual treatment, with variants and alternate versions and the careful redaction of manuscript and galley markings, that has already been lavished on Eliot's *The Waste Land* and more recently Ginsberg's *Howl*. But though such an edition is devoutly to be wished, what is needed is a readers' edition with notes that will allow people who want to read Crane's poems to pursue the ordinary interests that today's actual readers of poems have.

We need an edition with notes that will tell us that "Voyages I" was first written and published as a separate poem, called variously "Poster" and "The Bottom of the Sea Is Cruel." (Critics regularly discuss it under both titles.) We need notes that will tell us that "For the Marriage of Faustus and Helen II" was first written as a separate poem, "The Springs of Guilty Song." We need notes that will tell us that when "Recitative" was first written in 1923 it was three stanzas shorter than the final 1926 revision—and which three stanzas were added! We need a note to tell us that "Thou Canst Read Nothing Except Through Appetite . . ." was a poem Crane typed on the back of a piece of paper bearing a name and address someone had passed him in a heavy cruising venue (the baths? the bridge? the docks?), and that, in order to indicate its nature, long-time friend and confidant Sam Loveman, who did the textual editing on the poems for Weber's 1966 edition, gave it the title "Reply," which is clearly what it is, even if the title isn't Crane's. We need notes that will tell us that Crane sent the fragment "This Way Where November . . ." in a November 1923 letter to Jean Toomer, in which he described it as part of a long poem to be titled "White Buildings," centering on a catastrophic sexual encounter with a sailor that began at a drunken gathering of friends the night before Crane was to leave to spend the remainder of winter '23 in Woodstock, New York—and that Crane predicted the poem, when complete, would be unprintable; but that only this fragment survives.

An editor might *even* supply a note to the effect that Crane wrote the cycle of six "Voyages" as a set of meditations on Emil's sea-trips away . . .

We need notes that will give us both the 1926 version of "O Carib Isle," as well as the later 1929 version, not as a variorum exercise, but simply because they are distinct poems, sharing the first few and the last few lines. We need notes to tell us when and where the poems were written, when and where they were published—and under what title, when the final title is not the only one. If the situation in which a poem was written or to which it responds *is* known and can be explained easily and relevantly, why not note it?

Such information is far more important than notes explaining that, in "Possessions," Weber has corrected the spelling of "raze" to "rase," or that, in "Royal Palm," Marc Simon has corrected the spelling of "elaphantime" to "elephantine"—the sort of note which, in the absence of the other kind, clutters both Weber and Simon. Nothing is wrong with such textual minutiae. And for the carefully established text, we must be grateful to Simon. This is often a Herculean labor; one praises it as such. But notes on its establishment have no place in an edition devoid of that other information; in its absence, one would have preferred the fine points covered by a "have been corrected without comment" in the editor's "Note on the Editorial Method."

Likewise, we are grateful for the added poetic fragments—only noting that it is precisely such fragments and incomplete efforts for which readers generally *need* more extensive notes.

Both Simon and Weber tell us when the poems were published, and occasionally when written and revised. Maddeningly, however, neither says in what magazines or—far more important—gives us earlier titles. But the assumption that a general poetry reader exists today who will never encounter some article on Crane that quotes a poem in part (and in some earlier form illuminating something in the poet's development, for that's what such articles are made of), who will then turn to such an edition to find the final form of the poem in full, is absurd. And it is more absurd to assume that a specific reader who avoids all such articles will still want to know about the poet's—or a former typesetter's —misspellings!

In short, one wants among the notes for Crane the same sort of information that Edward Mendelson provides as "Appendix II: Variant Titles" in his *W. H. Auden: Collected Poems*, or that Donald Allen gives us in his notes to *The Collected Poems of Frank O'Hara*. When a writer like Pound or Eliot puts together his own collected poems, modesty perhaps excuses such omissions. Yet if the poet's work is interesting enough for a second party to undertake the task, what I've outlined represents what should be given first priority. And as specialists will know, in no way does that constitute a specialists' edition. But the assumption that there exists a Common Reader of poetry who comes from no place—and is going nowhere—is, besides preposterous, heuristically arrogant and pedagogically pernicious.[11] That, however, is what Simon's "reader's edition" seems to presuppose.

The supplementary selections of prose letters, essays, and reviews that

Weber included in his 1966 edition were immensely interesting. I should have thought Simon would have enlarged on them, rather than drop them altogether, (Even with minor poems, juvenilia, and fragments, Crane's poetic *opera omnia* are just not that voluminous.) Simon might well have added some of the letters to black writer Jean Toomer that were published in part in Unterecker's biography. One would have welcomed both the "White Buildings" letter and the "Heaven and Hell" letter; the latter threatens to achieve a measure of fame comparable only to Keats's letter on "negative capability" written on the 21st of December, 1817, from Hampstead to his brothers George and Tom.

It is all too easy to see the avoidance of such notes (or the exclusion of such letters) beginning in a kind of editorial exasperation with Crane's homosexuality. Where does one draw the line at good taste—more important, where did one draw that line in 1952, when Weber edited Crane's letters, or in '66, when he edited the poems? (That's what both the "Heaven and Hell" letter and the "White Buildings" letter are, after all, about.) To raise the question is, however, immediately to consider the oddly similar suppression by all three of Crane's major biographers of the fact that, in October 1923, Jean Toomer, after the publication of his novel *Cane* to critical, if not to popular, success, visited his white friend and supporter Waldo Frank (his and Crane's mutual mentor) at Frank's Connecticut home for the first time, whereupon Toomer fell passionately in love with Frank's wife, educator Margaret Naumberg. The passion was mutual. Weeks later, the two had run off together, hoping to leave America for the Gurdjieff Institute for the Harmonious Development of Man at the Chateau du Prieuré in Fontainbleau, France, in order to study with Georges Gurdjieff himself. Only days before Toomer's actual arrival, however, Gurdjieff died, but Toomer remained to study with Gurdjieff's disciples, while for months Naumberg wrote him heartfelt letters announcing her imminent arrival. In the end, she stayed in America.

The incident was the center of gossip in the Frank/Munson/Crane/Cowley/Toomer circle for months, if not years. But though certainly all three major biographers knew of it, neither Horton, Weber, nor Unterecker mentions it. One must go to recent biographies of Toomer to learn of it at all.

If it came to mean less to Crane once Toomer had given up writing for mysticism, the Crane/Toomer friendship was still an important one for Crane's early poethood—through, say, 1924. Though Toomer was three years older than Crane, the two were the youngest writers in the group. And heterosexual Toomer was one of the several straight men to whom Crane was (as the post-Stonewall generation would say) out. We know of incidents in which Toomer felt ill-understood by the group, notably by Frank and by publisher Horace Liveright, because of Toomer's racial make-up. And Crane suggests in that letter to Winters, already quoted, that homosexuality does not mean what Winters seems to think it does. With the speculations of all his friends about the topic rampant in their commentaries and memories, it is fairly certain Crane could not expect much more than superficial understanding there. Both men had reason, then, to feel themselves, however accepted, somehow still aliens in the group. It may well have brought them together. In 1937 and 1948 one can imagine biographers Horton and Weber not mentioning the Toomer/Naumberg affair from feelings of delicacy for Frank, if not for Toomer and Naumberg, all of whom were then still alive. But Toomer and Frank both died in 1967, and Unterecker's biography appeared in 1969 . . .

It's oddly paradoxical that if one looks at Toomer's all but inconsequential post-*Cane* writing, it might seem as though Toomer had turned to study, if not at Gurdjieff's knee, then at Winters's—though Kenneth Walker, in his study *Gurdjieff's Teaching* (Jonathan Cape, 1957), writes of Gurdjieff's conception of art: "I measure the merit of art by its consciousness, you by its unconsciousness. A work of objective art is a book which transmits the artist's ideas not directly through words or signs or hieroglyphics but through feelings which he evokes in the beholder consciously and with full knowledge of what he is doing and why he is doing it." Pursuing that "full knowledge," Toomer—as did Winters, pursuing his own aesthetic program—apparently purged himself of the verbal liveliness which, today, is the principal entrance through which one apprehends the pleasure in his writing; though by the time he broke with Crane, of course, Winters may not have been aware of Toomer's existence.

By then many had forgotten it.

But while one is clamoring for the Crane/Toomer letters, what of Crane's letters to Wilbur Underwood, Crane's older gay friend in Washington, D.C., of which we have had only snippets, accompanied by vague editorial suggestions that their subject matter is wholly beyond the pale? Such innuendo is certainly more damaging than any actual human activity possibly recounted could be.

Finally, just as we need an edition of Crane's poems with an apparatus that takes in the needs of actual poetry readers, we need a complete letters. (I am not the first person to make the favorable comparison between Crane's letters and Keats's.) Nor would it be a bad idea to put together a collection of letters and papers from *The Crane Circle* on the model of Hyder Edward Rollins's famous and rewarding 1948 paired volumes around Keats.

Samuel Bernhard Greenberg's notebooks, papers, and drawings are currently in the Fales Collection at New York University. Edited by Harold Holden and Jack McManis, with a preface by Allen Tate, a 117-page selection, *Poems by Samuel Greenberg*, was published by Henry Holt and Company (1947).

Crane's manuscripts, letters, and papers are largely stored at Columbia University. There are three full biographies of Crane[12] and currently four volumes of letters are generally available. Philip Horton published his *Hart Crane: The Life of an American Poet* in 1937. Brom Weber published his fine, if somewhat eccentric, biographical study of Crane and his work, *Hart Crane: A Biographical and*

Critical Study, in 1948. (Both Crane's birth- and death-dates are mentioned only in footnotes—added, in galleys, at editor Loveman's firm suggestion.) Weber also edited *The Letters of Hart Crane, 1916–1932* (largely those of literary interest) in 1952 and, as mentioned, *The Complete Poems and Selected Letters and Prose of Hart Crane* in 1966. Thomas S. W. Lewis edited *Letters of Hart Crane and His Family* in 1974, a book nearly three times the thickness of Weber's *Letters* and a fascinating family romance. *Hart Crane and Yvor Winters: Their Literary Correspondence* (1978), edited by Thomas Parkinson, is another important volume of Crane's letters and commentary. *Robber Rocks: Letters and Memories of Hart Crane, 1923–1932* (1969) by Susan Jenkins Brown (wife of William Slater Brown, formerly wife of Provincetown Playhouse director James Light) contains thirty-nine more of Crane's letters (there is some overlap here with Weber), as well as five auxiliary letters of the Crane circle. The volume concludes with Peggy Baird's devastating "The Last Days of Hart Crane," a reminiscence that makes Crane's final completed poem, "The Broken Tower," rise from the page and resonate (a poem whose title, if not the very idea for it, comes from "An Age of Dream," among the most popular sonnets of Lionel Johnson, another of Crane's adolescent enthusiasms.[13] We know the 1915 selection of Johnson's poems with the introduction by Pound was a treasured volume in Crane's adolescent library. Baird's memoir must be supplemented, however, by Unterecker's "Introduction" to the 1986 Marc Simon edition of Crane's poems: there Unterecker prints Gertrude E. Vogt's firsthand account of the talk on shipboard that morning and of watching from the *Orizaba*'s deck, with several other passengers, Crane's actual jump from the stern to his death—in a letter that reached Unterecker after his 1969 biography *Voyager* appeared. Marc Simon is also the author of *Samuel Greenberg, Hart Crane, and the Lost Manuscripts* (Humanities Press, 1978), an invaluable book for anyone interested in Greenberg or Crane or Greenberg's literary loans to Crane—and of which I have made extensive use here.

*   *   *

And now a note for a few special readers: Though my 1995 novel *Atlantis: Model 1924* is fiction, I tried to stay as close to fact as I could and still have a tale.

The lines Crane quotes in my text are an amalgam from early versions of "Atlantis," all of which were written by July 26, 1923—the summer prior to the spring in which the recitation takes place. (Crane had spent the previous evening with his father, Clarence Arthur, who was visiting the city; he would write his mother a letter later that afternoon and would see his father again the next day.) Crane's work method usually involved sending off copies of his just completed poems, along with letters to Waldo Frank, Jean Toomer, Gorham Munson, or the Rychtariks—a Prague painter and his wife who Crane said "really 'belong'—and are about the only people in this district that I enjoy seeing" ("Letter to Lorna Dietz," February 10, 1931). In 1926 he would take the poem up again and between January and August of that year work it far closer to the form present readers of *The Bridge* are familiar with. The final decision to change the title from "Finale" to "Atlantis" did not come, of course, till later. We know Crane had some of the Greenberg story wrong. In 1923 from Woodstock he'd written to Munson that Fisher had "nursed" Greenberg through his final illness at the paupers' hospital—which was untrue. During Greenberg's terminal weeks on Ward's Island he was attended only by his family and, on his final evening, the sparse and overworked hospital staff. Later Horton wrote that Fisher had "inherited" Greenberg's notebooks through "the indifference of the boy's relatives"—equally untrue: Morris had offered the notebooks to Fisher in the hope of getting the poems published. Samuel's family had been as appreciative and supportive of their youngest brother's talents as an impoverished family of Viennese Jews might be. They had always considered Samuel special.

We do not know for *sure* if Crane actually read either Fisher's essay on Greenberg, "Fragments of a Broken Lyre," in *The Plowshare*, or the ten poems published there. (Possibly Fisher just told him about them.) While it's certainly *probable* Fisher showed *The Plowshare*'s contents to Crane or at least talked about them, Crane does not mention them in his letters. (Nor does Marc Simon, in the reports of his interviews with Fisher on the topic before his death, recounted in Simon's book *Samuel Greenberg, Hart Crane, and the Lost Manuscripts*, clear up the question.) But possibly that's only because Fisher did not have a copy of the then four-year-old journal to give Crane to keep.

Besides knowing Samuel for the last seven years of the young poet's life, Fisher had known his brothers Morris and Daniel; and he had certainly known of, if he had not actually met, Adolf—which is to say, specific dates aside, Fisher knew pretty much everything my own tale recounts. Only four and a half months after the night that Fisher and Crane had sat up late in Woodstock talking about the tragic poet, Crane might well have remembered all the facts of Greenberg's life he tells in *Atlantis: Model 1924*. The misunderstandings and lacunae in Crane's knowledge, which—in the tale—I've made nothing of, could easily have been the result of drink and the random order of anecdotes around that December night's fire; or even the momentary pressure of a next day's quickly written letter. Why perpetuate them?

In that spirit, I mention: In his transcript of Greenberg's poem "Words," in the thirteenth line Crane typed "most" for "must." I've just assumed that in reading it over Crane recognized his error. In *Atlantis: Model 1924* he quotes the poem correctly.

This study grew—as did, indeed, my short novel—out of an observation my father several times made to me while I was a teenager: As late as 1924, just after he first came from Raleigh, North Carolina, to New York City—and shortly thereafter took his first walk across the Brooklyn Bridge—Brooklyn was nowhere near as built-up as it is today. Though, indeed, there were clusters of houses here and there, especially toward the water, my then-seventeen-year-old father was surprised, even somewhat appalled, that the road leading from the Bridge in those days decanted among meadows and by a cornfield. He was both surprised and appalled enough to mention it to me, with a self-deprecating laugh at his own astonishment at the time, some thirty-five years later.

The fields—and the corn—are both there (in the seventh and ninth stanzas) in Crane's "Atlantis."

But there is much more.

The bedlamite from the "*Proem*" (transfigured first into our superbly articulate Columbus, then, after myriad further changes, into the incoherent, aged sailor of "Cutty Sark") is, in "Atlantis," again aloft among the bridge lines, now as "Jason! hesting Shout!" (To "hest," the *OED* suggests, from *hātan*—to call upon—is to "bid, command . . . vow, promise . . . will, propose," or "determine . . ."—all of them obsolete.) The bridge in "Atlantis" spans a world as drenched in language as it is in moonlight: Cables whisper. Voices flicker. An arc calls. History has myriad mouths that pour forth a reply. Ships cry. Oceans answer. Spars hum. Spears laugh (though no traveler, searching that laughter, reads the "cipher-script of time" linked to it). Hammers whisper. Aeons cry. Beams yell. A choir translates. Sun and water fuse Verbs. And the many twain sing—for over all is song. But Crane's poem limns a world where not only the Poet, but almost every element of it, can apostrophize—can directly address —every other.

The "cordage" is there, from "Voyages I" (as well as a "Tall Vision-of-the-Voyage, tensely spare"), but this time "spiring" rather than "spry."

The one hitch in this articulating web is that the Bridge cannot speak directly to Love. But Love's white flower—the Anemone (first cousin to Novalis's blue amaranthus)—is the "Answerer" of all. Crane's final exhortation to the Anemone, which seems to sit apposite to (and is surely a metaphor for) Atlantis itself, is to "hold—(O Thou whose radiance doth inherit me) Atlantis—hold thy floating singer late!" Atlantis, hold the poet's floating attention late into the moon-drenched night. As well, hold him up as he floats on the turbulent waters, the chaos of language, beneath (that will finally receive everything of and from) the Bridge. The terminal question that the poem asks recalls the question that the title—with the poem following it—created (recall it: "What is 'Atlantis'?"): To what does this Bridge of Fire lead?

Asks the poem: "Is it Cathay . . . ?"

Since what the Choir translates the web of articulation into is a "Psalm of Cathay," many commentators have assumed Crane's question is rhetorical and, as such, the answer is a fairly unconsidered, "Yes, of course . . ." Often I have felt, however, as though, retrievable from the whisperings referred to by the poem's final sentence with its twin inversions ("Whispers antiphonal in azure swing" / "Antiphonal whispers swing in azure"), Crane all but exhorts us to construct some terminal antiphon of our own: No, friend: It is Atlantis that I sing.

The reader who can carefully architect an argument leading to such a terminus, above the liquid shift and flicker of Crane's rhetorical suspensions and spumings, has probably had an experience of the poem . . . that masters, that comprehends, that controls it? No, friend. Only one that is, likely, somewhat like mine.

But to articulate such a line in all its inescapable, referential banality is to close off the poem in precisely the way Crane wanted it left open. That openness—one is allowed into it (the Absolute) or not, at one's choice—is a fundamental, if not the fundamental, aspect of Crane's implied city, of Dreadful Night, of Dis or New Jerusalem, of God.

—November 1992–October 1993
Amherst/Ann Arbor/New York

NOTES

1. Greenberg's title was inspired by the musical titles of Whistler's paintings such as *Nocturn in Black and Gold* (*The Falling Rocket* [1875]), *Arrangement in Black and Grey* (*Whistler's Mother*) [1871], and *Symphony in Grey and Green* (*The Oceans*) [1866–1871], which all quickly gained popular titles (here in parentheses). At this point, Greenberg's social circle included several men who worked at the Met, where for certain he saw and learned the proper title for "Whistler's Mother" and heard about Whistler's titles for the others.

2. After the poet Michael Drayton (1563–1631).

3. Crane also supplies his range of titles: Tennessee Williams's play *Summer and Smoke* takes its title from Crane's poem "Emblems of Conduct" (indeed from the only three lines in the poem Crane apparently did *not* take from Greenberg); the title for Agnes de Mille's ballet *Appalachian Spring* comes from, appropriately enough, Crane's "The Dance"; Jim Morrison of The Doors took the title of his song "Riders on the Storm" from Crane's "Praise for an Urn"; and Harold Bloom's study of romantic poetry *The Visionary Company* takes its title from Crane's last poem, "The Broken Tower."

4. The use of Whitman promotes a tradition in which Crane has lived and struggled since his first poem: of rhetoric, reticence, and monologue as opposed to dialogue and clear dramatic statements; a poetic unity, if a historical disappointment.

5. We've mentioned the combination of prose poetry and verse in Novalis's *Hymnen an Die Nacht*. The recall might even remain with Crane's running, sometimes prose rubrics down the margins of "Ave Maria," "The Harbor Dawn," "Van Winkle," "The Rover," and "Indiana."

6. That task waited for Robert Hayden to take up, after Crane's death, with "Middle Passage." See page 223: "Note on Robert Hayden's 'Middle Passage.'"

7. "At sixteen I discovered (by reading a section of our history of English literature which we were *not* required to read) Thomson's *City of Dreadful Night*, and the poems of Ernest Dowson," Eliot wrote in "On Teaching the Appreciation of Poetry." "Each was a new and vivid experience." And in his 1961 Preface to *John Davidson: A Selection of his Poems*, Eliot wrote: "I feel a particular debt, towards poets whose work impressed me deeply in my formative years between the ages of sixteen and twenty. Some were of an earlier age—the late sixteenth and early seventeenth century—some of another language, and of these, two were Scots: The author of *The City of Dreadful Night* and the author of *Thirty Bob a Week*, "What exactly my debt is to John Davidson I cannot tell, any more than I can describe my debt to James Thomson: I only know that the two debts differ from each other."

8. A pre-internet library technology that had an immeasurable effect on the shape of hands-on research, which functions entirely differently from the OCS [On-Line Catalogue Service], as I can attest even in the preparation of this essay; as different as a listing of books vs. a week—or, indeed, a lifetime—in the stacks.

9. Since this essay was written, Thomson's translation of Novalis's *Hymns to the Night* has been published *in toto* in *Novalis and the Poets of Pessimism*, edited by Simon Reynolds (Norwich: Michael Russel, 1995).

10. Since this essay was written, Tom Leonard's magisterial work on Thomson, *Places of the Mind* (London: Jonathan Cape, 1993), has come to my attention. Brilliantly researched and persuasively argued, Leonard's work may be one of the great scholarly performances of our century, taking its place beside John Livingston Lowes's *Road to Xanadu* (1927) and Erich Auerbach's *Mimesis* (1946). Leonard holds that Thomson was drummed out of the army over this appallingly minor incident because he was a free thinker. He cites numerous other cases where men with such political leanings were treated equally unfairly. Yet the shadow of homosexuality still suggests itself in terms of Thomson: the overheard words of one lover to another that comprise §VI of *The City of Dreadful Night*, with neither speaker nor hearer identified as to gender, is an all but classical example of one of the homosexual genres alluded to above.

11. The Library of America edition, in its back matter notes, goes a long way in correcting some of these editorial problems.

12. A fourth biography is Clive Fischer's *Hart Crane: A Biography* (Yale University Press, 2002), which talks about Grace's purging of the letters, where confirmation for some of these questions might have lodged, along with suggestions about sex.

13. Johnson's sonnet, "The Age of Dream" (the second of a pair usually published together about an all but abandoned church; the first is "The Church of Dream"), concludes with the sestet:

Gone now, the carvern work! Ruined, the golden shrine!
No more the glorious organs pour their voice divine;
No more rich frankincense drifts through the Holy Place:
Now from the broken tower, what solemn bell still tolls,
Mourning what piteous death? Answer, O saddened souls!
Who mourn the death of beauty and the death of grace.

WORKS CONSULTED

Alvarez, A. *The Savage God: A Study of Suicide*. Bantam Books, 1982.
Beer, Thomas. *Stephen Crane: A Study in American Letters*. Knopf, 1923.
Blackmur, R. P. *Form and Value in Modern Poetry*. Doubleday Anchor, 1950.
————. "New Thresholds, New Anatomies: Notes on a Text by Hart Crane," in *Language as Gesture*. New York: Harcourt Brace and Company, 1952.
Bloom, Harold. *Agon: Towards a Theory of Revisionism*. New York: Oxford University Press, 1982.
————. "Hart Crane's Gnosis." In *Hart Crane: A Collection of Critical Essays*, edited by Allen Trachtenberg. Englewood Cliffs: Prentice-Hall, 1982.
Brown, Susan Jenkins. *Robber Rocks: Letters and Memories of Hart Crane, 1923–1932*. Middletown: Wesleyan University Press, 1969.
Brunner, Edward. *Splendid Failure: The Making of "The Bridge."* Urbana and Chicago: University of Illinois Press, 1985.
Butterfield, R. W. *The Broken Arc: A Study of Hart Crane*. Edinburgh: Oliver and Boyd Ltd., 1969.
Carlyle, Thomas. "Novalis," in *Foreign Review* VII (1829); also in *Critical and Miscellaneous Essays* (Philadelphia: A. Hart, 1852).
Clark, David R., ed. *Critical Essays on Hart Crane*. Boston: G. K. Hall and Co, 1982.
————, ed. *The Merrill Studies in "The Bridge."* Columbus: Charles E. Merrill Publishing Company, 1970.
Crane, Hart. "The Case Against Nietzsche." In *The Complete Poems and Selected Letters and Prose of Hart Crane*. Edited by Brom Weber. Garden City, NY: Anchor Books, 1966.
————. *The Complete Poems and Selected Letters and Prose of Hart Crane*. Edited and with an introduction by Brom Weber. Garden City, NY: Anchor Books, Doubleday and Company, 1966.
————. *The Letters of Hart Crane, 1916–1932*. Edited by Brom Weber. Berkeley and Los Angeles: University of California Press, 1965.
————. *The Poems of Hart Crane*. Edited by Marc Simon. New York: Liveright Publishing Corporation, 1986. (Reissued as *The Complete Poems of Hart Crane* in 1989.)
Dembo, L. S. *Crane's Sanskrit Charge: A Study of "The Bridge."* Ithaca: Cornell University Press, 1960.
Dowson, Ernest. *The Poems of Ernest Dowson*. With a Memoir by Arthur Symons. New York: John Lane Company, 1919.
Drew, Elizabeth. *Poetry: A Modern Guide to Its Understanding and Enjoyment*. New York: Dell Publishing Company, 1959.
Edelman, Lee. *Transmemberment of Song: Hart Crane's Anatomy and Rhetoric of Desire*. Stanford: Stanford University Press, 1987.
Eliot, T. S. "The Love Song of J. Alfred Prufrock." In *Selected Poems*. New York: Harcourt, Brace & World, 1936.
————. "The Waste Land." In *Selected Poems*. New York: Harcourt, Brace & World, 1936.
————. "Tradition and the Individual Talent." In *Selected Prose of T. S. Eliot*. Edited and with an introduction by Frank Kermode. New York: Harcourt, Brace & World, 1936.
Empson, William. *Seven Types of Ambiguity*. New York: New Directions, 1966.

(Fisher), William Murrell. "Fragments of a Broken Lyre: A Note on a dead and un-published poet, with ten selected poems following." In *The Plowshare*, January 1920.

Gilbert, Stuart. *James Joyce's "Ulysses": A Study*. New York: Vintage Books, 1955.

Giles, Paul. *Hart Crane: The Contexts of "The Bridge."* New York: Cambridge University Press, 1986.

Greenberg, Samuel B. *Poems by Samuel Greenberg: A Selection from the Manuscripts*. Edited and with an introduction by Harold Holden and Jack McManis. Preface by Allen Tate. New York: Henry Holt and Company, 1947.

————. *Poems from the Greenberg Manuscripts: A Selection from the Work of Samuel B. Greenberg*. Edited and with a commentary by James Laughlin. Norfolk: New Directions, 1939.

Hammer, Langdon. *Hart Crane and Allen Tate: Janus-Faced Modernism*. Princeton: Princeton University Press, 1993.

Hazo, Samuel. *Smithereened Apart: A Critique of Hart Crane*. Athens: Ohio University Press, 1963.

Horton, Philip. *Hart Crane: The Life of an American Poet*. New York: The Viking Press, 1937.

Johnson, Lionel Pigot. *The Collected Poems of Lionel Johnson*. Revised second ed. Edited by Ian Fletcher. New York: Garland Publishing, 1982.

Joyce, James. *Ulysses*. New York: Vintage Books, 1961.

Kerman, Cynthia Earl, and Richard Eldridge. *A Hunger for Wholeness: The Lives of Jean Toomer*. Baton Rouge: Louisiana State University Press, 1987.

Leibowitz, Herbert A. *Hart Crane: An Introduction to the Poetry*. New York: Columbia University Press, 1972.

Lewis, R. W. B. *The Poetry of Hart Crane: A Critical Study*. Princeton: Princeton University Press, 1967.

Lewis, Thomas S. W., ed. *Letters of Hart Crane and His Family*. New York: Columbia University Press, 1974.

Loveman, Sam. "A Conversation with Samuel Loveman." In *Hart Crane: A Conversation with Samuel Loveman*. Edited by Jay Socin and Kirby Congdon. New York: Interim Books, 1963.

————. Introduction to *The Hart Crane Voyages*, by Hunce Voelcker. New York: The Brownstone Press, 1967.

McKay, Nellie Y. *Jean Thome, Artist: A Study of His Literary Life and Work, 1894–1936*. Chapel Hill: University of North Carolina Press, 1984.

Nilsen, Helge Normann. "Memories of Hart Crane: A Talk with Emil Opffer." In *Hart Crane Newsletter* II, no. 1 (Summer 1978).

Novalis. *Henry von Osterdingen*. Translated by Palmer Hilty. New York: Frederick Unger Publishing Company, 1964.

————. *Hymns to the Night*. Translated by Dick Higgins. Kingston: McPherson & Company, 1988.

————. *Hymns to the Night*. Translated by James Thomson (B.V.). In *Novalis and the Poets of Pessimism*. Edited by Simon Reynolds. Norwich: Michael Russel, 1995.

————. *Pollen and Fragments*. Translated by Arthur Versluis. Grand Rapids: Phane Press, 1989.

Ouspensky, P. D. *Tertium Organum: A Key to the Enigmas of the World*. New York: Alfred A. Knopf, 1922.

Parkinson, Thomas. *Hart Crane and Yvor Winters: Their Literary Correspondence.* Berkeley: University of California Press, 1978.

Poe, Edgar Allan. "Drake and Halleck." In *Edgar Allan Poe: Representative Selections, with Introduction, Bibliography, and Notes.* Edited by Margaret Alterton and Hardin Craig. New York: American Book Company, 1935.

Pound, Ezra. "The Pisan Cantos, LXXIV–LXXXIV (1948)." In *The Cantos of Ezra Pound.* New York: New Directions, 1970.

Riffaterre, Michael. *Semiotics of Poetry.* Bloomington: Indiana University Press, 1978.

Salt, Henry S. *The Life of James Thomson ("B.V.").* London: Arthur C. Fifield, 1905.

Schaefer, William David. *James Thomson (B. V.): Beyond "The City."* Berkeley: University of California Press, 1965.

Shaw, George Bernard. *The Perfect Wagnerite: A Commentary on the Nibelung's Ring.* New York: Dover Publications, 1967.

Simon, Marc. *Samuel Greenberg, Hart Crane, and the Lost Manuscripts.* Atlantic Highlands: Humanities Press, 1978.

Socin, Jay, and Kirby Congdon, eds. *Hart Crane: A Conversation with Samuel Loveman.* New York: Interim Books, 1963.

Sugg, Richard P. *Hart Crane's "The Bridge": A Description of Its Life.* Tuscaloosa: The University of Alabama Press, 1976.

Thomson, James. *Poems of James Thomson, "B. V."* Edited by Gordon Hall Gerauld. New York: Henry Holt and Company, 1927.

———. *The Poetical Works of James Thomson (B. V.).* 2 vols. Edited by Bertram Dobell. London, 1895.

———. *The Speedy Extinction of Evil and Misery: Selected Prose of James Thomson (B. V.).* Edited by William David Schaefer. Berkeley: University of California Press, 1967.

Toomer, Jean, *Cane.* Edited by Darwin Turnder. New York: W. W. Norton, 1988. First published by Boni & Liveright, 1923.

Unterecker, John. "The Architecture of *"The Bridge."* In *The Merrill Studies in "The Bridge."* Edited by David R. Clark. Columbus: Charles E. Merrill Publishing Company, 1970.

———. *Voyager: A Life of Hart Crane.* New York: Farrar, Straus and Giroux, 1969.

Voelcker, Hunce. *The Hart Crane Voyages.* Introduction by Samuel Loveman. New York: The Brownstone Press, 1967.

Weber, Brom. *Hart Crane: A Biographical and Critical Study.* New York: The Bodley Press, 1948.

Winters, Yvor. "The Significance of *The Bridge* by Hart Crane, or What Are We to Think of Professor X?" In *On Modern Poets.* New York: New Directions, 1943.

Wordsworth, William. "Preface to *Lyrical Ballads.*" In *The Selected Poetry and Prose of Wordsworth.* Edited by Geoffrey Hartman. New York: New American Library, 1970.

Yingling, E. Thomas. *Hart Crane and the Homosexual Text: New Thresholds, New Anatomies.* Chicago: University of Chicago Press, 1990.

15

Afterword to Theodore Sturgeon's *Argyll*

New York City
June 10th, 1993

Dear Noël,

And after a cloudburst yesterday, when the city gutters flushed with rain, New York has finally turned over—today—into the heat and drench of summer. It was an odd and intensely involving experience, then, to reread the manuscript you sent me—Theodore Sturgeon's autobiographical account of his relation with his stepfather—that took me back, with such clarity, to a time before my own birth, the 1920s and '30s of our fast-fading century, to a borough of the city, Staten Island, I've only rarely visited, and to a Philadelphia wholly outside my experience.

This account of a battle royal, between a man—William Dicky Sturgeon—and a boy—Edward Hamilton Waldo—by the end of which neither has his own name any more, and both, one suspects, have been wounded to the depths of their very souls, is remarkable in so many ways. First, as with everything Sturgeon turned his pen to, I want simply to say what an extraordinary piece of writing it is! Cool, matter of fact, clear, and, like everything Sturgeon wrote, vivid; its cumulative effect is devastating.

To step back from it a moment, it is all too easy to see a brilliant stepfather, from the Depression '30s, who just didn't quite believe children were human. For one thing, they weren't supposed to have money—and if they did, as their parent, you were supposed to take it from them. (By law, after all, it was yours.) And because Argyll was intelligent, it was easier to wheedle it out of young Ted and Peter with promises to return it, later flagrantly broken, than to snatch it away brutally. Children were not supposed to be extraordinary, stand out, and attract attention to themselves. And when they did, you got rid of the offending object, threw it away, forbade them to reenter the situation, or simply chucked the problem. You fed and housed your child—and put the fear of God in him, by inculcating into him fear and respect for you. That is being a good father —and Argyll was a good father. There were so many of them in those days. (They are the fathers of armies.) But what was the effect on an equally brilliant and sensitive child?

A great wound to his self-confidence?

A crippling block to his ability to express anger directly and straightfor-wardly, so that it ultimately and repeatedly had to turn back against himself?

Well, someone might ask: But what does it matter if a merchant marine man, or a bulldozer operator, or a hotel manager, or even a guitar player is a little short on self-esteem, a bit too accommodating and polite? It just means he'll never get in trouble with the law; frankly, you've done the guy a favor, haven't you . . . ?

But if the merchant marine man, the bulldozer operator, the hotel manager, the guitar player is also one of the great short story writers—one of the mas-ter science fiction writers—of his age and country, well . . . then, it means a writer's career punctuated by painful periods of writer's block. It means that, at least once, he must produce a text or texts like this—and it is finally a very painful text—to extricate himself from the tortuous labyrinths of transference and self-subversion that have been woven by that severe childhood around him.

We're very fortunate to have it.

Like Franz Kafka's famous "Letter to His Father," it is a meticulous exam-ination of the relation between two people that one, the father, would say is centered on love, responsibility, and guidance, while the other can see in it only pain, fear, denial, scorn, betrayal, and humiliation. You may recall that Kafka's extraordinary letter, written in November of 1919, began when Kafka's father asked him, "But why do you always tell me you are so afraid of me?" and Kafka realized that he had no answer—because he was *too* afraid!

This is the moment of realization when we see that the labyrinth we have been enclosed in is much more complicated than the labyrinth maker ever suspected; that we have been building it from the inside just as vigorously as authority has been building it from without; and that, if we ever wish to escape it, we must begin a mighty examination and articulation of the intricacies it has thus acquired in its history.

Kafka never did find his way out. His letter was never delivered.

But what Sturgeon's letter shows us—the underpinning for this essay, written thirteen years later at the prompting of his psychotherapist—is that what waits at the labyrinth's entrance, like Ariadne with her ball of thread, is love.

In that, it is like so many of Sturgeon's wonderful stories. And that itself is a fine and luminous insight.

In its quiet and cumulative amassing of detail after detail, incident after incident, "Argyll" is fearful and moving.[1]

Thank you for sharing it with me before publication.

With gratitude,
Samuel R. Delany

—1993
New York City

NOTE

1. And still is: Rarely have I so identified with a tale of an emotionally tyrannical father who was once such a good provider (SRD, 2020).

16

Interview

Questions by Felice Picano

Felice Picano: Why science fiction? I mean we all read it when we were adolescents, but how did you decide this was your literary medium?

Samuel R. Delany: Of course we don't all read it. My career as a serious critic of science fiction started in 1975 at SUNY Buffalo with a chance to study the hard-edged differences between the reading processes of those who did read it and those who didn't. My basic discovery from that research was that written science fiction is a distinct sub-language of the greater language we all speak and read. Some of us learn it—as you say, usually in childhood or adolescence, when our language learning abilities are at their widest—and some of us don't. Paradoxically, it has little or nothing to do with any aptitude for science.

Whether or not we learn how to read science fiction may influence how we come to feel about science later on. But how we feel about science has nothing to do with whether or not we can read science fiction. Learning that these arrows ran in certain directions and not in others was very exciting for me in the mid-1970s.

But by then I *was* a science fiction writer. How I became one, you can read in my autobiography, *The Motion of Light in Water* (1988). Actually, as stories go, it's rather happenstance. I'd tried writing all sorts of things. The science fiction, however, sold. The other things didn't.[1] One day at twenty-one I realized that I'd written—and published—three SF novels already and was working on my fourth. Therefore I must be a science fiction writer.

But it was never something I decided I wanted to become.

FP: What kind of encouragement/discouragement did you get from those around you when you began writing SF?

SRD: When, in my late adolescence, it became clear I was seriously interested in writing, my parents were pretty mixed in their feelings. Both respected education greatly. In the 1910s and '20s, my father's father had been the vice-chancellor (vice principle, it was called then) of a black, southern college, Saint Augustine's. Many of his nine brothers and sisters had taught there. My mother enjoyed art, music, and literature. Like many black people at that time, they tended to see the actual writing of books as the salvation of the race and a process akin to magic. On the other hand, my father was a businessman (he ran a moderately successful Harlem funeral establishment), and was pretty clear on the limited possibilities of earning a living from writing. He couldn't have been less sanguine about writing as a career choice for me if I'd wanted to be an actor! When I won this or that high school literary contest, or received one or another scholarship because of my writing, my parents were very proud. But they were also worried—especially my father. So I got a lot of "mixed messages."

One of my father's closest friends, however, was a black writer of young people's books about black adolescents growing up in the American Midwest: Jesse Jackson. (No relation to the politician.) He and his family lived in the apartment directly below ours, from the time I was fifteen on. Jesse's regular income came from editing for a firm publishing immense economics reference books; he used to call them "door stoppers." But Jesse was always a vocal advocate of my creative work to my father. He predicted I would be in print before I was of age to vote—that was twenty-one, back then. His support kept a good deal of the tension down that might otherwise have exploded into something quite ugly—as, from time to time, the tensions between my father and me could.

My father died when I was eighteen, weeks after I started City College.[2]

But once my first novel was actually published—when I was twenty (Jesse's prediction had come true)—my mother, always the more pacific personality, was as supportive of my writing as possible. Though as far as I know, she never really read any of it.

She bought my books, displayed them in her house, gave them away as presents to everyone else in the family, and collected clippings of my reviews. But she was one of those people who simply had never learned to read science fiction.

FP: Did anyone say, "Wait a minute, how come you're not writing about being black in American Society Today?"

SRD: Eventually, yes—a few, white acquaintances. Science fiction was a pretty liberal field during the 1940s and '50s, however. And though some of those liberal gestures, by the '60s, looked pretty troglodytic, if you compare them to what else was going on at the same time, they come off pretty well.

Also, I was doing the best I could: my first SF novel to attract any serious attention, *Babel-17* (1966), featured a Chinese woman for its main character. The hero of my most popular novel within the SF field, *Nova* (1968), has a Senegalese mother and a Norwegian father. Because of that, and no other reason (the correspondence with my agent is still extant), John W. Campbell, one of the great editors in the field but also one of the field's most politically conservative voices, rejected the novel for serialization in *Analog Magazine*. The editor who took over *Analog* on Campbell's death, Ben Bova, several times told me that whenever he needed a reminder of just how stupid the most intelligent of us could be, he'd take out Campbell's rejection letter and reread it.

The hero of my most commercially successful novel, *Dhalgren*, is a half-breed American Indian. Many of the major characters in the book are black: I've always tended to deal with "marginal" groups of one sort or another—and black critics have been more appreciative of this than not.

FP: Were other pressures applied to you as you began to write? Say, to be another Richard Wright, or to be the African-American Saul Bellow?

SRD: No, not really—at least not seriously. The very fact that I was writing science fiction probably put me outside the scope of people—black or white—who would have been likely to offer such a criticism.

FP: How early on in your work did you figure out you could use science fiction analogues for homosexuals in your writing (the "goldens" in "The Star Pit," say, in 1966—or were there earlier versions?) . . .

SRD: I have to confess that I never saw—at least when I was writing it—the galaxy-hopping "golden" in "The Star Pit" as an analogue for gay men and women. That you did—or do—only confirms something I've been saying as a critic for some time: What we need is not so much radical writers as we need radical readers! And, regardless of my intentions, a very good reading that is!

The golden are marginal; they are hopelessly exploited by the rest of the society. But through that exploitation, they get to do things and see things and learn things that the rest of the society doesn't—and the result is that society both fears them and is hopelessly jealous of them.

What I had in mind at the time I wrote it—the tale is basically about Ratlitt and Allegra, the two deeply wounded children who desperately want to be golden, more than anything else in the world—was all the white kids in the '60s, when I wrote the story, who used to come up and explain to me, how, "Man, I'm really black! I mean, I don't feel like a white person. My soul is black . . . ," and would then wonder why I, a black person, was not impressed.

Those were the white folks who would suddenly back up and say, "Wait a minute, how come you're not writing about being Black in American Society Today?" Nobody else did.

FP: How much of your work did you see as subversive to the received WASP version of life? How much—or which particular works—were the most purely subversive"?

SRD: How much of my work is subversive? Oh, between eighty-seven and eighty-seven and a half-percent—seriously, I'm just not sure how to answer that.

The first story I wrote that I knew would be taken as dealing with an analogue for homosexuality was a 1966 story called "Aye, and Gomorrah." It won a Nebula Award for best SF short story of its year—and I was very surprised. But it emboldened me to write another story dealing with homosexuality, not indirectly, but directly, called "Time Considered as a Helix of Semi-Precious Stones." A year later that story won me another Nebula Award—and a Hugo. I say this story was direct—but it was also subtle: the word "homosexuality" is not used in it. But clearly the relation between the young boy Hawk and the narrator was once a sexual one. And a sexual one involving extreme sadomasochism: the boy carries his scars proudly from their time together and clearly is still in love with the narrator. It's pretty heady stuff, considering it was written a year before Stonewall.

The SFWA (Science Fiction Writers of America), who granted these stories their awards, is not a particularly gay organization; in fact, I'd go so far as to say it probably has a smaller percentage of gay members than most artistic guilds. But the awards that it granted—mirrored by the Hugo award, which is voted on by the general science fiction readership—was the first inkling I had of the overwhelming *hunger* of heterosexuals to know about what is going on within the realms of homosexuality!

Lesbianism is a huge and pervasive factor in straight male sexual fantasies. We know from the flood of K/S[3] pornography that gay male sexual practices form a great part of the sexual fantasizing of many heterosexual women. I've said it often: If gay men and women didn't exist, heterosexual men and women would have invented us!

Again, I think the subversiveness or the conservatism is in the reading, not in the writing. I've seen people give extremely conservative readings to pieces I thought were quite subversive. And I've seen people give highly subversive readings to pieces I didn't see as particularly subversive at all.

FP: My introduction to your work was *Dhalgren*, which I believe was a paperback bestseller for years. In the Bay Area in the mid-1970s it was sort of a cult book. How did reaching that new, much wider audience affect your following work?

SRD: It's sobering just how little effect writing a million-copy-seller actually has on a writer. For a couple of years or so your income goes up to an ordinary middle-class standard. You have a slightly easier time placing new work, even though from time to time your editor hints, ever so gently, it would be nice if your next book were in the same vein as the one that sold so well. Still, if it isn't, nobody sends goons around in the night to terrorize you and your lover.

Instead of the five or six fan letters you might receive during the entire life of a book that sells between sixty and ninety thousand copies in paperback, you get five or six letters a month—possibly five or six a week for the first two or three months of sales.

That's about it.

But unless the book gets a certain amount of intelligent, critical attention as well, the numbers really don't mean too much—unless those sales escalate into the realm of mega-bestseller: the Stephen Kings, or the Robert Ludlums.

It's funny. The largest-selling writer of all time in the English language— beating out Stephen King, Robert Ludlum, Barbara Cartland, Shakespeare, *and* the Bible—is a woman named Rosemary Rogers. Her books began to appear about the same time King's did—and, commercially, they wipe King off the page and make him look like a piker. But her readers are ninety-nine percent women. Her genre is romance—she created the current romance genre to the same extent King created the modern horror genre. But I can go to visit a new university to give a lecture and not an English professor on the faculty will have even heard of her, much less have read a word she's written!

I'd think they'd want to simply check her out as a phenomenon in the language that's supposed to be their speciality, whether she was any good or not.

But they don't.

FP: *Tales of Nevèrÿon* and *Neveryóna* were, I was told at the time they came out, the first "Gay Science Fiction." True or false? How purposeful were you in writing them to fill that bill? How did those books succeed, or not succeed, in breaking new ground?

SRD: The first two Nevèrÿon books (1978, 1982) are no more gay than, say, *Dhalgren* (1974)—which, after all, has a fair amount of bisexuality in it. My own stories ". . . Aye, and Gomorrah" and "Time Considered as a Helix of Semi-Precious Stones," preceded the first Nevèrÿon book by a decade. So the Nevèrÿon books don't have much in the line of credentials to be the first of anything.

The third and fourth books in the Nevèrÿon series, however, are a different story. The third volume, *Flight from Nevèrÿon* (1985), contains my 1984 novel "The Tale of Plagues and Carnivals," which, along with Paul Reed's *Facing It*, is the earliest novel to deal directly with AIDS in this country. The central story, "The

Mummer's Tale," is about homosexual prostitution. And the novel that fills up most of the fourth volume, "The Game of Time and Pain," is about gay sado-masochism and its effect on a politician who is working to end the institution of slavery in his country.

It's not really accurate to call the Nevèrÿon series "science fiction" at all. The stories come out of the tradition the late Fritz Leiber named "sword-and-sorcery," that swash-buckling genre that produced *Conan the Conqueror* and writers from Talbot Mundy and Edgar Rice Burroughs to Karl Edward Wagner and Michael Moorecock—though the writing and structuring of my tales is much closer in approach to, say, Isaak Dinesen, than it is to the traditional Gosh-Wow narrative of most sword-and-sorcery writers. Frankly, it leaves traditional sword-and-sorcery readers pretty confused the first time they try it.

Even if you've only encountered sword-and-sorcery through the Italian-made muscle epics that flooded the movie screens in the 1960s, we all realize it's a profoundly homoerotic genre—though the homosexuality is always latent and only suggested. It is also a profoundly sadomasochistic genre.

My enterprise was to bring these currents to the surface—and not in some blatant and blaring way. You know, the point of the story turns out to be that, once he's finished fighting off the barbarians, we catch Conan in skirts and eyeshadow waiting to be picked up at the local neolithic drag bar.

Rather, I wanted to ask some serious questions: How would a conscientious and considered predilection for whips, chains, and slave collars, say, influence a man who was actively and politically committed to ending slavery in his own country?

Although, really, in this case I don't think genre labels matter that much. If you're going to use them, I'd call Return to Nevèrÿon, my four-volume series, "fantasy" before I'd call it "science fiction." And I'd call it "sword-and-sorcery" before I'd call it "fantasy."

FP: The figure of older man/boy is a constant throughout your writing—*Triton*, *Nova*, "Star Pit," etc. How much of that is purposively reusing the Huck Finn/Nigger Jim and other young men/old men themes in American lit. And if that wasn't what it was about, was it standing in for gay relationships?

SRD: In my first half-a-dozen or so novels, that template—what we used to call the American Buddy Novel, which not only includes Huck and Jim but Natty Bumppo and Chingachgook from Cooper's Leatherstocking Tales—was precisely what I was trying to get away from.

From the time in 1960, when Leslie Fiedler published a chapter of his study *Love and Death in the American Novel* in the *New York Times Book Review* under the title "Come Back to the Raft, Huck Honey," it was clear to pretty much everybody that what these "buddy stories" were all doing (the most popular one since its 1957 publication was Kerouac's *On the Road*, about the narrator's transcendentally luminous "friendship" for Dean Moriarty/Neal Cassidy) was writing these tragic, homosexual love stories and then just incidentally either not mentioning the sex, or, worse, every once and a while throwing in something to convince the reader that the men were really straight, so it was all right for them to feel these overpowering emotions of longing and—hell, unnamed lust—after one another.

As a young gay reader, I felt betrayed by these stories—in their modern form—these (to quote D. H. Lawrence) "stark, stripped, human relationships of two men, deeper than the deeps of sex. Deeper than property, deeper than fatherhood, deeper than marriage, deeper than love."

I mean, *please!*

To gay readers, it was perfectly clear that it was only the proscription on the discussion of actual sex between men that made this endlessly unstated significance possible. I felt betrayed—I felt manipulated by them. Also, there were too many of them for the form to be aesthetically interesting anymore. And I resolved well before I hit twenty-one that if I ever wrote about such relationships, I would not suppress the sexuality.

Now what you discover is that such templates are much more pervasive than we give them credit for. Some of this begins, one way or the other, any time two men are presented as any sort of friends at all. But in both *Triton* and "The Star Pit," which you cite, the older man—Lawrence, in one case, and the narrator, Vyme, in the other—has had considerable homosexual experience, and is probably quite aware of what part that does or does not play in his relationship with the younger man. (In "The Star Pit," it's only implied; still, that's the point of the turn-about in the sex of Polotcki, and the bisexual "procreation groups" we learn both Vyme and Sandy have been involved with.) Lawrence, an older gay man, is sincerely fond of Bron, a hopelessly insensitive, younger heterosexual male, with endless personality problems. But Lawrence's gayness is not hidden; Lawrence is not letting himself be exploited by Bron through having to hide his gayness; and, in the end, heterosexual Bron is the one who ends up miserable, while Lawrence's story comes to a dazzlingly fairy-tale-like conclusion: now somewhere in his seventies, he becomes a rock star of incredible popularity, with a gorgeous young lover—and a set of male groupies—just mad for men of sixty-plus years and over!

(You could *only* do it in science fiction!)

So, no; these are *not* stand-ins for gay men. They *are* gay men—or they are bisexual men with a reasonable amount of gay experience, experience that influences both what they do and how things turn out for them.

FP: Can SF explore gay relationships more easily or more stylishly than other genres of non-genre writing?

SRD: I don't think so. I've always considered science fiction to be an actual form, like drama or poetry. The question has the structure, in my mind, of: "Can poetry explore gay relations more easily than novels? Can short stories explore gay relationships more easily than newspaper reporting?"

I don't see the specifically generic aspects of SF impinging on the content of the stories in the way your question suggests.

FP: *Stars in My Pocket* seems to be both a culmination of your previous work and a new direction. It was sold as the first part of a two-novel work. Is there a second part? If so, when can we hope to read it?

SRD: I'm still working on the second volume. When it's going to be finished, I can't say for certain. At my most optimistic, I think I might finish it in two or three years. But I've been working on it almost nine years now.

The pair of novels, which were conceived at the same time in the late 1970s, were intended to work as an allegory of the gay world—but both were inspired by a particular gay relationship I was then in; both were conceived well before the advent of AIDS. Shortly after I finished the first volume, that eight-year relationship ended—and AIDS became a reality which reshaped and refocused a lot of thinking about the gay world.[4]

Since then, I've conceived and executed the entire Return to Nevèrÿon series—seventeen hundred pages, in the most recent British edition—as well as two more novels (*They Fly at Ciron*, which appeared this past summer; and *Atlantis: Model 1924*, part of which just appeared in the current *Kenyon Review*). Yes, I still think the second volume in the Stars diptych would be worthwhile writing—but you can understand how it might look quite different, given the change of context, simply in terms of the urgency one feels to pursue it, nine —or, really, more than a dozen—years on.

FP: Do you want to talk about what happened with Bantam, with whom, I understand, you are no longer publishing and yet for whom you made a great deal of money in the past?

SRD: Like so many such situations, it's rather complex. I don't know if a brief discussion can reflect what the situation was at all. For one thing, I don't even think of it primarily as a situation with Bantam, but rather as a situation that obtained at B. Dalton and Waldenbooks, between 1985 and 1987—just before B. Dalton was bought by Barnes & Noble. Basically what happened is that Bantam printed and distributed many too many copies of the hardcover of *Stars in My Pocket Like Grains of Sand* over the Christmas 1984–85 season: twenty-eight thousand, to be exact, most of which went to B. Dalton and Walden. (If my own experience is a guide, many of those books never even got put out on the shelves, but simply remained in stock until they were sent back—that was certainly the case with Dalton in the Village, here in New York.) At the end of the season, the returns were fifty-four percent. And the book finally came in at about thirteen thousand copies sold in hardcover.

At the time Bantam was doing incredibly well with Louis L'Amour in hardcover—he was number one on the bestseller list for almost three years. And Bantam hoped to do with science fiction what it had done with westerns. One Bantam official was quoted as saying, "Bantam Books is not interested in doing hardcover books that sell under twenty thousand copies!" So my book (at only thirteen thousand copies) was considered pretty much a disaster—at least for the first seven or eight months of the program.

But after they'd done seven or eight more SF titles in hardcover, they realized they just were not going to reach sales of that size. After the four, six, or eight thousand copies they were selling of their other SF books, my thirteen thousand copies began to look pretty good. After all, it was one of the five best-selling hardcover SF novels of its year.

And of those five, certainly it had received the best critical reception.

Still, as I've explained, my own energies had all, by now, turned toward the Nevèrÿon series. These were gay; these were experimental. They were an odd and eccentric breed of fantasy, "sword-and-sorcery," which I was subverting by—I hoped—richly poeticizing its surface through both analysis and description and, at the same time, making its covert homosexuality and sadomasochistic currents overt and conscientious—all of which, I have to say, made traditional readers of sword-and-sorcery pretty uncomfortable. Though it delighted others. Bantam was publishing them, but they were also waiting for me to do another science fiction novel.

When the third Nevèrÿon volume, *Flight from Nevèrÿon*, came out in April 1985, containing my AIDS novel "The Tale of Plagues and Carnivals," that kind of did it for both Walden and Dalton's—as well as Bantam.

At about this time, at a science fiction convention in Madison, Wisconsin, in the discussion session after a panel on "Gay Science Fiction," a woman in her thirties, who explained she was a manager of a B. Dalton bookstore in a rural shopping mall, commented that her supervisor had told her that, if she was ever asked for books by Samuel Delany, Tannith Lee, or Barbara Hambley, she should tell the customer that B. Dalton did not stock these authors.

The word at Dalton and Walden was that I was "no longer a commercial writer" but was now writing "experimental" material, with a large gay component. Dalton and Walden both announced that they were no longer taking any Delany.

Did the gay content of the new books have anything to do with this decision? Certainly. But was it overt homophobia—a concerted decision not to stock books by writers dealing with gay themes? Urban outlets of both Dalton and Walden have sizable Gay Studies sections (But rural Daltons do not.) Nevertheless, the only thing the three authors cited by the supervisor have in common is that we all dealt regularly with gay material.

When I completed the fourth volume of the Nevèrÿon series, *Return to Nevèr-ÿon*, Bantam surprised me by saying they were not even interested in reading the new manuscript.

Now the actual sales on the Nevèrÿon series, once you looked at the figures, were pretty good: two hundred fifty thousand, over three printings, for the first volume, *Tales of Nevèrÿon*. Two hundred fifteen thousand for the second volume, *Neveryóna*. (Though it was substantially less than the first, sixty-five thousand of that was in a $8.95 trade paperback, and a hundred thousand (roughly) were in a $2.95 mass market edition, so that it actually made, in profits, substantially more than the first volume.) The third volume, *Flight from Nevèrÿon*—the one with the AIDS novel—sold only eighty-five thousand copies.

But the initial print run of one hundred fifty thousand copies on the third volume had been slashed in half to seventy-five thousand when a Bantam executive learned that the topic of the book was AIDS. It was probably not a bad idea: shortly afterward, Barnes & Noble cut *their* order in half (from twenty-thousand to ten thousand) when they too learned that the book reflected gay themes. I gather this was standard procedure around the chain bookstores. Even with the slashed order, however, eventually the book went back to press for a second printing of fifteen thousand copies. The net sales on the book were on the order of eight-five thousand.

If you look at the packaging of any of the first three volumes, however, there is nothing to suggest either "gay" or—on the third volume—"AIDS" (not to mention: "experimental") about any of them.

When it was learned that Bantam had rejected the fourth volume unread, after reviewing the sales figures on the first three volumes Tor Books made a verbal offer of twenty thousand dollars for the fourth volume, sight unseen, through editor David Hartwell. In the course of negotiations, Tom Dougherty phoned the buyer at Dalton to ask how many copies of a new Delany he would take. That was when he—and I—found out that Dalton would be taking no Delany, because Delany had become "experimental" and "non-commercial." A very embarrassed Tom Dougherty explained, through Hartwell, that the offer had to be withdrawn. Sixty percent of Tor's sales were through Dalton's, and if I had become an author that Dalton would no longer stock, they simply could not afford to publish me.

The word "gay" was never mentioned in either the conversation between Dougherty and the Dalton buyer, or between Dougherty and Hartwell, or, indeed, between Hartwell and me. But now I understood *why* Bantam had declined to consider the book before.

A week later, the book was bought by Arbor House at ten thousand dollars for hardcover publication, since it could only be sold in independent book-stores, but would not be taken by the two major chains.

Meanwhile, the fallout from the Madison SF convention was a letter-writing campaign in the gay community to the gay press—and, indeed, to B. Dalton and Waldenbooks. Articles appeared in the gay press by gay journalist Loren Mcgregor (in San Francisco's *Time Out*) and in the SF community by straight journalist Charles Platt (in the fanzine *Thrust*), both of which were basically accurate. And a letter appeared in a number of outlets in the gay press by Camilla Decarnin. At just about the same time, Dalton was sold to Barnes & Noble, and the buying staff underwent a major shake-up.

The new buyer, in an informal phone conversation with Hartwell, called the situation appalling. Nevertheless, when the book was published by Arbor House, Arbor House changed the title to *The Bridge of Lost Desire* in order to dissociate it in the minds of buyers and book people from the "tainted" series to which it was, in fact, the fourth and concluding volume.

Dalton took three hundred copies—a gesture, certainly, but (equally certainly) a bit below the hundred thousand plus orders for the first two volumes, or even the fifty-odd thousand they'd taken on the third volume . . . !

In late 1987, a gay fan group, the Gaylaxians, learned of the situation and made a fairly large, if somewhat confused, stink about it. But they were a year or two too late; the situation had had its time in the gay press already, and had been resolved by the sale of B. Dalton to Barnes & Noble. (Not understanding that, for better or for worse, the situation had been resolved more than a year before, the Gaylaxians wrote accusing letters to Dalton and Waldenbooks and were answered by publicity people there, all of whom had been hired *after* the B & N sale, and who didn't even know what the situtation being referred to was about! From there, the Gaylaxians turned on me, briefly deciding the whole thing must have been something *I* had invented (!)—until I wrote them a couple of long letters, and sent along with them copies of some of the documents involved (i.e., copies of the articles from a year before). The letters were eventually published in their fanzine. Things kind of settled down. But today people who know of the situation at all tend to know of it from that particular '87 brouhaha.

At the time these situations were forming and resolving, one must bear in mind the same forces that had caused the sale of Dalton were sweeping mightily through the field of American publishing. In the mid-1980s, Bantam was bought by the German multinational Bertelsmann and merged with Double-day, Dell, and Delacourt. Staff was constantly changing. Publishing policies were constantly being revised. (This is when the effects of the notorious Thor Power Tool Decision first began to be felt in publishing.) Similar mergers happened at Viking-Penguin, which merged with New American Library, Random House, and Knopf. At the end of the '70s there were something like seventy-nine independent trade book publishers in New York City. Though there are now almost as many—if not more—imprints today, in terms of corporate independence there are only about fifteen. With these mergers, publishers were seized by what has been called "the blockbuster publishing mentality," and turned a much higher percentage of their efforts to far fewer highly commercial/low literary properties. Most professional writers' careers spanning those years were deeply affected, most for the worse. Books that had sold moderately well—or even, in some cases, very well—were now judged to be no longer profitable and were all but abandoned by their publishers. Over a three-month period in 1988, six SF titles of mine (among many, many other titles by many, many others writers), continuously in print from between four to twenty years, were put out of print by Bantam Books so that they could devote everything from warehouse and catalogue space to advertising and shipping costs to a few new projects that would prove more profitable.

There are three ways you can look at what happened, all of which are correct as far as they go—yet none of which completely exhausts the situation.

(First) I was caught in a book-marketing situation which saw gay topics as substantially less commercial than straight topics; and because of this, I was, as such, punished for turning to openly gay subject matter. For a year and a half I was virtually blacklisted from the major chains—as were other such gay SF and fantasy writers, like Hambley and Lee, who also wrote about gay topics. It was only when pressure was put on Dalton, plus the fact that Dalton was sold, that they decided to take token numbers of my (and Hamley's and Lee's) books to avoid the ugly accusation of blatantly blacklisting gay SF and fantasy writers.

(Two) Because of the economic state of the country, the myriad publishing mergers of the early and middle 1980s (the German-based multinational corporation Bertelsmann's purchase of Bantam Books, Dell, Delacourt, and Doubleday, all of which now operate out of a single office at 666 Fifth Avenue) and concomitant changes in publishing policies, many quality writers who were making a decent living and commanding decent sales through the 1970s and '80s were suddenly demoted to the status of "mid-list writers," as publishers turned their attention and energies to "blockbuster bestsellers" and books that fell into the same category of (lack of) surface quality and sensational plot. It was not the gay content but the experimental form and literary surface that put my writing—along with that of many, many others—in this position, a position many writers across the country fell into, most with no gay commitments whatsoever.

(Three) Neither Bantam nor Dalton had any objections to my gay content, *per se.* Witness their initial support of *Stars in My Pocket Like Grains of Sand.* But fantasy is a far more conservative genre than science fiction. Bantam had not been able to support the experimental fantasy I have been doing for the last ten years. But I have burned no bridges at Bantam. The next time I do a science fiction novel (e.g., the second volume of *Stars in My Pocket*), they will be delighted to consider it seriously for publication, no matter how gay it is.

The fact is, Felice, all three analyses are equally true—and all three are equally partial.

There's even a fourth explanation—really an extension of explanation number two: the general contraction going on throughout the industry at the time. Between the time that the first Nevèrÿon volume was accepted and the time it was published, my editor left the company, and I became the property of the woman who had been her assistant. This woman was a very bright woman, but she was not a very strong personality. And just about the time the second volume in the series came out, she was fired—specifically because she wasn't able to hustle her books forward in the attention of the sales and marketing department. For the next six months, Bantam Books had no science fiction editor, and all the SF and fantasy was handled by a young publisher's assistant who had to oversee the SF with his left elbow while he did other things. Eventually he took over the SF, hired some editors, and created an extremely strong SF department. But I submitted the third volume of the series while the company was in this never-never-land state vis-à-vis the genre. I know he read the book. I know he liked the book, personally. But I also know he was completely at a loss how to market a collection of three sword-and-sorcery tales—part of a series—the longest of which was a direct analogue and commentary to the then-burgeoning AIDS situation! But the fact is, what happened to me has happened to any number of other writers whose editors have left the company—out from under them, as it were—even without the gay content.

But *with* the gay material, I didn't have a chance.

Shortly (i.e., eighteen months later, in 1987), Bantam returned the rights to me on all three Nevèrÿon books they owned—with some nudging. At first they didn't want to; but we said, "You've been jumping up and down now, saying how no homophobia is involved, but that the books are just not commercial. Now let's get your story straight, here." So, eventually, they got up off them. In the same period Arbor House was taken over by Avon/William Morrow, who sold *The Bridge of Lost Desire* to St. Martin's Press, who published it in paperback. The book went through two printings, but St. Martin's eventually discontinued its entire SF and fantasy line. There followed a three-year period during which I tried to get the rights back from Morrow, which involved a story as complicated as the one I've already told. Suffice it to say at the end of that time I succeeded. In that time the four books were published in England by HarperCollins/Grafton Books, with the title of the fourth put back as *Return to Nevèrÿon*.

In the meantime, the University of Minnesota Press contracted to do the four Nevèrÿon books. Then most of the senior staff was fired—and the result was that the project was held up for two years, and finally declined, even though contracts had been drawn up (though not signed). Basically, they fell victim to the same forces that were shaking everything else up and contracting publishing venues all around.

Recently, Wesleyan University Press took over the project. The first two books have just been released. I'm wholly pleased with how they are handling them. Whatever else you can say about them, Wesleyan is marketing and packaging the books as what they are—serious fiction with overt gay concerns and literary worth. They are not (as Bantam tried mightily to do) suppressing the literary side of the works in the packaging in order to make them commercially acceptable, nor are they suppressing the gay content to make them appeal to some notion of a mass readership.

Now we sit back and see if anybody buys them.

Many writers were hurt during the 1980s by a process that also, yes, hurt me. Because of the gay material in my books, and because of their seriousness, editors and readers have felt the books were important enough to rescue. That means I have been very, very lucky. Such rescues have not happened to everyone.

FP: Do you think that gay lit is developing in the right direction? What about Afro-American lit? What about gay/lesbian SF? What has or hasn't been done in the latter that you'd like to read?

SRD: What I want to read in all areas of writing are books and stories that make me go, "Wow!" Now that's a complex "Wow!"—and I can take it apart for you a little. I want a book or a story that, in the first few paragraphs or pages, makes me say: "Hey—this is really good!"

Then, when I close it, I want to say: "You know, it was even *better* than I *thought* it was going to be."

"*Macht Neues*" Wagner wrote to Liszt back in the 1850s—"Make it new!" Sixty-five years later Pound was quoting him in *Blast*!

In the 1920s, Cocteau said: "*Etonnez moi!*"—Astonish me!

Well, I'm looking for the same thing. I want to be astonished. But because what I want is going to be new, there's no way I can tell other writers—or even suggest to other writers—what they should be writing about.

Professional discussions of mysteries and science fiction are shot through with the pervasive, dull, deadening rhetoric of craft and competency. But a competent story is something only an editor cares about—and only when he or she is swamped with bad ones. Readers don't. Competent stories are stories readers read three to thirteen pages of then put down because they are without interest. The notion of a competent story is as silly as the notion of a competent poem. It's the astonishing you're after—or nothing.

At fifty-one, I confess, I have my suspicions about how to create such astonishment. It takes extremely clear observation of the world around you. And it involves extreme care in the language you choose to recount those observation. Care and clarity are always rare—that's why they can still astonish.

Randall Kenan's story "What Are Days" (1992) is an astonishing tale. So is Ethan Canin's "Emperor of the Air" (1985). Linda Shore's "The Horse" (1983) is astonishing. Guy Davenport's "*O Godjo Niglo*" (1983) is an astonishing tale.

In all the areas you cite, I'd like to read more stories that give me the same order of "Wow!" these do.

FP: The SF I've lately read in most of the popular magazines (*Amazing*, etc.) over the past four or five years seems to be seriously backtracking from the stylistic invention, structural creativity, and sheer imagination that character- ized the best SF of the 1970s. I find it pretty boring—definitely not in any way mind-stretching in its subject matter or ideas—even when it's well written. Do you agree? And if so, why is this happening?

SRD: I'm not sure I do. SF writers like Lucius Shepard, Karen Joy Fowler, Maureen McHugh, and Geoff Ryman have all produced their share of "Wow!- ers," at least for me. But, I confess, I haven't read as much science fiction in the last—say—half dozen years as I would have liked to. Part of the price you pay for being a professor is that you only have time to read the things you teach. But certainly your criticism is one I've heard before.

FP: Could this have to do with SF writers wanting to be thought of as "writers" first? (Few are: yourself, Le Guin, Ellison.) And does the need to be literarily accepted sound the death knell for SF?

SRD: I'm a little surprised to hear that one from you. It's the same argument, you know, as the one that laments: Once blacks start getting an education, acceptable housing, and decent paying jobs, won't that sound the death knell for jazz—and the general joys of black culture?

Give me a break.

The first half of that "Wow!" I spoke of, whether in science fiction or any- where else, the half that comes with the first few sentences or paragraphs or pages of the story, comes from the "style"—the energy of observation, as in the shape of the sentences and the choice of the words. Style is the first signal that the faculties of observation may just be, here, tuned a little higher than usual.

The second half of that "Wow!" is produced by the richness of structure.

Now, there are stories that produce the second half of that "Wow!" without producing the first. (And, Lord knows, there are enough that never produce either.) But these stories don't make it into the aesthetic halls of fame any more than the stories that produce the first half without the second.

What I think your question loses sight of is that *most* people who want to be thought of as writers don't succeed—at least in the long run—whether they start off in science fiction *or* in literature. That includes many of us—hell, *most* of us—who are published! It includes many of us who get a great deal of serious-sounding praise throughout our careers. What that means is—gay, straight, black, white, not to mention whatever genre you practice—all we can do is look closely, write carefully.

What we look at doesn't have to be out there in the real world, either. It can be an imaginary situation we choose to observe just as easily as we do a real one. In that case the intensity of observation becomes one with the imagination itself. Still, it *feels* like observing!

And we can pretty much forget about everything else.

—*November 14, 1993*
New York City

NOTES

1. Many of my early pieces were eventually lost by a very unhappy stroke of chance, part of which is discussed in *The Motion of Light in Water*.

2. On October 6, 1960, my father died of lung cancer at Harlem Hospital, where I was born.

3. K/S pornography expands to Kirk/Spock pornography and was an early and extremely popular form of fan fiction.

4. Shortly after this I stopped trying to write a sequel to *Stars in My Pocket Like Grains of Sand* and wrote a mainstream book called *The Mad Man* (1995) that deals with the same material directly. Some readers have recognized this book's relation to the earlier book, and so far that has been enough for me.

5. More accurately, we had been mid-list writers for twenty-plus years, but now mid-list writers suffered a change of status. Until then we'd been writers on the way up; now we were seen as writers on the way out. My personal way of handling this was to take the next university position offered to me—in my case a full professorship in the Comparative Literature Department of the University of Massachusetts at Amherst. This followed directly from my having been visiting Butler Chair Professor at SUNY Buffalo in 1975 and term-long fellowships at the University of Wisconsin's Center for 20th Century Studies and Cornell University's Andrew D. White House.

17

The *Loft* Interview

If you had to characterize yourself as a writer—for some prospective students in a creative writing workshop—how would you do it?

Samuel R. Delany: I'm a pretty cerebral writer. I enjoy theory and theorizing. For me, reading is something you do in your head. So is writing—largely. Having said that, the kind of theory I like is the sort that makes you do something—do something to the text you have in front of you that you're trying to write or rewrite. Something to make it better.

For me, the most interesting writing is born in the tension between imagination and observation. The famous creative writing workshop dictum "Write what you know" is only half the story. I'd say, rather, use what you know to make what you don't know come alive, stand up, and quiver.

There's a tendency for American writers to dismiss the theoretical, even the critical. But that strikes me as a pretty silly pose.

Whether we like it or not, writers are intellectuals. Now and again some primitive writers actually produce some interesting work. But the general stance of so many academic creative writers—"I just want to tell a good story"—is so patently insincere, and so clearly not what they're doing at all, that it's important for young writers to see another approach from time to time.

Most of your published writing has been science fiction—or sword-and-sorcery, a kind of fantasy. A lot of your work is also known for its exploration of alternative sexualities. As a writer, which of these represents your center?

SRD: I'm not sure I have a center. The illusory nature of most ideas of centrality is one of my favorite theories these days. Still, in one set of stories I tried to examine some of the real (and by "real" I mean political) problems the idea of sadomasochism brings up. They're the ones I'm still most likely to direct readers toward when they ask that sort of question.

What is fiction—realistic, genre, and literary—and how does it function?

SRD: Fiction exists as a complex of expectations. As soon as one writes, "The marquis went out at five o'clock . . ."[1] the problem is not then that you don't know what to write next. Rather, you have an immense choice of things you can follow it with. But an equal or greater number of things will produce, in those things that follow that sentence, a tiny, almost minuscule feeling of upset, violation, and the unexpected: "An anvil fell on his head from the roof and killed him." Or, "At that moment the Titanic sank." The problem is that the sense of expectation violated can be just as pleasurable, or even more so, than the sense of expectations fulfilled. And as soon as one choice is made (whether the writer goes with expectation or violation), a new set of expectations opens before the reader/writer. Which will the writer choose to develop: the sense of violation or the sense of fulfillment? But the expectations are always there, like a "tree search" lying in front of every writer (and reader) at the beginning (and all throughout, until the closing sentence) of every tale. The tree structure underlies every text. Any text represents only a specific path through it.

People who argue that genre fiction *per se* is valueless argue that, to be recognizably *of* a genre—science fiction, western, horror, mystery—the text must fulfill so many expectations that there is no room for the necessary violation that characterizes great literary works. The counter-argument is that, first, realistic fiction is just as much a set of expectations as any genre and requires just as much conformity to expectations to write. (People who argue against this usually see realistic fiction as simply "mirroring the world," rather than following a complex set of writerly expectations, the way traditional genre fiction does.) Second, the greater emphasis on *expectations fulfilled*, which, indeed, characterizes what we traditionally call genre fiction, means that when violations *are* worked into traditional genre tales, they register more forcefully on the reader than similar violations in tales belonging to the literary genres. Conversely, literary modernism, with its emphasis on *violation of expectation*, has produced an expectational field where violation is *so* expected that the differences in effect between *expectation met* and *expectation violated* are minimal. Thus, as an effective field, modernism (and by extension postmodern writing) is—affectively—moribund. I believe both arguments underestimate just how rich, complex, and vast the expectational field actually is. They're confining their view to the tiny range of expectations we call plot, character, style, theme, and setting. The fact is, there have always been moribund spots at every level: They're called clichés, and they've been with us at least since French printers coined the term. (*Cliché* means "clamp"; eighteenth-century newspaper printers would preset common words and phrases, keeping the type held in clamps and stored on a special shelf. When those phrases or words occurred in an article, the printer would find the right clamp, loose it, and slide the type into his type tray, instead of having to set the phrase letter by letter.) But the dismissal of entire genres as cliché rests on a blindness to the complexities of what it takes to ignite a genre and bring it life.

In any genre, literary or paraliterary, texts that go along merely fulfilling expectations register as moderately good or mediocre fiction, the sort one reads, more or less enjoys, and forgets. What strikes us as extraordinary, excellent, or superb fiction must fulfill some of those expectations and at the same time violate others. It's a very fancy dance of fulfillment and violation that produces the "Wow!" of wonder that greets a truly first-rate piece of writing—the inarguably wonderful story—no matter the genre it occurs in. The expectations I'm talking of cover everything from the progression of incidents that, in the course of the story, registers as plot, to the progression of sounds in the course of its sentences that registers as euphony. Such expectations occur at the level of metaphor and form, just as they occur at the level of character and motivation—and at many, many other levels besides.

The notion that plot or story exhausts what we can say about expectations across the whole range of narrative fiction, among all the various genres, literary and paraliteary, is about the same as the notion that, in music, the most expected note is always a fifth, fourth, or octave up or down within the same scale; thirds and sixths are also expected notes; second and sevenths are less expected; and the notes that lie outside the scale are unexpected. Now, with that as your only principle, create a rich subject for a Bach fugue, a pleasing melody for a Verdi aria, a satisfying row for a Schoenberg chamber symphony.

Taking off on Walter Pater's formalistic dictum, "All art aspires to the condition of music," philosophers like Richard Rorty and Donald Davidson are showing us that language is not less complex than music, but more so.

If you've got all those endless choices—expectations to fulfill or to violate—what do you do next?

SRD: It's easy to get *too* caught up in this tree-search model, of course. As early as 1958, in his groundbreaking little book *Syntactic Structures*, Noam Chomsky showed that the "end-stopped" (really, just another name for tree search) model of language was simply inadequate to generate all the well-formed sentences in a language. To counter this, Chomsky produces the model of "deep grammar," where complex sentences were generated on the surface of layers of vertical development. In terms of current computers, that means a tree search with a whole lot of loops, flags, go-tos, and other recursive features. But the fact is, we still don't have computers that, in a free dialogue situation, can generate original sentences of the range and complexity that your average six-year-old speaks easily. That suggests that even the deep grammar model is not adequate to language.

Indeed, it's the notion of language as well formed that seems to be the problem.

While a lucky few if us may write using only well-formed sentences more or less exclusively, none of us speaks only using well-formed sentences. In ordinary speech, some of us may come up, now and then, with three or four well-formed sentences in a row. But most of us, in actual dialogue situations, generate far more fragments and run-ons than we do well-formed sentences, with disagreements between verbs and nouns and incorrect tense progressions the norm rather than the rule, even though, if one of our ill-formed sentences is pulled out of context and we are asked to examined it carefully, we can usually tell that something or other is wrong with it, and often even what those errors are. "Grammar," even the most carefully constructed spoken grammar, as put together by the most careful linguists, is, in most actual speech situations, something that actual language aspires to, something that it approximates, but that spoken language is always falling short of—rather than something that controls language in some masterful way. And that goes for the language of the "competent speaker" as well as for the language of someone just learning it. (Of course the mistakes competent speakers make routinely are very different from the mistakes new learners make. But that is another topic.) Another way of saying the same thing: A grammar can never be a complete description of an actual language but must always be a reduction of it. One might go so far as to say: If you have a complete description of it, "it" is probably not a language but a much simpler communication object—a code. Still, another way of saying much the same is: It is only after we have an algorithm that can generate both well- and ill-formed sentences that we can likely develop a super-algorithm that can distinguish between them (i.e., a grammar); for, contrary to much linguistic speculation, a grammar is not something that, on some ideal Platonic level, is prior to the language and can be recovered by examination of specific language situations. If we ask a native informant what another native speaker means by a particular utterance, we will be given some translative paraphrase of, or possibly be told, "I don't know." If we ask, Did the second speaker say what she or he said correctly? We will be told, "Yes," "No," or "I'm not sure." It is from the second set of questions, or from assumptions that we know that the speaker was not making a mistake, from which we put together our grammar. But it is the idea of grammar that brings the idea of correctness and incorrectness to the language; the language is not founded on this idea. And the native informant will be able to paraphrase—that is, tell us the meaning of—many more utterances than those that, to a later question, he or she may deem correctly uttered. The informant will be able to give us at least some meanings of the pre-grammatical requests of little children, the slurred demands of the drunk, and the heated boasts or enthusiastic gossip or those speaking too quickly to care about the fine points of expression. The ability to understand a great deal of ill-formed language is not the accidental fallout of linguistic competence (i.e., the ability to speak in well-formed language), but is rather the anterior state necessary to have any concept of the well-formed in that language at all. Language does not follow grammar. Rather, grammar always follows language and is generated as an always partial description of what is actually there (i.e., a description of the parts there that are particularly useful in ways the concept of grammar defines). Thus, by extension, an algorithm that can generate only well-formed sentences but not generate both comprehensible (and incomprehensible) ill-formed sentences is simply not a complete language algorithm.

(If, provisionally, we describe science as the ability of the material world to excite highly logical and effective explanations for the way that world functions, then the ability to excite explanations, many or most of which will be illogical and incorrect, certainly precedes the ability to operationalize the logical and correct ones, through experimentation, picked out from among them.)

I may not be able to give you an immediate paraphrase of the meaning of these lines from Hart Crane's "Atlantis," taken from his poetic sequence *The Bridge*:

> Swift peal of secular light, intrinsic Myth
> Whose fell unshadow is death's utter wound,—
> O River-throated—iridescently upborn
> Through the bright drench and fabric of our veins . . .

But to ask whether, as a sentence, it is well-formed or ill-formed—whether it's correct or contains any mistakes of grammar, syntax, or diction—is simply hopeless. It's still poetry. More to our point, it's certainly still language—and language at a high and (to me and to many other readers) pleasurable level of expectational violation. Indeed, the only way to begin to talk about it productively as poetry is to read carefully the precise ways in which the language resists the fulfillment of expectations: "Swift peal of . . ." makes us expect, of course, ". . . thunder"—thunder being the mythic mode in which the god Zeus traditionally demonstrated his sacred power. But what we get instead is ". . . secular light." It's precisely the difference between the expected classically religious "thunder" and the actual violational "secular light" that starts to make the line—and, indeed, other words and phrases in the lines—meaningful, as it allows us to experience the specific play of differences that is Crane's vision.

Another semantic path that takes us more or less to the same place: The phrase "Swift peal of . . ." can also be easily completed within the field of expectation by the word "bells," which, in our society, would most likely be some form of church bells, and which again answers our expectations within an area of a religious aurality—which is violated by the phrase "secular light."

An even more extreme poetic example might be taken from Crane's friend, black writer Jean Toomer, who, at the start of the 1920s, experimented by writing a poem organized around a single letter ("Poem in C"):

> Go and see Carlowitz the Carthusian,
> Then pray bring the cartouche and place it
> On this cashmere, while I tell a story.
>
> The steaming casserole passed my way
> While I reclined beneath Castelay,
> Dreaming, ye gods, of castor oil . . .

Toomer also wrote, in a wholly invented language, "Sound Poem (1)":

> Mon sa me el karimoor,
> Ve dice kor, korrand ve deer,
> Leet vire or sand vite,
> Re sive tas tor;
> Ti tas tire or re sim bire,
> Rosan dire ras to por tantor,
> Dorosire, soron,
> Bas ber vind can sor, gosham,
> Mon sa me el, a som on oor.

To argue whether the first of these is well formed or not, or whether the second is actually language, is to miss the point: There is no way we can respond to them *other* than as language. In "Sound Poem (1)" there is no way to avoid hearing "wind" in the Germanic "vind," or hearing the line list toward English, with "vind can sor" ("wind can soar"). We hear "gosham" as a noun apostrophized, even though we don't know what noun it is. We hear the French forms of *my, pull,* and *say,* in *Mon, tire,* and *dire,* the Spanish for *the* in *el,* and the French for *cup of gold (tas d'or)* in *tas tor.* Words like *paramour* and *blackamoor* linger behind *karimoor,* and the proper name *Rosanne* lurks in *Rosan.* Indeed, the poem is nothing but semantic suggestions . . .

No, we can establish no easy narrative relations among the elements in either Toomer or Crane. But that is what both Crane and Toomer's poems have been crafted to do. And they do it not by avoiding language but by maneuvering—in all cases—fundamental language elements.

In all these cases, it is language expectations that are being violated—to highlight various poetic effects.

Robert Graves's delightful poem "¡Welcome to the Caves of Artá!" plays with the English/non-English all travelers in Europe are familiar with from local tourist brochures. And dialect poets from America's James Whitcomb Riley and Paul Lawrence Dunbar to Canada's William Henry Drummond have forced both meaning and emotion from the tensions in the speech of those challenged by one form or another of linguistic failing. Much linguistic work in the past has occurred within a paradigm which sees well-formed sentences as language but ill-formed sentences as, somehow, outside language (work that would certainly place Toomer's "Sound Poems," if not much of Crane, beyond the linguistic border); it sees them as some sort of non-language, when, on the one hand, the most cursory observation of actual language as it is spoken (or, with a poet such as Crane as a prime example, written) reveals that ill-formed sentences are just as much "within language" as are well-formed sentences, and are equally a part of the language process. The meticulous and careful readings by deconstructive critics of written language (writing: that bastion of the well-formed) reveal that the ideal derived from (but on which, rather, we mistakenly tend to ground) the whole notion of the "well-formed"—the sentence whose logic and clarity precludes all ambiguity, all semantic slippage—is itself an impossibility; that if such an ideal were achieved, rather than producing the phantasm of a perfect and mastered meaning, immediately present both to sender and to addressee, it would bring the communication process to a dead halt. The slippages, the ambiguities, the mistakes are finally what make language function in the first place. But even with this much of an overview of the ubiquity and utility of "mistakes," some will see that we are back at that very important notion of the violation of expectations—purposeful mistakes, if you will, that must reside in higher-level narrative grammars (even as slippages and ambiguities reside in well-formed sentences), if the narratives are to be in any way richly satisfying.

The much-beleaguered project of deconstruction can be looked at as a way of foregrounding the necessary and unavoidable "mistakes" (read: ambiguities, slippages) that reside in even the most well-formed sentences, and that must reside there if those sentences are to exist in time—and are to communicate anything at all over the time it takes to utter them.

But to return to our topic of fictive narrative: No one sits down and teaches you what fictive expectations are, much less which ones to conform to and which ones to violate.

Rarely have I been in a creative writing class that has talked about them at any length.

Where we learn them is from reading other fiction—other truly good fiction; and equally, or possible even more, from reading bad fiction.

Because violation has as much to do with success as does fulfillment, one "great work," or even a group of ideal "great works," can never teach you all the expectations at once. The artist, as T. S. Eliot wrote back in 1919 in "Tradition and the Individual Talent," must "familiarize himself with the tradition." In today's computer-oriented world, we might say: The artist (along with the critic) must, through broad exposure, become familiar with the overall structure of the possibilities of the tree . . .

And, remember, the tree (or the tradition) produces not only the good pieces but the bad pieces as well.

We learn those expectations not as a set of rules to follow or break—though, after a while, some writers can actually list a number of them in that form. Rather we learn them the way we learn a language when we live in another country: learn its grammar and syntax; learn what is expected of a competent speaker of that language.

And just to up the ante, languages change, including the language of fiction. What was perceived as violation yesterday is today a sedimented expectation. What was once an expectation is now honored only in the breach—or readers just giggle.

So while it's always good to know the history of the language you're speaking, and while that history will often tell you the reason why certain expectations are (or are not) still in place today—where, in effect, those expectations started out—the great stories of the past hold the key to writing the great stories of tomorrow no more than an oration by Cicero will tell a modern politician the specifics of what to mention in his next sound bite—even when Cicero and the modern politician can be seen as tackling similar problems.

All we can ever learn is what the language—of fiction, say—has been in the past. But every time we sit down to write a new text, we become involved, however blindly, in transforming the language into what it will be in the future.

—*1995*
New York

NOTE

1. The poet Paul Valéry used this phrase in the 1920s as an example of the quintessentially ordinary story. Eventually in 1951 Claude Mauriac wrote a novel with the title *The Marquise Went Out at Five.*

18

Note on Robert Hayden's
"Middle Passage"

Introduction to a reading from Robert Hayden's "Middle Passage" at the 92 Street Y on February 27, 1997, in honor of *The Norton Anthology of African American Literature*.

Robert Hayden was born in Detroit in August 1913. Sixty-six and a half years later in Ann Arbor, Michigan, not a hundred miles away, he died in 1980, in the same month—February—as we are in now. He was a much respected poet and professor of English at the University of Michigan.

Edited by Frederick Glaysher, Hayden's collected poems have recently been republished, also by Norton, with a new and very fine introduction by Arnold Rampersad, one of the editors of the anthology we honor this evening.

Hayden loved the black community, its history, its culture, as he loved the world community of art and artists. From reading his poems, I get a strong impression, however, that he was deeply aware that the center of love is desire, and that the center of desire is absence—so he also knew that a fundamental alienation lies between the poet and *whatever* the poet loves; and that the poem and the poet had to dwell—for long periods—within that absence, that alienation, if they were to return with anything capable of the necessary aesthetic shock.

More than any of the surface manifestations of political disagreement, this, I suspect, was what made Hayden uncomfortable with manifestos such as Larry Neal's—a memorable and powerful proclamation, also here in the *Norton Anthology of African American Literature* to inspire and instruct us—a 1968 manifesto that begins: "The Black Arts Movement is radically opposed to any concept of the artist that alienates him from his community . . ."

The 1962 poem by Robert Hayden I'm going to read tonight is baldly and simply the most extraordinary feat of prosopopoeia in the American tongue from this century's central decades.

In the 1920s when Hart Crane was struggling with his great poem-cycle *The Bridge*, one of Crane's early ambitions was to include, among its sections, one to center on a black Pullman porter named after John Brown that would be "a history of the Negro race." Eventually he abandoned this ambition and turned his poem to other things. The Hayden poem I shall be reading tonight always makes me realize *why* Crane couldn't do it—and how intelligent he was to leave that job to someone else:

Robert Hayden's "Middle Passage."

—*1997*

19

Beatitudes

§1. In his essay "Sodom: A Circuit Walk," Paul Hallam writes of a *Gay Sunshine* interview with Allen Ginsberg in which he "established, as a kind of Apostolic succession, his own homosexual decent from Whitman, by pointing out that he (Ginsberg) slept with Neal Cassady, who slept with Gavin Arthur, who slept with Edward Carpenter, who slept with Walt Whitman himself." Ginsberg added that this was "an interesting sort of thing to have as part of the mythology."

Well, back in 1965 I slept a couple of times with Chuck Bergman, then a very good-looking, thirty-five-year-old Lower East Side landlord, who from time to time was sleeping with Ginsberg . . .

Chuck had a charming Puerto Rican girlfriend on the side, but when he was in bed with me, *all* he talked about was screwing Ginsberg, who, at the time, was living in one of Chuck's apartments. Apparently the place was subject to lots of wear and tear, and Chuck was worried about his property, even though he was vastly honored by Ginsberg's presence—and quite happy to fall in bed with him. Chuck's constant talk of Ginsberg finally got kind of unnerving. I wonder if, at the time, I'd have felt differently had I known Carpenter and Whitman were in the picture.

§2. At the long-closed Endicott Book Shop on Columbus Avenue, in 1985 William Gass gave a reading from *Habitations of the Word*. William Gaddis came that evening. At one point a photographer who'd done some pictures of me the year before got a shot of all three of us, looking practically as if we knew each other. With the reading proper about to begin, I was in my seat in the fourth row when I looked up to see Ginsberg, squeezing between the files of folding wooden chairs on the green carpet. I was just about to move back, when he stepped squarely and heavily on my left foot—inadvertently, of course—and continued on to a chair further down.

Somehow that didn't seem the moment to run after him and mention that, twenty years before, we'd had a mutual bedmate.

§3. For the next half-dozen years I was able to say that was my only face-to-face encounter with Allen (this heavy-footed recomplication in our intimacy, I figured, allowed me to call him by his first name; everyone else did), though actually he'd been looking over my head.

That changed in February 1992, when I went down to Pennsylvania to participate in a gathering for the Associated Writing Programs. The '92 AWP Conference was honoring Ginsberg. I was part of a four-person panel on Gay Writing. At the reception upstairs in the Hershey Hotel after the panel was over, I was a bit surprised when, in his modest brown suit and tie, the scraggly-bearded Professor Ginsberg came over to me and, quite out of the blue, said: "Hello, Delany. How've you been?" At which point for me he became Ginsberg again, since I had become Delany—neither Chip (my nickname to all and sundry, or Samuel, the name for those who don't really know me).

"Fine," I said—and put my left foot quickly behind my right. "And you?"

We launched into a chat about the Cherry Valley Farm and the Naropa Institute, which he ran with Anne Waldman. Finally he reached into his canvas shoulder bag and handed me a flier for a series of readings he and Gwendolyn Brooks had organized of (mostly) black poets.

It was an impressive list. From me, certainly, he got points. Shortly someone called him to the front of the room where, with Ed Sanders and Tuli Kupferberg, the Fugs had reconvened for the event, and Ginsberg led the whole room in singing lustily along to some Blake "Songs of Innocence."

And all the Hills echoéd . . . we sang. And Sanders went around with a microphone and a portable tape recorder of his shoulder, recording us.

To this day I don't know who'd told Ginsberg what *my* name was.

The next and last time I saw him?

One warmish winter day in '94 or '95, when, a bit after three, I was leaving the office of Rhinoceros Books, one of my publishers, on 2nd Avenue just up from 43rd Street, I turned from under the gold marquee and saw Ginsberg walking among the afternoon crowd, in the same direction I was, eight or nine feet away.

I thought about saying hello, but finally held my peace, glancing at him now and then. (I assumed he didn't see or recognize me.) Soon, he was ahead of me. At 42nd Street he crossed over, to disappear among the people beyond the cars. Where might he have been be going? Where might he have been coming from? Would anyone ever find the note I made of it in my journal, with date and time? I thought about *The Poe Log* (Thomas and Jackson's *Documentary Life of Edgar Allan Poe 1809–1849*) and Jay Leda's *Melville Log*, which chronicle those writers day by day, sometimes hour by hour. Might my note solve, a century hence, some scholarly mystery about the poet's doings that day?

Ginsberg's death last month (April 5, 1997) means to me, more than anything, we are moving ahead into that century. We are leaving behind one which, for a hundred years, was *the* term for the indubitably new: It had named famous trains (The 20th Century Limited) and high-powered research centers (The Center for 20th Century Studies)—even as, with the 19th, the 18th, and the 17th, it gets ready to take its place in the past.

§4. An important psychological (if not sociological) transition the young writer must undergo is the mental move from envisioning a world where literature is produced Out There Somewhere, by mystical and mythical creatures who have no more reality than the characters in the books themselves, to a world where actual men and women write down those texts that so enthrall us—men and women who, besides having the talent or genius for making texts that delight, inform, or otherwise fascinate, and the ability to organize their lives so that these texts can find their way into print, are actual people, some Republicans, some Marxists, some with even stranger affiliations, living in actual houses, in specific neighborhoods. Some are even friends with one another. However Emily Dickinson effected such a mental transition in her second-story bedroom overlooking Main Street in Amherst, or how Hart Crane got through it in his tower room in his grandmother's house at 1709 115th Street in Cleveland, that transition alone is what allows the writer to harness her or his *Begeisterung* and write.

(The book that started the process off for me was Gertrude's Stein's endlessly wonderful *Autobiography of Alice B. Toklas*. I first read it in a Vintage paperback edition when, in 1959, I was seventeen.)

I had read Eliot and Pound and Hemingway and Cocteau; I had seen Picassos and Bracques and Matisses in the Museum of Modern Art. And two years before, in 1957, I had read—and practically memorized—the second issue of the *Evergreen Review*. But the notion—from the very first pages—that someone might have written to an author such as Henry James (as apparently once Alice did) about dramatizing *The Awkward Age*, and received a letter back was, until that moment, unthinkable to me . . . ! Living writers? Dead writers? It had never occurred to me that there was a fundamental difference between them, which had to do with their accessibility! Imagine learning that a writer like Gertrude Stein herself had a cleaning woman, Hélène, who sometimes cooked. (My *mother* had a cleaning woman who also did some cooking, Mary Boone, part of our household from my teenage years till nearly a decade after my father's death and I'd left home.) As various dinner parties and meetings with now this writer, now that, unrolled from Stein's simple-seeming prose, I got my first sense that writers were real people, and what's more many of them knew each other and liked or disliked one another—and perhaps, with the ones they liked, enjoyed spending time together, talked and hung out with one another.

At seventeen, going each day on the subway up to the Bronx High School of Science, taking every spare minute to write my short stories, just finishing my fourth book-length set of narrative scribblings, I knew now this world, real as it was, was somewhere on the other side of an ocean, and only decades in the past—which is to say, it had come much, much nearer.

For writers my age, a few years older, or up to a decade younger, who were not a part of it, the Beat Generation and its poetic cohort the San Francisco Renaissance (and, slightly less so, Black Mountain) was the first literary movement that we got to see, in the United States, up close.

(Stein had named the previous generation. "You are the lost generation," she had said to Hemingway, who had set her comment at the head of his first novel *The Sun Also Rises* [1926]. But the Lost Generation was specifically and insistently expatriate.)

What characterized the Beats more than anything else was (paradoxically) not that they were beat, but that they *were* a generation—far more so than, say, the often-chronicled "generation of 1914" or the target of Earnest Boyd's attack from the 1920s—"Aesthete: Model 1924," in the premiere edition of the *American Mercury*—on Gorham Munson, Hart Crane, Kenneth Burke, and Malcolm Cowley. These were a circle, yes. But a *generation* . . . ?

It's worthwhile asking, then, why the Beats took on their special relation to those of us who were five, ten, fifteen years their juniors . . .

§5. When I was twelve, and confined to my room, I wrote angrily in a green leatherette diary with a brass clip lock: "When you grow up, it's important to let your children *curse* around you!" My father, profligate with his "goddams" and occasional "shits" and even "nigger" (he was a black man living in Harlem and from the South), had sent me there because, in front of my Aunt Virginia, I'd let slip a "damn." His unfairness burned through my whole body.

What, in another five years, the Beats came to represent for us (yes, I *was* seventeen[1]—when, on one weekend, the student demonstrations against desegregation flared at Little Rock, the news of Sputnik's orbiting the earth broke across the world, and in that Saturday's *New York Times* Nathan Millstein's highly sympathetic review of Kerouac's *On the Road* launched it on its career as the novel that would end the '50s and usher in the '60s) were the good, the permissive, the ideally fair fathers, who said you *could* smoke dope, wear your old clothes, let your hair grow, and cuss as much as you wanted: Huck Finn's pap, without the drunken beatings.

Given that role, however, how could these free literary men and women, who grabbed our awareness by allowing the word to articulate any and every obscenity we kids could even consider (five years after *Howl* was dragged into the courts in 1956, I remember arguing with a dismissive post-thirty-year-old adult: "But don't you realize that was the first time a *poem* had been tried for obscenity since the fucking *Flowers of Evil*—and the *Saturday Review of Literature* never even *mentioned* it?"), possibly survive the process—not of *their* growing up (the Beats-and-associates who lived did that as well as they could), but of ours?

§6. I met my *first* Beat poet in the same seventeenth year—Diane di Prima. (At the time, of course, I didn't know she *was* Beat. Probably she didn't either.) I'd been told lots about her, that she was incredibly intelligent, that she was a physics major who'd switched to literature, that she was great friends with dancer Freddy Herko, that she had an extraordinary child named Jeanne (two syllables: as though "Jeanie"). When, one evening, she came upstairs from the printing shop where, with LeRoi Jones, she was putting together *Unmuzzled Ox* to drop in and sit, in one of the wooden folding chairs, in the front row (to the left) for the play and poetry reading I was directing and taking part in up at the Coffee Gallery (second floor, same address), she was distant, a bit gawky, certainly not very approachable—although, during the wine and soda afterward, I tried to be friendly.

She left quickly.

I doubt she was particularly impressed with the (most generous thing I can call it) neo-classical tone of the evening.

And she never knew that night she was speaking with a young man who had bought her first book[2] at the Eighth Street Bookshop and knew poems from it by heart:

> Monos they say
> could never have
> a lover.
>
> They say men turned
> to earth who touched
> his flesh.
>
> They say
> he never
> wept.

. . . from "The Life and Times of Monos." And, from the title poem:

> This kind of bird flies backwards,
> and this light breaks
> where no sun shines.

Yes, they were kind of Stephen Crane-like. But they'd meant a great deal to me—had even made me cry for dry-eyed Monos.

§7. In many ways, Freddy Herko was iconic of the Beat Generation.
Today he survives as a minor figure, a name surfacing now and again, with that of his fellow dancer Vincent Warren, in some of Frank O'Hara's poems, as anecdote after anecdote about him is forgotten or retired. Shortly after Freddy's suicide in October '64, the Judson Poets' Theater mounted a memorial program of his dances and choreographic works, organized by di Prima.

Both Warren and Herko danced regularly with James Waring's avant-garde troupe and took part in the extraordinary production of Waring's *Dances Before the Wall* at the Henry Street Settlement House. Warren and Herko roomed together for several years and were close friends during the period of Warren's affair with poet Frank O'Hara.

Warren had a steady job, in a time when dancers were even more socially "unsettled" than actors: He was a regular in the Metropolitan Opera's *corps de ballet*. Once, possibly three times, in the Sunday night production number that opened the Ed Sullivan variety show on CBS (Channel Two), among the all-male dancers that stepped brightly and walked lightly, Freddy was the second dancer from the far right. But he walked away from it, uninterested in doing the same thing week after week. He'd initially come to New York as a scholarship piano student at Juilliard and had only taken up dancing on his graduation. Largely he supported himself playing for dance classes and dance rehearsals.

Well, here's my own anecdote about him.

Understand, I have always loved dancing, to watch it, to do it. By the time I'd finished high school, I had made sure I'd seen every dance Balanchine had choreographed for the New York City Ballet—and most of those choreographed by Jerome Robbins. In those same years, twice I took the plunge and commenced lessons, once with a teacher of Indian dance at a local Harlem Community Center, and once at the American Ballet Theater School, with Madame Youskevitch—a class which, from time to time, her husband, the legendary Igor Youskevitch, took over.

Throughout my adolescence I was often struck by visions of complex evening-long dances—and though, half a dozen years later, I would help out through the summers of 1971 and '72 as one of two fairly beefy, black-clad (or occasionally naked) production assistants-cum-performers in the Charles Stanley Dance Company, I never got a chance to realize any of those Terpsichorean notions.

One day in June or July of 1964 at maybe ten in the morning (I was twenty-two), I was returning home to the Lower East Side after a night of sexual adventuring. At the 2nd Avenue subway station, as I was starting up the stairs to the street, Freddy Herko came loping down, two steps at a time.

As he all but fell toward me, I called, "Hello, Freddy!" and, at the bottom by the dirty tiling, he swung around to greet me—
"Hello!"
—clearly not sure what my name was.
Possibly because I was tired (possibly it had something to do with the air of raw sensitivity Freddy was projecting), it came blurting out: "Freddy—I keep getting all these ideas for dances. Only I'm not a trained dancer. I mean, I don't know what I should do. Maybe there's a class I should—"
But here Freddy dropped his hand on my shoulder and bent to say, "Oh, what you've got to do—you've got to get some people together. If they're dancers, fine. But that doesn't matter. And you have to make your dance, show them what you want them to do, and just do it. It doesn't matter whether you have any training or not—that's not what's important. What's important is that you *do* it! Just go ahead . . ." Now he stood up and, without even smiling, loped on into the subway station's concourse.
No "How are you?" No "How have you been?" That was the encounter's entirety.
I was astonished. Freddy was a superbly trained classical ballet dancer; I'd seen him dance half a dozen times in person—and I'd seen him on his Ed Sullivan gig. I'd been introduced to him perhaps three times, but always in backstage, post-performance confusion. We'd never even chatted at a party; there was really no reason for him to remember me. In an unwatered shot, however, he'd hurled at me an entire anti-establishment aesthetic. It left me rather reeling, and I hurried home hugely excited.
Years later I learned that this concept had originated with Waring and dancer-teacher David Dunn. But, in the 2nd Avenue subway station entrance, received in such a burst, it was among the things that tethered me to the New York countercultural aesthetic from my earliest years.
Other things also surprised me about the encounter, though they only registered among its flickering after-images. There at the bottom of the subway steps, Freddy had been wearing jeans and a dirty blue sweatshirt, the bronze hair of his chest a snarl in the V of the unzipped collar. He'd worn no shirt beneath. When he'd grasped my shoulder, I'd seen that his nails were very dirty. So was his face. His light brown hair was oily, and there had been a white crust at both corners of his mouth. More than a dancer's leanness had pared his body down to a state that was *too* thin, as he all but cantered off into the subway's darkness, where I glimpsed a soiled ankle under a jean cuff: He'd been wearing sneakers without socks.
"I just know," said Judy,[3] much closer to Freddy than I was, "that he was doing an *awful* lot of amphetamines at that time, just before he died."
All that keeps Freddy's death from being absolutely, even mythically, iconic for that generation is its lack of uniqueness. Too many others died too close

to the same way. I knew one personally (Doug Litwin, younger brother of my good friend Dave), and I'd been told of several more.

That afternoon, my musician friend, the late John-Herbert McDowell, was at lighting designer Johnny Dodd's Cornelia Street apartment, which had once been rented by W. H. Auden but had passed over the years down whatever aesthetic chain. That autumn afternoon John-Herbert, Eddie Barton (another dancer), Freddy, and half a dozen other people had stopped by. Someone had passed around tabs of LSD. Doubtless Freddy was already high on speed. Some-one had put Mozart's *Coronation Mass* on the hi-fi. Most of the dancers present, men and women, began to dance.

In the course of it, at a swell of music, in a move recalling the legendary entrance in *Le Spectre de la Rose*, Freddy rushed an open window and, surely convinced by the acid he would fly, called out Isadora Duncan's last words, "*Je vais à la gloire . . . !*" and did a *grand jeté* out into gold October sun.

The apartment was on the fifth floor.

Freddy's life arched on over another four or four-and-a-half airborne sec-onds. Striking—and seriously injuring—a pedestrian beneath him, Freddy himself was killed instantly on the curbside.

Though for several seasons I enjoyed the performances of the Grand Union Construction Company, a loosely organized dance troupe whose three- and four-hour evening programs were put together precisely with Herko's/War-ing's/Dunn's aesthetic, I have not choreographed a dance since I left my teens. From the morning when I ran into Freddy in the subway, however, my fiction became a lot more ambitious.

§8. George Preston was a black artist (and a decent banjo player), who, when he'd been eighteen or nineteen, had been my counselor at Camp Woodland. For several years in my early-middle twenties, when I would be standing in line, waiting for a teller (in those days before ATMs) at the Manufacturers' Ha-nover Bank on the corner of 8th Street and 6th Avenue, regularly I ran into him, wearing his jeans and blue denim jacket. Invariably I was coming from my agent's office on 10th Street, just off 6th. We'd exchange three minutes of pleasantries. George was doing okay. I was doing okay. He was having a show. I had a new book.

A year or too older than I, a stocky young man, all but an albino, with thick glasses before the palest of coral-colored eyes—another Woodland camper —worked at the news kiosk just outside the bank. We all said hello when we passed each other and smiled.

Along with Seymore Krim (who I later met through Judy Merril), artist Al Hanson (who visited me a couple of times on East Street with my friend Ana, and had tea), and Richard Seaver (whom I lunched with once when he was briefly interested in a novel of mine, during his tenure at Grove Press), George shows up now and again at parties or gatherings photographed and reprinted in collections devoted to the Beats as part of its almost endless cast of what Joyce Johnson has chronicled so brilliantly as *Minor Characters* (1983). What those pictures tell me today is that I was a little too young, a little too bumptuous and hard-working, and just not social enough at the time to have yet wandered into that particular circle.

§9. A few months after the reading where Ginsberg stepped on my foot, Beat generation maven William Burroughs gave me one of the few moments in which I was ever able to feel as if I were "in," though it was a decade after the Beats were themselves "in" by anyone's estimate. (Isn't that finally why we give names to groups like the Lost Generation, the Beat Generation—to sign the fact that *we're* not really in or of them?) In October 1986, the University of Kansas invited me to spend two weeks on its campus. I was vaguely aware Burroughs had retired to Lawrence, but I had no notion when I arrived that our paths would cross during my two weeks visiting creative writing workshops, science fiction classes, and graduate classes in literary theory. On my first weekend, then, I was surprised when I received a postcard and, a day later, a phone call from James Grauerholz, inviting me to Burroughs's house for Friday (I believe it was) afternoon. I said I'd be delighted—but asked, over the phone from my university motel room, what I'd done to deserve the honor.

Bill likes science fiction and science fiction writers, Jim told me. He wants to meet you—and actually has a few questions for you.

About 3:50 on Friday, Jim came by to pick me up and drove me to Burroughs's unimposing house. Burroughs himself was lean, angular, lively, and full of anecdotes about the various people who'd only recently dropped by to see him (the day before it had been Debbie Harry, from the pop group Blondie). His questions turned out to be about something I was actually able to throw some light on. Apparently, Burroughs had been retained by a production company to do a filmscript of William Gibson's SF novel *Neuromancer.* Had I read it? What did I think of it? How would I approach it for a film? Basically, we spent the afternoon brainstorming over possible filmic approaches to various parts of the novel—all of which I was happy to do. Burroughs was quite serious about producing a decent film script. I got regaled with stories of Brian Gyson and life back in the famous "Bunker" on the Bowery. Burroughs showed me his gun collection.

(Once I asked him how he had lost one finger joint, and he began to splutter, and was not happy answering, and I realized I had crossed a line in this social space, and so stored it away as later information with times I'd asked similar questions of others, and gotten similar or different responses . . . I apologized and we moved on; and thus we build up a picture of the social world.)

Finally he began to speak of lemurs.

He'd just acquired an extraordinary book of photographs of the animals, which had completely possessed his imagination. So lemurs it was, until, from the kitchen, Jim called in that dinner was ready. With a young friend of Jim's and another woman who'd been invited by, we sat down to some extraordinary tournedos Rossini that Jim had prepared, and some good red wine.

A little later, Jim and his friend drove me back to my motel.

It was a wholly pleasant afternoon and evening.

Had I felt *in*, however? No. I'd been too busy enjoying myself.

The moment of epiphany arrived three months later, when I was back in New York. My friend Ellen Datlow, the SF editor for *Omni Magazine*, invited me out for lunch—and a nice lunch it was. The conversation was miles away from Lawrence, when, offhandedly, she mentioned, "I got the strangest submission from William Burroughs, of all people—it's a story about . . . lemurs. Actually, it's rather interesting. I'm thinking of taking it."

And I found myself saying: "Oh, that's right. The last time I saw Bill, down in Lawrence, he'd gotten fascinated with them. He showed me a whole book on them. That's practically *all* he could talk about . . ."

Across a bit of sushi between the ends of her chopsticks, Ellen regarded me oddly for a moment: "You were down in Lawrence, Kansas, talking with William *Burroughs*—about lemurs . . . ?"

And for the most ephemeral of instants, I realized that, in the very lack of attention I had paid to it, I had passed through (and, alas, passed out of again) that ineffable moment of "in-ness," and had even brought back a bit of privileged information, the proof of my having, so fleetingly, been there.

§10. The Beats' two New York City stomping grounds, the West End Bar across from Columbia University, and the Ceder Street (on 8th Street, just west of University Place), were the two bars in the city where I could get served beer regularly before I was eighteen. But my hours and the late hours of those writers and artists who circulated around the Beat movement never overlapped enough for me to meet any of them—though, once, before I was twenty, I went to the Cedar specifically because a friend of mine had gotten into a conversation there with Samuel Beckett the previous evening, and I wanted to meet him.

He wasn't there, though—like Estragon, like Vladimir—I waited . . .

My distant "relationship" with Ginsberg, in its excessive spottiness, among the vast lacunae waiting for some imaginative in-filling, was pretty much characteristic of my relationship with the rest of the Beats and those associated with them. But the encounter with the writer is always a mythical occurrence. And there certainly was no more mythical *group* of American writers in this century's central forty years—say 1940 to 1980. I mean: Sexton, Plath, and Starbuck hanging out after the workshop with Lowell, talking about suicide . . . ?

The get-togethers of the Violet Plume (much as I might have loved them)? Jay McInerney having a drink with Raymond Carver when the creative writing class let out at Iowa . . . ?

No. I don't think so.

§11. Days before I took off for Europe in 1965, one autumn afternoon, I got picked up on Central Park West by a painter named William McNeill, who, in the first twenty minutes I knew him, dropped what seemed to me, at least at the time, a hundred names of Beat and peripheral-Beat writers: Gary Snyder, Joanne Kyger, Helen Adam, Robert Duncan, Jack Spicer, Lawrence Ferlinghetti, Michael McClure, Bob Kaufman . . . which is to say, the friends he was so anxious to let me know he had were writers and poets I had encountered in the *Evergreen Review*, including that famous 1957 Issue 2, the "San Francisco Scene," in which, eight years before, I'd first read *Howl*.

Three days later on October 18, I left for a six-month stay in Europe.

Four days in Luxembourg, two weeks in Paris, two weeks in Venice (now *those* were a couple of weeks to write about), and finally, by ferry, from Brindisi to Athens. . . . After a handful of days in that city, I was two months on the islands, first on isolate Melos, where the Venus di Milo had been discovered, then on more populous (but still, in the winter of 1965–66, fairly calm) Mykonos, and finally back in Athens by the second or third week of January.

A rough and vivid memory: sitting on the roof-patio of a small stone house in the picturesque neighborhood that, above the Plaka, clung to the back face of the Acropolis like a displaced island village, with my friend DeLys, a delicate, golden-haired woman from New Orleans. (Earthquake refugees from the island of Anafi had first built the little whitewashed stone houses, ran the city's lore, so that the neighborhood was known as Anaphiotika: Little Anafi.) While we sat, drinking Greek tea, someone down in the street shouted, "Hey—anybody home! Hey?" We looked over the roof-wall's edge.

Carrying some kind of dufflebag, a scruffy black-haired fellow in his thirties was doing the shouting. "Hey—it's Gregory! We're gonna crash here! Joyce said it was okay! Come on—let us in!"

Beside him stood a rangy blond guy, thumbs beneath wide, drab backpack straps, watching while the other shouted: "Open the fuckin' door, will you? Let us in!"

DeLys called: "Who *are* you? What do you want?"

"Come on—it's *Gregory!* You gonna let us in or not? We're tired. Let us in, now—"

"I'm sorry. I don't know you . . . I think you must have the wrong place!"

"This is the place," the black-haired man declared. "Come on and let us the fuck in, now—I don't have time for this—"

At which point the blond one said, "Hey, come on—man! Fuck the bitch!

We got those other places to try. Let's get goin'! Will you—?" He tugged the other by the arm. They turned—and loped off!

"Who in the *world*—" DeLys turned from the rail—"did *they* think they were?" She sat back down.

Though I'd only seen his picture on the back of his New Directions volumes (all of which I owned), *I'd* recognized him immediately: "That was Gregory Corso . . . !" I told her. (I had no idea who his companion was.) "I'm sure the Joyce he was talking about was your friend—the one whose book of poems you showed me . . . ?"

At one time Joyce had rented the same house, I'd gathered, before DeLys had taken it over.

"Well," declared DeLys huffily, "*I* never met him before." Grape leaves on the trellis whispered; her yolk-pale hair lifted in the afternoon's first breeze. "He didn't sound like anyone I'd want staying with *me*!"

In the early 1960s, Athens' itinerant winter internationals were just not that numerous. That same night I was at a party, somewhere nearer Colonaiki, where Gregory made an almost equally loud entrance, this time hanging all over the shoulders of an English redhead (briefly she'd been the girlfriend of another young Englishman I'd been traveling with, John Witten-Dorris) with whom he was now staying. Loud, opinionated, and probably stoned, he didn't remain long—and they left to a buzz.

"That man," DeLys said to me, "is just *awful*! What *is* his problem?"

"Well," I told her, "he's one of the two most famous poets in the United States, right now. And of the two—" the other was, of course, Ginsberg—"I think he's the more talented. That can't be a very easy job."

"Well, I'm glad I didn't let him in *my* house!"

Since I was now staying on DeLys's living room daybed, I was glad she hadn't, too.

I had three more encounters with Corso—two in Athens, one in New York.

A few days later, at an iron table in the yard of a *kafenion* at the bottom of Mnisicleos Street, across from Babba Stavros's restaurant on the edge of the Agora of Diogenes (the Tyrant, not the Philosopher),[4] conversation between half a dozen people interwove and tangled beneath the leaf-and-sun scumble that fell through some leaning, thick-trunked tree over the enameled metal table, when Gregory joined us—he knew someone or other I didn't know in the gathering. That day he wasn't particularly loud or unpleasant: he was talking to another man there about a translation he was going to do of Euripides's *Bacchantes*. Somehow I got into the conversation with some comments about a production I had heard of but not actually seen in which Dionysus had been played by a nude actor. The man to whom Gregory was expostulating was unimpressed: "I can't see why anyone would want to do *that*!" But Gregory

—possibly just to be eristic—thought it was a cool idea. Others at the table were leaving. Finally, the man said to Gregory: "Well—I'll see you for lunch at my place, then—tomorrow?"

With an explosion of enthusiasm, Gregory turned in his chair to grip high on my arm: "Can we bring this guy along? He sounds pretty interesting!"

The man smiled at me: "Certainly—if you'd like." And to me: "That is, if you'd like to come . . . ?"

I blurted, "I'd love to!" (By now I was twenty-three.)

He offered to write down his particulars in my notebook: Alan Ansen, followed by a Colonaiki address. He left, and a moment later, Gregory was up: "Come on . . ."

—and I spent the next two hours, as I remember, running all over Athens with, or just behind, Gregory. Where we went or what he was doing, I no longer remember. But it was all very important at the time. In the course of it we had a lot of beer at various cafés, and there was much agonizing—from Gregory—about his upcoming *Bacchantes* translation/adaptation. ("This is a *classic*, see? You can't just fuck around with it!") I felt wonderfully privileged.

By the time, alone, I wandered back through the National Gardens and up through the Plaka to DeLys's in Anaphiotika, I was also pretty drunk.

But the next day I made it to Ansen's.

The apartment was clean, cool, and off-white. Signed Cocteau drawings hung on the walls; I couldn't have been more impressed by Picassos. Gregory was already there—he was actually cooking lunch for us! It was to be a kind of casserole that he'd volunteered to make in the little kitchen in a large, blackened Dutch oven. We sat around over glasses of white wine, with Gregory darting to the stove now and then.

Ansen asked me what I did, and I told him I was writing a novel about Jean Harlow, Christ, Orpheus, and Billy the Kid.

Leaning forward on the white table, Gregory said: "Jean *Harlow*? Christ, Orpheus, Billy the Kid, those three I can understand. But what's a young spade writer like you doing all caught up with the Great White Bitch?" Then he frowned for a moment, sitting back. "Of course, I guess it's pretty obvious."

Then lunch came to the table.

The little red peppers that Gregory had used in the casserole turned out to be *really* hot. After one bite, Gregory put his fork down and declared: "Oh, Man —I fucked up! Come on. You guys don't have to eat this shit . . . !"

Actually, though, it was pretty good.

I was hungry, and I've always liked hot food. Ansen and I both persevered through a helping each, while Gregory drank cold retsina.

After a concluding snifter of Metaxa, I said thank you and left—and did not see Gregory again for half a dozen years.

§12. It was back in New York on the Lower East Side. It was summer; it was hot; it was muggy. Walking down 9th or 11th or one of those crowded streets over on A, B, or C, I saw a man in a dirty white shirt and ratty black jeans sitting in a doorway, with not a lot of teeth. Three steps later, I realized it was Gregory.

I went up and said hello, as people wandered by.

He was pretty out of it. Did he remember me? Or the over-peppered casserole at Ansen's? Had he ever seen the quote from our conversation that afternoon that had appeared, by now, as a chapter epigraph in my paperback novel *The Einstein Intersection*, published a year or so before by Ace Books? He answered no to all of them.

"Are you going to be sitting here for a while . . . ?" I asked tentatively,

"Man, I'm not going *anywhere* . . . !" he said thickly.

"I'll bring you a copy of the book!" I said. "I only live a few blocks from here." And I ran off to get him one. Though I was back with it in seven minutes by the clock, of course he was gone.

§13. Is there any point in telling the story of how, at a party on Henry Street, artist and set designer Robert LeVigne—his picture is in a dozen photograph books of the Beat writers of San Francisco—chased me around a table with sex on the brain? Fortunately guests arrived before he could catch me.

Or of my hopelessly unrequited infatuation, in 1969, with Ronnie Primak, the poet who worked as a bartender in North Beach, where, in the slant light through dim shutters, we'd sit and jaw with Richard Brautigan at the bar . . . Or how, at a drink-soaked dinner at Robert Berg's in San Francisco, I ended up falling into bed with poet Berg's roommate John Ryan—I'm sure increasing my "Apostolic succession" by dozens on dozens of dozens, as Ryan was rumored to have been in and out of bed with literally everyone!

Rather than anything sexual, though, my strongest memory of San Francisco—six or more years after the death of Jack Spicer—is of a reading Anne Waldman gave in that city, in that summer, where someone threw a beer can at the podium while she was in the midst of a poem, somebody else got sick in the audience, and someone *else*, drunk, staggered obstreperously, loudly in, reeled around a few minutes, then staggered out. Anne's reading was electric, extravagant, and wonderful as always. ("My God," she said, when she came off, "when that beer can came at me, I was scared to *death*!") As we were leaving, poet Jack Thibeau said to me: "This is the *dregs* of a scene! It's not even the end of one. It's the morning-after dregs . . . !"

§14. The connections between the world of science fiction writers and science fiction readers and the world of contemporary poetry and literature are not legion. Perhaps the most fascinating of them is that, when none of them was over twenty-five, SF writer Philip K. Dick (resolutely heterosexual) and San

Francisco poets Robert Duncan and Jack Spicer (both gay) were roommates for a season in the late 1940s and shared a single apartment on Berkeley's Telegraph Avenue.[5]

§15. In Brenda Knight's *Women of the Beat Generation*, the first entry is Helen Adam (1909–1993). I met Helen within a week or of my return from Europe in April 1966. Although I wasn't to learn of it till years after I first met her, Helen had been a child prodigy in Scotland, where her first book of ballads, *The Pegan Elf*, was published. She'd been twelve—and it had been made much of on *both* sides of the Atlantic! Her name speckles literary accounts of the 1920s, much like, in other times, the names Hilda Conkling, Minut Druet, Daisy Ashford, or Nathalia Crane. Such infantile precosity is a terrible weight for a serious artist to bear as an adult. That is probably a good deal of the reason that Helen, with her sister Pat and their mother, moved to the United States after World War II, settling in San Francisco.

Here is the critic William Rose Benét, writing in 1924:

> Some long time ago in Scotland there was a little girl named Marjori Fleming, and today a twelve-year-old, Helen Douglas Adam, the daughter of a Scotch parson and his wife of Dundee, is her successor to the juvenile purple. Miss Adam has now been published both in England and America.

Helen Douglas Adam lived a life committed to poetry—and to a concept of poetry that was, from time to time, in the words of Carolyn Kizer (describing the poet Judith Johnson), "splendidly unfashionable."

Her work was anthologized in the groundbreaking *New American Poetry* (1960) anthology put together by Donald Allen. Her influence on poets like the late Robert Duncan was mutual and profound. Certainly one of Duncan's most popular poems, "The Ballad of Mrs. Noah," began as a conscious and conscientious effort to write something in the genre that Helen had made so exciting to the poets who would eventually be labeled the San Francisco Renaissance, with her magical readings at the various galleries in San Francisco during the 1950s.[6]

Helen was a poet to whom music and magic were the most important things about language. Brocade was her fabric. Purple was her color. The ballad was her form.

To talk about Helen I have to repeat some of what I've already told. The first time I recall hearing Helen Adam's name was two nights before I left for Europe on October 18, 1965. Cruising inside Central Park one night, I met a painter named Bill McNeill who barraged me with names of poets and painters he'd known in San Francisco, many of whom—Spicer, Snyder, Duncan—I'd heard of. Some (Joanne Kyger, Ebbe Borregaard . . .) I hadn't. Five years before, as I mentioned, Adam had had work in Donald Allen's important anthology, but I would not hear of that book for more than another year. Adam had had no work yet in the *Evergreen Review*, nor had she published a volume with the Pocket Poet Series. And the fact that she lived on the West Coast meant hers was a name I didn't know.

A relatively detailed account of that night's meeting and the day it climaxed form section 59.8 toward the end of my autobiography, *The Motion of Light in Water*. I remembered it as strictly and as carefully as I could in 1987 when I wrote it. (The only thing I can think of that I possibly left out, as Bill and I sat together under the streetlight by the park bench at ten o'clock, outside its stone wall, was perhaps a mention by Bill that he and Helen had collaborated on a film together, *Daydream of Darkness*.) If you, the reader, are interested in timing and details, read my account in *Motion*. For better or for worse, timing and details are what constitute reality.

Six months later, on the evening of April 15, 1966, I returned to the States and the Lower East Side, and when I walked in, Marilyn Hacker, my wife, was sweeping the floor and Bill was getting ready to leave for his new apartment off Hudson Street. Things had changed, mostly for the good, I thought. But other things had remained unsettlingly the same.

Marilyn had prepared me for Helen's criticism of *Babel-17* on the first night I met her. Helen had read it, when it had come out—a month or so after *Empire Star*—while I'd been away in Greece.

At a side table in the back room of the Old Reliable, on my first visit to what would be the first regular bar I ever felt proprietary about, Helen sat with Russell and Dora FitzGerald and Lew Ellingham and Bill, who'd come again, at the west side of the back room.

"Marilyn said you'd read my book, *Babel-17*. And that you'd had some thoughts. I'd really like to know what they were."

"Well," she answered, "let me be honest." She was a gaunt, lively, older woman with iron gray hair, and a voice—resonant, Scottish-tinged—which, in another context, I once described (for a fictional character based on Helen) as "hair of tarnished silver; voice of scrap brass." She went on: "I thought it was a magical book, full of poets and monsters and ghosts and dragons all in the oddest places that were quite exciting. Then, in the last few pages, something happens: and it becomes a rather silly book about an intergalactic war nobody could possibly believe in or care about." She sighed, smiled, and shook her head. "There. That's it. I enjoyed it up until the end, though."

The main reason I remember is because I agreed.

I remember Helen at parties (a house-warming at Marilyn's on Henry Street, after which, a few days later, Marilyn and I decide we'd separate; a brunch at Bill McNeill's loft, where I met Barbara Wise and she asked me if I wanted to

do a film; an evening gathering at Barbara and Howard Wise's on 13th Street),
and I remember her at dinners at her tiny apartment with her sister Pat and
the numberless statues of Anubis, in the East 80s. And I remember, once,
shortly after I met her, in 1966, when she and some friends had come to my
7th Street apartment after brunch at Speedy's and the Old Reliable, and I had
been talking to her about James Thomson's *City of Dreadful Night*—which I'd
only read an anthologized fragment from.[7] Two days later, in the mail, arrived
the whole twenty-eight-page poem that Helen probably had Pat xerox for me,
and bound in a plastic cover (it was octavo size, of the sort used at the time to
protect library book jackets), in which she had put some gold foil and some
beautiful leaves, to make an extraordinary booklet of the poem.

I remember going night after night to her musical play, *San Francisco's Burning*, at the Judson Poets Theater, standing through it, squeezed in the side aisle,
because there was only standing room left, and applauding till my hands were
sore at its wonder and its life and its mighty and joyous mystery.

A production of *San Francisco's Burning* had already been mounted on the
West Coast, before Helen and Pat left California for New York. Among those
still alive, Dora FitzGerald, Joanne Kyger, Lewis Ellingham, William Alvin
Moore, and George Stanley were in attendance.

In New York, though Pat was somewhat reclusive, Helen was outgoing and
social. I remember Helen at a party at Marilyn Hacker's on Henry Street,
and I'm all but certain she was at Russell's day-long 1967 birthday party at his
and Dora's apartment on the fourth floor of 68 East 3rd Street. Possibly her
biographer Kristin Prevallet has the date of her arrival in the city.

My general sense is that the death of Spicer in 1965 in San Francisco all
but shattered the Spicer circle. Joanne Kyger with her husband Gary Snyder
returned from Japan, where, with McNeil, they'd lived at the same monastery.
Ebbe Borregaard went off with Joy to live in the woods. Harold Dull left the
city. And people like the FitzGeralds, McNeill, Ellingham, Link, and Hunce
Voelcker—all of whom knew Helen well and counted her part of their circle
—came to New York then, as Helen and Pat had done, to start over and build
new lives for themselves, now that the bubble of Spicer's magic had burst—
and, indeed, burst in such a sordid finale. (Read Louis Ellingham and Kevin
Killian's *Poet, Be Like God*. An hour's conversation with Ellingham or William
Alvin Moore [né Brodecky] or Dora FitzGerald about Helen would probably
yield ten times the hard-edged information about her that twenty pages of
my letters might give.) I think of this exodus as the diaspora of the remaining
fragments of the Magic Workshop from the '50s.

Ellingham returned shortly to San Francisco. The FitzGeralds left New
York in 1968 (or the beginning of '69) for Vancouver, where Stan Persky had
preceded them and George Stanley would soon follow. McNeill returned to
San Francisco a little later—but Helen and Pat (who were after all somewhat

older) stayed on at their East 82nd Street apartment in New York. But that's getting ahead of my story.

In the weeks after I first met her, Helen read my cards only once, I believe. (In later years, I *think* she did at least two more readings for me. . . . But that was in the 1970s.) She—and Russell, an old friend of hers from San Francisco—answered endless questions for me about the cards, however, over the autumn and winter of 1966–67, while I was writing and rewriting a novel called *Nova*. At Helen's suggestion, Russell loaned me his hardback copy of Arthur Edward Wait's book—not then available in paperback in every bookstore. Indeed, at that time, tarot decks themselves were rather hard to come by. The year following, Russell eventually created an entire deck, which he sometimes jokingly referred to as "the *Nova* tarot," and which grew out of his thoughts on the cards inspired by (among other things) my questions. McNeill also started a tarot deck, done from collages of magazines. But I don't think his was ever finished. Russell's widow Dora probably still has a few of Russell's decks at her home in Vancouver, B.C., where she's currently a social worker. Dora is a wonderful raconteur, by the bye, and is bound to have some fascinating stories of Helen. Have you seen the Helen Adam issue of *City* that Marilyn Hacker/Russell FitzGerald/Louis Ellingham published in 1968, which had a half dozen of Helen's ballads, illustrated with some of Russell's tarot cards? I can't seem to lay my hands on my own copy. But perhaps Marilyn Hacker may be able to help you.[8] Helen's influence is all over Russell's deck.

To repeat: The New York production of *San Francisco's Burning* (over the winter of 1966–67) was at the well-known Judson Poets Theater, on the south side of Washington Square. The book had a new musical score by Al Carmines. (Jean Rigg, currently at the Paula Cooper Gallery in New York City, was properties manager of the show.) Helen was not overjoyed at Carmines' upbeat, broad, and rather rinky-dink music. Her own more traditional ballad melodies had already been published (I think) with the first printing of the score with the Jess illustrations in San Francisco—and she would have preferred those, or at least something with the same feel. But she went along with it. And, despite Michael Smith's negative reviews in the *Village Voice*, the show received nightly standing ovations from a packed-house audience! My lover for much of 1966 into the first weeks of 1967, Ron Bowman, had a small part in the show—I think he played the Gentleman Caller—but the result was that I got to see full rehearsals, as well at least three performances, over its run. I never saw an audience less than completely carried away.

In black brocade, glittering with sequins, and a towering black medusoid-wire headdress, draped with black sequined gauze, Helen played the Worm Queen in *all* the performances!

"I am the Fair Forgetfulness
Whom men seek only in pain.
Who sleeps in the bed of the Worm Queen
Will never weep again . . ." (1961)

Several times over the years after the show, I was in *rooms* full of people,
where one started that line, and the rest joined in to finish chanting it! Once
having heard heard her, even thirty-one years ago, you weren't likely to forget
her rendition.

Julie Kernitz, who played Miss Dunn-Drummond (who "has no voice at
all!"), tells a story about rushing off the Judson stage during one performance,
on her rather dramatic exit, to bang smack full into Helen, in her Worm Queen
costume, who was making her way along the dark and narrow backstage passage, to get in position for her own entrance in the next scene. "Her headdress
fell off. Helen managed to get it back on and get out on stage," says Kernitz,
"though I don't know how. She must have been reeling. We knocked the wind
out of each other and practically fell down the both of us!"

Eventually *San Francisco's Burning* was reprinted with the Carmines score by
Hanging Loose Press. At various times, I've held both editions in my hands,
and even owned the first. But it vanished from my library many years ago
—more than thirty, now.

At about the time of the show, I recall Helen dropping in on Ron Bowman
and me—or perhaps coming by one afternoon with Ron—for coffee at his
St. Marks Place apartment.

I also remember attending readings Helen gave at St. Marks in the Bowery, in the downstairs hall, where Anne Waldman introduced her. Helen was
a lively and engaged woman pretty much all through the 1970s. During that
decade she accompanied Barbara Wise to Scotland—where she hiked to the
top of Ben Nevis. Barbara stayed at the bottom, in a guesthouse, not up to the
exertion. But Helen dashed right on up to the peak!

(Where decades later, Barbara's son David would scatter Helen's ashes, with
his wife Audrey and SF writer Lisa Tuttle, and report it on Facebook.)

Helen was the model for a character in a story I wrote in 1968, in which
her name was Edna Silem ("Melisande" spelled backwards, a *nom littéraire* I'd
borrowed from Marilyn), whose voice I described—thinking of Helen—as
"scrap brass." It was a wonderful voice. And I heard it ring out magically, here,
during rehearsals of *San Francisco's Burning*:

"I am the Fair Forgetfulness . . ." (1961)

And I heard it in the basement of St. Marks Church, during her incredibly
energetic poetry readings, where she made magic and music of whatever she
turned it to.

It's silent now—but still wonderful in memory.
For it still sounds in her splendidly evocative ballads and stories.

§16. Without ever knowing him well, I met Robert Duncan when, during 1969 and '70, I lived in San Francisco with Marilyn, and I attended a poetry workshop that, from time to time, met in our living room, run by Duncan and black poet Bill Anderson—though Duncan attended less and less over the time I was there. And he once came to a play I directed in my first months there (Genet's *Les Bonnes*, which we did in our rather sprawling front hall in French), where, after the show, he'd been quite generous to me in his praise of my directing. Nevertheless, Duncan could be an extremely preoccupied man—and the last two or three times in San Francisco I was in his presence, I very much got the impression that he'd forgotten completely who I was.

In the '60s, Marilyn and I were invited together a couple of times to Helen and Pat Adam's apartment for dinner. The place was tiny, lined with books, and set about all over with statues and pictures of Anubis, Helen's titular deity. Guests always dined in the living room at a small table, two or three sitting on the couch, with chairs for the others at the table's other three sides. Pat brought things in from the kitchen. I remember a wonderful pumpkin soup . . . I remember a veal roast with rosemary . . . and liqueur glasses of Cointreau. Because it was so small, it verged on the uncomfortable, though the conversation—and the food—invariably turned it into a wonderful night. Often there were tarot readings before dinner.

Sometime in 1973(?) when I was back in New York after my own stay in San Francscio, Duncan came to the City to do a reading at St. Marks, and Helen and Pat had him to dinner, along with Barbara and Howard Wise (Marilyn was in London, by then) and me. Other than a few more Anubis statuettes, the place hadn't really changed in the half dozen years since I'd last been there. Both Helen and Pat were wonderfully knowledgeable about literature —though Helen usually dominated the conversation. She had endless anecdotes about the lives of the poets, which were always amusing and instructive. Easily she could have taught literature on the university level, but she always pooh-poohed her knowledge when anyone praised her for it. I think she felt she might not have been able to keep it up under the pressure of formal weekly requirements. That evening, however, Duncan pretty much held his own. We left around ten, so that Pat could get to work the next day.

Duncan hadn't paid much more attention to me that night than he had the last few times he'd seen me. But apparently he enjoyed my company enough to show up unannounced (really, to sweep in, with his great cape: "I'm here . . . !" he declared, with a flourish, when, surprised, I opened the door) at my tenth-floor room in the Albert Hotel (where I lived that year) the next afternoon. You say you want the story . . . ? Let me rather draw a curtain of discretion. (Finally, nothing *really* happened except some pawing on his part. His boldness about the whole thing, however, I found just a *bit* appalling.) He left with a copy of *Nova*. I've often wondered whether he ever read it.

I never saw him in person again.

§17. Earlier in her life, Helen Adam's younger sister Pat also had literary aspirations. She wrote and published a novel, *Letters from Teg*, with the British publisher Hodder and Staunton, sometimes in the early 1950s, just before the sisters moved with their mother to America. In their major work, which I will come to in more detail soon, *San Francisco's Burning*, their collaborative "ballad opera" about the San Francisco Earthquake of 1906, although they did not take credit for individual poems, Pat was responsible for the cuttingly witty lyrics ("Talking," "Miss Dunn-Drummond Has No Talk at All," "Loving Lilly Babe," "I Must Have a Man," and some of the wittier songs of Mrs. Macky Rhodus—these are the titles of the numerous "showstoppers" in the piece that brought the audience to its feet), while Helen wrote the dark and drear verses. They never tried to hide this, if anyone asked—but they didn't bruit it about, either. The only way you would learn is if you got Pat alone and asked directly. I knew people who were much closer to them than I was, who were unaware of it.

Although she held a job and brought in most of their income, socially Pat was somewhat reclusive—especially during the 1960s and '70s. One would invite Helen and Pat to dinner regularly, stressing how much one wanted to see Pat. Helen would show up—and make excuses for absent Pat. After the first of four times, it would just be: "Well, you know Pat. . . ." Pat was, of course, working a steady office job, and Helen's employment—bike messenger jobs in San Francisco, and what she did to bring in money in New York, I'm not sure; the story is that in San Francisco on several occasions Duncan had secured Helen teaching jobs which she refused to take, claiming that while she could hold up her end at a dinner of literary folks with fascinating insights and stories about literary figures, she didn't have enough formal information to teach a class for an entire term—was more mercurial than Pat's, whatever it was. They had people to dinner regularly, where Pat did the cooking and was the soul of graciousness; I was at dinner three, possibly four times in the '60s and twice with the Wises in the '70s—the second time with Robert Duncan, when he made the trip to the city to read. (There's a story there, but it has more to do with Duncan than with Helen.) The only time I ever saw Pat on a social occasion outside their own home, however, was a small party given by Barbara and Howard, at their 13th Street house, some time in the early '70s. (Charles Naylor and Thomas Disch were both there. So were the Wises' painter friends, Ethel and Xavier Gonzales, from Castle Hill on Cape Cod. And I believe the playright Maria Irene Fernes was there that evening—a hero of mine, and as far as I was concerned, one of the great theatrical minds of the past thirty years. As well, their two youngest kids David and Juliette were also there, I'm sure. (Two older Wise boys, Danny and Jeremy, lived in the Amherst area, whom I would meet once I started teaching at U. Mass.) At any rate, when I had finished talking with Fernes, I came over to talk with Pat, who was sitting I remember on an ottoman. I started with asking her about her novel, which she had once mentioned at dinner, when Helen had been out of the room. That evening she was willing to tell me again, though she suggested that no one had read it and no one needed to remember it.

I persevered: How did she and Helen collaborate?

Oh, she and Helen just wrote the words for different songs.

You didn't work on each other's songs together . . . ?

No, she said. And suddenly I realized I had been thinking that they had; even though I had seen the show three times and watched a complete dress rehearsal.

The play had been borne to its success by half a dozen highly witty show-stoppers that got standing ovations throughout. One had been a song called "Talking" which had been a witty collection of general clichés, which Miss Dunn-Drummond and her young suitor sing together:

> "Talking, talking,
> Two can live as cheaply as one;
> Isn't it strange people marry on earth
> When it's rolling around—
> The Sun!"

Which one of you wrote that? I asked.

"That was me," Pat confessed.

Another of the high points was the song in which the prostitute Loving Lilly Babe, played by the wonderfully over-the-top Florence Tarlowe, sings about how she "must have a man." The song ends—

> "Who cares if a man has a hump on his back?
> "Who cares if he crawls on the floor?
> "I must have a man, a miserable man,
> "A dead-beat, down-and-out creepy-crawly man,
> "A broken-hearted man
> "To adore!"

"Which one of you wrote "I Must Have a Man" . . . ?"

Again Pat said, softly, "I did . . ."

"What about 'Miss Dunn-Drummond has No Talk at All . . .'?"

"That was mine . . ."

And so on, through all the numbers that were memorable for their wit!

To repeat: I had seen the play three times as well as a dress rehearsal, but until then I'd thought it an equal collaboration between the sisters, or even mostly Helen's. I told Pat how good I thought her contributions had been and how much I had enjoyed them. She said, "Thank you . . ." But with three minutes of questioning, I also saw that while Helen had provided the mysterious, and—yes—fascinating poetry that carried the story from scene to scene, and probably the overall plot, Pat had provided the considerable social sophistication and humor to which the show's blatant theatrical success had been anchored. I felt I had been let in on a secret that perhaps I was not supposed to know, or at least was not supposed to tell anyone. And the fact was, I didn't; as well, I still thought the play's totality was brilliant, in its music-hall manner.

But now I realized that most of the enthusiastic audiences at the Judson Poets Theater performances had seen it as a comic triumph with a mystical subplot—rather than a mystical extravaganza with moments of comic relief. Now I wondered how Helen herself had seen it.

§18. In the early 1980s, Pat had a stroke and died. The two had lived together much of their lives, for the New York leg of it in a very small space, with Pat the one who held down the nine-to-five job, and who as well took care of practical matters—shopping, cleaning, and cooking for company, in a combination of dependencies and freedoms—with Helen the one who brought romance and interesting variety and people into their lives. Helen was just not up to going on alone, I suppose. The last time I saw her was at lunch, with Barbara Wise at an East Side restaurant in New York, Maxwell's Plum. Barbara chose to take Helen there because the restaurant would be deserted at the time. A waiter, and our own mirror images across the room against the two-tone purple deco walls, were the only others there that day, at that early lunch hour. Barbara had chosen me as a lunch companion, because I had known Helen and liked her. Helen had liked me. And Barbara felt both would be good for a depressed and anxious woman. I couldn't tell you whether or not they were.

Though it was at least a year after Pat's death, Helen still seemed very depressed about it. "You have such a great talent," I told her, trying to make a little light of her low feeling. "And you've used it wonderfully. Doesn't that make you feel good?"

"No, Chip," she said. "I'm afraid I had a very small talent. And I don't think I've used it well at all—I wasted so much of it. And now I'm being punished for that." It was a harsh judgment on herself; but though I didn't agree, it was even harder to counter at the time.

Her anxieties became quite intense. Shortly Barbara, who took over taking Helen to the doctors, told me how Helen had developed what she thought was a bruise on her cheek, and she had become quite worried. Wasn't that how certain blood cancers manifested? Barbara arranged to take Helen to her own dermatologist. When the doctor was examining Helen, who had told him of her fears, he frowned at the dark spot, then he went and got a piece of gauze, poored some alcohol on it, went over, and rubbed the spot.

Moments later, the "bruise" was gone. It had simply been some dirt that Helen had missed over a few days of washing her face. Barbara thought it was amusing, when she told me. I don't know whether Helen was relieved, embarrassed, or if the anxieties simply moved on to something else.

The depression, however, become quite severe—and, a year or so later, she was put in a home. Last Sunday, after having refused all food for several weeks (she'd been hospitalized and fed artificially twice during the last month), she died.

Still writing this on the day I heard about Helen's death, I note: I have three books of her stories and poems (*Selected Poets & Ballads, Gone Sailing, Ghost and Grinning Shadows*) and was reading among them last night. (Would that I had more!) And, as I said, this morning I was left feeling pensive, pondering on time, old age, and mortality.

I just went through my copy of *Opening of the Field* and reread "The Ballad of Mrs. Noah" and "Atlantis"; and in *Roots and Branches*, "My Mother Would be a Falconress." All are poems in which it's easy to see Helen's wonderfully salutary influence on Duncan.)

§19. Years after Helen's death, one afternoon during 1999 or 2000, when I taught at Buffalo, I walked into the special poetry collection at the SUNY library, the day they had opened up several packages of hundreds of Helen Adam's full-sized, full-colored magazine collages. They had been stored in a warehouse since before she left San Francisco, in the wake of Jack Spicer's death, which in so many complex paths sent so many poets wandering. And that whole floor in the stacks was covered with gold and green and glimmering water and bats and boats and cats with wings and the astonishing generosity of genius that had slept in the darkness of a warehouse that surely, if Helen had not forgotten herself, must have left her certain they would never be seen by anyone else again. (The film *Daydream of Darkness* no longer exists, nor do most of McNeill's paintings . . .) At the point when I saw them, they had been gone into that warehouse more than forty years—and only a few people had remembered that Helen used to make them.

Well, it's fifteen years after that. Some of those collages are shortly to be published in a book. I've walked among the originals, laid out over the floor. They were rich and beautiful—beautiful and generous.

§20. I cannot present any of this as history. There are not enough people conveniently accessible who were also there to check for accuracy and contrasting view that comes with writing from whatever position we happen to hold. The differences among media and mode—letter, journal, email, screen, or paper —opens them to distortions as does age, the pleasure principle, the very forces that I see as driving me toward accuracy.

§21. When, in the late 1980s, Diane di Prima's collected poems appeared, I went (already a lover of her *Loba*) poring through the new volume in the St. Mark's Bookshop—to discover that di Prima had omitted *all* the poems from her initial book, *This Kind of Bird Flies Backwards*: among the first poems by a living writer that had spoken so sharply and pointedly to my adolescence.

(I had been in the audience when di Prima lectured about her last visit to Dr. Williams, just a week or so before his death.)

That's when the forty-five-year-old man realized articulately what a younger man had intuited for years: The Beat Generatation was not *my* movement. Precisely as it made the transition from scruffy chapbooks that had lain too long unsold in the "on-consignment" poetry shelves of the long-gone Brick Floor Book Shop, the New Yorker Book Shop, the *old*, old Eighth Street at the corner of Macdougal—volumes I was sure I alone in the city had purchased —to the officialdom of collected volumes and survey anthologies, what had spoken most directly to me, what had offered me my epiphanic moments of emotional and intellectual excitement, what had gotten *me* through the harsh nights and rainy dawns of youth was precisely what was being revised, elided, written out of it.

Corso's *Bacchantes* was never, after all, completed.

As the lived experience of one black, gay adolescent from Harlem fell away with time, history rushed in to fill the gap and obliterate anything the growing child might have found useful. It's not even the apparent contradiction between such omissions and an aesthetic that presumes to value spontaneity, the childlike in the world. Through those hours-long conversations over shrimp, steamed rice, white wine, and salad during those '60s evenings (dinners, nightmares . . .), over Auden's right to omit "Spain" and "September 1939" from his *oeuvre*, I always sided with the poet (along with our patrons of four years' time, Dick Entin, also our mentor, and his young wife Alice). As far as di Prima's right to select what she wanted for her book, I side with the poet now. Still, Auden omitted those poems because he felt, however inadvertently, they lied. The slide toward sentimentality in di Prima's early poems (a slide they now and again suggest, but seldom take) I can see. If there is a lie, however, I'm blind to it.

And their truth is still important.

But such considerations of content, of style, raise the question: *Is* there a central flaw in the Beat Generation, as image, as enterprise, that perhaps controls their larger mythic acceptance?

§21. Sometime in the 1980s I went to a film at MOMA devoted to Kerouac and reminiscences of him by his friends, John Cleland Holmes, Burroughs, Ginsberg, Johnson, the Charterses. I don't remember the title, but poet Lewis McAdams had been involved in its making.

It was something of a revelation.

The surprise was not that Kerouac had been—like Ginsberg, like Corso—as devoted and fanatical about literature and poetry as he was. (People who are *not* fanatical about literature do not produce works that strike people as new and energetic: rather they produce works just like everyone else's. Knowing what literature is is the only way one *can* change and develop it. We must give them that, at least: these writers had actually done that.) What surprised me was that, outside that fanaticism, Kerouac was such an extraordinarily ordinary *man*.

What he wanted to do—other than read and write—was to drink and fuck women. As far as I can gather, that was his only ambition for either the world or himself.

And this was the man that the circle—the generation around him—idolized.

To include drinking and fucking among one's ambitions is understandable. They are among mine. But to have *no* others seems limited, if not retrograde. Because he was charismatically handsome, I can understand how more-or-less heterosexual Kerouac provided a focus for the extraordinarily intelligent gay men who clustered around him—for a season, perhaps. An extraordinary writer? I grant it. That he wanted to learn from them about the literary—certainly that must have flattered them. But from all one hears, the only thing life held for him besides that was going into a bar and cutting out the woman he could get drunkest fastest and home to his place or hers—unless some guy, after *his* bod, managed to get him drunker faster.

Good food? Companionship? Theater? Dance? Teaching the young? Helping the poor, the oppressed? Changing the world—making it a better place either for art or for life (or just for drinking and fucking), or showing it the truth about itself . . . ? Power, evil, making money—even those, as ambitions, teach us *about* ambition and its range of successes and failures. But the cosmic yearning that informs so much of Kerouac's prose turns out, in the life, in the long run, to be only the desire for mom to take care of him—and the boozy search for that night's mom substitute. No, he was a monumentally ordinary and unambitious *man*—which is to say, he was an extraordinarily wounded one, a man whose only concern (perhaps it was the single one he could support) was with what, for most of us, are acts of self-healing. Yes, like all human actions not overtly unkind, such acts have their beauty. Still, once healed, to what end this body, this mind . . . ? To what task now . . . ?

I'm sorry. I don't get it.

These men's (and, indeed, women's) idolization of Kerouac the man—not the writer—strikes me as the great irony, if not the little tragedy, in that generation's tale.

—June 1997–February 2010
New York/Philadelphia

NOTES

1. What I had in mind was Rimbaud's famous line, *On n'est pas sérieux, quand on a dix-sept ans*. Frankly, I don't think I was ever more serious in my life. It is indeed that seriousness with which we approach the beginning of our lives that often renders us foolish, more or less charmingly so.

2. Diane di Prima's first book was a small white chapbook called *This Kind of Bird Flies Backward*.

3. "Judy" is Judith Ratner, herself a dancer from time to time with the James Waring Group, as well as an actress in the original Broadway production of Arthur Miller's *The Crucible*, and for forty-five-odd years my downstairs neighbor in New York City.

4. Diogenes the Tyrant, not the Philosopher: At least that's how someone tried to explain it to me. On my next trip back to Athens, someone else said of course that area had been the old slave market in the Greek Agora and was named for the famous philosopher/slave who'd lived there and left his sayings and anecdotes to the world.

5. I have since heard that both Jack Spicer and Larry Fagin were enthusiasts, at least, of Alfred Bester's *The Stars My Destination* (or *Tiger! Tiger!* in its original 1956 British release).

6. Another Robert Duncan poem that shows Helen Adam's influence is "My Mother Would Be a Falconress" (1968).

7. The anthologized fragment from Thomson's poem that I knew then was this: ". . . As I came through the desert thus it was, / As I came through the desert: All was black / In heaven no single star, on earth no track . . ."

8. The special Helen Adam issue of *City* is the source of Russell FitzGerald's interview with Adam in Kristin Prevallet, ed., *A Helen Adam Reader* (National Poetry Foundation, 2007), 331.

20

Dialogue with Octavia E. Butler

This conversation between Octavia Estelle Butler and Samuel R. Delany was conducted via email by Robert Morales, then an editor for *Vibe* magazine.

Robert Morales: What do you make of the market survey stating that the largest growing group of American consumers for home computers is middle-class blacks?

Octavia E. Butler: I'm glad of it. It's just that it's going to draw more of a line between the middle class and the working class. And that's not a good thing —the last thing the black community needs is more fractures.

Samuel R. Delany: With the new technologies, there are always new social divisions—between, let's say, the computer literate and the computer illiterate. In the past we've seen those divisions fall along racial lines. If, finally, these new divisions are starting to blur those lines, then it's another step in the proof of what we all know: On any absolute level, race doesn't exist. Class is all there is—and class can be changed.

RM: Does space research have any relevance to the daily lives of average people?

SRD: It should. The amount of storm and hurricane damage the country suffered was tremendous before the existence of weather satellites. The billions of dollars that have been saved in terms of avoiding hurricane damage have paid for the space program more than five times over. Perhaps the downside is that people don't have the sense of control of technology that they had forty years ago—when a bright little kid in every other elementary school class could take your radio home, change a bad tube, and get it working. That's fixing the hardware, not just programming. We're so dependent on our technologies today that when they do break down, we feel lost.

RM: Do you have any knowledge as to the uses of technology in contemporary Africa? For example, has televised media coverage made any significant contribution to the betterment of anyone?

SRD: One becomes painfully aware that it hasn't, any time there's a major catastrophe, from an earthquake to a war, in which thirty or eighty or a hundred-fifty thousand people lose their lives somewhere in that nebulous construction we call the Third World—and either you don't hear about it at all or you only run into your first mention of it six months or five years later. This promotes a very distorted view of the world. The growth of information means there's more chance for distorted deployments of information to move into our lives. Really, I do believe ours is the age of misinformation.

OEB: I once wrote a story about people who were telepathic and who were fighting with each other simply because they knew too much, each one, about what the other was thinking. Communication doesn't get rid of our biology, and I think all too often we're reacting out of biologically based feelings—attempting to dominate, or whatever—and we can't really talk about it because then we get into arguments about sociological theory about who has the biggest, the best, and the most.

SRD: In the women's dorm in the university where I'm teaching this fall, there are—all with the best intentions in the world—announcements all over the walls, "A Woman is Beaten Every Six Minutes." As you walk down the halls, on various bulletin boards the word "rape" appears every four feet. Now, obviously the reason for all this is to raise consciousness. But what it also does is create a general field of fear. If the subject were airline accidents rather than violence against women, try to imagine an airline terminal set up the same way . . .

OEB: They're living in a world that's out to get them . . .

RM: You've both written about biological roles and gender politics. What changes can you see impacting the lives—and/or attitudes—of the average person?

SRD: Things are backsliding. People are less adventurous in assuming whatever elements they want, to construct whatever gender identity that they have.

When I listen to kids talk in class, the girls will talk about what they feel and the boys will talk about what they think. You try to push the boys to talk about what they feel, often to the point where everybody gets to see what's happening and they actually start to laugh. But, even while they laugh at themselves, they still can't do it. Sure, it's social conditioning. But it's also a discourse in place that says if men discuss their feelings it's a sign of weakness.

RM: Is that a problem you find exaggerated among minorities?

OEB: I'm afraid so. Men who talk a lot in black culture are looked down on.

RM: What's the future of sex?

SRD: I think it'll endure. [*Laughter.*]

OEB: In the novel I'm working on now, I have a character hear on the news that in Australia the first baby has been born from an artificial womb. And she thinks, "If this catches on quickly, what will happen to all those women who make a living as surrogate mothers?" It's not something that plays a big part in the novel. . . . Right now, we have lots of ways to help conception along, but the old way is still the one most people use.

SRD: What changes the face of sex is how comfortable people feel about it. Again, I see divisions working through the country—not necessarily following racial lines—between people who feel sex is something that you play with and have fun with and those who feel it's a dirty, ugly prerequisite to procreation that happens to give you a kick for ten or twelve seconds before the shame sets in, and you have to get it done real fast and out of the way.

RM: You've both written about historical and future slavery. What manifestation of slavery do you see in the present day?

OEB: There was an article in the *New York Times Magazine* about female slavery in Mauritania. Some of these people have been enslaved for five hundred years, for so long they haven't just lost who they were before—they've lost any hope of being anybody else. To such a degree that a woman had been asked if she'd been raped, and at first she didn't understand the question. She said, "Of course, when it was time to breed us, they came at night—is that what you mean?" This is something I noticed when I was researching *Kindred*. Sometimes the suffering and the degradation has been so pervasive from the day you were born, that if someone doesn't cause you to feel physical pain all the time, you think he's kind! . . . These women are free now, but what does that mean? They're not free in their minds.

SRD: My aunts—my father's two oldest sisters—of the period between the 1890s and the 1910s of this century, when many black people still wandered around the landscape who, you know, had grown up under slavery. . . . These people were the objects of all the educational work that was the upside of Reconstruction.

OEB: My grandmother was an orphan who was raised by people who did not want her, and who mistreated her, so she got married at age twelve, so there was no chance at an education there. My mother had to be put to work at age ten because if a twelve-year-old married she's going to have a lot of children, so she's got to farm some of them out. But the attitude was: If you can just get an education, that you can have all these things—but somehow that's gone in a lot of the black community: "Oh, well, you can't win, so why try?"

I wanted to mention the modern slavery that we don't tend to think of as such. Consider how profitable running prisons has become? And think about the use to which prisoners can be put.

RM: Well, prisons are the choice construction contract these days, and prison guards make up the fastest growing segment of law enforcement in this country. It's like a human storage industry.

SRD: You look at the death penalty movement—it's incredibly expensive to kill someone. On the average it costs about five million dollars to kill a prisoner.

OEB: Don't you get the feeling that's a little bit like slavery was in the South? Where it was actually doing a lot of harm to poor whites, who were having trouble getting jobs because those jobs could be performed more cheaply by slaves. Perhaps in the future, here—more cheaply by a combination of prison workers and welfare workers. And it's the kind of work where you don't learn anything that will help you when you're released.

RM: So much for rehabilitation.

OEB: I remember an article about no longer offering college courses to prisoners.

SRD: Most of the country's problems, I think, finally become one version or another of problems in education. The information explosion doesn't seem to be working at all to get information that people need to the people who need it. And there's a real need to rethink the philosophy behind prison: Is it for revenge? Is it for protection? Is it for rehabilitation? What exactly is the purpose?

OEB: I think right now it's revenge.

RM: Will the U.S. ever have a black president—who isn't a Republican?

OEB: He will be a Republican when he comes along, which is too bad, because he's liable to be Clarence Thomas.

SRD: One of the things we have a sense of now is that when you have the first woman prime minister it's going to be Margaret Thatcher. It's not going to be someone who's an example of forward-crusading radical thought. It's going to be the most conservative among the newly empowered group.

OEB: It's somebody who's willing to do the Master's work for them, a driver.

RM: You often find among minorities an impulse to cast their hopes with one messianic figure, who'll solve all their problems.

OEB: All people do that, especially oppressed people—they need the symbol even more. There was a time when white people wanted a Great White Hope in boxing. . . . People need heroes.

SRD: The problem is that we don't have enough local heroes. The media tries to take this huge, social field that we have in the U.S. and come up with one or two heroes for the whole thing.

OEB: The media is a great tool for oversimplification in every direction.

SRD: The notion of a single hero for "the black community of the United States" is ludicrous—because the black community of the United States is not one community. It's many different communities, all interconnected.

OEB: And all the more so, as we get more integration from Africa and the Caribbean.

RM: Is there a future for black atheism?

SRD: I hope it's got a great one.

OEB: I think most black people are either afraid to be atheists, so every now and then they do something religious just in case. I'm not religious, and that's difficult sometimes. I was just at a conference, and one of the speakers said something about, "The two black atheists in the world"—and I have a feeling there're an awful lot of people who don't have any particular religious bent but keep their mouth shut about it.

RM: Is the Back-to-Africa movement basically science fiction?

OEB: Yes. [*Laughter.*]

RM: What's the appeal of apocalyptic fiction? What are people confronting when they read fortellings of an American race war—whether it's from SF novels or films, or from white supremacists, or from black nationalist leaders?

SRD: It's a psychological need to envision the possibility for a new beginning. The End is secondary to the fact that it gives you a chance to start all over. Even though the story may be about the death of society, people need that in order to grasp a mythical tool for thinking about the terminations of situations in their own lives so they can move on to the new.

RM: Is that all the excitement about the new millennium boils down to, people's need for another artificial demarcation?

OEB: Just another bit of silliness, yeah.

RM: What are your thoughts on the Illuminati, or the belief in mass conspiracies that control our lives?

OEB: Human evil and human good, they're both equally incompetent. That may be what saves us: When you get a Hitler, he's incompetent too. Even though he managed to accomplish a lot of horror, he didn't do as much as he expected.

It bothers me that people are willing to attribute any amount of intricate plotting—and successful plotting—to some cabal someplace that's so good at controlling everything and keeping itself out of sight that none of us can do anything about it.

SRD: Someone said, "Never assign to conspiracy what can be explained by stupidity." It reassures people to be able to think that all the bizarre things that go on in the world are the product of intelligence, rather than just random idiot acts interacting with each other.

OEB: I don't see it as random. I see people acting in their own behalf, however unenlightened.

RM: Last question. If Mike Tyson was as big as Godzilla, who'd win in a fair fight?

OEB: Considering that Tyson has only two weapons and Godzilla has quite a number more . . .— *Why* am I answering this question?! [*Laughter.*]

—*November 1997*

NOTE

This conversation precedes Delany's introduction of Butler (see page 309 in this volume) by three years.

21

Racism and Science Fiction

Racism for me has always appeared to be first and foremost a system, largely supported by material and economic conditions at work in a field of social traditions. Thus, though racism is always made manifest through individuals' decisions, actions, words, and feelings, when we have the luxury of looking at it with the longer view (and we don't, always), usually I don't see much point in blaming people personally, white or black, for their feelings or even for their specific actions—as long as they remain this side of the criminal. These are not what stabilize the system. These are not what promote and reproduce the system. These are not the points where the most lasting changes can be introduced to alter the system.

For better or for worse, I am often spoken of as the first African-American science fiction writer. But I wear that originary label as uneasily as any writer has worn the label of science fiction itself. Among the ranks of what is often referred to as proto-science fiction, there are a number of black writers. M. P. Shiel, whose *Purple Cloud* and *Lord of the Sea* are still read, was a Creole with some African ancestry. Black leader Martin Delany (1812–1885—alas, no relation) wrote his single and highly imaginative novel, *Blake, or The Huts of America* (1857) (still to be found on the shelves of Barnes & Noble today), about an imagined successful slave revolt in Cuba and the American South—which is about as close to an SF-style alternate history novel as you can get. Other black writers whose work certainly borders on science fiction include Sutton E. Griggs and his novel *Imperio in Imperium* (1899), in which an African-American secret society conspires to found a separate black state by taking over Texas; and Edward Johnson, who, following Bellamy's example in *Looking Backward* (1888), wrote *Light Ahead for the Negro* (1904), telling of a black man transported

into a socialist United States in the far future. I believe I first heard Harlan Ellison make the point that we know of dozens upon dozens of early pulp writers
only as names: They conducted their careers entirely by mail—in a field and
during an era when pen names were the rule rather than the exception. Among
the "Remmington C. Scotts" and the "Frank P. Joneses" who litter the contents
pages of the early pulps, we simply have no way of knowing if one, three, or
seven or them—or even many more—were not blacks, Hispanics, women,
native Americans, Asians, or whatever. Writing is like that.

Toward the end of the Harlem Renaissance, the black social critic George
Schuyler (1895–1977) published an acidic satire *Black No More: Being an Account of
the Strange and Wonderful Workings of Science in the Land of the Free, A.D. 1933–1940*
(The Macaulay Company, 1931), which hinges on a three-day treatment cost-
ing fifty dollars through which black people can turn themselves white. The
treatment involves "a formidable apparatus of sparkling nickel. It resembled a
cross between a dentist chair and an electric chair." The confusion this causes
throughout racist America (as well as among black folks themselves) gives
Schuyler a chance to satirize both white leaders and black. (Though W. E. B. Du
Bois was himself lampooned by Schuyler as the aloof, money-hungry hypocrite
Dr. Shakespeare Agamemnon Beard, Du Bois, in his column "The Browsing
Reader" [in *The Crisis*, March 1931] called the novel "an extremely significant
work" and "a rollicking, keen, good-natured criticism of the Negro problem in
the United States" that was bound to be "abundantly misunderstood," because
such was the fate of all satire.) The story follows the adventures of the dashing
black Max Dasher and his sidekick Bunny, who become white and make their
way through a world rendered topsy-turvy by the spreading racial ambiguity
and deception. Toward the climax, the two white perpetrators of the system
who have made themselves rich on the scheme are lynched (at a place called
Happy Hill) by a group of whites who believe the two men are blacks in dis-
guise. Though the term did not exist, here the "humor" becomes so "black"
as to take on elements of inchoate American horror. For his scene, Schuyler
simply used accounts of actual lynchings of black men at the time, with a few
changes in wording (bracketed phrases are sections of the text moved to make
the piece clearer):

> The two men . . . were stripped naked, held down by husky and willing farm hands
> and their ears and genitals cut off with jackknives. . . . Some wag sewed their ears
> to their backs and they were released to run . . . [but were immediately brought
> down with revolvers by the crowd] amidst the uproarious laughter of the congre-
> gation. . . . [Still living, the two were bound together at a stake while] little boys
> and girls gaily gathered excelsior, scrap paper, twigs and small branches, while
> their proud parents fetched logs, boxes, kerosene. . . . [Reverend McPhule said a
> prayer, the flames were lit, the victims screamed, and the] crowd whooped with

glee and Reverend McPhule beamed with satisfaction. . . . The odor of cooking meat permeated the clear, country air and many a nostril was guiltily distended. . . . When the roasting was over, the more adventurous members of Rev. Mc-Phule's flock rushed to the stake and groped in the two bodies for skeletal souvenirs such as forefingers, toes and teeth. Proudly their pastor looked on. (217–18)

Might this have been too much for the readers of *Amazing* and *Astounding?* As it does for many black folk today, such a tale, despite the '30s-style pulp diction, has a special place for me. Among the family stories I grew up with, one was an account of a similar lynching of a cousin of mine from only a decade or so before the year Schuyler's story is set. Even the racial ambiguity of Schuyler's victims speaks to the story. A woman who looked white, my cousin was several months pregnant and traveling with her much darker husband when they were set upon by white men (because they believed the marriage was miscegenous) and lynched in a manner equally gruesome; her husband's body was similarly mutilated. And her child was no longer in her body when their corpses, as my father recounted the incident to me in the 1940s, were returned in a wagon to the campus of the black Episcopal college where my grandparents were administrators. Hundreds on hundreds of such social murders were recorded in detail by witnesses and participants between the Civil War and the Second World War. Thousands on thousands more went unrecorded. (Billy the Kid claimed to have taken active part in a more than half a dozen such murders of "Mexicans, niggers, and injuns," which were not even counted among his famous twenty-one adolescent killings.) But this is (just one of) the horrors from which racism arises—and where it can still all too easily go.

In 1936 and 1938, under the pen name "Samuel I. Brooks," Schuyler had two long stories published in some sixty-three weekly installments in the *Pittsburgh Courier*, a black Pennsylvania newspaper, about a black organization led by a black Dr. Belsidus, who plots to take over the world—work that Schuyler considered "hokum and hack work of the purest vein." Schuyler was known as an extreme political conservative, though the trajectory to that conservatism was very similar to Robert Heinlein's. (Unlike Heinlein's, though, Schuyler's view of science fiction was as conservative as anything about him.) Schuyler's early socialist period was followed by a later conservatism that Schuyler himself, at least, felt in no way harbored any contradiction with his former principles, even though he joined the John Birch Society toward the start of the 1960s and wrote for its news organ, *American Opinion*. His second Dr. Belsidus story remained unfinished, and the two were only collected in book form later (George S. Schuyler, *Black Empire*, ed. Robert A. Hill and Kent Rasmussen (Boston: Northeastern University Press, 1991), fourteen years after his death.

Since I began to publish in 1962, I have often been asked, by people of all colors, what my experience of racial prejudice in the science fiction field has been. Has it been nonexistent? By no means: It was definitely there. A child of the political protests of the 1950s and '60s, I've frequently said to people who asked that question: As long as there are only one, two, or a handful of us, however, I presume in a field such as science fiction, where many of its writers come out of the liberal-Jewish tradition, prejudice will most likely remain a slight force—until, say, black writers start to number thirteen, fifteen, twenty percent of the total. At that point, where the competition might be perceived as having some economic heft, chances are we will have as much racism and prejudice here as in any other field.

We are still a long way away from such statistics.

But we are certainly moving closer.

After—briefly—being my student at the Clarion Science Fiction Writers' Workshop, Octavia E. Butler entered the field with her first story, "Crossover," in 1971 and her first novel, *Patternmaster*, in 1976—fourteen years after my own first novel appeared in the winter of '62. But she recounts her story with brio and insight. Everyone was very glad to see her! After several short-story sales, Steven Barnes first came to general attention in 1981 with *Dreampark* and other collaborations with Larry Niven. Charles Saunders published his *Imaro* novels with DAW Books in the early '80s. Even more recently in the collateral field of horror, Tananarive Due has published *The Between* (1996) and *My Soul to Keep* (1997). Last year all of us except Charles were present at the first African-American Science Fiction Writers Conference sponsored by Clarke-Atlanta University. This year Toronto-based writer Nalo Hopkinson (another whom I have the pleasure of being able to boast of having taught at Clarion) published her award-winning SF novel *Brown Girl in the Ring* (1998). Another black North American writer is Haitian-born Claude-Michel Prévost, a francophone writer who publishes out of Vancouver, British Columbia.

Since people ask me regularly what examples of prejudice have I experienced in the science fiction field, I thought this might be the time to answer, then—with a tale.

With five days to go in my twenty-fourth year, on March 25, 1967, my sixth science fiction novel, *Babel-17*, won a Nebula Award (a tie, actually) from the Science Fiction Writers of America. That same day the first copies of my eighth, *The Einstein Intersection*, became available at my publishers' office. (Because of publishing schedules, my seventh, *Empire Star*, had preceded the sixth into print the previous spring.) At home on my desk at the back of an apartment I shared on St. Mark's Place, my ninth, *Nova*, was a little more than three months from completion.

On February 10, a month and a half before the March awards, in its partially completed state *Nova* had been purchased by Doubleday. Three months after the awards banquet, in June, when it was done, with that first Nebula under my belt, I submitted *Nova* for serialization to the famous SF editor of

Analog Magazine, John W. Campbell Jr., who rejected it, with a note and phone call to my agent explaining that he didn't feel his readership would be able to relate to a black main character. That was one of my first direct encounters, as a professional writer, with the slippery and always commercialized form of liberal American prejudice: Campbell had nothing against my being black, you understand. (There reputedly exists a letter from him to horror writer Dean Koontz, from only a year or two later, in which Campbell argues in all seriousness that a technologically advanced black civilization is a social and a biological impossibility . . .) No, perish the thought! Surely there was not a prejudiced bone in his body! It's just that I had, by pure happenstance, chosen to write about someone whose mother was from Senegal (and whose father was from Norway), and it was the poor benighted readers, out there in America's heartland, who, in 1967, would be too upset . . .

It was all handled as though I'd just happened to have dressed my main character in a purple brocade dinner jacket. (In the phone call Campbell made it fairly clear that this was his only reason for rejecting the book. Otherwise, he rather liked it . . .) Purple brocade just wasn't big with the buyers that season. Sorry . . .

Today if something like that happened, I would probably give the information to those people who feel it's their job to make such things as widely known as possible. At the time, however, I swallowed it—a mark of both how the times, and I, have changed. I told myself I was too busy writing. The most profitable trajectory for a successful science fiction novel in those days was to start life as a magazine serial, move on to hardcover publication, and finally be reprinted as a mass market paperback. If you were writing a novel a year (or, say, three novels every two years, which was then almost what I was averaging), at the time that was the only way to push your annual income up, from four to five figures—and the low five figures at that. That was the point I began to realize I probably was not going to be able to make the kind of living (modest enough!) that, only a few months before, at the awards banquet, I'd let myself envision. The things I saw myself writing in the future, I already knew, were going to be more rather than less controversial. The percentage of purple brocade was only going to go up.

The second installment of my story here concerns the first time the word "Negro" was said to me, as a direct reference to my racial origins, by someone in the science-fiction community. Understand that, since the late 1930s, that community, that world had been largely Jewish, highly liberal, and with notable exceptions leaned well to the left. Even its right-wing mavens, Robert Heinlein or Poul Anderson (or, indeed, Campbell), would have far preferred to go to a leftist party and have a friendly argument with some smart socialists than actually to hang out with the right-wing and libertarian organizations which they may well have supported in principal and, in Heinlein's case, with donations.

April 14, 1968, a year and—perhaps—three weeks later, was the evening of the next Nebula awards banquet. A fortnight before, I had turned twenty-six. That year my eighth novel *The Einstein Intersection* (which had materialized as an object on the day of the previous year's banquet) and my short story, "Aye, and Gomorrah . . ." were both nominated.

In those days the Nebula banquet was a black tie affair with upwards of a hundred guests at a midtown hotel-restaurant. Quite incidentally, it was a time of upheaval and uncertainty in my personal life (which, I suspect, is tantamount to saying I was a twenty-six-year-old writer). But that evening my mother and sister and a friend as well as my wife were at my table. My novel won—and the presentation of the glittering Lucite trophy was followed by a discomfiting speech from Fred Pohl, an eminent member of SFWA.

Perhaps you've heard such disgruntled talks. They begin, as did this one, "What I have to say tonight, many of you are not going to like . . ." and went on to castigate the organization for letting itself be taken in by (the phrase was, or was something very like) "pretentious literary nonsense" unto granting it awards, and abandoning the old values of good, solid, craftsmanlike storytelling. My name was not mentioned, but it was evident I was (along with Roger Zelazny, not present) the prime target of this fusillade. It's an odd experience, I must tell you, to accept an award from a hall full of people in tuxedos and evening gowns and then, from the same podium at which you accepted it, hear a half-hour jeremiad from an *eminence gris* declaring that award to be worthless and the people who voted it to you duped fools. It's not paranoia: By count I caught more than a dozen sets of eyes sweeping between me and the speaker going on about the triviality of work such as mine and the foolishness of the hundred-plus writers who had voted for it.

As you might imagine, the applause was slight, uncomfortable, and scattered. There was more coughing and chair scraping than clapping. By the end of the speech, I was drenched with the tricklings of mortification and wondering what I'd done to deserve them. The master of ceremonies, Robert Silverberg, took the podium and said, "Well, I guess we've all been put in our place." There was a bitter chuckle. And the next award was announced.

It again went to me—for my short story, "Aye, and Gomorrah . . . ," which I had, by that time, forgotten was in the running. For the second time that evening I got up and went to the podium to accept my trophy (it sits on a shelf above my desk about two feet away from me as I write), but, in dazzled embarrassment, it occurred to me as I was walking to the front of the hall that I must say something in my defense, though mistily I perceived it had best be as indirect as the attack. With my sweat-soaked undershirt beneath my formal turtleneck peeling and unpeeling from my back at each step, I took the podium and my second trophy of the evening. Into the microphone I said, as calmly as I could manage: "I write the novels and stories that I do and work on them as hard as I can to make them the best I can. That you've chosen to honor them —and twice in one night—is warming. Thank you."

I received a standing ovation—though I was aware it was as much in reaction to the upbraiding of the naysayer as it was in support of anything I had done. I walked back down toward my seat, but as I passed one of the tables, Virginia Kidd, an agent (not my own) who had several times written me and been supportive of my work, took my arm as I went by and pulled me down to say, "That was elegant, Chip . . . !" while the applause continued. At the same time, I felt a hand on my other sleeve—in the arm that held the Lucite block of the Nebula itself—and I turned to Isaac Asimov (whom I'd met for the first time at the banquet the year before), sitting on the other side and now pulling me toward him. With a large smile, wholly saturated with evident self-irony, he leaned toward me to say: "You know, Chip, we only voted you those awards because you're Negro . . . !" (This was 1968; the term 'black' was not yet common parlance.) I smiled back (there was no possibility he had intended the remark in any way seriously—as anything other than an attempt to cut through the evening's many tensions. . . . Still, part of me rolled my eyes silently to heaven and said: Do I really need to hear this right at this moment?) and returned to my table.

The way I read his statement then, and the way I read it today—indeed, anything else would be a historical misreading—is that Ike was trying to use a self-evidently tasteless absurdity (he was famous for them) to defuse some of the considerable anxiety in the hall that night; it is a standard male trope, needless to say. I think he was trying to say that race probably took little or no part in his or any other of the writer's minds who had voted for me.

But such ironies cut in several directions. I don't know whether Asimov realized he was saying this as well, but as an old historical materialist, if only as an afterthought, he must have realized that he was saying, too: No one here will ever look at you, read a word you write, or consider you in any situation, no matter whether the roof is falling in or the money is pouring in, without saying to him- or herself (whether in an attempt to count it or to discount it), "Negro . . ." The racial situation, permeable as it might sometimes seem (and it is, yes, highly permeable), is nevertheless your total surround. Don't you ever forget it . . . ! And I never have.

The fact that this particular "joke" emerged just then, at that most anxiety-torn moment, when the only three-year-old, volatile organization of feisty science fiction writers saw itself under a virulent battering from internal conflicts over shifting aesthetic values, meant that, though the word had not yet been said to me or written about me till then (and, from then on, it was, interestingly, written regularly, though I did not in any way change my own self presentation: Judy Merril had already referred to me in print as "a handsome Negro," and James Blish would soon write of me as "a merry Negro"; I mean, can you imagine anyone at the same time writing of "a merry Jew"?), it had clearly inhered in every step and stage of my then just six years as a professional writer.

Here the story takes a sanguine turn.

When Fred Pohl wrote his speech, he had apparently not yet actually read my nominated novel. He had merely had it described to him by a friend, a notoriously eccentric reader, who had fulminated that the work was clearly and obviously beneath consideration as a serious science fiction novel: Each chapter began with a set of quotes from literary texts that had nothing to do with science at all! Our naysayer had gone along with this evaluation, at least as far as putting together his rebarbative speech.

When, a week or two later, he decided to read the book for himself (in case he was challenged on specifics), he found, to his surprise, he liked it—and, from what embarrassment I can only guess, became one of my staunchest and most articulate supporters, as an editor and a critic. (A lesson about reading here: Do your share, and you can save yourself and others a lot of embarrassment.) And *Nova*, after its Doubleday appearance in 1968 and some pretty stunning reviews, the paperback garnered from Bantam Books what was then a record advance for an SF novel paid to date (a record broken shortly thereafter by Philip K. Dick's *Do Androids Dream of Electric Sheep*), ushering in the twenty years when I could actually support myself (almost) by writing alone.

(Algis J. Budrys, who also had been there that evening, wrote in his January 1969 review in *Galaxy*, "Samuel R. Delany, right now, as of this book, *Nova*, not as of some future book or some accumulated body of work, is the best science fiction writer in the world, at a time when competition for that status is intense. I don't see how a science fiction writer can do more than wring your heart while telling you how it works. No writer can. . . ." Even then I knew enough not to take such hyperbole seriously. I mention it to suggest the pressures around against which one had to keep one's head straight—and, yes, to brag just a little. But it's that desire to have it both ways—to realize it's meaningless, but to take some straited pleasure nevertheless from the fact that, at least, somebody was inspired to say it—that defines the field in which the dangerous slippages in your reality picture start, slippages that lead to that monstrous and insufferable egotism so ugly in so many much-praised artists.)

But what Asimov's quip also tells us is that, for any black artist (and you'll forgive me if I stick to the nomenclature of my young manhood, which my friends and contemporaries, appropriating it from Dr. Du Bois, fought to set in place, breaking into libraries through the summer of '68 and taking down the signs saying Negro Literature and replacing them with signs saying "black literature"—the small "b" on "black" is a very significant letter, an attempt to ironize and de-transcendentalize the whole concept of race, to render it provisional and contingent, a significance that many young people today, white and black, who lackadaisically capitalize it, have lost track of) the concept of

race informed everything about me, so that it could surface—and did surface
—precisely at those moments of highest anxiety, a manifesting brought about
precisely by the white gaze, if you will, whenever it turned, discommoded for
whatever reason, in my direction. Some have asked if I perceived my entrance
into science fiction as a transgression.

Certainly not at the entrance point, in any way. But it's clear from my story,
I hope (and I have told many others about that fraught evening), transgression
inheres, however unarticulated, in every aspect of the black writer's career in
America. That it emerged in such a charged moment is, if anything, only to be
expected in such a society as ours. How could it be otherwise?

A question that I am asked nowhere near as frequently—and that the recounting of tales such as the above tends to obviate and, as it were, put to sleep
—is the question: If that was the first time you were aware of direct racism,
when is the last time?

The fact is, to live in the United States as a black man or woman, the answer
to that question is rarely other than: A few hours ago, a few days, a few weeks.
. . . So, my hypothetical interlocutor persists, when is the last time you were
aware of racism in the science fiction field *per se*. Well, I would have to say, I just
spent last weekend attending Readercon 10, a fine and rich convention of concerned and alert people, a wonderful and stimulating convocation of high-level
panels and quality programming with, this year, almost a hundred professionals,
some dozen of whom were editors and the rest of whom were writers.

In the Dealers' room was an Autograph Table where, throughout the convention, pairs of writers were assigned an hour to make themselves available
for book signing. The hours the writers would be at the table was part of the
program. At 12:30 on Saturday, I came to sit down just as Nalo Hopkinson
came to join me.

Understand, on a personal level, I could not be more delighted to be signing
with Nalo. My student years ago, she is charming, talented, and today I think
of her as a friend. We both enjoyed our hour together. That is not in question.
After our hour was up, however, and we went and had some lunch together
with her friend David, we both found ourselves more amused than not that
the two black American SF writers at Readercon, out of nearly eighty professionals, had ended up at the autograph table in the same hour. Let me repeat:
I don't think you can have racism as a positive system until you have the socio-
economic support suggested by that (rather arbitrary) 20 percent black / 80 percent white proportion. But what racism as a system does is isolate and segregate
the people of one race, or group, or ethnos from another. As a system, it can
be fueled by chance as much as by hostility or by the best of intentions. ("I
thought they would be more comfortable together. I thought they would want
to be with each other . . .") And certainly one of its strongest manifestations is
as a socio-visual system in which people become used to always seeing blacks

with other blacks and so—because people are used to it—being uncomfortable whenever they see blacks mixed in, at whatever proportion, with whites.

My friend of a decade's standing, Eric Van, had charge of programming the coffee klatches, readings, and autograph sessions at this year's Readercon. One of the goals—facilitated by computer—was not only to assign the visiting writers to the panels they wanted to be on, but to try, when possible, not to schedule those panels when other panels the same writers wanted to hear were also scheduled. This made some tight windows. After the con I called Eric, who kindly pulled up grids and schedule sheets on his computer. "Well," he said, "lots of writers, of course, asked to sign together. But certainly neither you nor Nalo did that. As I recall, Nalo had a particularly tight schedule. She wasn't arriving until late Friday night. Saturday at 12:30 was pretty much the only time she could sign—so, of the two of you, she was scheduled first. When I consulted the grid, the first two names that came up who were free at the same time were you and Jonathan Lethem. You came first in the alphabet—and so I put you down. I remember looking at the two of you, you and Nalo, and saying: Well, certainly there's nothing wrong with that pairing. But the point is, I wasn't thinking along racial lines. I probably should have been more sensitive to the possible racial implications . . ."

Let me reiterate: Racism is a system. As such, it is fueled as much by chance as by hostile intentions—and equally by the best intentions, as well. It is whatever systematically acclimates people, of all colors, to become comfortable with the isolation and segregation of the races, on a visual, social, or economic level —which in turn supports and is supported by socio-economic discrimination. Because it is a system, however, I believe personal guilt is almost never the proper response in such a situation. Certainly, personal guilt will never replace a bit of well-founded systems analysis. And one does not have to be a particularly inventive science fiction writer to see a time, when we are much closer to that 20 percent division, where we black writers all hang out together, sign our books together, have our separate tracks of programming, if we don't have our own segregated conventions, till we just never bother to show up at yours because we make you uncomfortable and you don't really want us; and you make us feel the same way . . .

One fact that adds its own shadowing to the discussion is the attention that has devolved on Octavia Butler since her 1995 receipt of a MacArthur "genius" award. But the interest has largely been articulated in terms of interest in "African-American Science Fiction," whether it be among the halls of MIT, where Butler and I appeared last, or the University of Chicago, where we are scheduled to appear together in a few months. Now Butler is a gracious, intelligent, and wonderfully impressive writer. But if she were a jot less great-hearted than she is, she might very well wonder: "Why, when you invite me, do you always invite that guy, Delany?"

The fact is, while it is always a personal pleasure to appear with her, Butler and I are very different writers, interested in very different things. And because I am the one who benefits by this highly artificial generalization of the literary interest in Butler's work into this in-many-ways-artificial interest in African-American science fiction (I'm not the one who won the MacArthur, after all), I think it's incumbent upon me to be the one publicly to question it. And while it provides generous honoraria for us both, I think that the nature of the generalization (since we have an extraordinarily talented black woman SF writer, why don't we generalize that interest to all black SF writers, male and female) has elements of both racism and sexism about it.

One other thing allows me to question it in this manner. When, last year, there was an African-American Science Fiction Conference at Clark-Atlanta University, where, with Steve Barnes and Tananarive Due, Butler and I met with each other, talked and exchanged conversation and ideas, spoke and interacted with the university students and teachers and the other writers in that historic black university; all of us present had the kind of rich and lively experience that was much more likely to forge common interests and that, indeed, at a later date could easily leave shared themes in our subsequent work. This aware and vital meeting to respond specifically to black youth in Atlanta is not, however, what usually occurs at an academic presentation in a largely white university doing an evening on African-American SF. Butler and I, born and raised on opposite sides of the country, half a dozen years apart, share many of the experiences of racial exclusion and the familial and social responses to that exclusion which constitute a race. But as long a racism functions as a system, it is still fueled from aspects of the perfectly laudable desires of interested whites to observe this thing, however dubious its reality, that exists largely by means of its having been named: African-American science fiction.

To pose a comparison of some heft: In the days of cyberpunk, I was often cited by both the writers involved and the critics writing about them as an influence. As a critic, several times I wrote about the cyberpunk writers. And Bill Gibson wrote a gracious and appreciative introduction to the 1996 reprint of my novel *Dhalgren*. Thus you might think that there were a fair number of reasons for me to appear on panels with those writers or to be involved in programs with them. With all the attention that has come on her in recent years, Butler has been careful (and accurate) in not claiming that I am any sort of influence on her. I have never written specifically about her work. Nor, as far as I know, has she ever mentioned me in print.

Nevertheless: Throughout all of cyberpunk's active history, I only recall being asked to sit on one cyberpunk panel with Bill, and that was largely a media-focused event at the Kennedy Center. In the past ten years, however, I have been invited to appear with Octavia at least six times, with another appearance scheduled in a few months and a joint interview with the both of us scheduled for a national magazine. All the comparison points out is the pure and unmitigated strength of the discourse of race in our country vis-à-vis any other. In a society such as ours, the discourse of race is so involved and embraided with the discourse of racism that I would defy anyone ultimately and authoritatively to distinguish them in any absolute manner once and for all.

Well, then, how does one combat racism in science fiction, even in such a nascent form as it might be fibrillating, here and there. The best way is to build a certain social vigilance into the system—and that means into conventions such as Readercon: Certainly racism in its current and sometimes difficult form becomes a good topic for panels. Because race is a touchy subject, in situations such as the above-mentioned Readercon autographing session where chance and propinquity alone threw blacks together, you simply ask: Is this all right, or are there other people that, in this case, you would rather be paired with for whatever reason—even if that reason is only for breaking up the appearance of possible racism, since the appearance of possible racism can be just as much a factor in reproducing and promoting racism as anything else. Racism is as much about accustoming people to becoming used to certain racial configurations, so that they are specifically not used to others, as it is about anything else. Indeed, we have to remember that what we are combatting is called prejudice: prejudice is pre-judgment—in this case, the prejudgment that the way things just happen to fall out are "all right," when there well may be reasons for setting them up otherwise. Editors and writers need to be alerted to the socioeconomic pressure on such gatherings of social groups to reproduce inside a new racist system inside, by virtue of "outside pressures." Because we still live in a racist society, the only way to combat racism in any systematic way is to establish—and repeatedly revamp—anti-racist institutions and traditions. That means actively encouraging the attendance of nonwhite readers and writers at conventions. It means actively presenting nonwhite writers with a forum to discuss precisely these problems in the con programming. (It seems absurd to have to point out that racism is by no means exhausted simply by black/white differences: indeed, one might argue that it is only touched on here.) And it means encouraging dialogue among, and encouraging intermixing with, the many sorts of writers who make up the SF community.

It means supporting those traditions.

I've already started discussing this with Eric. I will be going on to speak about it with next year's programmers.

Readercon is certainly as good a place as any, not to start but to continue.

—*1998*

22

Some Queer Notions about Race

Race is a fracturing trauma in the body politic of the nation—
and in the mortal bodies of its people. Race kills, liberally and
unequally; and race privileges, unspeakably and abundantly. Like
nature, race has much to answer for; and the tab is still running for
both categories. Race, like nature, is at the heart of stories about
the origins and purposes of the nation. Race, at once an uncanny
unreality and an inescapable presence, frightens me; and I am not
alone in this paralyzing historical pathology of body and soul. Like
nature, race is the kind of category about which no one is neutral,
no one unscathed, no one sure of their ground, if there is a ground.
Race is a peculiar kind of object of knowledge and practice. The
meanings of the word are unstable and protean; the status of the
word's referent has wobbled—and still wobbles—from being considered real and rooted in the natural, physical body to being
considered illusory and utterly socially constructed. In the United
States, race immediately evokes the grammars of purity and mixing, compounding and differentiating, segregating and bonding,
lynching and marrying. Race, like nature and sex, is replete with
all the rituals of guilt and innocence in the stories of nation, family,
and species. Race, like nature, is about roots, pollution, and origins.
An inherently dubious notion, race, like sex, is about the purity
of lineage; the legitimacy of passage; the drama of inheritance of
bodies, property, and stories.
    —Donna Haraway, *Modest Witness@Second Millennium*

I.

I don't remember ever being unaware of racial injustice as a major problem in America. My family talked about it constantly. My Uncle Hubert, a New York judge and a crusading politician, fought it passionately. My Uncle Myles, my mother's brother-in-law and another judge in Brooklyn, fought it too. In 1950, when I was eight, our Park Avenue school sent my whole, largely white (besides me, there were three other black students in my class of twenty-three: Linda Anderson, Peggy Dammond, and Mary MacDougal) third-grade class on a weeklong trip north to an Otis, Massachusetts, farmhouse owned by a friendly white couple, George and Lois. Our first night in the country, Lois proposed to entertain us by reading some of Joel Chandler Harris's Uncle Remus tales in dialect. When she was about three sentences into the story of "Br'er Rabbit an da Tar Baby," I raised my hand vigorously. Surprised, she called on me, and I stood up from the rug where we sat listening and announced, "My father says that those stories are insulting to Negroes and are just a white writer making fun of Negro speech so that white people can laugh at us. And you shouldn't do that." Then, among Robert and Wendy and Johnny and Pricilla and Nancy, I dropped back down, cross-legged on the rug.

I'm not sure what response I expected. What shocked me, however, as Lois sat there on a wood-frame chair in her heavy sweater and long winter skirt, was her sudden embarrassment, her quick agreement ("You're perfectly right. I know that . . . I just wasn't . . . Really, I didn't mean to offend any of you—any of you at all."), and the speed with which she jumped up and turned to go to the wall bookshelf—while on the rug in the sprawling farmhouse library, among my equally surprised classmates, black and white, I was struck by the presence of extraordinary power, suddenly and surprisingly.

For a third grader, such power is *hugely* uncomfortable.

The discomfort was enough to make me mumble now, with embarrassment, "Of course, I don't really care. I mean, it's just my parents . . ." But, with me as their mediator, my parents had already won.

Understand, I knew those stories. My father had read me the "Br'er Rabbit" tales and had often laughed out loud in spite of himself. Years before, my mother had read me about "Li'l Black Sambo." Both had explained the problems with their racial humor—even as the tigers melting into a pool of butter around the palm tree had remained with me as a delicious bit of fantasy. If Lois has been prepared to read them, even enjoy them with provisos, caveats, and explanations, I would not have objected. But she was doing precisely what my parents had warned me white people did with those tales: present them as language to laugh at, and at the very end, be surprised that such funny speech could actually yield a maxim that made sense, wholly detachable from the human experiences that had taught it. But now Lois slid the orange-covered volume back into the bookcase and, a moment later, returned to the chair with another book.

The memory of my power, and the strangeness with which it sat—the part of it now mine—in my body for the rest of the evening, blots out all recollection of what Lois finally read that night.

II.

Strongly aware of my own homosexual feelings by the time I was nine, ten, eleven, I learned with the feelings themselves, however, that I must keep them secret. About my sexual feelings I couldn't possibly have stood up for myself against another unthinking child's comments, much less an adult's. A couple of times during my adolescence, I had one or another experience when, believing I was discovered, I learned only how anxious and even determined the straight world was not to see or acknowledge such feelings in anyone—and I felt as if I were being given a boon, a gift, another sort of power to aid me in my secrecy.

In 1961 at nineteen I married a white woman of eighteen, a poet, with whom I had gone to high school. Paradoxically, she was the person with whom I would share these feelings the most. For the previous two years, she had been the one person whom I could tell all about my gay feelings, experiences, and confusions. But it wasn't until I was twenty-two, when I'd had what at that point was called a "nervous breakdown," brought on largely by the pressure of having written and sold five novels in three years, and exacerbated by the added pressures of trying to negotiate a heterosexual relationship along with whatever homosexual outlets were available to me, that I began to realize, more than half a dozen years before Stonewall, that the oppression all women in our society in general and gay men in particular suffered was something other than the psychological *Sturm und Drang* Lillian Hellman had portrayed in *The Children's Hour*, but was a centrally political problem.

Since then, both problems have focused a great deal of my thinking and my writing. Only ten months ago, in Texas in June 1998, a black man, James Byrd, was chained to a truck and dragged to his death by a group of white men for the crime of being black. Six months ago, an openly gay student in Wyoming, Matthew Shepherd, was beaten, burned, roped to a fence on a cold Wyoming road, and left to die for the crime of being gay. And the murder of pediatrician Barnett Schlepian in his own upstate New York home by an antiabortionist—seven months back—makes clear how threatening the notion of any structural change in the status of women is to many.

Yet I have always felt a difficulty in discussing these problems together. The ability to be clear and logical about any one of them at any one time has always come to me as a feeling of power. But the others have tended to stay silent within, a discomfort whose articulation might subvert that power, reveal flaws in its logic, and ultimately negate the socially beneficial authority of my position. The distance between New York, Texas, and Wyoming is, if anything, the allegorical marker informed by the difficulty of bridging the topics throughout my own articulation.

To speak of gay oppression in the context of racial oppression always seemed an embarrassment. Somehow it was to speak of the personal and the mechanics of desire in the face of material deprivation and vast political and imperialist and nationalist systemics.

I remember clearly when to speak of women's oppression in the context of racial oppression seemed to be speaking of something selfish, personal, not large-hearted enough. After all, men took care of women. If you improved the lot of one group of men, wouldn't you of necessity improve the lot of "their" women, "their" children? Pointing out that the very discursive structure that such an argument, such a perception appealed to was the locus of rampant abuse to women as it denied them full autonomy in the family, the society, the race—and the obvious and awful extent of the abuse to women it occasioned in all the country's races—seemed like moving a millstone up a hill—or even a huge heap of sand—just with your shoulder.

Similarly, to speak of racial oppression in the midst of discussing gay liberation was to confront an embarrassing reminder of the huge amount of homophobia that manifested itself most forcefully right at the strongest areas of black nationalism and the fight to end racial power imbalances.

How, then, was one supposed to negotiate, as it were, the road from New York to Texas to Wyoming? How could we look at the highways between them, their intricate and interconnecting side paths, their main lanes and alternate routes, their service roads, much less the political ecology of their interdependencies?

III.

Functioning as a kind of momentary historical vision of the fall of some never-experienced utopia, a childhood story I grew up with, told and retold a dozen times, came from my Aunt Amaza Reed—a woman on my mother's side of the family who, among my black and brown cousins, was blonde and had green eyes.

Actually a second or third cousin, twenty or thirty years older than my mother, Aunt Amaza was from a small town near Salem, North Carolina, and her story centered around a town meeting of the then much smaller city, which she had attended with her parents when she was a little girl of seven or eight —a meeting that must have occurred around 1896, when the Jim Crow laws mandating separate but equal schooling were first instituted throughout the South. As Aunt Amaza described it, "Salem was one of those little southern towns where everybody was related to everybody else. At the town meeting in the church where they announced that, by law from now on, they would have separate but equal facilities, after the mayor explained the 'one drop of Negro blood makes you Negro' rule, he added, 'But we'd go crazy here if we all try to figure that one out.' So he told the eighty or so people gathered that night: 'All right, what we'll do is: Everybody who wants to be Negro get on this side of the room and everybody who wants to be white get on that side.' Now—" my Aunt Amaza continued—"if cousin Henry was not speaking to Aunt Clem that month, and if Aunt Clem had decided she was white, then cousin Henry was fit to be tied if he was going to be the same race as that hard-headed woman, and went over to the Negro side. People went with their friends, and saw it as a fine opportunity to get away from their enemies, their nuisance relatives. That's pretty much how the decisions on who was which race were made. And I'll tell you, by the end of the evening, there were an awful lot of pretty dark people on the white side of the room, and an awful lot of pretty light people on the Negro side. And don't *talk* to me about families! But they took all the names down in a book." Here my Aunt grew pensive. "They didn't know, back then, what it was all going to mean, you see. They just didn't know."

By the time I was nine or ten, I had heard the story several times. I'm sure I was not more than ten or eleven when I began to realize that the "single drop of blood" rule, while its intentions were strictly prophylactic, also managed legally to fix the vector of racial pollution in one direction alone. Black contaminates white—but not the other way around. Over the *longue durée*, then, this seemed certain to be a legal mandate that eventually the country must be all black.

IV.

I was nowhere near as lucky in my political education about gay oppression. I had no early vision of a prelapsarian utopia to fall back on. The topic would have bewildered my otherwise politically liberal parents. Even Freud's notion of pre-pubescent "polymorphous perversity" was evoked not to explain child-hood sexual behavior but rather to explain it away. What my early education in that matter actually was, was only brought home to me not a full year back at the February 1998 OutWrite Conference of Lesbian and Gay Writers in Boston, Massachusetts. One of the Sunday morning programs began with two questions.

"Why is there homophobia?" and "What makes us gay?"

As I listened to the discussion over the next hour and a half, I found myself troubled: Rather than attack both questions head on, the discussants tended to veer away from them, as if those questions were somehow logically congruent to the two great philosophical conundrums, ontological and epistemological, that grounded western philosophy—"Why is there something rather than nothing?" and, "How can we know it?"—and, as such, could only be approached by elaborate indirection.

It seems to me there are pointed answers to be given to both the questions. "Why is there homophobia?" and "What makes us gay?" These are answers it is imperative we understand, historify, and contextualize if gay and lesbian men and women are to make any progress in passing from what Urvashti Vaid has called, so tellingly, "virtual equality" (the appearance of equality with few or none of the material benefits) to a material and legal-based equality.

By the time I was ten or eleven, I knew why "prostitutes and perverts" were to be hated, if not feared. My Uncle Myles—Judge Paige, a black man who had graduated from Tuskegee, a Republican, a Catholic, and as I've said, a respected judge in Brooklyn's Domestic Relations Court—told us the reason repeatedly throughout the 1940s and '50s, during a dozen family dinners, over the roast lamb, the macaroni and cheese, the creamed onions, and the kale (this was how I knew I had to hide those sexual feelings; this is what I had to hide them from), where he sat at the head of the dinner table.

"Prostitutes and perverts," he explained, "destroy, undermine, and rot the foundations of Society." I remember his saying, again and again, that, if he had his way, "I would take all those people out and shoot 'em!" while his more liberal wife—my mother's sister—protested futilely. "Well," my uncle grumbled, "I would." The implication was that he had some arcane and secret information about "prostitutes and perverts" that, while it justified the ferocity of his position, could not to be shared at the dinner table with women and children. But I entered adolescence knowing the law alone, and my uncle's judicial position in it, kept his anger, and by extension the anger of all right-thinking men like him, in check—kept it from breaking out in a concerted attack on "those people," who were destroying, undermining, and rotting the foundations of society; which meant, as far as I understood it, menacing my right to sit there in the dining room in the Brooklyn row house on MacDonough Street and eat our generous, even lavish Sunday dinner, which my aunt and grandmother had fixed over the afternoon . . .

These were the years between, say, 1949 and 1953, that I—and I'm sure, many, many others—heard this repeatedly as the general social judgment on sex workers and/or homosexuals. That is to say, it was about half a dozen years after the end of World War II. Besides being a judge, my Uncle Myles had also been a captain in the U.S. Army.

What homosexuality and prostitution represented for my uncle was the untrammeled pursuit of pleasure; and the untrammeled pursuit of pleasure was the opposite of social responsibility. Nor was this simply some abstract principal to the generation so recently home from European military combat. Many had begun to wake, however uncomfortably, to a fact that problematizes much of the discourse around sadomasochism today. In the words of Bruce Benderson, writing in the *Lambda Book Report* 12: "The true Eden where all desires are satisfied is red, not green. It is a bloodbath of instincts, a gaping maw of orality, and a basin of gushing bodily fluids." Too many had seen "nice, ordinary American boys" let loose in some tiny French or German or Italian town where, with the failure of the social contract, there was no longer any law —and there had seen all too much of that red "Eden." Nor—in World War II —were these situations officially interrogated, with attempts to tame them for the public with images such as "Lt. Calley" and "My Lai," as they would be a decade and a half later in Vietnam. Rather they circulated as an unstated and inarticulate horror whose lessons were supposed to be brought back to the States while their specificity was, in any collective narrativity, unspeakable, left in the foreign outside, safely beyond the pale, a purely masculine knowledge of an extra-social horror which was somehow at once presumed to be both in the American male and what American males had to save civil American society (i.e., an abstraction that contained both women as bodies, capable of reproduction, and all institutions as systems) from.

The clear and obvious answer (especially to a Catholic Republican army officer and judge) was that pleasure must be socially doled out in minuscule amounts, tied by rigorous contracts to responsibility. Good people were people who accepted this contractual system. Anyone who rebelled was a prostitute or a pervert, or both. (And, yes, my uncle was painfully aware that prostitutes and pimps—if not perverts—were strongly associated in the minds of many in those years, black and white, with blacks.) Anyone who actively pursued prostitution or perversion was working, whether knowingly or not, to unleash precisely those red Edenic forces of desire that could only topple society, destroy all responsibility, and produce a nation without families, without soldiers, without workers—indeed, a crazed, drunken, libertine chaos that was itself no state, for clearly no such space of social turbulence (which, turned loose for group fun, so much of the military—indeed any all-male group—had shown itself at any moment capable of becoming) could maintain any but the most feudal state apparatus.

The male-gang mentality that causes groups of men to attack women, or gay men, or anyone perceived as different seems to turn on some "deep" idea homosexual component—which to call "homosocial" is only to fit it with a shadow mask for an interim moment of analysis, a component for a certain conservative *Weltanschauung*—and might even have been assumed to have social use.

That was and will remain the answer to the question, "Why is there hatred and fear of homosexuals (homophobia)?"—as long as this is the systematic relation between pleasure and responsibility in which "prostitution and perversion" are seen to be caught up. The herd of teenage boys who stalk the street with their clubs, looking for a faggot to beat bloody and senseless, or the employer who fires the worker who is revealed to be gay, or the landlord who turns the gay tenant out of his or her apartment, or the social circle who refuses to associate with someone who is found out to be gay, or the young murderers of Wyoming, are simply the Valkyries—the *Wunschmädchen*—to my uncle's legally constrained Woton.

What I saw in the conversation at OutWrite was that the argument exists today largely at the level of discourse, and that younger gay activists find it hard to articulate the greater discursive structure they are fighting to dismantle, as do those conservatives today who uphold one part of it or the other without being aware of its overall form. But discourses in such conditions tend to remain at their most stable.

The overall principal that must be appealed to in order to dismantle such a discourse is the principal that claims desire is *never* "outside all social constraint." Desire may be outside one set of constraints or another, but social constraints are what engender desire; and, one way or another, even at its most apparently catastrophic, they contour desire's expression.

V.

A 1993 cover of *Time* magazine ("The New Face of America") most recently morphed that softly brown face of the future, which Donna Haraway, in the same chapter from which I've taken my epigraph, has reread as the face of SimEve. ("Never has there been a better toy for playing out sexualized racial fantasies, anxieties, and dreams.") That face, as Haraway points out, allows us to see the results of myriad micro-pollutions as it cajoles us into forgetting the bloody history of miscegenation that brings it about.

If one of the reasons I am black is because my grandfather, Henry Beard Delany, was born a slave in Georgia (as were six out of eight of my *great*-grandparents), another reason is because black members of my family had been lynched by white people for looking like my Aunt Amaza—or even like me.

Two among its many qualities make the concept of race theoretically problematic—and I mean theoretically in the sense of something to be theorized.

First, of the "three races of mankind"—Caucasian, Mongoloid, and Negroid, as they were once known: white, yellow, and black—the black race among them, at least within the bounds of the white United States (thanks to that one-drop rule), at the level of the law functions entirely as a hereditary pollutant.

Second, race is a concept that has no opposite. It has no negative. The word "race" comes from the Spanish *raza*—a large, old family of many generations. By the beginning of sixteenth century it had spread around the northern rim of the Mediterranean, so that in Italy one spoke of "the Sforza race" or "the Medici race," while on the back of his pen-and-ink drawing with wash over traces of black and red chalk, done between 1510 and 1512, "The Fetus in the Womb," Leonardo da Vinci could write:

> The black races of Ethiopia are not the product of the sun; for if black gets black with child in Scythia, the offspring is black; but if a black gets a white woman with child, the offspring is gray.

Here the term "races"—and note the plural—simply means the great old families that comprise Ethiopia. That such an observation about racial mixing appears even before, historically, the term means race, endorses an image of conception, hereditary, and birth is not without its significance. Not until the eighteenth century was the term, however, "racialized," when writers like Oliver Goldsmith begin to use phrases such as "the Tarter race" (in *The Natural History of Animals*, 1774). It is not without significance that, along with *The Vicar of Wakefield*, *She Stoops to Conquer*, and *The Deserted Village*, the works by which we are likely to know him today, twelve years before in 1762 Goldsmith had written a series of travel letters, presumably from China, that were republished under the title "The Citizen of the World." The eighteenth century's totalization of the world begins to pull forward the modern concept of race, i.e., "The major divisions of mankind" (as the OED characterizes the word in section "d" of definition 2).

But compare this notion of "race" (a major division of mankind) to the earlier notion, race as family, whether progenitors or progeny. Race as family allows of an opposite.

"He has no family. . . . All his family are dead. . . . She is without family." All these are rational sentences. But once the term becomes racialized, that rationality is precisely what the negative looses: "He has no race. . . . All his race is dead. . . . She is without race." These sentences are irrational, meaningless. At best (in the case say, of "All his race is dead") they throw us back to the specifically *pre*-racial, family meaning of the term. This is a semantic sign, I would hazard, that race has now become something—an essence—that suffuses the body of the subject and deeply affects the mind, rather than remains caught solely in the process (as with the concept of family) by which the subject is reproduced or reproduces itself.

It would appear, then, that the concept of race develops to assuage the anxiety at the absence of a term for a group larger than a single family, as a term that is specifically not coextensive with the idea of a nation but is nevertheless mediated by heredity rather than by geography.

At this point, the relation of sex to race becomes self-evident: You can't very well have heredity *without* sex.

But here we are at the verge of the polluting powers of race. For if family is taken to be the form of the process by which heredity occurs, then race is the thing-in-the-body that is inherited: but the "thing-inherited" always turns out to be its own pollutability—sometimes called purity. Indeed, even without appealing to the "one-drop" rule (the United States' historical, if inanely pyrrhic, method for policing racial borders), we can see that the inescapable imbrication of race and sex via the concept of heredity makes race itself nothing more than a field of potential pollutions.

The polluting power of race is simply another name for the inclusionary power of a great family: One cannot marry out of such families; one can only marry into them. The concept of race arises, however, when the great family becomes so large that it loses its boundaries and the relation between members becomes purely sexual—natural, transcendental, essential—rather than contractual; as a corollary to the same transformation, inclusion then everts into pollution.

Is it a paradox, then, that in so many narratives of racial impurity, the sign of pollution actualized is the emergence of homosexuality? In the conceptual field of race, a field that has no necessary existence apart from the threat of pollution, of sexual infiltration, the dramatic proof that pollution has occurred is the emergence of men and women whose commitment to heredity, to preserving the threat of pollution to other races (marked or unmarked) that maintains the racial field in its stable/unstable existence, is, at least in the popular imagination where much of my narrative calculus takes place, radically in question.

The difficulty of speaking of racism and homophobia together is precisely this: While the machinery of oppression to both races and sexual orientations is distressingly the same, the underlying desire to end racism is seen as the desire to lift the proscription on pollution itself, allowing it to run wild, even self-destruct, into the micro-pollutions represented by the grid of constitutive photographs behind SimEve's benign (as a vampire's expression is benign, as homosexual Walter Pater noted of the Giaconda, the Renaissance model of all-woman that, with revolution, Republicanism, and Romanticism had already transmuted into Goethe's eternal feminine) smile. The desire to end homophobia is seen, however, as the desire to remove the stigma on opting out of the pollution game entirely.

Black men coupling with white women—in this country—extend the black race. Black women coupling with white men weaken, pollute, dilute the black race. The difficulties of speaking about the relationship between the oppression of one sex by the other and the oppression of one race by the other is the fear that an oscillating system of exploitation of women, white and black, by black and by white men, which alone is what allows race to be, will be revealed.

Race exists through potential pollution/procreation.

Same-sex relations threaten to bring pollution/procreation to a halt.

Woman is the cherished/guarded/enslaved ground on which this game of pollution/procreation is played out.

What we are doing, I hope it should be clear by now, is tracing out the negative calculus of desire underlying the positive arithmetics of the discourse falling out of patriarchal inheritances. But this sense of a contradiction at the level of desire is what paralyzes so many of us in speaking about both oppressions at the same time and relating them in any rational hierarchy. What we can be certain of is that, in any discussion of any one field, however forward-looking we believe our statements and position to be, if any discomfort lingers about either of the other two, however silent, then some aspect or other of our articulated positions are, in some manner, acceding to this spurious, fatal calculus.

The power of race is that it grows, strengthens, spreads, reproduces itself, takes all into itself, revels in its ability to include—which, again, is its ability to pollute given another name. (Quite probably for certain white slaveholders, what now and again went on in their black breeding pens, sequestered across the fields from the main house, played the same discursive role for them as what went on in the European theater did for my uncle, the judge.) To believe that race exists is to believe that its energy—specifically its sexual energy as a potential for procreation—is a real and potent force, for good or ill. But by the same uncritical calculus, homosexuality is seen as the element that is at once within it but that which, at the same time, denies procreation its all-important outlet. (This articulation parenthesizes women in the equation just as smartly, just as sharply, as choosing to murder a male abortion doctor becomes a metonym for women's oppression.) Breeding is, after all, what white slave owners in the early years of slavery wanted their slaves to do. Presumably having same-sex relationships is what they didn't want them to do or didn't care about.

VI.

From some time in the 1970s comes one of my most vivid memories of that paralysis—well after I had come out—in this case, sitting at the blond wood tables of the Schomburg library on 135th Street, where a brother who had come into the library to read soon engaged me in a heated and pressing conversation, and where I felt I could do nothing but listen. "Don't you realize," he declared, leaning forward and taking my forearm, "homosexuality is the white man's evil that he has inflicted on us to help destroy us. Black men ain't gay—unless they've been paying too much attention and listening to white men. There ain't no gay people in Africa. . . ."

Ten years later, again in the Schomburg, this time when I'd been invited to give a reading there with Octavia Butler, in the Q and A session afterward our community audience was upset by a young man in dashiki and batiked cap presenting the same set of concepts, which evoked mumblings both of disapproval and approval.

Mumblings, yes—but no one said anything clear and articulate. And the moderator chose that moment to bring the session to a close.

Today (October '98), anyone interested can go to the 42nd Street area and listen to the street preaching of a black sect, decked out in leather, turbans, and metal studs, calling itself the Nation of Zion, whose preachers stand flanked by two or more guards. While their rhetoric begins with a historically reasoned critique of the image of a "white" Christ, they soon move on to openly exhort, as they have almost daily for more than a decade now, the extermination of all mixed-blooded blacks, all homosexuals black and white, and all blacks with vitiligo (the disease where the pigment-producing cells break down while blotches appear on the face and hands and eventually over much of the skin) as unclean and polluted.

Wherever we find it, the hidden calculus supporting this argument remains invariant: Homosexuality pollutes the family, the race, the nation *precisely because* it appears to reduce the threat or menace of pollution to others—the mutual menace that holds the boundaries of a given family, race, or nation in tense stability. And "woman" is an undifferentiated, wholly invaginated ground of reparation/procreation that, as it perfuses all as an essence, is simply absent on any other level: material, bodily, intellectual, economic, political . . . an absence often designated in a false positivity by the "social."

VII.

Interestingly, the first time I encountered these ideas, and the paralysis they sometimes engender, was, of all places, in Greece—a location that, throughout the rest of European culture, is historically associated with homosexuality as much as it is, inextricably, with the origins of European culture in Greek literature and art.

In the months I lived in Greece, during the middle 1960s (I was twenty-three), one of the places I visited regularly in Athens was a pair of movie theaters, one right next to the other, about three or four blocks off Omonoia Square. Both screened Steve Reeves–style Italian muscle epics alternating with American westerns. To say that one was slightly rougher than the other simply meant there were more young Greek men there, often from the army or the navy, actively hustling the procession of middle-aged Greek businessmen in and out. One day I noticed a young man sitting on the balcony in—for that place and time—an uncharacteristic suit and tie, rare among the work clothes, military uniforms, and slouch jackets most of the patrons wore. He seemed a bit too proper for this milieu. But, after observing him for twenty minutes, I saw that he knew a number of the people moving about from seat to seat in the balcony; and a bit later, once we had passed each other on the narrow stairway up to the balcony, he came over to talk to me! Petros was a student (was he nineteen? was he twenty?) and turned out to be extraordinarily intelligent. Committed to being a doctor, he was nevertheless a lover of literature. At the movies and, later, back at the Boltetziou Street room that my three (straight) traveling companions (an Englishman, a Canadian, and another American) and I were sharing—while my roommates were out exploring the city—over four or five days Petros and I had sex some three or four times. "Are you really black?" he wanted to know.

I explained as best I could that, according to American law and culture, I was. His response was to leap on me for another session of lovemaking, which merely confirmed what I'd already learned, really, in France and Italy: that the racial myths of sexuality were, if anything, even more alive in European urban centers that they were in the cities of the United States.

Almost as soon as we finished, Petros asked me would I give him English lessons, though he already spoke the language fairly well. In return, he said, he would help me with my Greek.

Could he take one of the novels I had written home with him to try to read? Certainly, I said. The four or five sessions over which I helped Petros unscramble the syntax of various paragraphs in my fifth novel, *City of a Thousands Suns*, were some of the most useful lessons in the writing of English *I* have ever had. And for my first Greek lesson, a day or two later, Petros came over to my rooms after his university classes with a chapbook of Yannis Ritsos's 1956 *Hē sonata tou selēnophōtos* (The Moonlight Sonata). In that high-ceilinged room, with its four cot beds and tall, shuttered windows, we sat down to begin.

"If you are going to learn Greek, you start with very good Greek—very great Greek poetry." Petros explained. "You know Ritsos? A great modern poet."

In some ways reminiscent in both tone and matter of T. S. Eliot's "Portrait of a Lady," *Hē sonata tou selēnophōtos* is a good deal longer and—finally—more complex. The speaker, an old woman in a house (which may, after all, be empty), keeps looking out the French windows, wanting to go with someone in the moonlight as far as "the bend in the road," "*o streve tou dromou.*" No literary slouch, Petros spent an hour and a half explicating the phrase "let me come with you," which tolls repeatedly through the poem, each time modulated in its nuance—the phrase with which, as he reminded me with a grin, he'd first invited himself to my room.

By the end of two weeks, sex had fallen out of our relationship; poetry had taken its place. Then, with a burst of warm weather, now at my excuse, now at his, even the language lessons dropped off. But the friendship endured.

One evening, some weeks on in our now Platonic friendship, Petros and I decided to go for dinner down to Piraeus—a few stops out on the subway that began at Omonoia Square, with its dozens of lottery salesmen with their sticks and streaming ticket strips, strolling around the underground concourse.

Along the docks, as the clouds striped the east with evening, we hunted out the smallest and most pleasant of places we could find: a wooden structure, built out over the dock boards. Inside, it was painted green, with screening at the windows rather than glass. At places you could look down between the floorboards and see water flicker.

At a picnic-style, or perhaps barracks-style, bench, we got beer and a plate of *mezie*—hors d'oeuvres. As we sat, talking, jabbing toothpicks into oily bits of octopus, artichokes, and stuffed grape leaves, somehow we got into the politics of Greek-American relations.

What pushed us across the transition from the amiable converse of two young, gay men out in the purple evening to something entirely other, I've never been able to reconstruct (though it must have been some unformed or insensitive statement, or even argument, of mine), but suddenly Petros was leaning across the table toward me, both his fists on the boards. "Even this place—" he was saying. "What could be more Greek than this place—eh? You think, yes? Here on the Piraeus docks? Eh? Well, I tell you—everything you see here is American! The paint on the walls—American! The screening in the windows—American! The nails in the boards—American! The fixtures on the sink over there—American! Even the calendar on the wall, there—even you can see that's American!"—he pointed to a pin-up calendar, in Greek, advertising Coca-Cola. "The blades that cut the paper mats we're eating on! The machinery that puts the electroplating on this knife and fork. None of that is Greek. Look out the windows at the boats in the harbor. Even if some of them are Italian-built, their hull paint is American. Everything, the floor, the ceiling, everything you look at, every surface that you see—in this Greekest of Greek places—is American! I have no country! You—you Americans—have it all!"

To say I was taken aback just doesn't cover my response.

Somehow, incensed as he was, Petros and then I recovered. Soon, we were more or less amiable. We finished eating. Then we went for a walk outside by the water. But it was as if I had come so far along an evening road, only to round a certain bend—to discover a waterfall or an ocean or a mountain beyond that I had never seen before, so that even on the return trip, nothing looked quite the same.

As we walked back to the Piraeus subway station, I told Petros where I had to go the next afternoon—a street that made him raise an eyebrow, then laugh.

It was famous in the city for its cross-dressers. But, I explained to Petros, "No—that's not why I'm going. There's an English-language school down there, where a British friend of mine teaches. Because I write books, he's asked me to come and visit his class. He wants me to read them something of mine. And to talk about writing English with them."

"Will you talk to them about some of the things you spoke to me about, in your book that we read?

"Probably," I told him.

"Good!" Petros pronounced.

On the ill-lit platform, with wedges of light from above, we caught the subway back to Athens, and I hiked up steep *Ippokratous* to 'Odos Boltetziou, trying to keep hold of the fact that what I was seeing—much of it, at any rate—was not what I had thought I was seeing when I'd left to go to dinner.

The next afternoon at twenty to four, I threaded my way out from Omonoia Square to the glass door with the venetian blinds inside it, hurried up to the second floor of what was called something very like the Panipistemiou Ethnike Anglike, and my British friend John Witten-Dorris let me into the room, where his fourteen pupils—two girls and twelve boys, all about seventeen or so—had been in session for twenty minutes of their hour-and-a-half English lesson.

The pages I read them from one of my science fiction novels and our discussion of it were nowhere near as interesting as Petros's exegesis on Ritsos. But the students made a brave attempt to question me intelligently, ("How much money you make from writing of a book in America?" At the time, I made a thousand dollars a novel—seven-hundred-fifty if it was under sixty thousand words. "Are writers very rich in America—they are not so rich in Greece, I think.") Then my part of the lesson was more or less over, and John turned to other material.

One of the students or John, I don't remember, at some point made a joke about the cross-dressers who would soon be strolling up and down the evening street outside. Then one thick-set, dark-eyed youngster leaned forward. "I must say . . ." he began three times: "I must say . . . I must say, because we have a guest today, I must say—must explain: there is not homosexuality in Greece!" In concentration, his fists knotted on the school-desk table before him, as he leaned with an intensity that mirrored Petros's from the night before, though this young man was a year younger, a head taller, and weighed, I'm sure, half again as much. "There is not homosexuality in Greece! The Greeks must not —cannot do that. It is dirty. It is bad. It is bad and disgusting they who do that. The Greeks do not do that. There is homosexuality only from foreigners! It is all the bad and dirty tourists that make—that bring homosexuality in Greece. The Englishmen. The Americans. The Germans. The tourists! Not Greeks —you know, now!"

John knew that I was gay—though I doubt the students did. Perhaps, as someone who had invited me to his class, he felt he had to defend me, though I would have been perfectly happy to let it ride. "That just doesn't make sense to me, Costa. When you all go home from here, the people you see down on the street, most of them are pretty obviously Greek. You hear them talking with one another, joking. That's Greek I hear, downstairs."

"You don't see that!" Costa insisted, "you don't see that! Not Greeks. Not Greeks! If Greeks do that, it is only because of the foreigners. They do it, sometimes, maybe for need money—maybe, that the foreigners pay them. But Greeks not do that. It is bad. It is very bad. Why would Greeks do that? It— how you say, doesn't make sense!"

I watched this impassioned young man. I looked at the other youngsters around the room: one girl in a dark sweater rubbed the edge if a book with a foreknuckle. A boy with a bush of light hair slouched back, one hand forward over the front edge of his desk. Some smiled. Some just looked uncomfortable without smiling. The room's walls were gray. A ceiling fan hung from the center, not turned on. Blinds were raised halfway up the windows. Costa's white shirt was open at the neck; his sleeves were rolled up his forearms. Beneath his desk, he wore dark socks beneath broad-strapped sandals, which now he slid back under his chair. I wondered what surfaces of Greece, if any, I was seeing.

After the class, I walked home with English John, who was rather breezy about it all, though even he seemed troubled. "You know, he manages to make that speech to us almost every other week. I wasn't expecting it today though, but—like he said—we had a guest."

Over the next days, I found myself thinking about both experiences. What was particularly bothersome to me was the way the second seemed posed to obliterate the first—to impugn the very social conduit by which my new vision had been gained. If, indeed, as Costa insisted. I "didn't see that," what was I to make of what I did see?

At any rate, this is certainly the young man I remembered when my tablemate at the Schomburg seized my forearm to insist, so passionately: "Homosexuality is the white man's evil. Black men ain't gay—unless they've been paying too much attention to white men. They ain't no gay people in Africa." Just as, when America takes so much pride in pointing out the influences of black culture on its music, fashion, and language, it was Petros who first alerted me to all the white surfaces that already make up so much of black, melanist culture, even to its most virulent homophobic protestations—by teaching me to see the American surfaces of Greece.

VIII.

Because, at the level of cultural myth, in terms of the calculus of desire, within the silent space of discourse, homosexuality represents an opting out of the pollution game altogether; because, at the same symbolic level, the only uniquely racial power that exists is specifically the power to pollute (all others can be reread in terms of class, culture, sociality); because the only patriarchal discursive power to be seized by women is that which directly or indirectly holds stable "the race" (black or white or Asian, it makes no difference), gay liberation is, I believe, in its small way, privileged—in that there can be no advance on that front until there have been advances, changes, and material shifts on the fronts of both racism and sexism. (It is no accident that gay male culture only began to change its place in the larger cultural map with the socio-economic unchatteling of women). I think this is the (most partial) explanation of why the gay rights movement followed the civil rights movement and the feminist movement in time as it emerged into postmodern consciousness—even though, as a movement itself, it goes back to the very nineteenth-century coinage of the terms homosexual and heterosexual. From here on in, advances in one cannot proceed much further without advances on the other two fronts. Conceptually, they are inextricably linked.

On the particular level where the argument must proceed case by case, incident by incident, before it reaches discursive (or counter-discursive) mass, we must look at how that principle operates in the answer to our second question: "What makes us gay?"

The question "What makes us gay?" has at least three different levels where an answer can be posed.

First, the question "What makes us gay?" might be interpreted to mean, "What do we do, what qualities do we possess, that signal the fact that we partake of the pre-existing essence of 'gayness' that gives us our gay identity and that, in most folks' minds, means that we belong to the category of those who are gay." This is the semiotic or epistemological level: How do we—or other people—know we are gay?

There is a second level, however, on which the question "What makes us gay?" might be interpreted: "What forces or conditions in the world take the potentially 'normal' and 'ordinary' person—a child, a fetus, the egg and sperm before they even conjoin as a zygote—and 'pervert' them (i.e., turn them away) from that 'normal' condition so that eventually we have someone who does some or many or all of the things we call gay—or at least wants to, or feels compelled to, even if she or he would rather not." This is the ontological level: What makes these odd, statistically unusual but ever-present gay people exist in the first place?

The confusion between questions one and two, the epistemological and the ontological, is already enough to muddle many arguments. People who think they are asking question two are often given (very frustrating) answers to question one—and vice versa.

But there is a third level where this question "What makes us gay?" can be interpreted, which is often associated with queer theory and academics of a poststructuralist bent. Many such academics have claimed that their answer to (and thus their interpretation of) the question is the most important one, and that this answer absorbs and explains what is really going on at the first two levels.

This last is not, incidentally, a claim that I make. But I do think that this third level of interpretation (which, yes, is an aspect of the epistemological, but might be more intelligibly designated today as the theoretical) is imperative if we are to explain to a significant number of people what is wrong with a discourse that places pleasure and the body in fundamental opposition to some notion of a legally constrained social responsibility, even as the same view is reduced, under conditions of oppression, to seeing homosexuality as an abnegation of the racial imperative to produce and multiply—rather than a discourse that sees that pleasure and the body are constitutive elements of the social as much as the law and responsibility themselves—and sees the racial as a remnant of the most hidden, violent, and ruthless of class divisions, as well as a systematic imposition of cultural and economic divisions between genders and families: "Everybody who wants to be Negro get on this side of the room and everybody who wants to be white . . ."

One problem with this third-level interpretation of "What makes us gay?" that many of us academic folk have come up with is that it puts considerable strain on the ordinary meaning of "makes."

The argument against our interpretation might start along these lines (I begin here because, by the polemic against it, the reader may have an easier time recognizing it when it arrives in its positive form): "'To make' is an active verb. You seem to be describing a much more passive process. It sounds like you're describing some answer to the question 'What allows us to be gay?' or 'What facilitates our being gay?' or even 'What allows people to speak about people as gay?' Indeed, the answer you propose doesn't seem to have anything to do with making at all. It seems to be all about language and social habit."

To which, if we're lucky enough for the opposition to take its objection to this point, we can answer back: "You're right! That's exactly our point. We now believe that language and social habit are much more important than heretofore, historically, they have been assumed to be. Both language and social habit perform many more jobs, intricately, efficiently, and powerfully, in shaping not just what we call social reality, but even what we call reality itself (against which we used to set social reality in order to look at it as a separate situation from material reality). Language and social habit don't produce only the appearance of social categories—rich, poor, educated, uneducated, well-mannered, ill-bred: those signs that, according to Professor Henry Higgins in *My Fair Lady*, can be learned and therefore faked. They produce as well what heretofore were considered ontological categories—male, female, black, white, Asian, straight, gay, normal, and abnormal . . . as well as trees, books, dogs, wars, rainstorms, and mosquitoes—and they empower us to put those ironizing quotation marks around words such as 'normal,' 'ordinary,' and 'pervert' in our paragraph describing the ontological level.

"Because we realize just how powerful the socio/linguistic process is, we insist on coupling it to those active verbs, 'to make,' 'to produce,' 'to create'; early in the dialogue, there was another common verb for this particular meaning of 'to make' that paid its due to the slow, sedentary, and passive (as well as inexorable and adamantine) quality of the process: 'to sediment,' a verb that fell away because it did not suit the polemical nature of the argument, but that at this point it might be well to retrieve—'What makes us gay?' in the sense of, 'What produces us as gay? What creates us as gay? What sediments us as gay?'"

It is at the level where those last four questions overlap that our interpretation of the question—and our answer to it—falls.

Consider a large ballroom full of people.

At various places around the walls there are doors. If one of the doors is open, and the ballroom is crowded enough, after a certain amount of time there will be a certain number of people in that other room on the far side of the open door (assuming the lights are on and nothing is going on in there to keep them out). The third-level theoretical answer to the question, "What makes us gay?" troubles the ordinary man or woman on the street for much the same reason it would trouble him or her if you said, of the ballroom and the room beside it, "The open door is what makes people go into the other room."

Most folks are likely to respond, "Sure, I kind of see what you mean. But aren't you just playing with words? Isn't it really the density of the ballroom's crowd, the heat, the noise, the bustle in the ballroom that drives (i.e., that *makes*) people go into the adjoining room? I'm sure you could come up with experiments where, if on successive nights you raised or lowered the temperature and/or the noise level, you could even correlate that to how much faster or slower people were driven out of the ballroom and into the adjoining room —thus proving crowd, heat, and noise were the causative factors, rather than the open door, which is finally just a facilitator, *n'est-ce pas?*"

The answer to this objection is: "You're answering the question as though it were being asked at level two. And for level two, your answer is fine. The question I am asking, however, on level three, is: "What makes the people go into that room rather than any number of other possible rooms that they might have entered, behind any of the other closed doors around the ballroom?" And the actual answer to that question really is, "That particular open door."

Now, it's time to turn with the actual and troubling answer we have come up with to the newly interpreted question, "What makes us gay?" The answer is usually some version of the concept: "We are made gay because that is how we have been interpellated."

"Interpellate" is a term that was revived by Louis Althusser in his 1969 essay,

"Ideology and Ideological State Apparatus" (in *Lenin and Philosophy* [New York: Monthly Review Press, 1971]). The word once meant "to interrupt with a petition." Prior to the modern era, the aristocrats who served as royal courtiers could be presented with petitions by members of the *haute bourgeoisie*. These aristocrats fulfilled their tasks as subjects of the king by reading over the petitions presented to them, judging them, and acting on them in accord with the petitions' perceived merit. Althusser's point is that "we become subjects when we are interpellated." In the same paragraph, he offers the word "hailed" as a synonym, and goes on to give what has become a rather notorious example of a policeman calling out or hailing "Hey, you!" on the street. Observes Althusser: In the process of saying, "He must mean me . . . ," we cohere into a self, rather than being, presumably, simply a point of view drifting down the street.

That awareness of "He must mean me" is the constitutive *sine qua non* of the subject. It is the mental door through which we pass into subjectivity and selfhood. And (maintains Althusser) this cannot be a spontaneous process but is always a response to some hailing, some interpellation, by some aspect of the social.

In that sense, it doesn't really matter whether someone catches you in the bathroom, looking at a same-sex nude, then blurts out, "Hey, you're gay!" and you look up and realize "you" ("He means me!") have been caught, or if you're reading a description of homosexuality in a textbook and "you" think, "Hey, they're describing me!" The point is that anyone who self-identifies as gay must have been interpellated, at some point, as gay by some individual or social speech or text to which he or she responded, "He/she/it/they must mean me." That is the door opening. Without it, nobody can say, proudly, "I am gay!" Without it, nobody can think guiltily and in horror, "Oh, my God, I'm gay . . . !" Without it, one cannot remember idly or in passing, "Well, I'm gay."

Because interpellation only talks about one aspect of the meaning of "making" / "producing" / "creating" / "sedimenting," it does not tell the whole story. It is simply one of the more important things that happen to subjects at the level of discourse. And in general, discourse constitutes and is constituted by what Walter Pater once called, in the Conclusion to *The Renaissance*, "a roughness of the eye." Thus, without a great deal more elaboration the notion of interpellation is as reductive as any other theoretical move. But it locates a powerful and pivotal point in the process. And it makes it clear that the process is, as are all the creative powers of discourse, irrevocably anchored within the social rather than somehow involved with some fancied breaking out of the social into an uncharted and unmapped beyond, which only awaits the release of police surveillance to erupt into that red Eden of total unconstraint.

What the priority of the social says about those times in war where that vision of hell was first encountered by people like my uncle, possibly among our own soldiers: Look, if you spend six months socializing young men to "kill, kill,

kill," it's naive to be surprised when some of them, in the course of pursuing their pleasure, do. It is not because of some essentialist factor in "perversion" or "prostitution" (or sexuality in general) that always struggles to break loose.

It is language (*and* and *as* social habit) that cuts the world up into the elements, objects, and categories we so glibly call reality—a reality that includes the varieties of desire; a reality where what is real is what must be dealt with, and which is one with the political. The world is what it is cut up into—all else is metaphysics. That is all that is meant by that troubling poststructuralist assertion that the world is constituted of and by language and nothing more that we have any direct access to.

The problem with this assertion is that one of the easiest things to understand about it is that if language/social habit makes/produces/sediments anything, it makes/produces/sediments the meanings of words. Thus, the meaning of "makes" on the semiological/epistemological level is a socio/linguistic sedimentation. The meaning of "makes" on the ontological level is a socio/linguistic sedimentation. And, finally, the meaning of "makes" on the theoretical (i.e., socio/linguistic) level is also a socio/linguistic sedimentation. This is all those who claim the third meaning encompasses and explains the other two are saying. When I said above I do not make that claim, what I was saying in effect was: I am not convinced this is an important observation telling us something truly interesting about ontology or epistemology. It may just be an empty tautology that can be set aside and paid no more attention to. Personally, I think the decision as to whether it is or is not interesting is to be found in ontology and epistemology themselves, rather than in theory—that is to say, if the observation emboldens us to explore the world, cut it up into new and different ways, and learn what new and useful relationships can result, then the observation is of use and interest; but it is not interesting to the extent it leads only to materially unattended theoretical restatements of itself.

I would hope that, without having to go through the same argument again, we can see that at this theoretical level it is the same process of interpellation that "makes us gay" that also "makes us black." Such a process is the social construction that, like the weather, everyone so often speaks of, and no one ever seems to do anything about. And when race is cut up ontologically—specifically by the science of genetics—we simply find nothing there: the genes for dark skin, full lips, broad noses, and kinky hair are irrevocably tied neither to each other nor to anything else. They are merely physical traits. They fall together in the people where they do merely because, historically, people with those traits have been sexually segregated; so do blond hair and blue eyes, or epicanthic folds and straight black hair. When the sexual segregation is lifted, they flow and disseminate through the population, and reconvene in wholly different arrangements as a few generations of natural selection bring them together.

IX.

Homophobia is not a natural distaste. It is learned. It is supported by lack of familiarity, yes. But, even more, it is supported by a structure of logic. It occupies a place on a conceptual map. That is to say, it is part of a discourse. Such discursive elements are transcendentalized—attached to nature or religion—only when the larger discursive logic is lost sight of. To dismantle such discourses, as a step toward remapping them, requires that we begin by retrieving precisely that overall discursive logic—by showing precisely how it relates to images of man and woman in their functional descriptions; how it relates to the tribe, to the race, to the state, to the nation. What is difficult to internalize is that for the same reasons and on the same theoretical level, homosexuality is no more natural than the homophobia that counters it.

The natural in our rhetorical gallery is directly connected to the good.

If homophobia is "natural," then what it counters—homosexuality—must be bad.

If homosexuality is "natural," then it must be good, and attempts to counter it must be bad.

But this, of course, is the system that we are fundamentally trying to dismantle—and must dismantle—if we are to institute more functional conceptual mapping, one that sees homosexuality as pleasurable and useful to a number of people, some of them gay, some of them not, and of no particular consequence to anyone else; though "pleasurable," "useful," and "indifferent," just as much as "harmful" and "dangerous," are also all socially constructed categories. The larger social job—which slowly but surely is coming about—is to demonstrate that in the greater world today, such ideas leave the whole nation better off and closer to what I think it can be fairly easily shown is a more functional and efficient national model. Given our current level of technology (where, indeed, war becomes a far smaller profession of a much more specialized subgroup than anything close to the standing armies of the nineteenth century) and the world's population problem, it seems self-evident that the nations that divorce sex from procreation (and distance themselves from the nineteenth-century discourse in which the country with the largest and the most violent male population of necessity wins out over its neighbors) are the most likely to endure. I also think, by the bye, that a level of international cooperation and assistance also must replace the nineteenth-century imperialistic logic that even makes such a statement as the above comprehensible today. But that is for a later elaboration, and we have to start somewhere.

Let me end with another tale, then, from a few months ago.

In Michigan, where I taught last term, a traveling gay discussion seminar came to the women's dorm where the administration had housed Dennis and me. The evening's topic was "coming out." At the beginning of the seminar, a black freshman woman in the audience got up and announced, clearly and strongly, that she felt homosexuality was wrong—contravening the laws of God and nature. If, however, we all understood that she felt that way, she would consent to sit there and listen.

And she did.

I do not know what she made of the discussion from the four young people in the seminar, all within a year or two of her age, who told of their fears and moments of bravery in the course of coming to terms with their own homosexuality: of the problems dealing with parents, school mates, friends at home, of the moments of frightening hostility, of the times of unexpected support and understanding. There was one young Asian man on the panel. There was a Mexican woman. The one white boy was the son of a minister. There were no blacks. As I sat there, a gay black man of fifty-five who had spent half of his life before Stonewall and the other half since, listening to them talk, I found much of what they said moving. I found much of it—yes—naive. Some of it I thought was insightful. There were things they said that I agreed with. There were things they said that I felt could be further thought through.

And all of them, I thought, were very brave.

But what was probably clear both to me and to the young woman who'd made her initial statement is that these were sincere young people saying how they'd felt, how the world looked to them. They were clearly people of goodwill, who clearly wanted the world to be better for themselves and for those around them.

When we actually change our political ideas, most of us change them fairly slowly. Exposure is as much a factor as logic.

In a democracy, the respect the young woman asked for must be granted if she is ever to change her thinking. That is as much a democratic right as the right of the brave youngsters in the seminar to be heard.

Somewhere, in Michigan then, as it does here and has done before, as it has so many times now, sedimentation continues, sedimentation begins.

—October 1988
New York

23

The Star-Pit Notes

These are an updating of my notes that accompanied my two-hour radio play *The Star-Pit* (WBAI, 1967), based on my novella of the same title. WBAI and the Pacifica chain of radio stations were among the last proponents of radio drama in the country during the 1960s. KPFA, a Pacifica station in Berkeley, California, broadcast a San Francisco production of Jean Genet's *Les Bonnes* (in French) that I directed, which first played in our front-hall impromptu theater for three weekends, then moved to a church basement for the next three months.

In early spring of 1967, when I was living intermittently with Marilyn on East 13th Street, I received a phone call from someone who said he was Baird Searles —Drama and Literature Director for radio station WBAI-FM. His name was unfamiliar, but I knew of WBAI and had listened to it on and off. In the year of my father's death, in the autumn of 1960, it had been his favorite radio station. "I really enjoyed that story of yours in *Worlds of Tomorrow* this last winter—'The Star-Pit,'" Mr. Searles told me. "I was wondering whether you might like to write something on that order as, say, a radio play."

I responded immediately: "Why not simply do 'The Star-Pit' itself?"

"Well, actually," Searles said, in his oboe-esque voice, "that sounds wonderful! Why don't you come in, and we'll talk about it?"

The next Thursday, I went to the private house at 30 East 39th Street, three blocks from Grand Central Terminal, where at that time WBAI-FM had its offices and studios on the top two floors—and where I discovered, sitting at a desk in Searles's office, my old friend Judy Ratner, whom I hadn't seen in some four or five years. Judy was now Searles's assistant. When Baird had mentioned to her he'd been impressed with the story, she mentioned that we'd been friends. Searles's phone call had been the result.

During a vegetarian lunch shared among the three of us that afternoon, Judy (who had been a child actress on Broadway) said she'd love to play Allegra in the story. I said that sounded good to me, and shortly she gave me a copy of *Madness, Sanity, and Civilization* (later republished by Vintage Books as *Madness and Civilization*), a Signet-Mentor paperback with an orange cover, showing a badly reproduced woodcut of a medieval "Ship of Fools" in black. The book was by someone I'd never heard of before, Michel Foucault, though I'd seen the volume on the psychology shelf at the Eighth Street Bookshop, then on the corner of MacDougal Street and 8th. But when, at home I plunged into the book, I was totally befuddled by its rhetorical pace and density.

Everyone called Baird "Bai" (pronounced "Bay"), the same way they called me "Chip." A neat and compact man with strawberry blond hair, Bai had once been a ballet dancer, but now smoked almost nonstop. (He was to die in Canada, twenty-five years later, of emphysema complicated by lung cancer.) Initially at that first lunch I projected the play's running time at an hour.

"Fine," Baird said. "How much help do you need putting together a cast . . . ?"

An energetic twenty-five-year-old back then, soon I had gotten in touch with an old high school friend, Daniel Weiseman—who had played Voice Three in Marilyn's play *Perseus: An Exercise for Three Voices*, when we'd performed it six years before at the 10th Street Coffee Gallery, half a flight up from a printing shop. A year older than the rest of us in the play, Danny had seemed to know a good deal about theater back then. (Each night backstage, in the gallery's wooden-walled washroom that served as our backstage area, he'd done our makeup for *Perseus*.) A chain of phone calls got a number from his parents in the Bronx, and I learned that, now using the name Daniel Landau, Danny was living in the East Village himself and was, indeed, acting and directing. I called him. Would he be interested in directing a play for WBAI?

"Sure," he told me. "Bring it over."

So I did.

In his apartment, just off 2nd Avenue, I read Danny a few pages of my story, and he decided immediately what I'd hoped he would: I was an adequate enough actor to do the protagonist and narrator. By the beginning of the following week, he had found five other actors. (Later I explained to Judy that because Danny had put together the cast and because of all the work he was doing—none of us was getting paid for his or her considerable labor—I felt I had to let him choose the actors that he wanted. Judy would have been fine, but Danny's Allegra, Randa Haynes, was very good. Although she understood, still Judy was disappointed.) We decided to assign multiple parts, and Danny dealt them out to each. A wonderful woman with a somewhat mannish voice, Phoebe Wray—who, back then, because I was twenty-five, I thought of as older; *now*, of course, we're exactly the same age—got the somewhat sexually ambiguous part of Poloscki.

Young Walter Harris agreed to do the twin roles of Ratlet and Androcles. Walter was a student at the (old) High School of Music and Art, then at the top of the steps up through St. Nicholas Park, the same steps up which I had often walked to get to City College in the single year I'd attended. He knew Phoebe already from performances they'd done together at the Judson Poets Theater. The Harris family was (and still is) something of a Greenwich Village legend in that neighborhood's extensive little-theater circles. Walter's father, George Harris Sr., his mother, Evelyn Harris, and all five children (Walter, his older brother George Jr., and three sisters) were actors. What's more, they were actors particularly interested in experimental and avant-garde theater. At the time, Walter had been having a run of luck: fifteen years old, blond, and handsome, he was in the midst of a string of fourteen nationally televised commercials; also he was understudying for a part in the pre-Broadway incarnation of the '60s smash-hit musical *Hair* at New York's then relatively new Joseph Pap Public Theater. That same year, he also worked with and composed music for Robert Patrick as well as for Tom Eyen—names, along with that of Tom O'Horgan (who directed the legendary *Hair*), that would reverberate on and off Broadway over the next two decades, Patrick with *Kennedy's Children*, Eyen with *Dreamgirls*, and O'Horgan with *Jesus Christ Superstar*, once *Hair* was done. But since, as a radio drama, my play did not require memorizing lines—and the parts were interesting—Walter threw himself into *The Star-Pit* with an intriguing combination of adolescent energy and laid-back professionalism.

Three years later, at eighteen, Walter would come down with bone cancer, lose his right leg, and become (in his own words) "a new-age monk for thirteen years" in a late '60s/early '70s religious movement called the Holy Order of MANS. Today, the most widely known member of the Harris family is Walter's older brother George Harris Jr., who went to San Francisco (where I knew him slightly in the '70s) and who, under the name Hibiscus, started the Cockettes Theater Troupe. George/Hibiscus returned to New York, formed the Angels of Light Troupe, and in 1983 was one of the first men to die of AIDS. The article reporting his death in the *Village Voice* was the first time in print I saw the acronym "AIDS," followed by its then-obligatory parenthetical expansion, "(Acquired Immune Deficiency Syndrome)."

My agent Henry Morrison had recently moved to new and bigger offices on East 53rd Street and had actually gotten his own Xerox copier machine. (This was an age when there were no copy shops.) Kindly, he let me copy out pages from the magazine for the actors, with pages ready for them by the second rehearsal.

Though I still have trouble with a small number of Walter's line readings (it was sometimes difficult for Danny to get him to hit the right word), he was fun to work with. Along with all the other actors he worked very hard. Despite any of my quibbles, it's a fine job. Forty-eight years later when I asked him, now an actor in Seattle, what he remembered from his time working on *The Star-Pit*, Walter wrote to me: "What I remember most about *The Star-Pit* was how much fun it was playing those cool roles, and characters like those I knew from my reading, and interacting with you and your Afro hairdo—the first Afro I remember seeing on anyone!"

Jerry and Randa were also wonderfully personable to work with. Over all, we had some six rehearsals in Danny's living room, and Danny managed several other sessions just with me, since my part was three times as long as anyone else's. Although it's a bit dated, as old acting styles often become, the ensemble performance still generates some nice moments. Over the next couple of weeks, the piece began to pull together, developing an overall dramatic arc.

Phoebe Wray—our Poloscki—joined the cast late. A playwright as well as an actress, she would do work at the legendary Café Cino, that astonishing node of Off-Off Broadway creativity, still talked about today. I have the vaguest memory of her arriving at one rehearsal where she could only make the last half hour.

As for her own memories, thirty-odd years later: "Chip says there were rehearsals; I don't remember any. My recollection is that I had not read the story and hadn't had the script very long and wasn't at all sure who I was in it."

Once we began to find our way in the story, after a discussion with Danny and the other actors, I phoned Bai. "Would you like to sit in on a rehearsal?"

"Nope," he said. "I trust you."

At the next rehearsal, I told Danny and the rest: "Baird says he trusts us. He's going to let us do what we want." There was some surprise, and even some discussion; but the result was that all of us—already working hard—began working even harder.

Finally, on an afternoon in the first days of July, we all filed into a recording studio on the top floor of wbai's 39th Street townhouse.

Until that point, my several visits to wbai-fm had been suffused with the palest green. Bai's office was on the second floor, and until then my comings and goings had been dominated by sunny office windows, white plastic pots hung with ivy and spiderplants, light green runners on the stairs and along the halls, and pale green walls.

But now, as I climbed up to the third floor, wbai turned black.

The uppermost studio spaces, in which until now I'd never been, were walled with dark masonite or black foam rubber, covered with hand-sized black cones, to increase the wall area that could absorb extraneous sound. Today, in its offices and studios on the twenty-third floor of an office building at the east end of Wall Street, WBAI has at least eight studios. In 1967, on 39th Street, there were only three. One studio was always broadcasting. Another often housed the engineers for the current show.

During those weeks, we'd fill up the third.

At the end of an hour, being asked to move into another studio was such a regular occurrence, we got used to it. For the next three months, I would dash through the smoke-hued lower chambers and rush up into these dark rooms with their turning reels, their little lights, their dials.

On our first studio day, I'd requested three hours of recording time for the actors.

Wisely Baird had booked us four—and, even more wisely, he had made sure it was on a day when no one was booked in *after* us. We'd been promised the best and most creative engineer at the WBAI studios, a young man named David Rabkin. At the end of two hours of recording, however, David packed up, said a brisk good-bye—he was expected somewhere in Jersey—and left. Now Rabkin's assistant, Ed Woodward, a friendly bear of a guy with glasses and a warm smile, took over.

We never saw Rabkin again. Woodard would remain with the project through a couple of hundred hours of post-production work. Three months later, when it came to assigning credits, some of us wondered why we needed to put Rabkin's name on the piece at all. Bai said it was obligatory, though. Well, could we at least put Woodard's name first, then? No, Bai told us: Alphabetical order was the WBAI way. (It wasn't that Rabkin *hadn't* worked while he was there. It was that Woodard had worked so long and so hard.) Bai only recanted because, on the best and most usable of his own takes, accidentally he read it with Woodard's name first. In all the printed announcements for the show, Rabkin leads.

As soon as Rabkin was gone, Woodard suggested we record all the dialogue that takes place in the various starship hangers with a slight echo, to give the lines a sense of place and give the place a sense of size. When we played them back, immediately those scenes opened up and sounded far more authentic. Woodard suggested a dozen more technical ideas, actually, which enriched the show. Toward the end of the session, I recall standing around in the studio with all the actors, while Ed recorded five minutes of room tone. When, a week later, Sue and I returned to lay in the sound effects, that small, clear plastic reel of "silent" tape made editing them possible. (A baker's dozen years on, working on Frank Romeo's two films *Bye-Bye Love* and *The Aunts*, I was the one who made sure we'd recorded enough room tone to edit the sound.)

Here are Phoebe's recollections of what turned into a day-long session:

"What I remember of the day of recording—and it is darkened at the top and sides, like a mold growing down from the ceiling—is the very dark room in a brownstone. . . . It took a long time to do, I remember that. Lots of coffee.

Laughter. Sneaking off into a (dark) corner to work on my lines. Overhearing someone, a woman, who didn't like what I was doing, or at least I thought that's what she said, and getting paranoid. Maybe I was just anxious anyway because I'm usually very thorough in preparing a role. But I was working with Walter Harris and Danny, so at least I had friends there. I know they liked my androgynous voice, but I expected that. (I sang second tenor in junior high.) We all wanted it to be right, to be good, to be exciting."

With second and third takes, misreadings, coughs, excuse-me's, and false starts, we finished laying down the naked dialogue somewhat before two that morning. Joan Tanner's part had been finished by seven, and she had gone home. Walter and Jerry were done about ten thirty, and left. Phoebe, Randa, and I—with indefatigable Danny—stuck it out till after one. A couple of Randa's "Allegra" monologues had to be done three or four times. We'd been in the studio nonstop a bit over nine hours—and had recorded just under five hours of tape.

That night Danny and I cleaned up the pizza boxes and soda cans. Randa, Phoebe, and I said something about finding a place to have a cup of coffee. (Phoebe: "Then there was the release of walking out of the artificial darkness into the night-time Manhattan street. New York at night always thrilled me. The streets were quiet, but the energy was trembling underfoot, like a dragon in the subways, snoozing with one eye open a slit.") After looking around the midtown streets just below Grand Central Terminal for five minutes, though, we decided we were all too exhausted and instead went home. (Phoebe: "I went home to my beloved wire fox terrier, Morgan, and didn't think about *The Star-Pit* very often, had it on my resume for a while, and then dropped it off. Unsure of my performances, I think. I had a rehearsal and couldn't listen when it was first broadcast. Or was I there with Danny? I can't remember.")

That hot, hot summer, Marilyn was pretty much taken up by a stormy affair with a twenty-one-year-old half–American Indian poet named Link, himself the live-in lover of another writer, a cadaverous-looking twenty-eight-year-old, Hunce Voelcker. Both Hunce and Link had been part of the Jack Spicer circle in San Francisco. My comings and goings in the second floor apartment at 10th Street got little attention.

Now and again Marilyn found herself involved with another of Link's lovers, a bisexual twenty-six-year-old Irish-American printer, Harvey—four months out of the Navy and on his way to becoming a serious alcoholic. Though Harvey was a big, friendly, wonderfully nice guy, a couple of times I woke up on the foldout couch, where most of us slept, to find him snoring away while (*Ahem . . .*) urinating against my leg. That same summer, during the time I was not working on *The Star-Pit* or off rehearsing with the Heavenly Breakfast, a music group that later became the center of an East Village commune across and to the east from the fire house on East 2nd Street, Harvey and I published

Marilyn's first book of poems, an eight-and-a-half-by-eleven-inch pamphlet called *The Terrible Children*. On the cover was a photograph I'd taken back while I was in high school. The lettering was by our friend, the artist Russell Fitz-Gerald (another one-time member of the late Spicer's circle). We printed five hundred copies. Together with Marilyn, we distributed finished copies to half a dozen bookstores in the Village and East Village area, where thirty or forty of them actually sold.

Forty-eight hours after our marathon *Star-Pit* taping session, I came back into the studio with Sue Schweers and the then nineteen-year-old redheaded associate producer, Neal Conan. With Ed coaching us for the first hour or so, we began what turned into three ten-hour days of editing the five hours of naked tape, which produced the hour-and-fifty-minute dialogue-and-narration track that forms the play's basis.

Sue was an extraordinary flute player. She had dozens of instruments, some of which she had made herself. A number of them are described in my book *Heavenly Breakfast* (Bamberger Books, 1992), where she appears as "Lee." She played the show's breathy lyric prelude on a length of industrial hosing with an inch-and-a-half bore and arbitrarily cut-in finger holes. Among the piccolos, tenor recorders, and shawms, the only classical silver flute you hear in the play is in the arpeggios accompanying some of Allegra's radiant fantasies. A week later, over a few more hours of recording time, we laid down tracks for all the special effects: Everything from the "world wind" to the computer beeping in Vyme's office is one or another (or a combination) of Sue's flutes, sometimes electronically distorted.

I've never quite understood why, but the editing and the placing of the music and special effects took almost ten times as many studio hours to put together and lay in as had the editing of the dialogue. Moments I recall from the whole? We worked late in the studio every night during the week the Beatles' new 45-rpm record of "I Am the Walrus" was released. Listening to it on the corner speaker high on the wall over the workbench, we laid in the computer blippings. On the other side of "Walrus" was "Hey Jude." The next day, when Sue and I were in the studio again, somebody—possibly it was Ed—put together a tape loop of the today famous but then unknown (I'd only heard it perhaps three times before, on the radio that week) all but endless ending and started it playing over the studio speakers. We'd been working about twenty minutes, with the thing running on and on and on . . . when one or the other of us looked up, realized what was happening, and began to laugh.

The Star-Pit was recorded when four-track, reel-to-reel recorders were the usual thing in studio equipment. Back then only a few *very* big music studios had eight-track equipment.

A previous Mind's Eye Theater project had been a production of ten hour-long readings covering the whole of Christopher Morley's wonderfully witty novel from the 1930s, *The Trojan Horse*. Some twenty-six actors had been involved in that high-jinks project. Then living in New York City and fresh from the Yale drama school, with a degree in playwriting, the spectacularly talented writer Joanna Russ had worked on that project as "continuity girl." Baird was the model for the character Jai Vhed in Russ's second novel *And Chaos Died* (1972). (By the end of the Morley project, she'd had something of a crush on him.) That had been a logistics nightmare—mostly in terms of getting all the actors to show up when needed. The music had been canned, however, occurring only at each episode's beginning and end; nor were there any sound effects—so that, as Baird finally confessed to us, *our* project was the most technically complicated The Mind's Eye Theater had undertaken. Twenty-six actors not withstanding, certainly ours ended up requiring the most hours of studio time.

When we were in sight of the end and tempers were fraying (because we were all beginning to see it was going to require still *another* few sessions), our nineteen-year-old production assistant Neal suddenly exploded at me: "You know, Chip, you have the *ugliest* laugh of *anyone* I have ever heard in my *life*—and if I have to stay in the same room with you for five more minutes, I'm going to go crazy or punch you in your fucking jaw . . . if you laugh again at *anything!*" Then, overturning (accidentally) a blue cardboard coffee container with white Greek pillars on it that was sitting at the end of the desk, he stalked from the tiny studio—leaving both Sue and me *quite* surprised, with coffee splattered over the black vinyl floor.

Five minutes later, Neal was back—with a grumpy apology and a fistfull of paper towels.

But a day later I was out visiting my sister in Brooklyn, when all of a sudden she laughed at something—and I realized we Delanys *do* have an . . . eccentric laugh. Indeed, it might be rough, cooped up with it in a tiny workspace, hour after hour, day after day, as Neal had been.

The music/special effects accompanied maybe a half an hour of the dialogue and expanded the show by a full six and a half minutes. Now, with everything in place, *The Star-Pit* ran an hour and fifty-seven minutes.

I assumed we had a "director's cut" and that next we had to set ourselves a reasonable playing time, then start trimming it down. The last things added to the show were Bai's heads-in and tails-out announcements. That final afternoon Bai invited Sue and me to come to his Upper West Side apartment for dinner the following Saturday night, to celebrate the project's completion.

In 1967, two years prior to Stonewall, on the written page the most notable thing about "The Star-Pit" had been its gender skewing. Several fanzines and two or three prozine articles had made that a topic of comment. Today, of course, it's almost invisible. But Jerry Matts—that *rara avis*, a twenty-nine-year-old straight male actor—was particularly tickled with it. "Now here, Chip, I'm playing your . . . husband? Wow!" He sat back on Danny's living room couch and laughed. "I mean, am I supposed to play it kind of . . . you know, swishy?" (At the time—two years before Stonewall—the word "gay" was not in use.)

"No, darling," Danny said. "You're just supposed to play your own, dear, sweet, straight, *very* butch self. *That's* the whole point!"

"Okay," he said. And he did.

The greatest gender skewing in the printed version is, of course, the penultimate scene's revelation that Poloscki is a woman—which revelation does not arrive on the page until halfway through her dialogue with Vyme. But even though we'd picked Phoebe for her somewhat masculine voice, because it was a radio play there was no way to preserve the ambiguity till the proper dramatic moment. As soon as Phoebe/Poloscki spoke her first line ("Who's over there?"), her gender was clear—and we had to let the effect go. Even at the final recording session, however, where we simply needed Bai to read, deadpan, the list of actors and actresses and their parts, we had to take it two or three extra times, because the same thing that had occasioned so much wonder from Jerry —"Vyme's husband, Jerry Matts"—now kept breaking Bai up. But not only was this a time without any notions of "gender skewing" or "gender bending," along with the word "gay" the word "gender" itself was rarely or never heard.

In 1967 Baird lived with his lover Martin Last in the apartment just across the air shaft from the apartment I live in with mine today, on the Upper West Side's 82nd Street.[1] That Saturday evening Sue and I left the Heavenly Breakfast commune on Second Street and took the IND subway up to the Museum of Natural History stop, by Central Park on the Upper West Side.

(Among the "musical" distortions of my essay about the commune ("Heavenly Breakfast," 1979): Our trip to visit "January House" is actually our trip to Bai and Martin's for dinner, with an account of a dinner at a cooperative in San Francisco run by painter Knute Styles, which we visited—Sue and I—a couple of years later during 1969 substituted for dinner at Bai's in New York.)

In the living room over drinks, Bai and Martin had showed off their new clear-plastic, inflatable furniture. Then, moving to the kitchen, with Sandra Lay—daughter of popular science writer and government rocketry advisor Willie Lay—as a fifth guest, we sat down for a steak fondue. Conversation was largely about the Science Fiction Shop that Bai was planning to open up on Hudson Street, with Sandra as one of the partners.

What *would* be the final running time for the radio play, I asked Baird at one point.

"If it's an hour and fifty-seven minutes long—" Bai shrugged—"then that's how long it'll run. No, we're not cutting a second from it."

I was astonished—and delighted.

The Star-Pit first aired on WBAI-FM in late November of '67. It ran at prime time, five to seven o'clock in the evening.

Back at the Heavenly Breakfast, seated or lying on the Second Street apartment's kitchen floor, everyone in the commune huddled around our old vacuum-tube radio. I don't think that day there was much heat. I recall some sweaters, a few overcoats. Once the show started, Janet's three-year-old son Andy announced: "Chip is in the radio," then put his head down on it (because it was warm) and went to sleep for the remainder of the program. As I recall, there were only three brief station-identification breaks in the whole two hours' running time.

It was repeated the following Sunday afternoon (from three to five), when I caught most of it a second time while I was up visiting my mom.

After skipping a year, for the next six years *The Star-Pit* played annually over WBAI, usually around Thanksgiving—running from four to six in the morning, or sometimes from three till five a.m. For a while it was something of a New York autumn tradition. I stayed up (or got up) to hear it twice in that time. There was another year break. Then it ran for three more years.

By the show's tenth anniversary, WBAI had relocated to a large church basement on East 58th Street. That year I came in when they ran it, to reminisce for the listeners, before and after it aired. Since then, every two or three years, WBAI's Jim Freund has found a post-midnight slot for it on one holiday or another, when someone working at the station wanted to take a night off.

Twenty years later, in 1987, Barbara Wise and I did a two-person reading for WBAI, almost as complex as *The Star-Pit*, of an hour-long section from my 1985 AIDS novel *The Tale of Plagues and Carnivals*. Sadly, there were some technical problems. Although the acting was good, some all-too-elaborate sound effects were added by the overzealous young woman who produced it, and who thought that, because I was a science fiction writer, anything I wrote should sound "weird and strange and creepy"; and the idea that there were characters and a story, with motivations and relationships that had to be understood by the listeners, had not occurred to her. She overlaid weird music arbitrarily through the whole piece and electronically distorted all the voices, until eighty percent of the words were unintelligible.

Around 1990, I learned that Danny Landau had died of AIDS.

Phoebe again: "I met Danny when I was working as an actress Off-Off-Broadway in New York in the 1960s, and I loved him. He was flaky and creative and great fun to be around. He once gave me an odd assortment of pieces from a mah jong set and a horn-handled Italian switchblade. I have no idea why, or why I took them. Gifts, I guess, given with a smile, not to be refused."

Though WBAI-FM has played it twice or possibly three times since then, in the last decade *The Star-Pit* has been largely silent.

Jim Freund (whom I run into regularly, now recording a Dixon Place reading, now recording a set of readings at Readercon) has been promising to get me a cassette of *The Star-Pit* for a dozen years. Last month, when two Saturdays in a row I came in to do his 4 a.m. morning show *The Hour of the Wolf*, kindly he transferred the drama to cassette. Coming out of their worn white cardboard boxes from the upper shelves of the WBAI-FM archives, the two ten-inch aluminum reels on which the master tapes are still wound—so modern in 1967 —today look like what they are: dinosaurs from another century. But with my partner Dennis's help, here at home we've made some dubs.

Phoebe: "There's a heart-tug around it. . . . One reason that I kept pushing it away was that it had an unfinished feeling for me. Perhaps all these years later, there will be a completeness in it. I wish Danny were here to share in that."

So do I.

I hope you enjoy this thirty-year-old glimpse into the future.

—1960, updated November 1998
New York City

NOTES

1. The apartment in which I wrote this and where I lived upstairs from Judy Ratner for forty-odd years has now been renovated, as has hers. She now has moved to Northampton, and I and my partner of twenty-seven-odd years are now in Philadelphia. The windows of Baird and Martin's apartment, which I could look through for most of my time there, have been walled up, and the building they lived in is now several floors taller.

In October 2016, Walter Harris sent me a largely photographic history of his family's little-theater efforts, with lots of information about his older brother, George/Hibiscus. "The Star Pit" gets a mention in the Appendix under "radio." Apparently Walter had not been aware of what I'd written about his extraordinary brother in *Flight From Nevèrÿon* (Bantam, 1985). I read it to him over the phone (SRD 2016).

2. This chapter's text originally appeared at: www.pseudopodium.org/repress /TheStarPit/SamuelRDelany-NotesOnTheStarPit.html/.

3. Audio files of the radio play can be downloaded at Ray Davis's website, https:// pseudopodium.org/repress/TheStarPit/index.html/.

4. What follows are the original program notes for the radio broadcast.

> *The Star-Pit* was first broadcast by *The Mind's Eye Theater* over WBAI-FM in
>   New York City, November 1967
> Produced by Baird Searles
> Production Assistant Neal Conan
> Directed by Daniel Landau
> Music and Sound Effects by Susan Schweers
> Technical Direction by David Rabkin and Ed Woodward
> Announcer . . . Baird Searles

Vyme (narrator) . . . Samuel R. Delany
Vyme's Wife, Golden Girl, and Allegra . . . Randa Haynes
Ratlet, Golden Boy, and Androcles . . . Walter Harris
Vyme's Husband, Pilot, Sandy, Golden Man, and Sailor in Bar . . . Jerry Matts
Antonni and Assorted Children . . . Joan Tanner
Vyme's Mother, Joseph, Sailor in Bar, Poloscki, and Lady from Carlson's Lab . . .
   Phoebe Wray

24

A Note on Bruce Nugent's
"Smoke, Lilies and Jade"

Putting together the notes for this republication of Bruce Nugent's best-known story, I was surprised—no, I was startled—to learn that Bruce, whom I first met in 1959 when I was seventeen and whom I knew on and off up until his death in 1987, was actually the same age as my father. Both were born in 1906. But during my adolescence and young manhood, this tall, soft-spoken, black, gay man, a multilingual artist and writer, so wonderfully sophisticated about dance and theater and literature, had seemed to me everything fathers were not.

Half a dozen years before Bruce's death, when he was in his seventies, I went to a program honoring him. Along with Langston Hughes (1902–1967) and Zora Neale Hurston (1891–1960), Bruce had been one of the younger figures of the Harlem Renaissance, a jazz-age literary movement that, in many ways, grew up in a complex reaction to W. E. B. Du Bois's focus on "the talented tenth."

The day of the program, my good friend Bernie Kay was ill with lung cancer. Bernie had first met Bruce when he was nineteen and Bruce was twenty-three. For the decade before Bernie's final illness, when he had run Mrs. Cavenaugh's translation bureau on the nineteenth floor of the Candler Building on 42nd Street, Bernie had hired Bruce to translate from the Italian. Bruce was enamored of all things Italianate, as Bernie was enamored of all things Hispanic. On a dozen visits, I would come into the office to find Bernie working on the typewriter near the door and Bruce busy on the other, in a grid of sunlight from the wide venetian blinds, in that narrow office no more than seventeen feet end to end. Though he had to get up out of a sick bed to do it, Bernie was determined

to see Bruce receive his honors; so my then-lover Frank and I drove him down to
that extraordinary loft and library on New York's Lower Broadway—the Hatch-
Billops Collection—that houses so much of African-American theater history.

In the interview that went along with the afternoon's ceremony, I heard
Bruce tell the story about the writing of "Smoke, Lilies and Jade," the earliest
story by an African-American writer on a gay theme—a tale that I had heard
him tell several times before in Bernie's living room. When in 1926 they were
planning *Fire!!*, which was to appear that November, twenty-four-year-old editor Wallace Thurman (1902–1934, another gay black writer) was discussing
with Bruce, then twenty, what might assure that magazine's success. Well, if
they included stories about scandalous and salacious topics, everyone would
want to read it. What were the two most scandalous topics they could think
of? What about homosexuality and prostitution? But who, then, should write
which? According to Bruce, they'd flipped a coin. Bruce won the assignment
to write a gay tale, and Thurman won prostitution as his topic (with a story
called "Cordelia the Crude," which a year later he turned into the successful
Broadway play *Harlem*, which ran for a hundred performances).

That same afternoon at the Hatch-Billops, I heard Bernie, during the questions and comments, tell another story about Bruce that has always stayed
with me.

One snowy night in the 1920s, Bruce knocked on Bernie's door—and came
in, shoeless. Back in Harlem, he had found a black man walking in the snow,
barefoot. Bruce had given him his own shoes, then walked three-quarters of a
mile through the snow himself to Bernie's, to get a pair from his friend. "After
all, I knew I *could* get another pair—whereas that poor man had nobody to get
shoes from at all." This is an emblem of Bruce's extraordinary generosity, a
generosity that explains to some extent why so little of his work is extant today.

Bruce was as much (or more) of an artist than a writer, and, according to
Bernie, vast amounts of his work had been given away or lost, in fires, evictions,
and hastily abandoned apartments over the years, so that little of it remains.

Contemporary accounts and letters from the Harlem Renaissance are full of
tales of Bruce; Nugent's own accounts of his contemporaries were invaluable
to a whole generation of Harlem Renaissance scholars. His next-best-known
literary piece is a scenario, *Sahdji: An African Ballet* (1932), also a piece with many
gay resonances. He had two poems in Countee Cullen's (1903–1946) historic
anthology of '20s black poets, *Caroling Dusk* (1927), as well as an autobiographical statement, written just after "Smoke, Lilies and Jade" but prior to the first
of his several trips to Italy—all years before, when still a high school student, I
was introduced to him one afternoon when he dropped by Bernie's West End
Avenue apartment.

Here is Bruce Nugent's autobiograhical statement from Countee Cullen's
1927 anthology *Caroling Dusk*:

I was born in Washington, D.C., on the second of July, 1906, and have never ceased to marvel at the fact. After attending public school with very good marks (I was thrashed if I did not lead my class), I attended the Dunbar High School of the same city. When I was thirteen my father died, my greatest impression being the crowded church and vault. My mother left Washington for New York where my brother and I joined her in a few months. New York was an adventure and still is. A glorious something torn from a novel. Even the first hard winter with mother ill and my feet on the ground was just a part of it. My gathering bits of fur to paste on newspaper to cut out for inner soles for my shoes, the walking to work to save carfare, and getting lunch as best I could, all seemed romantic and highly colored. Weren't there theaters and lights, Broadway, Fifth Avenue . . . and more lights? Noise and bustle and high silk hats and flowers in pots in the Bowery. Hobble cars creeping like caterpillars up Broadway. Taxis and people and forty-second street. Traffic towers and tall buildings. Wasn't this New York? A year later I discovered Harlem. I was at that time an art apprentice at seven fifty a week. But that was too little money. So I became an errand boy for ten dollars, bell hop in an all womens' hotel for eleven fifty-five, eighteen with tips, secretary and confidence man for a modiste for twenty-five, ornamental iron worker and designer for twenty-eight, and elevator operator for thirty. Then I had the mumps and despite the glamor of New York, I wanted to go, just go somewhere. So I went to Panama working my way. Then New York again and a costume design class. A visit home to D.C. where I met Langston Hughes. *Opportunity* accepted my first poem. Washington for eleven months then New York again. I arrived penniless and have remained so. The few drawings and sketches made on these trips were either destroyed, lost, or given away en route. I began to write seriously and to paint just as seriously; I entered contests but never won. I am still penniless and happy and planning to go to Paris and Vienna by hook or by crook.

—December 4, 1998

25

Introducing Octavia E. Butler

What a pleasure it is for me tonight to introduce to you Octavia Estelle Butler.

The first time I saw Octavia, in 1970, she was a face among the twenty-odd faces around the circle on the first morning of the Clarion SF writer's workshop at Clarion College in Clarion, Pennsylvania. By the end of my week as an instructor, my picture of her was of someone shy, sharp, and wonderfully curious.

Her short story "Crossover" appeared in Robin Scott Wilson's 1970 *Clarion* anthology. Six years later came her first novel, *Patternmaster* (1976). A brief decade on, Butler and I were asked to appear together in a program at the Schomburg Center, that fabled gathering of African-American literature a few blocks from my old home in Harlem, where I lived on 133rd Street and 7th Avenue. Years before, when the Schomburg collection had been housed in the old George Bruce Branch of the New York Public Library, my mother had worked there as a library clerk. Many times I'd visited her there, so I felt that I was, in a sense, going home. But what I found on the corner of 135th and Lenox Avenue was a brand new library building. The collection, always astonishing, had grown and been added to and was now an affair of worldwide fame. And the shy young woman who had been my student more than a decade before had become an astonishingly articulate and awesomely impressive presence. I left the library that evening aware that I had been honored to take part in a program with a truly extraordinary woman.

In the early part of this decade, when I began to teach comparative literature at the University of Massachusetts, I taught Butler's Hugo-winning story "Speech Sounds" (1983) and her Hugo and Nebula Award-winning "Bloodchild" (1984). I taught them again. And I taught them again.

The reason I taught them so frequently is because, of all the science fiction stories we read over those years, they prompted the most interesting discussions among my students by far. Once the discussions began, again and again the students would return to them, till those tales became the benchmark texts with which they judged what was going on in the other stories we dealt with. Butler's tales became the measure for all their thinking about what science fiction might do.

In 1993 Butler's novel *The Parable of the Sower* increased the rhetorical range, density, and variety of a writerly voice that already rang as resonantly as any writer's in the country. In 1995 with the presentation of a MacArthur Fellowship, or "Genius" award as it is sometimes known, many more people began to realize what a mind, what a measure, what a writer we had in our midst. This year we have the long-awaited continuation of that dual novelistic project: *The Parable of the Talents* (1998).

And tonight, with us, we have . . . Octavia E. Butler.

—January 14, 1999

NOTE

This was read at a party at the modest ground-floor offices of Seven Stories Press, Octavia E. Butler's publisher. Whoever was supposed to introduce *me* had not shown up. Was there anyone who could say anything about me? Suddenly a young Dominican writer emerged and delivered extempore a perfectly adequate summary of my career. His name was Junot Díaz, and that night marks the beginning of what was to grow into a very warm friendship.

26

Poetry Project Interview

A Silent Interview

Interviewer from the Poetry Project at St. Marks: What form/shape will writing of the twenty-first century take?

Samuel R. Delany: I can't believe you're really frivolous enough to think that, because I'm a science fiction writer, I have some privileged, informed, or even interesting take on the future, more than do ditch diggers, dry cleaners, insurance salesmen — or, indeed, the run-of-the-mill poet or novelist. The only thing SF writers are apt to know about the future that the ordinary woman or man on the street does not is that it's *really* unpredictable.

That alone is what allows our genre to be.

Once, about twenty-five years ago, some people in Missoula, Montana, flew SF writers Frank Herbert (*Dune*), Frederik Pohl (*Gateway*), and me out to their city to take part in an audience-packed, Saturday-night panel that addressed the question "What is the future of Montana geological study and mining?" They were incredibly impressed with their own cleverness and originality in inviting some science fiction writers along with the geologists and mining engineers who were the program's other participants. The organizers were quite convinced no one had ever done such a thing before. We were each paid five hundred dollars for our appearance.

But I'm doing *this* interview for free. Therefore, you have to compensate me with intelligent and reasonable questions about which it's possible to say something interesting, based on something I might conceivably know.

Interviewer: How does the creating and making (or unmaking) of myth function in your work? Or how might this function in our postmillennial writing?

SRD: For me, myths are what we tend to believe when there's no direct sensory proof of that belief available. Thus, when I'm in New York, Paris functions in my life largely as a myth. When I'm in London, New York functions for me as a myth. And, of course, there's all of what we take as history. The myths that concern me, of course, are the ones we believe, the ones we hold true. Since the evidence for most of our modern beliefs about the universe is not immediately available, most of contemporary life is fundamentally mythic. (Heidegger calls this the "inauthentic," but I'm not so sure that's the best term for it—at least in English.)

Because of the myriad ways and the multiple trajectories through which they are communally enforced, myths are very similar to discourses on the one hand and to ideologies on the other.

A communal task that art accomplishes—particularly the verbal arts of fiction, poetry, and criticism—is to help with the all-important shifts in discourse that must occur for there to be meaningful historical change.

Because it *is* a communal task, because no *single* work of art can accomplish such a discursive shift by itself, the artist (responsible only for her or his own work) *doesn't* have to worry about preaching. It does no good; don't waste your time. It's far more effective to look at a situation and dramatize, in however complex allegorical terms you'd like, what it is you've seen.

Science fiction's kerygma contains a story about SF editor H. L. Gold and the great SF writer Theodore Sturgeon, during the early 1950s—the McCarthy period. Sturgeon found himself so upset about what was happening to people all around him, the lives and livelihoods of his friends that had been destroyed, that he could no longer write. When Gold asked him for a story, Sturgeon told him, in despair, "Unless I let everybody know what that evil demagogue is doing to the country, writing fiction doesn't seem worth it."

Gold told him: "Look. You write me a story about a man who, unbeknownst to his wife, goes to meet her at the bus station when she's returning from a visit to her mother's. He sees a strange man meet her, and follows them through the city . . . and I *promise* you: By the end of that story, *everyone* who reads it will know what you feel about that demagogue there in Washington." Well, that's how writing works—and it works because what validates a McCarthy (or a Hitler, for that matter) is a *discourse* that says such behavior is or is not acceptable. That same discourse controls how A treats B when they meet in a store on opposite sides of a counter and one tries to buy something from the other.

For the same reason that poets and artists don't have to worry about preaching, the general public doesn't need to worry about imposing censorship. "For poetry makes nothing happen," W. H. Auden wrote in his elegy for Yeats. That privileged lack of power of the single work of art—the single poem, say—is precisely what, I feel, Auden was getting at.

Many works of art taken together, however, through the very process by which we learn to read them, establish discourses—discourses of the possible, discourses of the probable, discourses of desire. Discourses are the conceptual tools with which we socially construct our world, materially and imaginatively. That's what I think the late-Victorian poet Arthur William Edgar O'Shaughnessey (1844–1881) was getting at when *he* wrote in his poem "Ode":

> We are the music makers,
> We are the dreamers of dreams,
> Wandering by lone sea-breakers,
> Sitting by desolate streams . . .
> World losers and world forsakers,
> On whom the cold moon gleams:
> But we are the movers and shakers
> Of the world forever, it seems.

Both Auden and O'Shaughnessey are true at the same time. But one was referring to art as an individual enterprise of powerless separate works. The other was referring to art as a collective enterprise facilitating social mentation. The two function differently in two different conceptual spaces: the space of individual appreciation and the space of shared discourse.

Interviewer: List your favorite utopias.

SRD: I don't very much like utopias as a form. I much prefer science fiction—which, as a genre, is fundamentally antiutopian (and equally antidystopian) in the thinking it supports. I suspect, indeed, that's why science fiction has largely displaced utopian fiction as a genre. Again, Auden is the one who spelled out the explanation for us, in "Vespers," from his poetic sequence *Horae Canonicae*, and again in some of his essays in *The Dyer's Hand*.

For city lovers, the city is New Jerusalem—the site of knowledge, sophistication, freedom of action, as well as all true learning and culture. For the urban-oriented temperament the country, the rural landscape, is the location of the superstition-, disease-, fire-, flood-, and earthquake-ridden Land of the Flies. There life is harsh and brutal and all society is bound by the chains of gossip and village opinion.

For country lovers, the rural world is Arcadia and the city is, rather, the dirty, shabby, mechanized, and inhuman place where everyone wears the same uniform and does the same repetitive and meaningless tasks in quintessentially boring settings: Brave New World. As Auden points out, the decision as to whether you are more comfortable in the city or the country is largely a matter of temperament and/or habitation.

It is not a matter of objective facts. You pay for the culture, variety, and freedom of cities by having to toil in Brave New World. You pay for the beauties of nature by having to live in a relatively small-minded and oppressive township.

Science fiction—unlike utopia/dystopia—has traditionally taken its images from all four forms and integrated them into single visions of a rich and complex world. (After all, temperaments change, sometimes hour by hour.) The best and most characteristic SF novels (Bester's *The Stars My Destination*, Pangborn's *Mirror for Observers*, Harness's *The Paradox Men*, Sturgeon's *More Than Human* . . .) allegorize complex possible relations among all four. More recently, since cyberpunk, two more image clusters have added themselves to the mix: both Techno Junk City and the Empire of the Afternoon have joined with New Jerusalem, Brave New World, Arcadia, and the Land of the Flies. But such complexity—the hallmark of science-fictional thinking—leaves the simplistic templates of "utopia (good) / dystopia (bad)" far behind.

If only because of their insufferable and insulting arrogance, time-hogging utopian monologists don't command much of a place anymore. Rather we need to encourage a polyvocalic politics, through dialogue and an appreciation of multiple prospectives, which is what science fiction as a genre does—and by science fiction I specifically do not mean "speculative fiction," which is, at least today, a monologic imposition by which one or another academic tries to privilege the particular science fiction he or she most prefers (cyberpunk, social, feminist, or what have you), at the expense of the overall genre's range and richness, a range and richness that make the individual novels and stories in any or all of those parenthetical subcategories signify in a dialogic and polyvocalic process.

Interviewer: In your autobiography you state that you are "neither black nor white . . . male nor female. And you are that most ambiguous of citizens, the writer." Explain. What roles does or will that most ambiguous of citizens play in our public or private culture(s), or in our potential utopias?

SRD: I've always found it interesting the way people misread that passage, the way they pull it out of context. You'll remember, in *The Motion of Light in Water*, my autobiography, I present that as an *error* in my thinking that I got trapped into when I was at an emotional nadir—and on my way to a nervous breakdown that eventually landed me in a mental hospital.

Only when I began to get it back together and was in the midst of the kind of thinking that got me out of the hospital and, at twenty-three, back into the world—and that started me writing again—did I realize that I was a "black man, a gay man, a writer"; that these were specific, if complex, categories.

As categories, they were social impositions—not essences. They were what had always already given me my identity; and an identity was something to be examined, interrogated, analyzed: vigilance and, often, resistance were the conditions of being able to function.

Now people desperately love all that wonderful-sounding ambiguity—just as I desperately desired it when I was beaten and confused and exhausted by life and overwork. "I belong to no category; I straddle them all . . ." It sounds romantic/decadent, but somehow still transcendent. When we pursue such ambiguity, mistakenly we feel it's a way to escape social accountability. That we crave such ambiguity is the sign of just how wounding the categories can be or have been. Still, espousing that ambiguity was and is a way of saying: 'Not me . . . I'm above all that, outside of it, not a part of it.'"

What I learned is that precisely when one says, "I'm not a part," one is most trapped by one's identity, most paralyzed and most limited by the greater society, and that is the sign one has given up, given in; that one is precisely not in a condition of freedom—but of entrapment. Saying, "I am not a part" is very different from saying, "Because I am a part, I will not participate in that manner." The first is delusion. The second is power—which is inimical to the cry of powerlessness that you quote—and is the other way discourses are changed.

Interviewer: In your collection of essays *Longer Views*, you name a dozen poets whose work you have enjoyed over the last few years. How has poetry influenced your work? What is the connection, for you, between, say, poetry and science fiction writing?

SRD: You'll have to excuse me. Auden is on my mind, because only yesterday someone sent me an audiotape of two TV programs that featured him, which I first watched in 1953 when I was eleven years old. The second one in particular—in which Auden was interviewed—made a great impression on me as a child. One of my best friends in elementary school was a boy named Johnny Kronenberger, whose father, Louis Kronenberger, had collaborated with Auden on *The Oxford Book of Aphorisms*. From time to time Auden babysat for Johnny and his sister Liza. So, by the time I was eleven, I already knew of Auden and knew he was a famous poet—that, indeed, he was queer and lived with Chester Kallman. (The kids at my New York private school were quite a bunch of gossips.) With great glee, Johnny had described to me Chester's imitations of Diana Trilling at his parents' annual Christmas party.

I'd mentioned seeing the *Camera Three* program in my autobiography. Involved in collecting all the extant Auden interviews, Auden scholar Jacek Niecko had recently read my book, phoned me up, and offered to send a copy of the programs to me.

I listened to the soundtrack of the programs just last night—for the first time in forty-five years. Hearing the voice of Jim McAndrew, the *Camera Three* spokesperson (in the 1950s McAndrew was the poor man's Alistair Cooke) for the first time since before I entered puberty, last night I was most aware of how people use poetry for their own purposes—which may or may not have anything to do with what the poet is interested in, writing his or her poem.

Camera Three was a wonderful show. There I saw my first modern dance. There I first heard the poetry—in both English and Spanish—of Federico García Lorca. There I first saw Balanchine's choreography. But it was, I also realized last night (as are so many attempts to "bring Art to the People," of which *Camera Three* was a classic example), in many ways an aesthetically conservative program.

In 1953, McAndrew was probably somewhere between thirty-eight and forty-two. He'd graduated from college just before World War II, in that age when not everybody went to college and when the mark of intelligence was merely having a high school diploma. He'd missed out, doubtless, on the "New Criticism" and probably regarded it as a suspicious order of recent academic nonsense—the way someone who'd graduated from college in the 1950s might have regarded poststructuralist literary theory ten or fifteen years ago. When, during the second program devoted to the poet, he got around to interviewing Auden in person, clearly he had an intellectual agenda already in place. What I realized last night, however, which needless to say had completely escaped me at eleven, was that his only interest in Auden was in how Auden was going to validate that agenda. Moreover, equally clearly, he couldn't imagine Auden himself having any other interest than to validate it. With every "question/ statement" McAndrew poses, his point is that the historical purpose of the poet has been to provide images of heroes for the nation. Clearly that's what Homer did. Clearly that's what Shakespeare did. Thus, that's what Auden must be doing, too. ("The poet must speak from a position of strength," he begins by declaring.) "Okay, Mr. Auden, tell our audience just how you go about doing this." And whenever Auden tries, however politely, to move the conversation toward something that might actually be interesting about poetry (at one point, while describing how technology changes the structure of the personal act, Auden explains that pressing a button to drop a bomb is far different from Achilles fighting a one-to-one combat with Hector), McAndrew diligently takes it back to this narrow and straited notion: "Of course the people must find a hero in the midst of something technological. They might pick the tailgunner of the plane that dropped the bomb on Japan twelve years ago. But the poet wouldn't be interested in the tailgunner, of course."

Realizing he's been completely misunderstood, Auden declares: "Oh, he might . . ."

McAndrew's tailgunner was certainly a not-so-veiled dig at a then much-discussed World War II poem by Randall Jarrell, "The Death of the Ball Turret

Gunner," about an insistently unheroic death (Jarrell's poem ends, "When I died they washed me out of the turret with a hose"), but I was eleven and oblivious.

McAndrew reminds us, however, how relatively new and troubling for the modern critic the poetic task of protesting the ironic futility of so much modern life—not to mention modern death—actually was; it was as new and difficult to deal with as, a hundred years before, Browning's celebration of the barren and ugly and insistently unbeautiful landscape in "Childe Roland to the Dark Tower Came" (1855) had once been. I don't believe McAndrew would have been able then to conceive of the flowering of such a poetic task in a poem, only a handful of years later, such as Allen Ginsberg's *Howl* (1956), a protest Auden's own poems had taken on in works such as *For the Time Being* (1942): "If, on account of the political situation, / There are quite a number of houses without roofs, and men / Lying about in the landscape neither drunk nor asleep . . .")—and "The Shield of Achilles" (1952), which he read that same morning on the show.

Today McAndrew sounds unbelievably clunky, dated—and incredibly dictatorial: he knows what poetry is for, and that's all he's interested in hearing about. At the time (to repeat), the establishment critical position was that the purpose of poets was to write great poems about great political leaders; and the fact that no poet whom anyone actually wanted to read was even vaguely interested in doing anything like this was a sign of the decadent times in which we lived.

Against this, Auden tries to maintain a demeanor that is at once light, conversational, erudite, and not too appalled. Within the margins of civility, he protests all this strait-laced intellectual flapdoodle. At one point, when McAndrew is going on piously about Shakespeare, and says, "Henry the fifth was a popular hero—"

Auden interrupts: "And rather a bore!"—and McAndrew, you can hear it, is actually shocked!

If you are familiar with the history of criticism, you realize that McAndrew's thematic dogmatism is precisely what the "New Critics" of the late 1940s and early '50s were—really—just then in rebellion against.

(The earlier program, in which half a dozen actors declaimed Auden's poems like a bunch of nineteenth-century Shakespearean hams, ranges between the comic and the pathetic. But this is what people thought poetry was, back then. Even recordings of Sylvia Plath, reading her own poems in that decade, fall into that same mode. Auden's great love lyric to Chester Kallman, "Lay your sleeping head my love . . . ," was read out by a woman to a snoozing man: the directors probably thought they were being quite daring, if not revolutionary. Auden, as he reads "The Shield of Achilles" and "In Memory of William Butler Yeats," alone comes anywhere near the tone of intelligent conversation in which the vast majority of his poems are actually written. And, forty-five years later, that was what I remembered.)

While there are *more* poets today, and people have become *somewhat* more comfortable with them, conversing with them, hearing them read, and perhaps a little more polite to them, I don't know whether the fundamental situation has changed. We find lines that we love and quote them out of context—only to reread the entire poem a decade later and discover that the poet was telling us that is something we must never do or think!

The very brilliance of expression was the poet's attempt to allegorize its seductiveness as a dangerous idea.

In his essay "Writing," Auden tells us: "The English-speaking peoples have always felt that the difference between poetic speech and the conventional speech of everyday should be kept very small, and, whenever poets have felt that the gap between poetic and ordinary speech was growing too wide, there has been a stylistic revolution to bring them closer again." Auden was writing this—and I first read it—during the ascendancy of Dylan Thomas. Auden's poetry was, of course, insistently a poetry of highly intelligent conversation, whereas Thomas was a surreal and flashy ranter. But with observations such as the one I quote above, by the time (a shy decade after watching him on *Camera Three*) I had begun to publish, Auden's work was there to help make me aware that the language labors that produce poetry were not very different from those necessary for prose.

That fundamental closeness between poetry and prose in English is what allowed me to see poets laboring over their poems and to put like labor into my prose. What differentiates the two is the discourses that control the way in which the two are read. Though there's some, of course, there's much less difference in the way the two are written than it would otherwise seem.

Interviewer: Define silence.

SRD: I won't try to define it, because silence—at least in the way it interests me—is one of those objects that resists definition. But I can certainly make some descriptive statements about it so that we might be more likely recognize it the next time we encounter it in one of its many forms.

Today silence is a rather beleaguered state.

And silence is the necessary context in which, alone, information can signify —in short, it's the opposite of "noise."

As such, it's seldom, if ever, neutral. It's pervaded by assumptions, by expectations, by discourses—what the Russian poet Osip Mandelstam (born the same year as our Zora Neale Hurston, 1891) called *shum vremeni*, "the *hubbub* (or *buzz*; or *swoosh*) of time." As such, silence is the only state in which the *shum* that pervades it can be studied.

Since Wagner at least, silence has been considered the proper mode in which to appreciate the work of art: Wagner was the first major artist to forbid talking in the theater during his concerts and operas. He began the custom of not applauding between movements of a symphony, sonata, concerto, suite, or string quartet. Also, he was the first person, during performances of his operas at Bayreuth, to turn off the house lights in the theater and have illumination only on the stage.

Silence.

Darkness.

For better or worse, this aligns art more closely with death: it moves us formally toward a merger with the unknown.

Carnival, circus, and social festival are the lively arts that fight the morbidity of that early modernism/late romanticism. They are the arts around which one is expected to make noise, point, cry out "Oh, look!," then buy cotton candy from a passing vendor, and generally have a life, while the artists satirize it in simultaneous distortion, as clown, acrobat, and animal trainer—with silly prizes to the people for random effort and skill.

But, whether one is looking at comic books or construing philosophy, silence is still the state in which the best reading takes place; not to mention the writing —or revising—of a story or a poem.

—January 1999
New York City

27

How to Do Well in This Class

The key to doing well in this class is much the one you need to do well in all your classes:

Organize Your Study Time!

Doubtless, you've heard this before. But what does it mean? It means a number of things. Here are some of the most important.

It means set aside time for having fun and just hanging out. That's very important. But also set aside time for study—and for attending your classes! It may be self-evident and a little silly to have to say it, but the work really is as important as the fun!

Here, however, in order to explain why these are so important, we have to say a few words about how students mess up. A very few students don't care how well they do and just don't try from the beginning. But I know most of you want to do well. The overwhelming majority of students who fail their courses, or do poorly, do so not because they don't care, but because they go through some version of the following process. When I describe it, perhaps you'll recognize it, or recognize part of it.

Possibly because you've neglected to do some earlier work for the first week or two, sometimes toward the beginning of the term, in order to catch up you try to study too hard and too long. But because you haven't set any time limits on that study, it's more than you (or anyone else!) can possibly do comfortably in a single sitting. Therefore, after a few hours, in order to compensate you go out and try to have a good time. But because you haven't set any time limits on your good times either, you spend too much time at *that* (a couple of days, say, without going back and doing any studying at all) so that you fall even *further* behind! Eventually, a week or two later, you make another stab at studying —but, again, because you haven't set it up in terms of reasonable time limits, the process just repeats, with longer and longer periods between the attempts to study, as you have more and more to catch up with. The end result is a failed course or two—and your good times are marred by your nagging anxiety about classes not going well, or skipped or missing or poor papers, and bad test results.

The process is strong, stable, and extraordinarily efficient—efficient enough to remove several hundred or a thousand students a year from among the twenty-five thousand that attend the University of Massachusetts. The thing to understand if you get caught up in this process is that what is messing up your marks and doing in your grades is not your intelligence. (As I'm sure you've noticed, if you've gotten a chance to look around: People a lot less swift than you are often doing pretty well.) If you first got caught in this process back in high school, then almost certainly one person or another—a relative or a friend— has told you that it has something to do with your character or your personality. ("You just don't try! Don't be so lazy! You *could* do it if you *really* wanted to . . .") Well, sad news for them: It's not your character, either. (Having gotten caught in this process without really understanding what it is and how it works, you may have decided that you yourself can't get out of it and so have decided to give up. But that's another story.) Though it is hard for people to grasp this, it is the *process itself* that is responsible for your doing poorly. Put pretty much anyone inside this process—exceptionally smart or pretty ordinary—and the results will be the same.

The most important thing to remember if you're trapped in this process and want to get out of it is that you can't fight the process from inside it. If you say, "Okay. As soon as I've had my fill of fun, I'm going to sit down and study," you might as well forget it. You're still inside the process—the process of failure. If you say: "Okay! Enough of this. I'm going out and walk around, look for a friend, and go hang out at a bar," you're *still* within the process.

The process of failure is, you see, one of setting up *unorganized, open-ended* units of time. The way to get out of the process is to set up organized, end-stopped units of time. That's the only thing that will halt it. If you want me to put it in terms of rules, I can.

Don't sit down to study without planning a specific time at which to stop. When you go out to have fun, set a specific time by which to be back.

If, in the middle of things, you decide you want to change to a new time, fine: Do that—set a new time to stop; set a new time to be back. But to get out of the process, you have to stop living in a world of open-ended time units and start living in a world of end-stopped time units. Hard as it may be to believe, *that's* the fundamental difference between what the people who are getting those As and Bs and maintaining a 3.5 or higher GPA are doing—and what *you're* doing.

If you're caught up in the process of failure, you'll do better if you set yourself three half-hour study sessions every other day (that's three half hours that start here and end there: once in the morning, once in the afternoon, and once at night) than you will if you go on doing what you're doing now: that is, sometime on Sunday or even Monday night, deciding maybe you better sit down and do some catching up, which, for a few minutes or even a few hours, you actually do . . .

The fact is, organizing your time and setting limits on your periods of fun and your periods of work constitute a process too. It's a process that frees what intelligence you have to exercise itself in its most constructive mode on the problem to hand. It makes it easier for you to study, and, more important, it makes it possible for you to study *again*—whereas the process of failure not only makes it harder for you to study but makes it even harder (indeed, all but impossible) for you to study again. In a school situation where you are not working on a single, overall, encompassing, obsessive problem, but rather on several limited and usually more or less separate fields (math, chemistry, history, French, economics . . .), it's the only process likely to let you negotiate them all with any combined efficiency. But if you don't organize your time, other forces—powerful forces that Sigmund Freud grouped together under the term "the Pleasure Principle"—will take over and organize it for you; and (as Freud himself was quick to note) those forces will organize it in ways that, in the long run, produce some unpleasurable results, like flunking out of school.

Organizing your time and setting limits is not only a process. It's also a habit. If you haven't done it before, the first ten times you do it, it's going to feel like eating with the wrong hand. Do it anyway. The next ten will be easier —and the ten after that, easier still. By then, however, you will be starting to experience the rewards from living your life this way.

Again: The solution is to organize your study time from the start—*and* your fun time. Set limits on both.

What kind of limits? First, understand: Studying more than four hours straight without at least an hour break is generally not going to help you too much. After a certain amount of time (different for each one of us), things simply stop sticking in your memory. You start making mistakes or misremembering things without knowing it.

A full fifteen-credit course load is the equivalent of a full 40-hour-a-week job —and if you want to do particularly well, you'll have to put in some overtime. If you have a part-time or full-time job as well as classes, you have to take that into account.

Again: Organize your time. Write down the hours you intend to study and the hours you have set aside for yourself. Try to stick to that schedule. After you've tried it for a week or two, decide if it's working or not. If it's not, adjust it where you need to.

Here's my suggestion: Depending on whether you think of yourself as a slow reader or a fast reader, start by setting aside between an hour and an hour and a half, three nights a week, to read and take notes for this class. The four long stories that we read over the term ("Heart of Darkness," "The Time Machine," "The Turn of the Screw," and "The Metamorphosis") may easily take you between eight and fourteen hours each to read. So, as well as your regular reading time, be prepared to give a good part of one weekend day (before the lecture!) to each of those four longer stories as well.

When a paper is due, break out your reading diary and look at your notes on details, set yourself a full six hours on one day to write it (eight hours if you have to re-read the whole story), and at least two hours on another day to go over the paper and revise it, once you've had a night's sleep and can look at it with fresh eyes. Figure in break times.

Besides being a professor, I'm also a professional writer. I wouldn't think of handing in a piece of writing without going over it to revise and correct it, a day after I'd "finished" it. You shouldn't either. Revising is part of the writing process. I have a couple of friends I show all my writing to and ask them to suggest improvements. Try that, too, and see if your papers aren't better.

And go to a movie with a friend at least once a week!

Try it, and see how it works out. You may well find you don't need as much time as I've suggested. If so, adjust your schedule down. But just because it starts off easy, don't abandon your schedule altogether! If you do, even if you're someone who finds the work easy, you may still fall behind.

The only human endeavors I know that don't profit from being done in end-stopped time units are works of art—specifically novels, non-fiction pieces, and long poems. Creative work alone seems to thrive on long, uninterrupted, obsessive periods of work. (Novels seem to require the process of failure from which to grow!) Even there, sometimes breaks and forced stopping periods can benefit such projects. It's the rare novel that doesn't benefit from the artist having her or his nose rubbed in the realities of daily life a handful of times, at least, during its creation.

—February 1999
New York City

NOTE

The date of a first draft of this essay is unknown; probably in my early years at the University of Massachusetts, Amherst.

28

His Wing, His Claw
Beneath the Arc of Day

One functional description of a religion useful in distinguishing it from a philosophy is that a religion is a system of thoughts and images in which elements of the human body combine with elements of animal bodies to produce a conjunction before which people must reconsider their behavior. Such a description suggests that, in Christianity at least, the bird wings on angels and the horns, hooves, tails, and goat-eyes on devils and demons are more to the point than the preachings of the insistently human Jesus and his disciples.

The year 1885 gave us in whole or in part three great critiques of bourgeois morality, critiques that suggest their own alternatives without recourse to the notion of a personal afterlife to provide either ultimate rewards or ultimate punishments: Friederich Nietzsche's tract *Also sprach Zarathustra*, Walter Pater's novel *Marius the Epicurean: His Sensations and Ideas*, and Georges Seurat's great painting *Un dimanche après-midi à l'Île de la Grande Jatte* (1884–1886). All three lean on those human/animal correspondences that suggest religion. In all three, images of humans and animals—horses, serpents, monkeys, wolves, dogs— threaten to conjoin in some proto-religious figure.

Heaven can be menaced by a tower—by the concerted work of mankind speaking some prelapserian language of political unity.

The sky cannot.

Currently among U.S. English-language writers of science fiction and fantasy, by far the most interesting to take on the Judeo-Christian kerygma as his field of interrogation is James Morrow (1953–). But in the range of that work, heaven gets fairly short shrift. In *Towing Jehovah* (1993), God has fallen *out* of the sky and his tremendous carcass floats in the sea, waiting to be pulled by a steamship to its Antarctic burial site. Whether it be the material air of Robert Boyle (1627–91) or in the airs of the spirit, in the sky of early meteorologists, or in the skies of today's airlines companies, in the space of the astrophysicist and the rocket scientist, or in the universe of the theoretical physicist, the concept of "heaven" (along with that of "paradise") gets bypassed somewhere along this conceptual measure. In English, the terms "heaven" and "heavenly" carry a huge connotation of the feminine and femininity—and in a patriarchal society such as ours, often that is a sign that such concepts have moved wholly into the superstructure of discourse to become all but conceptually irrelevant, unless their use remains that of lying about something darker and less pleasant in advertising and popular songs. A good deal of nineteenth-century romanticism (and its immediate forerunners in the eighteenth) is a matter of coming to terms with the common-sense and scientific improbability of any sort of personal afterlife, realizations that went hand and hand with the expanding concept of the sky, the atmosphere, the space of the solar system, the deployment of stars in the galaxy, the range of galaxies in our corner of the universe: in short, the hugely extended concept of the night. Novalis introduced it into the gallery of romantic images. Wagner (in Act II of *Tristan*) set it to music and allied it with sex. Indeed romantic night can be seen to displace a pre-romantic heaven. The older theological question about where to put all those bodily resurrections is displaced by the scientific realization that there are simply no material relations either to translate them or sustain them. Here heaven withers and, if it does not die, at least grows moribund.

Today, as the world becomes smaller and smaller and, at the same time, falls more and more under the control of unconscious forces, heavenly and demonic chimera in their mediate position between human and animal (and many others between human and machine) have been on the increase in whole ranges of comic books and other popular iconographies, where they function as signs (rather than metaphors) of impossibility, paradox, contradiction, and negation itself—those operations that alone make logic and reason possible, but which operations (Freud reminded us) do *not* exist in the unconscious. These marvelous monsters picture the power, the mystery, the incomprehensibility of those symbolic, logic-facilitating operations unique to consciousness. These creatures inhabit a set of narratives that open to an all too easy decoding, brawn standing for brain and brain standing for brawn. That such apparitions are often pictured in the sky should not, I think, be taken as a sign for their heavenly luminosity; rather their locations make them part of a pre-enlightenment image of materiality: they inhabit fire, water, earth, and air. For almost as soon as the sky grows any larger than the local arc of light or ark that stretches horizon to horizon, heaven (as it were) collapses, tears loose from it, and falls in fragments to the earth.

—February 1999
New York City

29

Student of Desire

David Wojnarowicz was a sexual radical.

What does that mean? He tried to write about sex honestly. He tried to picture it accurately. Although it doesn't say so, the wash illustrations for his book *Memories That Smell Like Gasoline* (1992) are largely from the back balcony of the Variety Photoplays Theater on Third Avenue below 14th Street, before it was closed down as a porn house and remodeled. You can recognize the particular space from among New York City's several sex theaters because of the chairs and the wall on which a man leans, pants down around his ankles, waiting to be fucked.

Being a sexual radical means focusing a certain amount of attention on the details of the act. It means presenting those details without letting them be swept up either by a discourse of sentimentality or by an equally pervasive discourse of horror—discourses that wait to gather everything to themselves and prevaricate shamelessly about the topic to all who would listen.

Some things most of us would find pretty horrible happened to Wojnarowicz. He was raped by a trucker in New Jersey when he was a kid. Wojnarowicz details some of these adventures in the comic book *Seven Miles a Second* (Fantagraphics, 1996), with artists James Romberger and Marguerite Van Cook, and in *Memories that Smell Like Gasoline* (Artspace Books, 1992):

I had been drugged, tossed out a second story window, strangled, smacked in the head with a slab of marble, punched in the face at least seventeen times, almost stabbed four times, beat about my face too many times to recount, almost completely suffocated, and woken up once tied to a hotel bed with my head over the side[;] all the blood rushed down into it making it feel like it was going to explode, all this before I turned fifteen. (15)

Out of context, there's no way to read this except as a confirmation of the horror. In context, however, it becomes a confirmation of the horror survived: survived not as some form of sentimental uplift, but simply in the manner one survives the most boring afternoons in the July heat or the equally dull February midnight. Wojnarowicz got hold of a truth that French novelist Flaubert also knew wonderfully well: sex manifests through desire, and desire functions through absence. Like language, desire is a complex structure of what, just now, we don't have. (That's why we talk about it; that's why we want it.) We may see it, we may pursue it, we may wander in search of it along a foggy evening waterfront or through the East Village at dawn or along the back balcony of a pornographic movie house at four in the afternoon. But even when we clasp the lover to our body, even when one body enters another, and the fluids of one mix with the fluids of the other, absence lies at the core of each. In his prose works, *Close to the Knives* (1991) and the posthumous *Waterfront Journals* (1996), Wojnarowicz the writer made his awareness of this essential absence palpable, page by page.

—*March 1999*
New York City

30

A Centennial Life from
the Roaring Twenties

On *The Broken Tower: The Life of Hart Crane* by Paul Mariani

I.

Approximately ten miles off the Florida coast, on April 27, 1932, minutes past noon, as the steamship *Orizaba* churned from Mexico back to the United States (eight bells had just sounded), with the other passengers gathered on the rear deck to hear the announcement of the winners of the ship's daily pool, Gertrude E. Vogt saw the American poet Harold Hart Crane (1899–1932) step from the cabin door. He wore a topcoat over his pajamas. With a black eye, he looked generally disheveled.

In the two days of the trip so far, traveling with his "fiancée" Peggy Baird Cowley (waiting for her divorce from Crane's friend Malcolm to come through), the not-quite thirty-two-year-old young man had already established himself as the shipboard character, if not nuisance. At the previous day's stopover at Havana, Crane and Peggy had gotten off the boat. Crane had sent two postcards, one to a professor of Spanish he'd known in Mexico, another to his mother's old housekeeper on the Isle of Pines, both named Simpson. Then he and Peggy had gone drinking. Back on the boat (everybody on shipboard now knew) the Purser had had to lock the drunken, rowdy Crane in his cabin, though he'd gotten out again that evening and gone down into the sailors' quarters, where he'd been robbed of watch, ring, and wallet—and gotten the black eye.

What Vogt did not know, however, was that, only minutes before, Crane had left Peggy in her cabin, where she'd been confined since the previous day with a burned arm from an accident with a box of Cuban matches (ten years older than Crane, she was as much of a drunk as he was), with the words: "Darling, I'm not going to make it."

Peggy's response had been a motherly, "Put your clothes on, dear. You'll feel better."

In the bright April sun over the back deck, Vogt saw Crane walk to the ship's stern, remove his top coat, fold it over the rail, put his hands on the bar, and step out of his bedroom slippers. He raised himself on tiptoes, lowered himself once more—

Then Crane vaulted over, to drop from sight!

After some five astonished seconds, the cry went up: "Man overboard!"

Vogt and the others ran to the rail.

Down among the wake's billows (thirty-five years later, Vogt would write to Crane's third biographer John Unterecker, nearly a year after *Voyager*, his biography of Crane, had appeared), she saw Crane "swimming strongly." Then she lost sight of him. The ship's bell was ringing. Moments later, the ship shuddered, as the officer on the ship's bridge managed to disengage the propeller. Shortly, the steamship began to troll back and forth, searching for Crane or—as an hour unfolded toward two—his remains.

It is still unclear whether he was sucked down into the wake, whether he was backwashed into the ship's screw, or whether sharks got him and ate him (they were rampant in those waters), but no one ever saw Crane again.

Five years later, W. W. Norton published the first of what is now five full-length biographies of the poet: Philip Horton's *Hart Crane: The Life of an American Poet* (1937) is still the most sprightly—though its creation was surely the most stifled. While Horton was researching and writing his book, many people who knew Crane, as well as a number of Crane's relatives, were still alive. In effect looking over Horton's shoulder as he worked, some of those friends and relatives had aspects of the poet he—or she—wished to stress, or other aspects he or she (especially Crane's obsessive, depressive, spoiled, but always extraordinary mother, Grace Hart Crane) would have preferred did not see print.

To start by placing him in a perfectly arbitrary context, Crane was eleven years older than Jean Genet. He was born in the same year as Jorge Luis Borges.

Crane was a homosexual, sexually active, and with a thing for seafood. If gossip and some of his letters are to be trusted, for Crane sex meant sailors.

Coded by a variety of means, homosexual concerns sequin Crane's poems, starting with the very first he published (in *Bruno's Weekly*, out of Greenwich Village, in September 1916, when Crane was seventeen and still living at home in Cleveland): "c33"—the number of the jail cell in which Oscar Wilde was confined at Reading. They are there in the splendid sequence "Voyages" to his sailor lover, Emil Opffer (with whom Crane lived in Brooklyn in 1924 on Columbia Heights, the back of the building opening on what today is the Promenade, and whom he once described in a letter as "the Word made Flesh"), as well as some of the equally searing poems in his major poetic sequence *The Bridge* ("Harbor Dawn"—about waking with his lover in bed; "Cutty Sark"—about an unsuccessful pick-up of a sailor on South Street, who, after Crane keeps the man drunk and talking in the bar till dawn, starts back to his dock—his ship pulled out at three—instead of going home with Crane). Even the line, broken in two, from Whitman's "Passage to India," which serves as epigraph to "Cape Hattaras" but which, even more importantly, forms a bridge with the previous "Cutty Sark"—

> The seas all crossed,
> weathered the capes, the voyage done . . .
> —Walt Whitman

—is a fragment Crane expected would prompt a certain sort of reader (as Scholar Robert Martin noted more than fifteen years ago) to recall the incestuous homoerotic lines that terminal ellipsis stands in for, from the end of the poem's (Whitman's, that is) section eight:

> The seas all crossed, weathered the capes, the voyage done,
> Surrounded, copest, frontest God, yieldest, the aim attain'd,
> As filled with friendship, love complete, the Elder Brother found,
> The Younger melts in fondness in his arms.

Finished some two months before his death, Crane's last poem, "The Broken Tower," includes among the many allegories nested in the vivid fragments that comprise the poem at least one of a gay man who has just learned he can perform heterosexually (if he gets drunk enough)—and who seems *very* happy about it.

The night before his leap into the *Orizaba*'s wake, when the drunken Crane had broken out of his cabin and gone down among the largely Spanish-speaking crew, quite possibly he tried to read his poems to this one, or even put the make on the same one or another. (Although he had not seen Opffer in a year and a half, April 26—the afternoon his last binge began—had been his sailor lover's birthday.) On that hung-over morning, robbed and beaten, Crane may well have felt both forms of sexuality impossible; and the tension between them—after all, he'd made much of marrying Peggy—finally drove him over the rail.

Crane had been open about his homosexuality with any number of his straight friends: novelist and critic Waldo Frank; critic Gorham Munson; black writer Jean Toomer, author of *Cane* (1923); poet and critic Yvor Winters and later, poet Allen Tate; as well as women such as Lorna Deitz and Susan Jenkins Light (later Susan Jenkins Brown), married to James Light, himself a gay man and a director at New York City's Provincetown Playhouse; and probably Peggy. Crane was a loud and difficult drunk, who, especially in his last years, got into street brawls and bar fights and was sometimes punched out. Many assumed these were butch numbers Crane propositioned who didn't appreciate it, so that some of his acquaintances, including the poet Leonie Adams and her husband, on whose couch Crane ended up the morning after a number of those nights, were sure (especially after tales began to filter back of his final night on shipboard) that the beatings were, for him, part of or even the most important part of his sexual adventurings.

One reason I suspect this is over-extended armchair psychologizing by the staunchly Catholic Adams and spouse is, however, that Crane nowhere mentions any such S/M leanings in his letters. Even after the expanded 1997 edition of Crane's selected letters, *O My Land, My Friends*, edited by Brom Weber and Langdon Hammer, there are still some unpublished letters from Crane to one of his gay friends, Wilber Underwood, reputed to focus on sex. Though the Hammer-Weber edition overlaps with both Weber's 1965 edition of the literary letters and the larger 1974 compilation by Thomas S. W. Lewis of the letters between Crane and his family, we still need a complete correspondence—and could also use a couple of "Crane Circle" volumes, modeled after the ones Hyder Edward Rollins gave us for Keats in 1948. Unless the remaining letters to Underwood contain major surprises, however, rather than simply "scandalous" details—and, as each new set has come into print, though all have enriched our knowledge, none has surprised—we can probably assume Crane's street fights and bar fights and nights in jail (with, at thirty, prematurely gray hair, a puffy face, and the enlarged knuckles of a street brawler rather than a poet) were the result of drink, not sex, however frequently the search for sex (after all, often successful) initiated them.

Brom Weber's *Hart Crane: A Biographical and Critical Study* appeared in 1948 from the Bodley Press, New York, eleven years after Horton's initial biography. Weber would go on to edit his own edition of Crane's poems (as well as the first selection of Crane's letters, mentioned above). Weber's is what, today, we would call an intellectual biography. Its eccentricities are, however, notorious: Crane's birth and death dates are given only as footnotes, added in galleys at the insistence of Weber's in-house editor Sam Loveman (another of Crane's gay friends), when the publisher noticed they were absent. Weber had been prepared to leave them out entirely.

Well, Crane needed an intellectual biography. People delighted in telling tales about him. A serious drinker since his twenty-third year, and in his final a hopeless alcoholic and eventual suicide, Crane was loud and loved to party.

Often a nuisance, he smashed furniture and tossed typewriters out of windows with regularity. He was also a warm, supportive, and enthusiastic friend. In his early years, people respected him, loved him, forgave him—and forgave him again and again, until he was an unforgivably obstreperous lush. After Crane agreed to winter with them, a few weeks on Allen Tate and his wife Caroline Gordon ejected him from their home in Patterson, New York, as an intolerable guest. One of Crane's landladies, who had all but fallen in love with him the previous year, now locked the door against him when at a party (again in Patterson) he commenced another chair-smashing session. In Mexico, Katherine Anne Porter said she would simply not see him any more if he came around sloshed again—and stuck to it. Because he had no formal schooling and—though he left hundreds of pages of letters to friends and family—because he left so little sustained critical prose, it's easy to lose track of the fact that Crane was also an intellectual. He read widely, thought deeply, and regularly revised and reworked his poems in the light of his thoughts about poetry. But it was far easier to think of him simply as a character, and that's what Weber's book tries to counteract.

As an intellectual biography, among the early incidents Weber recounts is a visit during Crane's fifteenth year by writer and eccentric publisher Elbert Hubbard, who came to Cleveland to write up the story of Crane's father's success in the candy business, in the process charming Clarence Arthur Crane (C. A., to his friends and family) and fascinating his budding poet son. Hubbard was an American phenomenon. Born in 1856 on a dirt-poor midwestern farm, he went into journalism (he was a friend of Stephen Crane's when Crane was struggling in the same profession in New York City in the early 1890s) and became famous with an 1899 essay, "A Message to Garcia," which, reprinted in newspapers, pamphlets, and anthologies, had appeared in more than thirty million copies by 1913 and was still read in conservative elementary schools up through the 1950s. At some point during the visit, Hubbard doubtless suggested Crane come spend some time at Roycroft, Hubbard and his wife Alice's successful work cooperative. Crane was clearly taken with the notion.

Here's what Weber writes:

During the summer of 1914, Hart successfully managed to spend a few weeks, with his parents' reluctant approval, at Roycroft, the East Aurora, New York, establishment of Elbert Hubbard. It was the first of his flights from home, and resulted from a meeting with Hubbard, who had come to Cleveland to write a success story about the Crane chocolate business. The career of Hubbard is one of the low points in American cultural history. [. . .] As advertising copywriter, vaudeville actor, columnist, and publisher, he fought vigorously for the principles of conservatism. At the same time, his "artistic" appearance with its Windsor tie, long hair, and unpressed clothes . . . his surface obeisance to the ideas of William Morris . . .

his sponsorship of Stephen Crane's free verse . . . his reports of visits to the home of writers like Emerson, Poe, and Ruskin and of his meeting with Whitman, as well as his frequent quotations from their works . . . gave an air of ingenuousness to his commercial activities. To Hart, he was a fresh and liberating figure as he made his habitual scoffing remarks about businessmen, attacked Christian Science [Crane's mother and grandmother were devout Christian Scientists], and perhaps impressed him with his friendship for Stephen Crane. At East Aurora, Hart lived with the Hubbard family, eating at their table, and participating in their discussions. In accordance with Hubbard's baronial ideas, Hart worked in the Roycroft bookbindery mornings and spent his afternoons on the Roycroft farm doing odd jobs in the open air. Though the days spent in Hubbard's company speedily destroyed the illusion of the man as a literary genius, there is no doubt that Hart's decision in the 1920s to enter advertising as a profession, as well as his familiarity, if not his initial acquaintance, with the works and ideas of America's classic poets, were encouraged by this summer interlude. (8) [bracketed ellipses, mine; additions in brackets, mine; non-bracketed ellipses, Weber's.]

Hubbard was a political conservative and supported big business. When, in Colorado, the state militia fired on men, women, and children to "protect" the property of John D. Rockefeller, thereafter known as the Ludlow Massacre, in an exchange of letters in *Harper's Weekly* Hubbard defended the founder of Standard Oil, whom by then he counted as a golfing friend. Liberal writers like Weber found him loathsome.

Hubbard had been a "vaudevillian" when three-hour vaudeville shows included uplifting twenty-minute "recitations" on moderately serious topics, like "American Business," "Motherhood," and "Education Today." These had to be delivered with considerable histrionics; their purpose was to make the audience weep. Often they were billed in the program as "Lectures." By 1900 they had fallen out of the usual vaudeville fare. But they helped Hubbard to become a compelling public speaker as well as writer.

Eleven years before Weber's account, in 1937 Horton had given a somewhat different—and briefer—mention of the visit to Hubbard's.

Once [Hart] was caught at the train in the act of running away to visit Elbert Hubbard, his only literary acquaintance, the quaint journeyman of American letters, who had made one of his "little journeys" to the Crane chocolate factory. Although [Hart] finally had his way, he returned after a few weeks, recalcitrant as ever, thoroughly disillusioned, it seemed, by his pilgrimage to East Aurora, but without having sacrificed his enthusiasm for poetry. (28)

Horton was writing at a time when most literate Americans still remembered the popular Hubbard series (written in the years after the uplifting "Message"):

A Little Journey to the Home of Eminent Artists, A Little Journey to the Home of Eminent Scientists, A Little Journey to the Home of Famous Women, A Little Journey to the Home of American Statesmen. Over a dozen volumes, each containing six to ten profiles; like many pre–World War I books they were (maddeningly) undated, but were beautifully printed—and regularly reprinted—often bound in red Morocco, at Roycroft in East Aurora. Their style is highly rhetorical and comes out of the tradition that includes the rhetorical eloquence of W. E. B. DuBois and William James. Though I have not yet seen it explored, this is interesting in terms of Crane's own relation to rhetoric *per se.*

Horton was interested in the emotional situation *around* the trip to Roycroft. Weber was interested in what, intellectually, Crane got from the trip: what, in effect, he brought home from East Aurora to Cleveland. However by 1948, Hart's running away to find it was no longer prologue to the story.

Horton placed the visit to Hubbard in the summer of 1915, when the young Crane was particularly moody, largely over the growing tension between his parents that, in 1916, would lead to their divorce proceedings. But, as we shall shortly see, this date is impossible.

Twenty-one years after Weber's "Biographical and Critical Study" (that book's subtitle), in 1969 John Unterecker published the third of the five biographies, his eight-hundred-thirty-one-page National Book Award–winning *Voyager: A Life of Hart Crane.* (This was and remains the most detailed and accurate.) Here is Unterecker's account of the not-yet-sixteen-year-old Crane's East Aurora visit:

> [Hart] had met only one professional writer, Elbert Hubbard, whom his father admired and who had once written enthusiastically of C. A.'s spreading business ventures. Hubbard in his Cleveland visit must have seemed to young Harold artist incarnate: eloquent, largely and "artistically" unkempt—his unpressed jacket set off by a flowing Windsor tie and a long, carefully mussed shock of leonine hair. Almost weekly after Hubbard's return to East Aurora, New York, where he ran what for a time was an internationally famous inn-farm-workshop-publishing house loosely modeled on William Morris's ventures in late-nineteenth-century England, Harold had badgered his parents to let him visit the great man. Finally, probably in the fall of 1914, they had consented, Grace [Crane's mother] most reluctantly.
>
> Though the visit seemed to have been disillusioning, it gave Crane an insight into the practical side of a successful writer's life. Living, as most apprentices did, with Hubbard's family, working mornings in the Roycroft bookbindery (where he helped produce sumptuous editions of Hubbard's own works) and afternoons on the spreading, level farm associated with the inn, Harold came to know firsthand how manuscripts could be marketed, how newspaper editors could be cajoled into accepting columns, how books could be publicized. Like Harold's father, Hubbard was a phrase maker. His books, abounding in quotable "sayings," seem now the

product of an extrovert ad-man, but at the time they struck many Americans as mines of profundity. Though at first attracted to Hubbard by his praise of Emerson, Whitman, and Poe, Harold returned home convinced that Hubbard's output was pompous and shallow. Ironically, C. A.—who had first been unsympathetic to the visit to East Aurora—later regularly quoted Hubbard in letters to his son, usually on the importance of a steady job and cash in his pocket. (39)

Note that by 1969, Hubbard's personal meeting with Whitman and the visits to the homes of Poe and Emerson have fallen out of Unterecker's account to be replaced here with "praise" of them.

From my own sense of young writers, the direct contact Hubbard could boast with the past was probably more to the point: "Ah, did you once see Shelley plain? / And did he stop and speak to you . . ." wrote Browning.

Seven years ago, in the centennial of Crane's birth, Paul Mariani's biography *The Broken Tower: The Life of Hart Crane* ("The Life" it says on the book jacket; "A Life," it says on the title page) appeared from W. W. Norton, the corporate heir of the publisher who had put out Horton's biography. Though longer than either Horton's or Weber's, Mariani's biography pretty much eschews all problems of intellectual biography. It collects a lot of gossip thought to be—at least till recent years—unprintable. It may well be the most readable, but it achieves its readability at a steep price.

Here is Mariani's account of Hubbard and the East Aurora visit:

In the summer of 1914, a writer and self-promoter from East Aurora, New York, one Elbert Hubbard, a man who'd modeled himself after William Morris by dabbling in everything from bookbinding to textiles and design, visited the Cranes in Cleveland. Because Hubbard was a self-styled entrepreneur as well as an artist, C. A. hailed him as someone after whom Harold might model himself. If one had to dabble in writing, C. A. reasoned, Hubbard's was the way to go. For years after, in fact, C. A. would quote Hubbard's Yankee self-start maxims in letters to his son. As for Harold, it did not take him long to realize how little substance there was to Hubbard. Whatever the artist was, he understood, Hubbard was not it. (26)

As Mariani has decided that Hubbard's visit to Cleveland must have been in 1914, he puts the trip to East Aurora in April of 1915:

In April 1915 Harold spent several weeks as an apprentice at Roycroft, Hubbard's art colony in western New York. Three months later, the boy escorted his mother on a tour of the east United States, staying at posh hotels in Rye Beach and Boston. (27)

and we are finished with all mention of Hubbard. The first thing to note is that the incident that first recommended Hubbard to Crane's parents in Cleveland

—Hubbard's article on C. A.'s business success—has dropped away. As well, there's no speculation on what Crane might have taken from his East Aurora trip. Indeed, the single sentence on the trip per se is so condensed that, really, one must know the story already in order to understand why Mariani even mentions it. And the description of the Roycroft workers' community, print works, furniture factory, and farm as an "art colony" is, at the mildest, strained.

Now for the April 1915 date: Both Unterecker and Horton have Crane with his mother and grandmother on the Isle of Pines until "late spring" of that year. And both Unterecker and Horton have the trips to Boston and Rye Beach coming before the trip to the Isle of Pines in January of 1915, not after. Neither Unterecker nor Horton tells the incidents in those years in strict chronological order, and they are hard to untangle. If one is not following along and making careful notes, it's difficult to tell the precise chronology in either of their versions. But that only suggests more strongly that Mariani's is just a careless reading of the earlier biographies. True, Unterecker mentions the trip to Boston and Rye Beach after he mentions the 1915 Isle of Pines journey. But Mariani has confused where Unterecker mentions it with *when* Unterecker says it occurred.

Weber and Unterecker both revised Horton's 1915 date for Crane's weeks at Roycroft back to 1914—and Unterecker put it in the fall, rather than in April —for, I can only assume, the following reason: After the June 1914 assassination at Sarajevo, Hubbard became more and more obsessed with the war and with world peace, as he saw it. On April 25th, 1915, Hubbard addressed the entire Roycroft community (it numbered at the time almost five hundred, a fact the reader is not likely to pick up from any of the extant biographies). Later that same day, he and his wife Alice departed on a trip intended to take them to England and then Europe, where Hubbard wanted to inspect the war effort firsthand.

The two of them left the States on the *Lusitania*.

By May 7 both were dead, having gone down with the great liner when the Germans sank it off the Irish coast. The Roycroft community weathered the shock, stayed together, and went on publishing Hubbard's works well into the '20s. But, to recapitulate, in "late spring of 1915" Crane and his mother are just getting back into the country. By the end of the first week of May, Hubbard and his wife are dead, having quit East Aurora on the 25th of April. Thus Crane's visit almost certainly occurred at least a year before. All the details about Hubbard can be verified in the 1940 biography *Elbert Hubbard: Genius of Roycroft* by David Arnold Balch, which is shelved on the 11th floor of the University of Massachusetts's library, where Professor Mariani and I both taught. Indeed, Balch writes of an extended trip Hubbard made to Cleveland in 1908, when Hubbard first met Rockefeller—though C. A. is not mentioned. With, admittedly, only an hour in the stacks, I could not find C. A.'s profile in the six-odd *Little Journey* volumes shelved there. Nor is it contained in the fourteen-volume "memorial edition" reprinted in 1928 (by William H. Wise & Co.) I ran into, three months later at a secondhand bookstore, driving back to New York City from Waltham. But neither set was a complete works.

However, a trip to what today is known as the "Roycroft Campus" in East Aurora, New York, and some conversation with someone familiar with the institution's history is revealing about what those weeks may have been like for the fourteen- or fifteen-year-old Crane. At first he probably stayed in a room at what is today the Roycroft Inn, where Alice and Elbert Hubbard also had their suite; at the time it was the central commons building, housing the offices and the stream of dignitaries who regularly visited Roycroft. After a few days there, he was likely assigned a room in a building called Emerson Hall (probably with a roommate near his own age), just a little away from the center of the complex—a long, three-story structure, which after World War I was to serve as a dormitory for the young women working at Roycroft. Before that, it housed the adolescent male interns. The statement that Crane "ate with the Hubbards" might give a somewhat inaccurate image to those unaware of how Roycroft was set up: Alice and Elbert took their meals nightly in a communal dining hall, in what is today the Inn's main dining room. Although workers with families generally took their meals at their homes, about a hundred of the single workers ate there with the Hubbards. The mottoes carved on wooden plaques that hung over the heads of the Roycroft workers as they dined still hang from the beams today. Alice and Elbert were always personally concerned with the young workers and took a personal interest in them. A number of the interns, male and female (and Crane was likely one), ate at their table.

At one point or another, walking through the building, the young Crane must have looked up at the murals of Venice and other places in Europe that Hubbard had commissioned for the commons room to inspire his workers with a sense of the greater world in which they lived and labored. He probably browsed in the library that was open to all the Roycroft workers. For all Hubbard's conservatism, Crane would have seen—as he moved about the communal workplace during his stay—the slogan VOTES FOR WOMEN! in two-foot-high wooden letters, which Alice Hubbard had set up by the main road outside the dining hall, near the public well that provided much of the community's water, for all who came through the town to read. The sign stayed there from 1906 until her 1915 death.

Today a visitor can look at archival photographs of young workers in the printing shop, laboring on new editions of Hubbard's "Message to Garcia," *The Little Journey* series, and the collected volumes of Hubbard's articles. One can look at pictures taken in the carpentry hall, where the idealistic young men and women built the solid furniture, marked with the circled R, which before the Great War sold for such reasonable prices across the country. (Basically, this is what produced the place's income.) That was what Crane observed and took part in. Roycroft was a place where good work and the good life were felt to be intimately connected. Whatever Crane's personal disillusions with Hubbard's politics or literary output, this basic idea—even from a visit of weeks—surely stayed with Crane, as Weber suggests, a positive principle for the remaining decade and a half of his life.

Somehow, the biographer must gather all such data, sift through them, and (1) decide which of them are relevant to Crane, (2) decide which are necessary to the contemporary reader's understanding (Horton's references to Hubbard as a "quaint journeyman" and his "little journeys" were clear to American readers in 1937—and are opaque today), then (3) work his or her rhetorical magic, to represent his selection, rendering it concise, accurate, and vivid. My suspicion here is, however, that Mariani failed at (1), with the result that (2), in spite of his considerable talent at (3), has suffered.

If there's new evidence for dating, we need to know what it is. Otherwise, the specialist can only assume that Mariani has erred—and that newcomers to Crane are being misinformed.[1]

In the acknowledgments that close out his book, Mariani writes: "In the past thirty years, more material on Crane—letters, memoirs, critical commentary —has become available, so that both Horton and Unterecker must be revised and Unterecker streamlined" (464). But here the streamlining may be so great that, in Mariani, we lose incidents, accuracy, and insight—if not understanding. I shall present more evidence for this as we move forward. First, however, we must look at Mariani's presentation of Crane-as-poet.

The adult Crane was an endless reviser of his poems. For his longest, "Cape Hatteras" (235 lines), which fills seven-and-a-half printed pages and forms the fourth major section of his poetic sequence *The Bridge*, more than thirty-three pages of drafts and work notes, many of them typed, some filling up both sides of the page, have survived, along with a page-long synopsis for an abandoned earlier version. One Appendix to Weber's study contains sixteen printed pages of previous drafts and work notes for "Atlantis," the finale of *The Bridge*. The finished poem is only a stanza over three pages. Running from 1923 to 1929, these drafts cover six years.

Much of the scholarly work on Crane in the past twenty-five years has been spent in retrieving the process of construction—how Crane moved from draft to draft, often over weeks, many times over months, and frequently, as with "Atlantis," over years. (Notable among the book-length efforts in this direction are Paul Gile's *Hart Crane: The Contexts of The Bridge* (1986), Edward Brunner's *Splendid Failure: The Making of The Bridge* (1985), and Lee Edleman's *Transmemberment of Song: Hart Crane's Anatomy and Rhetoric of Desire* (1987). Mariani's book reflects almost none of this work.

We're not talking of Flaubertian labors over the text here, but we're not talking first-, second-, or even third-draft throwaways, either. Crane was a poet who worked on his poems and did not let them go until he had something that at least came near satisfying him. Though a first draft may have erupted at a boozy gathering when Crane ran off into the next room to type while the Victrola blared, these poems (as Malcolm Cowley reminds us in *Exile's Return*) were meticulously reworked over the following days and weeks.

When, in Mariani's narrative, Crane writes a poem, instead of an account of the details through which the text was garnered, Mariani gives us three to five pages of critical rhapsody about what, to him, the poem means. Some two-thirds of this is interesting—and about a third seems as loopy and off-the-mark as most interpretations of Crane. Crane is a difficult writer. He gets more than his share of critical nonsense written about him. I suppose, then, Mariani actually does pretty well. But the picture we get of Crane "struggling" through his poems is always as though that struggle progressed only from first line to last, when the truth was a more complicated, revisionary, and, indeed, holistically visionary process—so that Mariani's reader misses out on an important aspect of Crane's creative method.

There are not many complexities in Mariani's biography. The traditional stories are there. We have Crane's father, racketing between millionaire candy manufacturer (Clarence Arthur Crane invented the peppermint Life Saver) and scuffling near-bankrupt several times during Crane's life, now hopelessly jealous and possessive of his wife, now trying to separate himself from Crane's mother and start a new life with a new woman, and always bemused by his poet son. Why couldn't Crane get a good job and write poems in his evening hours? We have Crane's mother and grandmother, refined and intelligent women, but one simply old and the other prone to depression, both deeply into Christian Science; and the mother made her son her escort and confidant even before her husband began to stray.

Throughout Crane's life away from them, both his mother and father deluged their son with what must have been pounds of letters, trying rationally to present their own positions as they careened through divorce, remarriage with one another, a second divorce, and finally Crane's father's remarriage and, not long afterward, death by stroke. Clarence Arthur's letters are bemused, long-suffering, and finally obtuse. Crane's and Grace's are passionate, high-spirited, and often jaw-droppingly manipulative. And there are Crane's peregrinations, from Cleveland to New York, to the Isle of Pines, to Paris and Mexico. (Weber sees Crane's whole life as a series of flights to escape his parents, whom he was usually financially dependent on, anyway.) Also there are the volatile friendships with Greenwich Village and literary friends from the 1920s. Mariani has added a number of new anecdotes about Crane's sexual escapades. All involve sailors. Is this simply part of Crane's (or the 1920s') code, i.e., a way of talking about something more general? Was is it an exclusive fetish on Crane's part or just a preference, socially imposed by the fact that the Navy got the lion's share of gay young men in those years? Is it some combination? You won't learn the answers from Mariani.

My sense is that Professor Mariani wanted to tell Crane's story straightforwardly, not stopping for critical fine points or to weigh alternate versions or to assess conjectural evidence. But that presumes all the story is known—and it isn't. Crane's homosexuality is only one reason much of it was kept hidden. A Crane poetic fragment, for example, "Thou canst read nothing except through appetite . . ." consists of some lines Crane wrote down on the back of an address an admirer (presumably unwanted) passed him in a heavy cruising venue—the baths, the docks, a bar, the back of some movie theater. After Crane's death, Sam Loveman, his gay friend, literary executor, and working editor for Weber's edition of the poems, who knew the fragment's genesis, titled it somewhat coyly "Reply," though in the 1986 Marc Simon edition of the poems, Loveman's title is dropped. Today the fragment appears with no explanatory note (or title) at all. Another untitled fragment—"The alert pillow, the hayseed spreads" —would seem to chronicle a sleepless night in a country hotel; it's written on the back of a piece of hotel stationary. But it too appears with only the most maddeningly, even arrogantly, uninformative of notes in the current Simon edition. And none of the five biographies—Mariani's included—enlightens us even this much about either. But that is the sort of information that resides in the odd scholarly article and critical ephemera that Mariani has not used.

Like that of any other actual woman or man, Crane's life abounds in mysteries no biographer can ever solve for good. In his adult years, Crane mentioned to several friends an adolescent suicide attempt on his trip as a fifteen-year-old to the Isle of Pines, when, he claimed, he took all his mother's sleeping powders.

After her son's death, when Horton questioned her, Grace had no memory of any such incident.

She did, however, recall a bizarre occurrence on the island that involved her waking her son, late one night, to shoo off an untoward invasion of cattle into the yard, which ended with the "sensitive" young Crane reappearing from the jungle only to collapse and have to be taken, unconscious, to the doctor's, as prologue to a three-day recovery.

Are the night of the cows and Crane's claimed suicide attempt connected? Among Grace's letters to her husband from the Isle of Pines, one from spring 1915 requests he send her more sleeping medication, as a large portion of hers had gone missing . . .

One can speculate. But one cannot know. Besides the homosexuality, the alcoholism was another reason the earlier biographers were uncomfortable with much of Crane's brief life. And finally there was the level of emotional chaos at which Crane lived, especially during his last years. As we get further and further from Crane's three decades, more and more context is necessary to make that life make sense. A word that appears only in the most passing manner in Mariani's book is "Prohibition," though Crane's life as a suicidal alcoholic can't be understood outside it. As Malcolm Cowley explains in *Exile's Return* (1951)—this is another thing you won't learn from Mariani's book—between 1920 and 1933, while the Eighteenth Amendment prohibited the sale of alcoholic beverages (having ridden in alongside of, that same year, the Nineteenth Amendment, which gave women the vote, thereby doubling the United States' voting population), so much illegal liquor was available that the problem was not how to get hold of it. Rather, because everyone had his or her secret gallon in every office desk drawer or kitchen or closet, his or her stash in every home, his or her jug in every back room, and where at every meeting, private or even public, you were offered a swig from the ubiquitous hip flask, the problem was how to stay sober enough to transact the ordinary business of day-to-day life. The ubiquity of alcohol during prohibition years claimed many thousands of victims. F. Scott Fitzgerald was one; Hart Crane was another.

Finally, it is not just facts that we do or do not have access to. Entire modes of social behavior need to be made clear—discourses, if you will. Though none of the biographers stresses this, the fact is that Peggy Baird Cowley, ten years older than Crane (Malcolm Cowley was her second husband), was as much of a drinker as Crane was—at least when the two were living and traveling together in Mexico. Her own account, "The Last Days of Hart Crane" (republished in *Robber Rocks*, Susan Jenkins Brown's 1969 memoir and letter collection centering on Crane, published the same year as Unterecker's biography), is a fascinating piece of writing, even a devastating one. Crane's final poem, "The Broken Tower," takes on great resonance in light of it. Peggy later told several people that, while she was terribly fond of her loud and difficult friend and was grateful for his companionship during an emotionally hard time for her, she had no serious intentions of marrying him; he was, after all, gay, and she was quite aware of it. In 1970, at age eighty-three, after two further marriages, Peggy died in an upstate New York home for the destitute called Tivoli.

After quitting a job at J. Walter Thompson's advertising agency, at the beginning of November 1923, the twenty-four-year-old Crane planned a visit to the Rector House in Woodstock with Edward Nagle and William Slater Brown. The night before he left New York, near midnight Crane wandered out of his send-off party to end up in an encounter involving a sailor named Jerry and a boat to Antwerp. Unterecker assumes the encounter was sexual. The next day, however, en route to Ridgeway, Connecticut, Crane wrote to his gay friend Wilber Underwood about it, and also to the straight Jean Toomer: "I am still overwhelmed by the appalling tragedy of last night. I never even undressed, and it will be weeks until I can get the thing out of my mind. No need to say more . . ." Shortly after Crane wrote his letter to Toomer, after a party at

Eugene O'Neill's in Ridgeway, the incident catapulted him into a poem—once he reached Woodstock and settled in.

On November 23, 1923, Crane sent Toomer some twenty-one lines (a fragment, "This way where November takes the leaf . . ."), with an explanatory letter:

> The boat for Antwerp and Jerry still haunt me. Aside from the three briefers [short book reviews] I have done for the *Dial*, that poem has been my only immediate concern. It is growing very slowly. I doubt the possibility of ever printing it, but don't care. Significances gradually lift themselves from the trial lines. I send you some of the poem as it stands at this hour, as you are fine enough to be concerned. It was great to have your inquiry about it. I think I shall call it "White Buildings," perhaps. Certainly it is one of the most consciously written things I have ever attempted, whether or not it has any sense, direction or interest to anyone but myself. Let me know if anything in it gets through at all to an outsider.

By "an outsider," one of the things Crane may well have meant was "a heterosexual."

II.

Mariani only mentions Weber's 1948 "biographical and critical study" once, and designates it "a critical study" only. But Weber's book contains a number of biographical incidents Unterecker chose to overlook. One is a report by Mrs. Isabel Lachaise, Edward Nagle's mother, that winter a frequent visitor to Edward, Bill, and Hart at the Rector House. She tells of a drunken semi-suicide attempt by Crane.

Isabel and her husband, the well-known sculptor Gaston Lachaise (Edward's stepfather), had been invited to the young men's for dinner:

> After the meal was finished, [the Lachaises] were sitting together with Brown, Nagle, and Crane and talking, when Crane suddenly burst from the room, caught up an ax used for wood chopping on his way out, and ran out of the cottage into the surrounding woods. Nagle and Brown, familiar with Crane's suicidal frame of mind, were very much alarmed and followed after to find and restrain him." (212)

Weber's point is that, even if the incident was just "a plea for help" by an unstable young man, it shows that even in the relatively calm period of his Woodstock stay, Crane was concerned with death on a personal level, which throws into relief his insistent pursuit of "life" in his poems of this period. The story is also interesting in terms of a like tale from later in Crane's life, which

Horton and Unterecker also leave out, but that Mariani includes. We shall get to it soon.

Crane never finished "White Buildings," at least not under that name, though he salvaged the title from his fragment for his first published poetry collection in 1926.

Something that possibly helped derail him, while still in Woodstock, was a poetic encounter many commentators have found important to Crane's work. When Crane's friend Gorham Munson visited Woodstock, he stayed with the art critic William Fisher in a cabin about half a mile away. The three young men had the two older men over for a huge Thanksgiving dinner. Fisher later dropped over to the Rector House several times for tea, and invited Nagle, William Slater Brown, and Crane to avail themselves of his library, where Crane made a discovery that has been made by many readers, before and since.

Crane wrote to Munson: "I have been amazed at the finesse and depth of Pater in his *Plato and Platonism* which Fisher has subsequently loaned me. I think it beats *The Renaissance* all hollow for style and ratiocination." (It does.)

About a week before Christmas, Crane stopped by Fisher's place one afternoon, where Fisher showed Crane some manuscript notebooks, full of poems, by a young poet named Samuel Greenberg. Greenberg had died of tuberculosis, aged twenty-three, in the pauper hospital on Wards Island, on August 16 or 17, back in 1917. Crane was so fascinated by the poems that he stayed till nearly midnight.

Fisher was something of a champion of Greenberg's work. As a promising youth of seventeen, Samuel Greenberg had first been sent to meet Fisher by a friend, George Halprin, who had been engaged by the Greenberg family to give piano lessons to Samuel's older brother Daniel. When Halprin arrived at the Greenbergs' cramped apartment in the neighborhood of Delancey Street, he heard the then-teenaged "Sammy" playing a Chopin ballad in the backroom, far more expressively than he had any reason to expect—and discovered a shy, sensitive, large-eyed boy with glasses, who played only by ear, who could draw exquisitely well, and who also wrote poems.

In a letter to Gorham Munson written on December 20, Crane wrote, "This poet, Grünberg [Crane's spelling], which Fisher nursed until he died of consumption at a Jewish Hospital in New York was a Rimbaud in embryo. . . . Fisher has shown me an amazing amount of material, some of which I am copying and will show you when I get back." Fisher's nursing of Sammy (as Fisher and his friends had called him) through his terminal illness was either Crane's real misunderstanding or a quick fiction for a quick letter. While Fisher doubtless visited his young friend during his last illness, the hospital's overworked staff and the Greenberg family were the only people who had attended Greenberg's final days on Wards Island.

Fourteen years after Crane's Woodstock visit, Horton further confounded posterity's understanding of matters by writing in his 1937 biography that Fisher had "inherited the notebooks through the indifference of the boy's relatives" (160)—and while Crane never believed *that*, it too turns out to have been false. Greenberg's brother Morris had entrusted five of Samuel's notebooks to Fisher in hopes of seeing his younger brother's work published, including one in which, with an eye to publication, the young poet had made fair copies, some time before his death, of much of his completed work. (Thirty-five more of Samuel's notebooks, some filled with first or early drafts of the same material, were in possession of Samuel's older brother Daniel; they would end up, with Fisher's five, in the Greenberg Collection in the Fales Library at New York University.) Fisher edited his own magazine out of Woodstock, *The Plowshare*, and in it he had published first one Greenberg poem, "The Charming Maiden," then a selection of ten more (all of which Fisher had more or less heavily edited), along with an appreciation, "Fragments of a Broken Lyre," by the time, in 1923, Crane came to winter in the lively upstate artists' colony.

Crane was enthralled by Fisher's stories of the impoverished, precocious Jewish youngster. And he was fascinated by the poems. Borrowing a number of the notebooks, Crane typed up forty-two of Greenberg's poems from the fair copies in Samuel's hand, returning the notebooks to Fisher just before he left Woodstock on January 2, 1924, to go back to New York City with William Slater Brown.

Horton's biography claims that Crane brought the Greenberg notebooks down with him, from Woodstock to New York, because, years later, William Slater Brown remembered that Crane had read him out some of Greenberg's poems on the train trip home. Eventually finding the typescript among some possessions left on the Isle of Pines during Crane's 1926 visit, Horton assumed Crane had made his typescript in New York, then returned the notebooks to Fisher at an unspecified date. Years later, however, Marc Simon interviewed Fisher, who said, no, Crane definitely returned the notebooks before he left Woodstock. Fisher simply would not have given them to someone who was going to take them out of the little town. Thus the Greenberg poems that Slater Brown remembered hearing are doubtless from the typed copies that Crane made himself on his manual typewriter while staying at the Rector House.

Like Crane, Greenberg was a confirmed dictionary reader and a connoisseur of unusual words. Unlike Crane, Greenberg sometimes made words up, such as the adverb "orbly" (from "orb") and the adjective "wrapt" (which seems to be a cross between wrapped and rapt). Crane's eccentric vocabulary came from the dictionary and other writers. Crane took several words from Greenberg (and possibly whole concepts that he associated with those words, among them "gates," "script," and, indeed, "wrapt") for his "Voyages" and, later, *The Bridge*.

Crane went so far as to create an entire poem by taking lines from several of Greenberg's, and arranging them in his own form, like a found-object poem.

The Crane poem, from which Tennessee Williams took the title for his play "Summer and Smoke" (a phrase from one of the few lines in the poem by Crane and not by Greenberg), was called "Emblems of Conduct" and is the third poem in Crane's collection *White Buildings*. Crane was dubious about the poem and finally used it only because Allen Tate and Malcolm Cowley both urged him to include it. Eventually "Emblems of Conduct" produced a lot of silly talk about possible plagiarism. To my mind the most obvious reason for printing the poem is that Crane wanted to attract attention to the all but unknown Greenberg.

Well, why didn't he put a footnote or something on it? asks the self-righteous pundit. Answer: Because Crane knew it would be more exciting to discover the source for oneself without a nudge. Already he had the example of Eliot's *Waste Land*, before him, and he was reviewing this for the *Dial*, where two years before in 1926 *The Waste Land* had first been published, which by the inclusion of a few lines from Webster and Kyd had practically started a renaissance in scholarly interest in Elizabethan dramas other than those by Shakespeare, Marlowe, or Jonson. Given the fact that, after Crane's death, Greenberg's poems were finally published in their own volume in 1947, with a "Preface" by Allen Tate, fundamentally Crane was successful.

In 1948 Weber's account of Greenberg stressed the fact that, however Rimbaldian his reader Crane might have found him, Crane's was the stronger talent — which, for Weber, excused any use Crane might have made of Greenberg's work. (A phrase from Greenberg, "the varnished lily grove," was included in an early version of "Voyages II," though dropped from the final draft.)

Unterecker devotes a characteristically detailed sixteen pages to that two months in Woodstock, from the initial party at O'Neill's in Connecticut to the ebullient Thanksgiving dinner with Munson and Fisher, and on to Crane's work on the poems "Recitative" and the "White Buildings" fragment, as well as an intelligent consideration of Simon's reconstruction of Crane's work on Greenberg, with some speculation on what Greenberg's work meant to Crane and a smart description of Greenberg's poems for those who don't know them. "Samuel Greenberg's primitive, half-formed work showed an artist's vision but a vision relatively unshaped by technique," Unterecker wrote. "Had he lived, had he had time to read, time to perfect his art, he might, Crane felt, have become a poet much like Crane himself. The same interest in language, the same exploration of the possibilities of metaphor show up in the tumbled-out phrases, and as Crane laboriously copied them he was swept with pity for their maker" (336). Only the after-dinner incident with the ax, as recounted by Mrs. Lachaise in Weber, Unterecker omits.

Because of the various words Crane borrowed from Greenberg, we must count Greenberg one of Crane's influences. However far one wants to extend that influence, it's clear Crane spent time *thinking* about Greenberg (he typed thirty-two pages of them from Fisher's notebooks), thinking about his poems and mulling over his condition as an all but undiscovered artist, so close to Crane's own age, and probably identifying with him.

Unterecker gives us, as mentioned, sixteen pages on Crane and Greenberg.

Mariani gives us nineteen lines on Crane's discovery of Greenberg, and fifteen lines on the assembling of "Emblems of Conduct," the last four of which are: "Crane's attempt to take by eminent domain the scattered remains of a dead young poet was not, finally, one of his best efforts, and he may have included the poem in his first collection merely as an accent mark to eke out the required number of pages he needed for a book" (144). In Mariani's version, Tate's and Cowley's urgings to include the poem have gone the way of Elbert Hubbard's article on C. A.

Greenberg is not mentioned in the remainder of Mariani's book. But if I miss anything in Mariani's account of those Woodstock weeks, it's all indication that Crane spent a goodly while—months, on and off throughout his creative life—thinking about Samuel Barnard Greenberg and the significance of his tragic life, his work, and his words.

Mariani's book includes a photograph of Crane in Woodstock, captioned "Hart Crane in woodsman's clothing and Chinese moustache, Woodstock, late 1924." But Crane's Woodstock visit was in late 1923. If the picture was taken on New Year's Day, or possibly on the morning Crane left (January 2), then it might indeed be dated early 1924. Unterecker used the same photograph, captioned "In Woodstock, New York, winter 1923." Mariani's text offers no reason for the change in date. Without a good one, however, "late 1924" is wildly improbable.

After Crane returned—on January 2—from the eight-odd weeks in Woodstock and floundered about jobless in Greenwich Village for the first months of 1924, in April Malcolm Crowley secured him a job as a copywriter at Sweet's Catalogue Service.

In mid-April, with a sailor named Emil Opffer, three years his senior, who lived with his father (also Emil, a retired sailor "distinguished as an editor [of a Danish-language newspaper *Nordlyset*] and anarchist," Crane wrote his mother) and a younger brother, Ivan. Crane moved into rented rooms in a house Opffer senior owned at 10 Columbia Heights on the Brooklyn shore. The view from the back windows encompassed (off to the right) the Brooklyn Bridge.

The affair with Emil was one of the most poetically productive relationships of Crane's life. "Voyages," a cycle of six poems, pose themselves as meditations on six trips away his sailor lover makes. (When Emil was home, as Crane made it clear to his friends, writing was *not* what they did.) Here's how Horton handles the move into the house in which the engineer Washington Roebling, who'd built the bridge to the designs of his late father, John A. Roebling, had once lived with his wife.

He [Crane] was not alone there, for he had living with him a person whom he had fallen deeply in love with over the preceding weeks. This was a young man of his own age whom he had recently met through mutual friends and from whom he had received not a little help during the last weeks of his unemployment. He was quiet and retiring, but Crane soon discovered in him a sensitive knowledge and appreciation of music, which led to their attending a few concerts together. His almost bashful reticence in company, Crane learned, was due to the fact that he had grown up in the army and had subsequently taken to the sea to earn his living by making periodic "Voyages" as ship's printer or checker of cargo. As their intimacy deepened, Crane found more and more to attract him in his new friend, until suddenly a relationship developed which for a time at least was of supreme importance in his life.

Though it is not necessary or even important to investigate Crane's sexual life in detail, in this one case exception should be made, for it must be considered as more than a casual "affair." (165)

When Horton was writing, Opffer was still alive. (In 1976, indeed, Emil—now aged eighty-one—married for the first time in Denmark.) In 1937, when homosexuality was a crime, at least in this country, there was no particular reason to out him. Though Horton is off in the ages (again, Opffer was three years older—and two inches shorter—than Crane), besides "concerts" there were also some performances at the Metropolitan Opera, at its old home on Broadway and 7th Avenue. Emil was friends with the great Danish tenor Lauritz Melchior; fond of the two young friends, Melchior gave Emil and Hart a number of passes to see his performances from backstage.

I would assume Horton's description is more or less accurate, including Opffer's relatively passive personality vis-à-vis Crane's far more ebullient carriage. As far back as November, Crane had written Jean Toomer (as we've noted) about his homosexuality—and there had been no unpleasant repercussions.

Something of a womanizer, Toomer had just run off with Waldo Frank's wife, Margaret Naumberg. Both Toomer and Crane were in relationships requiring a bit of understanding from their friends. Now Crane wrote to both Gorham Munson and Waldo Frank, married men *and* straight, about his love for Emil. Part of the reason was doubtless practical. Though a sailor, Emil was already a member of the social circle, largely through his father. Crane had first met Emil (so claimed Crane's friend and eventual literary executor, Sam Loveman) at a party given by Elinore Fitzgerald, the director of the Provincetown Playhouse. Emil had been generous (claims Horton) to the foundering, jobless, all but homeless young poet. This was the sophisticated '20s. If the two men now lived together and moved about socially with one another, the relationship would have been impossible to hide. Another reason is one that, in our more cynical age, sounds a bit mawkish, but, as Horton makes the point, was likely true:

Crane was temperamentally incapable of hypocrisy or dissimulation, and after his arrival in New York had gradually confessed himself to one after another of his intimates. Consequently there was no secrecy concerning the relationship in question, and it was accepted by his friends, if not with respect at least with complete tolerance and equanimity. (166)

Because Horton is so careful not to out Opffer as Crane's lover, surprisingly Horton does give Emil a single mention by name in his book. Crane spent the winter of 1927–28 in Los Angeles as the secretary/companion to a gay stockbroker, Herbert Wise, which left Crane plenty of free time and nights out. The passionate portion of Crane's and Opffer's relationship had come to a more or less pacific end a couple of years before. But now Opffer arrived on a boat, and the two met and began a night of joint carousing and drinking in the Los Angeles waterfront area, San Pedro, which ended with violence. Horton writes:

> One night . . . he and his friend Emil Opffer, who had just arrived in port on a ship from New York, were severely beaten and robbed in one of the dark waterfront streets by a group of sailors who had been enjoying drinks with them at one of the bars. (240)

As the less damaged of the two, Crane managed, with another sailor friend, to get Emil back on his boat by the time it pulled out. The sexual component to the evening, if there was any, is not "investigated," and there is no way to tell from Horton that Opffer is a *particular* friend, i.e., Crane's lover from 110 Columbia Heights, and the "onlie begetter" of the brilliant "Voyages."

Mariani too gives an account of Crane's 1928 reunion in San Pedro with Emil, which started with both men missing each other by eight hours and ended, when they finally got together, with both of them beaten and robbed in the street by five sailors. The source for the account is a full but still somewhat telegraphic letter Crane wrote (dated March 27, 1928) to Sue and William Slater Brown. Mariani, in elaborating the account, again muffs details. Crane wrote that after the beating he had—"with a sailor friend whom I had run into earlier in the evening while waiting for E"—got the all but unconscious Emil back from the police station to his ship, then roused some sailors on board to look after his friend, once Crane left him. Crane woke the next morning in a Salvation Army hotel. Mariani, however, has Crane and several sailors getting Emil back to the boat, having incorrectly assumed that the sailors were rousted somewhere en route while returning Emil to the boat. Again, none of this is major. But Crane's poems and his letters need to be read with care.

Here's a critical notion:

Recall the obscure incident with the sailor Jerry and the boat to Antwerp from the night of Crane's send-off party to Woodstock. Given the Antwerp reference the poem contains ("It's the S. S. *Ala*—Antwerp—now remember kid / to put me out at three she sails on time."), *The Bridge*'s "Cutty Sark" might just be a (printable) version of the original "White Buildings," with sailor "Jerry," that whole incident recalled from '23—when, after all, no one gets undressed. The truncated lines from Whitman, which close out "Cutty Sark" as much as they introduce "Cape Hatteras," may be Crane's way of saying that the night-long session did *not* end with the young man (Crane) melting in the older sailor's (Jerry's?) arms. Indeed, that may be one of the reasons *why* the lines are truncated, i.e., so that they function to suggest a missed possibility rather than to make a direct statement. Such would be very much in keeping with Crane's method of "indirect mention"—by which he sometimes dealt with matters queer.

Here's another.

"Quaker Hill" is generally taken to be about an abandoned hotel in the vicinity of Sue and William Slater Brown's country house, Robber Rocks—"the old Mizzentop." But the poem also has many resonances with the "night of the cows" from Crane's fifteenth summer on the Isle of Pines, and his mother's decaying mansion there. Was Crane possibly writing about correspondences (and/or differences) between the two times in his life?

Here's a third:

Contrary to what is suggested by the title of Unterecker's biography—as well as to what is stated at the opening of Voelcker's study, *The Hart Crane "Voyages"* ("the poet is the voyager" [8])—the poet is not the voyager in the poetic sequence "Voyages." In commentary on Crane, critical homily often ends up displacing common sense: The "voyager" among the poems is, rather, the "you," the "other," the "beloved." The poet and speaker of the sequence is the stay-at-home narrator, the geographically fixed consciousness that meditates on (and sometimes identifies with) the voyaging beloved.

And finally:

When, in Denmark in 1978, Helge Norman Nilsen interviewed Emil Opffer, then in his eighties, Opffer told of a story of how, when he and Crane had lived at 110 Columbia Heights, Opffer's father had recounted a tale to the amusement of both men. Once, when Emil senior had been a sailor, as a joke he'd jumped overboard just to see how long it would take for his fellows to pick him up. Was this tale of a sailorly jape perhaps in Crane's mind that noon of April 27, 1932? (Had he indeed forgotten that Emil senior had leaped from a sailing ship and not one with a propeller? Or had Crane erroneously assumed that the propeller's wake would push him away from the ship, rather than suck him down amidst its multiple, braiding currents . . . ?) Neither postcard Crane sent the day before reveals any hint of depression . . .

Weber was not anxious to dwell on Crane's homosexuality; In his edition of the letters, Emil is always "E—." But when, with "Voyages," it becomes inescapable, he quotes in full Crane's letter to Waldo Frank of April 21, 1924, which begins, "Dear Waldo: For many days now I have been quite dumb with something for which 'happiness' must be too mild a term . . . ," and goes on to tell of his joy with Emil.

Look it up.

It's a humdinger.

With the letter, Crane included a copy of a new poem, "Lachrymae Christi," as well as one entitled "Sonnet"—which, expanded by four lines, would soon be revised to become "Voyages III," including its poignant terminal exhortation: "Permit me voyage, love, into your hands."

Mariani's account of the beginning of Crane's and Emil's relationship is full, informative, and accurate. And there is some new stuff. (Although I'd known the Opffers were already part of Crane's circle, I hadn't known that younger brother Ivan Opffer was a sometimes musician with the Provincetown Playhouse.) Loveman alone has given us any account of the progression of the relationship itself between Emil and Crane, in his introduction to Hunce Voelcker's 1967 study, *The Hart Crane "Voyages."* There Loveman suggests that the poetic sequence only really got going when Emil came home unexpectedly to find Crane in bed with someone else. This changed the color of their relationship, though not its practical form. They continued to live together. But Crane's poetic sequence was, according to Loveman, a response to that change.

But there's always the possibility that Loveman was wrong. Unterecker clearly believed at several points he was. Whether sex did or did not fall out of the relationship at that point is, finally, anybody's guess. Crane was wondering about his own health in terms of venereal diseases in '25 (in which he spoke of the possibility of having to give up Emil)—and was pleased to discover it was a false alarm. But hints—a phrase here, a phrase there—suggest that sex was not at the center of their relationship, while others suggest that it was.

We have said the "Voyages" pose themselves as meditations during six of Emil's successive "Voyages" away. But that is not how they were actually written. The first of the poems was composed before Crane even knew Emil existed (and was initially called "Poster"). Once Crane decided to create a longer work, the first new poem written was actually "Voyages III." But the details of the writing of "Voyages" are not what concern Mariani. If, however, you want to know what moving into 110 Columbia Heights was like for Crane, between the extant letters written at the time and Mariani's account, you have here about as much as we can know. For many, this will be the test case for a biography of Crane. And this test, yes, Mariani's volume passes as well as any of the others —though it should be supplemented by Loveman's account in Voelcker (which neither Unterecker nor Mariani makes use of).

The affair between Jean Toomer and Waldo Frank's wife, educator Margaret Naumberg, was rigorously suppressed from the three previous biographies, but is now at least mentioned by Mariani.

When Toomer first visited his and Crane's mentor, Frank, back in October 1923, the electricity that generated between the handsome black writer and Frank's wife was so intense, the two ran off together before two weeks were out.

Whenever Crane wrote to Toomer subsequently, he always included best wishes to Margey and, in letters to others, mentioned that he was concerned with Naumberg's precarious position. It *was* 1923, after all, and she had just left her husband for a black man, however light-skinned.

Horton avoided speaking of her. Unterecker removed all references to her. He even blotted Crane's regularly repeated "Give my love to Margey" with ellipses from the letters he quotes to Toomer, like a Soviet secret-police censor under Stalin, rendering Naumberg a nonperson.

Though Mariani mentions the absconding, there's no mention of Crane's concern for Margey, nor is there any speculation as to why the three previous biographers felt it necessary to suppress all reference to her.

Mariani relates an account of a suicide attempt in the presence of Sam Loveman in the autumn of 1928, not used by Unterecker, Weber, or Horton. Suicide attempts are of course biographically important—especially since, just short of four years later, Crane would finally kill himself on his return trip from Mexico.

Although Mariani does not say so, I assume the source for this new account is an interview that Sam Loveman gave, edited by Kirby Congdon and Jay Socin and published as *Hart Crane: A Conversation with Samuel Loveman*. (This is in error: Loveman's first name was Sam, not Samuel.) Although the interviewer is not identified, I've always assumed it was Congdon. (With it first appeared Crane's poetic fragment, "The alert pillow, the hayseed spreads—.") Here is the passage from Loveman's account:

> Once—I don't know whether I ever told you—[Crane] tried to commit suicide in my presence. We had been out having dinner; he got raffishly high and we went to a lovely restaurant in the Village. No one was there but Dudley Digges, the actor,[2] in one corner. Hart waltzed me over to him and introduced me with a low bow. Then he began to dance mazurkas on the floor. He loved to dance. It was a big room, and we had an excellent dinner. He got a little higher, and then we went out, as usual, he bargained with a taxi driver. He would never pay more than two dollars fare to Brooklyn. And then, usually, because he always forgot that he hadn't money with him, the person with him had to pay. Through some mishap we landed at the Williamsburg Bridge. I think there is a monument or a column there, and Hart went up and as a matter of rite or sacrilege, pissed against it. Then we started across to Columbia Heights. He lived at Number 110. When we got to Henry Street, it was around eleven or eleven-thirty. In one of the doorways we saw

four legs sticking out and a sign, "We are not bums." They were going to an early market and their wagon was parked in the street. Hart became hysterical with laughter. Well, when we got to Columbia Heights, the mood changed. The entire situation changed. He broke away from me and ran straight up the three flights of stairs, then up the ladder to the roof, and I followed him. I was capable of doing it then. As we got to the top he threw himself over the roof and I grabbed his leg, one leg, and, oh, I was scared to death. And I said, "You son of a bitch! Don't you ever try that on me again!" So he picked himself up and said, "I might as well, I'm only writing rhetoric."

I[nterviewer]: That's what was bothering him.

S[am] L[oveman]: He could no longer write without the aid of music or of liquor. It was impossible. He had reached that horrible impasse. So, we went downstairs to his room. I lived a couple of doors away. I worried myself sick about him. He poured himself some Dago Red, turned on the Victrola, and I left him. (12) [bracketed insertions mine]

We can make one correction in Loveman's account right away: Almost certainly Loveman meant to say "kazotsky," not "muzurkas." Crane had learned the athletically impressive squat-and-kick from a Russian dancer, Stanislaw Portapovitch, and performed it all throughout the decade of his adulthood at pretty much every opportunity. (And the murzurka would just not be described as danced "on the floor.") For the rest, however, probably we should take Loveman at his word.

To follow the details of his account, however, you have to know a bit about the geography of New York's Lower East Side, and the relationship of its various bridges to various parts of Brooklyn. You have to know that just below the old Lower East Side market district of Hester Street, Orchard Street, and Fulton Street (back then home of the famous Fulton Fish Market), a few blocks below Delancey, you cross Henry Street on the way to the Brooklyn Bridge, which takes you across into Brooklyn Heights. You have to know the Brooklyn Bridge connects what was once Murray Street in Manhattan to, on the Brooklyn side, Sand Street, running up into the Navy Yard, with Columbia Heights just off the other way. As well, you have to know that the Williamsburg Bridge at Delancey Street crosses the East River to plunge into Brooklyn's Williamsburg, somewhat distant from the Heights: The Brooklyn ends of the two bridges are two-and-a-half-times farther apart than are their Manhattan entrances.

Once Crane and Loveman left the Village restaurant and got a cab, the initial instructions to the cab driver must have been some form of "Take us across the Bridge to Brooklyn Heights" (or, possibly back then, to Columbia Heights). A knowledgeable cab driver would certainly have known that the bridge involved in such instructions would be the Brooklyn Bridge, not the Williamsburg. But instead of taking them to the Brooklyn Bridge, the cab took them to Delancey Street and the mouth of the Williamsburg Bridge, whereupon, realizing the mistake, they abandoned the taxi (before it actually started across) and decided to walk down the three-quarters of a mile through Manhattan to City Hall Park, where they would cross over the river to Brooklyn—in this case over the Brooklyn Bridge, by foot—and on home, once Crane finished taking a leak on a column or monument in the entrance plaza (demolished more than a decade ago, along with the elevated concourse before the bridge's walkway). In their walk down through the city, they crossed Henry Street, around the corner from the Fulton Fish Market, where they encountered the two men sleeping in the doorway with the sign, near their cart. They continued on, most likely taking the Rose Street entrance to the Bridge's walkway, beside the red-brick tower of the old Pulitzer Building (now torn down), and crossed the Brooklyn Bridge into the Heights, then to cover the short distance to 110—where "the entire situation changed."

Though, true, Loveman makes no direct mention of that night's walk across the Bridge, this is the only itinerary that connects all the mentioned points in any reasonable way.

Well, here is Mariani's version of Loveman's account:

One night, after dining with Sam Loveman in Lower Manhattan, Crane hailed a taxi for the ride back across the Brooklyn Bridge. Two bucks, he told the cabbie, two bucks was all he was going to pay for the trip. He seemed in high spirits, though he was upset when the cabbie took the Williamsburg Bridge across the river by mistake. On the bridge Crane ordered the cabbie to stop. Then he got out, staggered to one of the bridge supports, and urinated on it, either by way of mock baptism or to mark his displeasure, Loveman wasn't sure. When they got to Columbia Heights, Crane discovered, once again, that he had no money, so Loveman was left to settle the bill. By then Loveman notice that his friend's mood had shifted into a kind of depression. Screw it, Crane shouted. He was finished, all used up. There was nothing left to do but to jump. He took off at a run toward the apartment, the older Loveman ten years Crane's senior in panting pursuit. Crane made it to 110, then began taking the steps by two—the first floor, the second, the third, then the ladder and onto the flat tar roof. He headed straight for the roof's edge and was about to go over when Loveman managed to reach out and grab his leg. Loveman was shaking with fury. Don't you ever pull that on me again, he shouted at Crane. You sonofabitch, don't ever do something like that to me again. Finally, when they were off the roof and he had settled down, Crane blurted out the reason for his insane action. What the hell, he said, all he was capable of writing any more was rhetoric. Why live? (313)

Now scholars make mistakes. In writing about Crane myself, I've called one of his Woodstock roommates at the Rector House "John" Nagle, when his name was actually Edward. I've inadvertently dropped an "f" from Opffer's name. Following Socin, I have written Loveman's first name as "Samuel" instead of "Sam." And once I even put in print that Horton's judgment about the indifference of Greenberg's relatives had its origins in one of Crane's letters. It doesn't. It's just Horton. But every one of these errors, once I'd discovered it, has lost me nights of sleep.

(Even Unterecker can err: His mention of Hubbard's "praise" of Emerson to the young Crane is extremely unlikely. Though Hubbard wrote a more or less respectful profile of the Sage of Concord for his "Little Journeys" series, throughout his life Hubbard openly criticized Emerson's philosophy, as did Crane's critic correspondent Yvor Winters, and regularly and publically derided Emerson's "Self-Reliance" as preposterous nonsense.)

To list the discrepancies between Loveman's account and Mariani's would fill pages. The most major is that Mariani has missed the whole walk home —easy enough to do, unless you know the lay of the city; or unless you've taken that walk yourself on many, many Indian Summer nights, as I did when I lived in the East Village during the '60s and had friends in Brooklyn Heights. Did Crane piss on the bridge supports (as Mariani says) or on a "column or monument" (as Loveman says) . . . ? There's no real evidence for who hailed the cab that evening—or even for who, that particular night, actually paid. Was the comment about rhetoric made on the roof (as Loveman says) or back in the apartment (as Mariani says). . . . Both Crane's "Screw it," as well as the rest of his indirect dialogue, along with Loveman's "Don't you ever pull that on me again," and, "Don't ever do something like that to me again," though certainly warranted by the situation, are just not what Loveman says he said. And Loveman mentions no shouting and no running at all—until they were within the building.

Anyone can pick out half a dozen more. Just to make things more complicated, there *is* a Henry Street in Brooklyn Heights that runs perpendicular to Clarke Street and that Crane and Loveman may have passed the very end of on their way to Columbia Heights, after they "started across." But the mention of an "early market," as well as the placement of the Henry Street episode before they "reached the Heights," makes it all but certain Loveman is referring to the far better-known Henry Street in Manhattan.

Now, finally, are any of these details important?

Possibly not—save that, the way Mariani has described it, both men would have been exhausted before they reached the roof, if they'd started running a block away from the building. (I take Crane's comment as Loveman renders it—". . . I'm only writing rhetoric"—to indicate a major doubt about Crane's entire poetic enterprise to date, and not, as Mariani does, merely a weakening of his poetic powers, however distressing.[3]) What the discrepancies do tell us is that (1) Mariani did not understand Loveman's account, in terms of the geography; nor (2) did he check the account to confirm the details of what he did understand, but gave only a rough version from memory. To detail completely the places where this sort of thing—can we call it anything other than carelessness?—pervades his book would take many, many pages. This is particularly sad because there is, indeed, so much data here not in the other biographies, much of it concerned with Crane's sexual carryings-on. But the carelessness makes it hard to tell where Mariani has new facts or a new interpretation worth considering, where he's novelizing for effect, where he's abridging for economy, or where he just got it wrong, didn't know, or forgot.

Unterecker had access to Loveman's story—as he did to Isabel Lachaise's tale of the unsuccessful suicide attempt with the ax that night in Woodstock. He chose not to use either, possibly because he suspected both Loveman and Mrs. Lachaise of exaggerating, and possibly because the earlier incident, at any rate, seemed out of keeping with Crane's self-presentation during those Woodstock weeks as a generally happy young man. As Crane's behavior became more and more extreme, people inflated some of his earlier escapades to bring them in line with the suicidal alcoholic he became. But also Unterecker did not want to present Crane as too fragile or neurotic, for fear it would undercut the poet's reputation, which was simply not as solid in the 1950s and '60s as it is today.

Myself, I think that both incidents, carefully recounted, need to be included in Crane's biography, since they suggest recurrent behavior of a similar type for a man who, after all, did kill himself. But I think both should be accompanied by whatever reservations the biographer has about the sources. That's the biographer's call.

Well, Mariani uses one.

III.

Finally, what about our five biographers' attitudes toward homosexuality?

Horton's we've already had: It's neither important nor "necessary to investigate," with the exception of the biographical background for "Voyages." Weber will not use the term (it creates a rather interesting effect in the course of his book, which alternates between sounding hopelessly old-fashioned then, for pages at a time, astonishingly enlightened), but allows Crane to speak about it, in the case of "Voyages," in (some of) his own words.

Though published in 1969, the massive accumulation of Unterecker's *Voyager* is, much of it, a '50s document. Just before World War II and continuing for the decade after, led by popular men of letters such as Louis Untermeyer in an effort to co-opt "culture" to the war effort and thence the effort to "get America back on its feet," a cultural current emerged that maintained poets (and male ballet dancers) were really all—at least if they were any good—terribly manly fellows who could not only drink you under the table but also beat you at arm wrestling. The 1950s, in which much of the research for Unterecker's book was carried out, was the decade that valued security and conformity. Unterecker does not espouse any of this nonsense directly, but he is fairly careful not to go out of his way to violate these then-popular cultural notions. As well, when supportive evidence came along, he was happy to foreground it. ("Poetry must speak from a position of strength . . ." is a cultural tag-line for establishment poetry in the early '50s, against which the Beats, Black Mountain, and the Berkeley Renaissance would rebel, or were already rebelling.) This is to say, a normalizing urge moves through the Unterecker book, which may reflect either its author's studied belief or simply his suspicion that if Crane were presented as any wilder and more neurotic, no one would take him seriously.

Unterecker appends this note to his account of Crane's first homosexual experience:

> Crane "confessed" the history of his homosexuality to many people, and their memories are not in agreement as to what he said. My guess is that he didn't always tell the same story. According to one recollection, the first contact was with a chauffeur. Grace told a woman for whom she worked late in her life that Hart confessed a "handyman" has seduced him. Horton repeats Hart's one-time bragging account that the young man had been a "tutor" and that Hart himself was the seducer. Whatever the circumstances of his introduction to homosexual activities, it is important to keep in mind that not until he was twenty, when he found himself in love with a boy very near his own age, did homosexuality seem a real problem. From that time until his year in Mexico and his affair with Peggy Cowley, he did regard himself as a homosexual. In no way effeminate, he was contemptuous of effeminate men. Perhaps it is significant that his first homosexual love affair followed his parents' divorce and that his first "normal" love affair followed a break with his mother and reconciliation with his father. (777)

As a gay man, I read this with a cold eye today. As far as homosexuality not being a problem till Crane was twenty, I find myself muttering: "A problem for whom?" Homosexuality was the greatest problem for me between the ages of ten and eighteen: Once I started doing it, believe me, it became less problematic by whole orders of magnitude!

As far as Crane's contempt for effeminate men (which Loveman repeats later in his *Conversation* and Susan Jenkins Brown echoes in *Robber Rocks*), the only problem with it as a blanket statement is Loveman himself. I can't speak for Loveman's self-presentation at age thirty or forty (the height of his friendship with Crane), but the single time I met him, with poet and critic Hunce Voelcker and when Loveman was on the far side of seventy, he was a wonderfully warm and friendly old gentleman who looked as if he were moments from flying off through the sun-shot leaves above Greenwich Avenue on twinkle-toed slippers. And Crane had felt nothing but affection for him.

For better or worse, Mariani and I inhabit the same contemporary view of homosexuality. It might be summed up: "Because things have changed and now it's all out, we can all just use our own experiences and write from what we know." All three of the previous biographers were, in one way or the other, as Mariani puts it about Horton and Unterecker, more or less writing "around Crane's homosexuality" (464).

No matter how open we feel we are today about sexual matters, much about Crane's sexual behavior remains unknown. None of Crane's letters to Opffer and few or none to any of his other lovers have survived. The need to destroy them in the years after they were written is a sign of our just-finished century's sexual repressiveness in its earlier half. Much of what remains is gossip, conjecture, not written down or only written down years later.

Lincoln Kirstein's charming, if self-deflating, memoir of Carl Carlson is a rare point of attested fact in a field that is otherwise all vapors and waterfront fog and Cuban music heard through late-night summer mists. (This is another of Mariani's sources: in other accounts Carlson sometimes becomes "Bob Thompson," transformed by friends who did not want to out him, as he was also an aspiring writer and sexually involved with women.) Carlson was a sailor who'd once been a lover of Crane's and who, two years after Crane's death, was briefly Kirstein's lover.

A gay man of sixty-four with a sexually active life behind me, I first started reading Crane in my teens. Sailors and alcoholism aside (and the fact that I married at nineteen), I've always assumed that my sex life between the ages of twenty and thirty-two shared much with Crane's.

Mariani is a straight man who has identified with Crane for many years —and has doubtless known, more or less well, gay men who he thought were either like, or different from, Crane in their sexual proclivities.

Well, who hasn't?

Ten or fifteen years ago, I would have said that such differences meant that I could write intelligently about Crane's sexuality, whereas a straight critic such as Mariani probably could not. Today, my suspicion is that we are both hamstrung by our experiences and share far more assumptions in matters of the writerly discourse that controls how we speak about homosexuality than not.

I don't think we would say the same things—only that we are both likely to be wrong, and for the same reasons.

If the last twenty years of gay and queer studies had impressed me with anything, it is that the social construction of homosexuality has been particularly fluid, precisely because it has been as socially marginal as it has, and has not been subject to the same discursive forces that would stabilize its social forms the way forms of patriarchal heterosexuality have been stabilized. Today, my gay graduate students have almost no idea what it was like to be a gay, sexually active nineteen-year-old in a major American city ten years before Stonewall.

How, then, is anyone today, straight or gay, supposed to get a good grip on what being gay meant in the American Midwest, or in New York, or in Paris, or in the Caribbean, or in Mexico during the century's first three decades— Crane's decades, Crane's venues.

In the late 1950s and early '60s (just for an example), after dark the walkways of all three of Manhattan's downtown bridges to Brooklyn were extremely active cruising sites.

What does "extremely active" mean?

It means that, if you were under forty and of middling to average looks, in the spring, summer, and fall months, you could expect to encounter someone who wanted to have sex with you within an hour of arriving—and, if you were not too choosy, within ten or fifteen minutes you could find someone perfectly acceptable, either to go home with or to have sex with in some shadowed corner on, near, or under the bridge.

Older visitors—and colder months—might extend considerably the time needed to make contact. And there were often early birds looking to make assignations during the day.

The first time when, at nineteen, I walked from Delancey Street onto one of Manhattan's Williamsburg Bridge walkways at about ten-forty of an autumn night and, in the course or some three minutes, saw (first) that, while not at all crowded, between four and five times as many people were out—all male, ambling back and forth—as I might have expected, and that (secondly) a group of four effeminate men were leaning against one rail, chatting and laughing ("camping it up," as one might have said back then), and that (thirdly) ten yards later, someone walking past gave me a heavy stare—heavy enough to make me, a few steps on, look back to see that he had stopped, turned, and was still watching me. Well, one of the first things to go through my mind was: So *this* is what was hidden in Hart Crane's *The Bridge*. Now I was sure I knew what "Harbor Dawn" had been the "morning-after" of.

Since the late '60s, this has not been the case with the bridges. When I discovered them, of course, I assumed that they had been active meeting places as far back as World War I. My only evidence, however, was that they were active when I got there in '61. But were the nineteen-, the twenty-one-, the twenty-four-year-old Crane's experiences of Manhattan and Brooklyn, forty years before, at all similar to mine? I assumed they must be . . .

George Chauncey . . .

Jonathan Ned Katz . . .

Where are you when we need you?

Similarly, when, as a twenty-three-year-old I first read Horton, I assumed

Crane's entire social circle was queer: It seemed to me self-evident that Frank and Munson, though married, must be older gay men of letters, supporting and encouraging the young gay poet, Crane. Certainly Fisher was gay. The one exception to this (again, to me, self-evident) was the notably younger couple who'd befriended Crane, Sue and James Light. Certainly they were straight. For one thing, eventually they got divorced. Older married gay men (who had, of course arranged everything with their spouses beforehand) did not.

Indeed, in 1963 or thereabout, my reason for assuming this was simply: That's what my own social experience had been. In 1963 this seemed so self-evident to a young (married) gay man in New York City that I must have told fifty people, as though I had firsthand evidence that of course Munson and Frank were gay . . .

They weren't. And Sue Light is the one person in the "Crane Circle" who, we now know, was married to a gay man. Once director James left Sue to live with another man, Sue and he maintained a close and friendly relationship (she regularly held dinner parties for James and his friends) till Susan married William Slater Brown. So much for the self-evident. If those are my demonstrably incorrect assumptions, I can only wonder what Mariani's are.

But all this sidesteps perhaps the greatest reason why a new biography of Crane is needed: It is not just that the 1950s' view of homosexuality dominates the most scholarly account of Crane's life—Unterecker's. Rather, the general '50s view as to what the "great artist" himself must be is in evidence all through Unterecker, a view contoured profoundly by the postwar mentality. The major problem with Unterecker's biography might be designated as its attempt to protect the reader from the complexity of Crane's personality.

Crane was what, a few decades ago, most people would have designated as an extreme anxiety neurotic.

Because the medical explanation it suggests is so clearly absurd ("neurosis" means "an inflammation of the nerves"), the term has tended to fall out of use. But this does not mean the condition it names, however inadequately, doesn't exist.

At various times in his life, people gave Crane jobs, now at advertising companies, now at magazines, then watched him try to perform these, only to realize within days, sometimes within hours, that it was hopeless. The problem was not Crane's intelligence. Rather it was the debacle authority and its handmaid, regimen, made of his life. People like Crane, especially when they are brilliant and personable, can be delightful friends. But they can be counted on for very little. Moreover, their self-destructive contradictions make such folks extremely painful to love.

The contradictions that cripple the anxiety neurotic usually make for a miserable person—and often (when coupled with something like alcoholism) for a largely dysfunctional one. On paper, however, it's fairly easy to make the anxiety neurotic appear comparatively normal: simply give his own version of his own life.

There is a fragile surface logic and coherence to the actions and reactions of the neurotic, a coherence that no one can follow better than the anxiety neurotic himself. (Since we are exemplifying Crane, I will use the masculine exemplary.) What makes him contradictory is his intensity, with the attendant pain that engenders. But of course that same intensity—'40s and '50s mavens of cultural health and manly art notwithstanding—can also demand an aesthetic response; can command the excess articulation that *is* poetry or art.

"There was something about that restaurant last night that just made me uncomfortable, a funny smell or something," the severe neurotic explains to a friend the next day, "so I left without ordering—and finally, a little later, I stopped and picked up a hamburger."

What he does not bother to say is that his leaving the restaurant entailed suddenly leaping from his chair, overturning it behind him, as well as knocking over a glass of water just set out on the table, and bolting from the place, bumping into a waiter in the process; nor does he mention two other restaurants he tried to go into, from which he made equally untoward exits, panicked and precipitous, unsure if he smelled the same odor or not; nor does he explain that the hamburger he finally ate came, three hours later, after standing in front of a hamburger joint for twenty minutes, afraid to go inside, until he finally gave the money to another customer who was just going in, and asked him to buy and bring it out to him.

"A couple of weeks ago I was in a bakery, where this saleswoman completely refused to look at me while she was serving me, till I just had to tell her, you can't treat customers that way," the same anxiety neurotic explains to a friend, a month after the fact. "But, I'll tell you, having to talk to her that way, it bothered me for the rest of the week." What he does not tell his friend, however, is that the saleswoman's preoccupied "Okay, honey, what do you want, now?" elicited ten minutes of shouting and intense raving on his part, storming back and forth and banging his fist on the glass counter, till—at the threat of police retaliation—he ran from the shop to stand shaking in the street for twenty minutes, finally to make his way home, whereupon he went to bed and stayed there, only desultorily getting up to eat or go to the bathroom, for the next five and a half days, overwhelmed with thoughts now of revenge, now of suicide.

If you should catch him out (say you're actually with him during one of these episodes), the anxiety neurotic takes refuge in the supreme rationality of his own responses. There was some annoying smell, some sound, or some behavior on the part of someone else—he isn't making it up—that would have upset anyone. Just ask anyone else if he or she doesn't find similar things annoying. His distress, he will maintain, is perfectly understandable, perfectly normal. What he remains all but blind to, and is all but incapable of understanding should you try to explain it to him, is that some lack of motivation is not what earmarks his behavior as irrational; rather it is the intensity, the extremity of his response, and finally the misery it causes him, which makes it appear to most other people extreme or inappropriate, and thus probably in need of change, whether through therapy or medication.

The anxiety neurotic's response, however, is to hide the behavior whenever possible and otherwise normalize it through retelling and rationalization.

Unterecker's dropping of both the Woodstock and Brooklyn suicide attempts (because, presumably, Crane himself never mentioned them in print or in a letter) is in complicity with the anxiety neurotic's general self-presentation as a rational being. This complicity works all through Unterecker's biography. Unterecker tells us that Crane quit his job at J. Walter Thompson's advertising agency after three months because he didn't like the regimentation and the time it took away from his writing; but he doesn't mention the row on the final day or that Crane threw everything in his office desk drawers out his window before leaving.

The point is, there is a psychological relation between the young man who angrily tossed the contents of his desk out the window on his last day of work at Thompson's and the one who, three or six weeks later, astonished Mrs. Lachaise with his attempt to ax himself drunkenly to death after dinner, however ineffectually—as there is a relation with the young man who normalized these tales out of his own conversational and epistolary self-presentation. Unterecker's is as much a deception as Crane's protests to his mother and father in countless letters that he was looking for work, that he was seeking a job, were a deception. Possibly as that necessity to work became greater and greater, it became self-deception. But the fact was, for more than a few months at a time, Crane *couldn't* work (certainly not at any job entailing responsibility)—and we know this because of the disastrous results that occurred (indeed that became more and more disastrous) every time he tried. Yet Crane could never admit it; and his father and mother could never let themselves see it.

The problem of our knowing where one epoch or another places such a condition on the three-dimensional grid cut through by ethics, illness, and contingency is a matter of our understanding that particular epoch's psychosocial discourse. But when either the anxiety neurotic himself or the sympathetic biographer attempt to smooth such a condition out of existence, and the only traces remaining are the overall pattern, then the ability to look through the material and judge it properly requires some psychological perspicacity.

If Crane couldn't work, he could, for a while, write poetry. And he wrote it committedly, intelligently, and brilliantly. That Crane was as neurotic as he was makes the fact that he could control his poetic output as carefully as he did only the more heroic. But this is perhaps the greatest reason we need a new biography, one in which the internal demons against which Crane labored can be explored and his triumphs and failures before them appreciated for what they were—rather than one in which they are systematically suppressed because they are not deemed appropriate for the creation of "truly healthy" (or, for that matter, "authentically sick") art. Any uneasiness Unterecker has about dealing with Crane's homosexuality or alcoholism is finally, I believe, only a smaller part of this larger problem; and it is the larger problem that calls for another careful review of Crane's life—one that will acknowledge what he suffered.

There are neurotic homosexuals and non-neurotic homosexuals, though Unterecker (himself gay) probably was not sure this was the case when he was writing. Crane was one of the former. What Unterecker's uncertainty finally causes him to do is indulge the identical suppressions and self-normalization characteristic of the anxiety neurotic. In that sense, what we need is a less neurotically self-protective biography of Crane, done with similar care and scholarship. The revelation of Crane's neurosis, if anything, does not make Crane's pleas to his father for financial support any less moving. Rather it makes his father's failure to provide him with regular financial support the more tragic —nor is either side's position improved by the fact that neither could see, nor admit, Crane's condition directly.

But here I turn to summarize and recapitulate. Mariani's new biography *The Broken Tower* is a good read. A single word kept surfacing and resurfacing in my mind while I was reading, however: Under-articulated. While the overall shape of Crane's story is largely here, often Mariani's account fails to foreground (or, in many cases, even include) the details that make the given incident meaningful. The thinness of his account of Crane's visit to Elbert Hubbard's Roycroft or the inclusion of one suicide attempt (and his treatment of it) but his overlooking of another are just particular cases in point, which could be added to endlessly.

Crane was a modernist poet, an experimental poet. His work is fundamentally different from the relatively referentially "transparent" work of his near contemporaries, Frost, Millay, Benét, or Robinson—all of whom received Pulitzer Prizes in the same decade that Crane's work was making the laborious journey from all but unknown to literary scandal. Crane's poetics directly underlie the currents leading to our contemporary L=A=N=G=U=A=G=E poets, such as Ron Silliman, Lyn Hejinian, Charles Bernstein, Bruce Andrews, and Susan Howe, a poetics grounded in what Silliman has called "the materiality of the signifier." Crane's poems have the interest outside their own historical moment that they do because Crane was so intensely a product of that history. ("Cape Hatteras" is as much "about" the international twenty-fifth-anniversary celebration of the Wright Brothers' 1903 triumph at Kitty Hawk—headline news around the world in 1928, with endless celebrations and aeronautics demonstrations, three months before Crane launched into the poem's final version—as it is about Kitty Hawk or the Cape *per se*; though the celebration is not mentioned by Mariani.) Thus it is precisely the sort of uncontentious biography that Mariani here attempts that needs to be most expertly grounded in history and poetics, however lightly they are appealed to in the course of the work.

In Mariani I miss both sorely.

Paradoxically, the legacy of Pound and Eliot, the great experimenters, is today a kind of neoclassicism: often beautiful, but more frequently pallid, with all that made Pound and Eliot experimental (the erudition, the willed obscurity, the collage techniques, the anti-narrative fragmentation) today set aside as affectations of their times, and replaced by a fetishization of Flaubertian clarity —precisely the "structural clarity" championed by Crane's one-time supporter and eventual adversary Yvor Winters.

Today Crane, along with William Carlos Williams, seems rather the source of all that is alive and changing in poetry—possibly because, more than either Eliot or Pound, Crane and Williams risked coming closer to those two rich sources of poetic renewal: in Williams's case, "the language really used by men," and, in Crane's, the creation of a wholly invented language, which, while it was supremely attentive to the mechanics of actual speech (what makes it so alive), was finally a language so radically artifactual that it could never be uttered by any actual living human.

For all its new material about Crane's sex life, Mariani's biography makes no attempt to supersede, say, Unterecker's, and many passages come to us as if through a children's game of round-robin telephone, with pointless errors and distortions creeping in throughout. If we are to gain insight into, or even get a meaningful picture of, who Crane was, we need a biography that faces Crane's sexual and psychological situation with more detail and care than Unterecker's, not less. Moreover, we need one with more psychological—not to mention textual—acuteness *and* historical sensitivity than Mariani's.

—*April 1999 / June 2006*
New York City

NOTES

I would like to thank the docents of the Roycroft Campus Museum, who were obliging and informative when I visited East Aurora, New York, during my researching of Crane, and who showed me the dining room where the young Crane ate at Elbert and Alice's table, and the dormitory in which he lived, and the library where he doubtless browsed, during the time he was Hubbard's "Valued Helper," as Hubbard called him in the signed gift that remained in Crane's possession until his death.

1. Crane's most recent and thorough biographer Clive Fisher (*Hart Crane: A Life*. Yale University Press, 2002) resolves the problem by citing a copy of Hubbard's *Little Journeys to the Homes of English Authors*, presumably given Crane on his leaving East Aurora and signed, "To Harold Crane My Valued helper at Roycroft Elbert Hubbard April 20 1915." Thus Horton and Mariani are right; Weber, Unterecker, and I are wrong. My apologies, Professor M. But even Fisher calls the seventeen days between April 20, the date of the gift, and May 7, the date of Elbert and Alice's death, "three weeks" (SRD, 2005). It's closer to two by a day.

2. Today Dudley Digges is best known for his supporting role in the 1933 film of H. G. Wells's *The Invisible Man*, starring Claude Rains.

3. See my "Atlantis Rose . . . Notes on Hart Crane," previously included in *Longer Views* (Wesleyan University Press, 1995), and in this volume: see page 122.

WORKS CONSULTED

Balch, David Arnold. *Elbert Hubbard: Genius of Roycroft*. New York: Frederick A. Stokes Company, 1940.
Brown, Susan Jenkins. *Robber Rocks: Letters and Memories of Hart Crane, 1923–1932*. Middletown: Wesleyan University Press, 1969.
Browning, Robert. "Memorabilia," from *Men and Women* (1855), in *Robert Browning: The Poems*. Volume One. New York: Penguin Books, 1981.
Brunner, Edward. *Splendid Failure: The Making of "The Bridge."* Urbana: University of Illinois Press, 1985.
Cowley, Malcolm. *Exile's Return*. New York: Viking Press, 1951.
Crane, Hart, *The Collected Poems of Hart Crane*, ed. with an Introduction by Waldo Frank, Liveright Publishing Corporation, New York, 1933.
———. *The Complete Poems and Selected Letters and Prose of Hart Crane*. Edited by Brom Weber. New York: Liveright Publishing Corporation, 1966.
———. *The Letters of Hart Crane, 1916–1932*. Edited by Brom Weber. Berkeley: University of California Press, 1965.
———. *Letters of Hart Crane and His Family*. Edited by Thomas S. W. Lewis. New York and London: Columbia University Press, 1974.
———. *O My Land, My Friends: The Selected Letters of Hart Crane*. Edited by Langdon Hammer and Brom Weber. New York: Four Walls, Eight Windows, 1997.
———. *The Poems of Hart Crane*. Edited by Marc Simon. Introduction by John Unterecker. New York: Liveright Publishing Corporation, 1986; reissued as *Complete Poems of Hart Crane*, 1993.
Crane, Hart, and Yvor Winters. *Hart Crane and Yvor Winters: Their Literary Correspondence*. Edited by Thomas Parkinson. Berkeley: University of California Press, 1978.
Edleman, Lee. *Transmemberment of Song: Hart Crane's Anatomy and Rhetoric of Desire*. Stanford: Stanford University Press, 1987.
Fisher, Clive. *Hart Crane: A Life*. New Haven: Yale University Press, 2002.

Gile, Paul. *Hart Crane: The Contexts of "The Bridge."* Cambridge: Cambridge University Press, 1986.

Greenberg, Samuel. *Poems by Samuel Greenberg: A Selection from the Manuscripts.* Edited by Harold Holden and Jack McManis. Preface by Allen Tate. New York: Henry Holt and Company, 1947.

Horton, Philip. *Hart Crane: The Life of an American Poet.* W. W. Norton, 1937.

Loveman, Sam. *Hart Crane: A Conversation with Samuel Loveman.* Edited by Kirby Congdon and Jay Socin. New York: Interim Books, 1963.

Mariani, Paul. *The Broken Tower: The Life of Hart Crane.* New York: W. W. Norton Company, 1999.

Unterecker, John. *Voyager: The Life of Hart Crane.* New York: Farrar, Straus and Giroux, 1969; paperback edition: Liveright, 1987.

Voelcker, Hunce. *The Hart Crane "Voyages."* Introduction by Sam Loveman. New York: The Brownstone Press, 1967.

Weber, Brom. *Hart Crane: A Critical and Biographical Study.* New York: The Bodley Press, 1948.

31

9/11: Echoes

Against the echoes of our feet in the stairwell—she was coming up; I was going down, holding the banister, step at a time, with my cane—it brought back those seventeen months of queues in which they tried to get food to the prisoners without which they would have starved, and a woman who'd learned that the one beside her was Akhmatova leaned to whisper: "Can you write this . . . ?" with all the situation's intense differences, then, now.

In our stairwell, a decade younger than my soon-to-be-sixty, Lois looked up, smiled, stopped: "Hello, Chip. How are you? Ah . . . You know my daughter, Lois. She has the same name as mine. I was going to tell you this. Really, I'm so glad I ran into you. I know you've seen her in the building here: my daughter Lois—she's twenty-two. You know, she worked in the World Trade Center. She was engaged to a fireman. David, he was twenty-five."

"Is she all *right?*" Then I thought I was being too bumptious.

"Well, sort of. They were planning to get married, just this October. Her and David. That morning, three weeks ago, you know, because she wasn't feeling well, she called in about twenty to nine to say she would be coming in late that morning—maybe she would be there by ten-thirty. So, of course five minutes after she hung up, the first plane hit. At the firehouse David heard there was trouble; he didn't know she'd stayed home. He had his whole ladder company up and running down there to offer help and see what they could do—and, of course, to get her out of there. Well, when the buildings went down, he was killed—and the other boys. They were men, but I call them boys—because, you know, I'm fifty-two."

"Oh . . ." I said, as sincerely as I could, "Lois, that's . . . awful!" How many times that month did we say or think or write, *That's awful!* "How's Lois doing . . . ?"

"How do you think?" elder Lois said too quickly, this plump Latin woman with champagne-colored hair. "She's a basket case! She's seeing a therapist— but I don't know if it's doing much good. Oh, she just cries . . ." Lois shook her head. "David was going to get her a dog for a wedding present. They'd picked it out together, but it was going to stay in the kennel until they moved into their own place—this month, in October. Well, the other boys in the ladder company, the ones who were left—they got the dog for her and gave it to her. For David. Oh, Chip—I just don't know what to do for her. You're a writer, aren't you?"

"Yes. That's right."

Lois looked at me.

"I mean, do you think there is any way you could write . . . ? I mean, write something? To tell people that story? I don't know—I just would like it if people knew, somehow. That things like that happened." Lois shook her head again.

Over the next weeks I've thought of other things I would also like to write about: About Vince's Turkish wife, Asude, going back to Istanbul to help after the earthquakes. About a piece of music that made me stop and listen to it, as it tumbled out among a dozen unmemorable songs from the speakers beside my computer. About Blanche McCreary Boyd saying, "Write your story as simply as you can for the most intelligent person in the room." About why it is so much easier to tell Lois's mother's tale (which I have, among a dozen others, certainly more than a dozen times, now) than it is to write it. About how, at Paul's party where the two artists were about to do the video and computer demonstration of their memorial laser columns, the Iranian woman interrupted to ask us for a minute's silence for those bombed in her country. About crossing Broadway at 79th and going from bright sun into the shadow of a building, where—now that the light was off my dusty glasses—I saw people coming toward me over the street, and a smoky blue afterimage pulsed over the face of a young woman stepping off the corner, lighting a cigarette: Lois (Lois's daughter) smokes—I've seen her smoking in the stairwell; though not for three months.

But on the steps, I said to Lois (her mother, Lois), "Lois. You know. I don't really know—really. But. I mean, well . . ."

Well, but, there is some of the story.

—October 2002
New York City

32

Eleusis

A Note on Friedrich Hölderlin

Two years older than Coleridge and Novalis (they were exact contemporaries), eighteen years older than Byron, twenty-two years older than Shelley, and twenty-five years older than Keats, Johann Christian Freidrich Hölderlin was born in Lauffen, Swabia, a town on the Neckar River, on March 20, 1770 — the same year as the births of Beethoven, Beethoven's lifelong friendly rival Atron Reicha, and Hegel in Germany, and of Wordsworth in England.

The poet's mother was a pious German woman, Johanna Christiana Heyn. His father was Heinrich Freidrich Hölderlin. Heinrich Friedrich died when Hölderlin was two. When he was four his mother married Johann Christoff Gok, of the nearby town of Nürtingen. Two years later, Gok became Nürtingen's mayor. The poet Hölderlin was the eldest of four: he had sister, a brother, and a half-brother by his stepfather. The mayor died when Hölderlin was nine. For the rest of his life, Hölderlin's mother seems to have been the major figure for him. He corresponded with her extensively, generally warmly and lovingly, giving her many details of his doings in his letters to her, up until his madness.

Even so, in Hölderlin's biography she does not come off too well. She and her son by the mayor, Karl Gok, withheld a major legacy Hölderlin was supposed to inherit. When he went mad and was in the care of the generous and good-hearted carpenter Zimmer, they contributed nothing to his upkeep — not even the interest on his legacy. Johanna died in 1827. On Hölderlin's death in 1843, Karl Gok took the considerable inheritance for himself. It had been due the poet, back in 1791, when he'd turned twenty-one. Had Hölderlin received it, certainly it would have made the decade and a half of his creativity far easier and less traumatic than it was, as well as the subsequent thirty-six years of his confinement. As far as we know, the poet may never even have realized this sum was due him. The money is unmentioned in his correspondence with his mother or anyone else.

During his childhood, everyone assumed Hölderlin would be a minister. At twelve and thirteen, in preparation for his entrance examination, he received private tutoring in Latin, Greek, Hebrew, and rhetoric, as well as music. In 1784 he entered the Lower Monastery School at Deckendorf, to begin the courses that would lead to his becoming a Lutheran minister. There he befriended the young Schelling—age seven—whom on several occasions he protected from the teasings and tauntings of the older children, which started a lifelong friendship between the two boys. He began to read travel literature, which became major nourishment for his imagination.

Hölderlin's passionate and influential childhood reading included Klopstock, Young, and (of course, like everyone else—they were the *Lord of the Rings* of their day!) McPherson's *Ossian* prose-poems/forgeries. In 1786 he moved on to the Higher Monastery School at Malbourn, where he met and fell in love with Louise Nast. In 1787 he had his first doubts as to whether or not the ministry was his calling. Now, at Louise Nast's urging, he added Schiller's revolutionary drama *Don Carlos* to his reading.

When he was eighteen, in 1788, along with G. W. F. Hegel, Hölderlin entered a theological academy, the Stift in Tübingen, where the budding philosopher and the burgeoning poet were soon roommates. Warm and enthusiastic letters passed between them when they were apart during the holidays and over summer vacations. At the Stift, young Schelling entered the seminary and became the third member of their group. Hölderlin's more mature reading would include Rousseau, Plato, Leibnitz, and Spinoza. There at the Stift, Hölderlin became a fine classicist, even as authorities kept greater and greater surveillance over the theological students, so that their enthusiasm for France's 1789 revolution did not translate into political activity at home. By 1790, among the students the most revered writer was Immanuel Kant, whose philosophy (wrote Hölderlin's fellow student Magenau) "made our heads spin, and the pulpit echoed of space and time."

Hölderlin's engagement with Louise Nast broke off in 1789, the year of the French Revolution. "I wish you happiness if you choose one more worthy than I, and then surely you will understand that you could never have been happy with your morose, ill-humored, sick friend," he wrote her on their separation. His next passion was for Elise Lebret. One German biographer insists that Hölderlin—and most of his circle—was gay. Similar to many gay men, his mother was by far the most important person in Hölderlin's life, and some people have speculated that all these passionate friendships with women were basically platonic.

In 1791, the year after he passed his Magister exams, Hölderlin's first poems saw print ("Holderlin's muse is a solemn muse," wrote Christian Schubart, the editor of the magazine, in his introduction to the issue). Traveling with friends in Switzerland, he contemplated leaving the Stift, and he wrote his mother of a series of terrible headaches and his first doubts as to his religious calling: "And then one's inner life no longer enjoys its youthful vigor."

In 1792, the same year he began work on his novel *Hyperion*, at the outbreak of war between France and the Austro-Prussian coalition Hölderlin wrote to his sister Ricke, "Believe me, dear sister, we will face grim times, should the Austrians be victorious. The abuse of princely power will be terrible. You must believe me and pray for the French, the defenders of human rights."

After Hegel's departure from the Stift in 1793, Hölderlin witnessed many aspects and examples of the pain and the stupidity of war. As he wrote to his half-brother Karl:

My affections are now less directed toward particular individuals. The object of my love is the entire human race, though not, of course, as we so often find it, namely in the condition of corruption, servility and inertia. . . . I love the race of coming centuries. For this is my deepest hope, the faith that keeps me strong and vital: our grandchildren will have it better than we, freedom must finally come, and virtue will better flourish in the warmth of freedom's sacred light than in the ice-cold zone of despotism. We live in times when all things are working toward better days. These seeds to enlightenment, these still wishes and strivings of iso-lated individuals for the development of the human race, will spread and grow strong and bear marvelous fruit . . . this is the sacred purpose of my wishes and my activity: that I might stir the seeds of change that will ripen in a future age.

This same year Hölderlin met Schiller, who was impressed enough with the twenty-three-year-old poet to recommend him as a tutor (with some reserva-tions) to Charlotte von Kalb for her son Fritz. Hölderlin took up the position at the beginning of 1794. Though he began his duties with great enthusiasm, Fritz's masturbation became a major block to his education. From the euphe-misms of the letters it is hard to tell whether the practice was truly excessive on the boy's part or whether it was Hölderlin's and Fritz's parents' (at least by today's standards) overreaction. In one 1795 letter to his mother, Hölderlin explained that he would sit up all night long, guarding the boy to prevent his self-indulgence, with the result that he was too exhausted to tutor him during the day. Finally Charlotte relieved Hölderlin of his responsibility for her son and terminated his employment, providing him with enough money to live for several more months in Jena. During that year he went on to meet Herder and attended Fichte's lectures, as had the German poet Novalis only a few years before. In Jena, Hölderlin was befriended by Isaac von Sinclair, a student in whose garden house the poet took a room for several weeks. Sinclair was shortly expelled from the university for his radical political activity, but the poet and the firy republican remained close friends. About this time, having heard a reading of part of the novel at Sinclair's, the publisher Cotta agreed to bring out *Hyperion* on its completion. After sending a letter entreating his mother to allow him to put his full energies into his writing, in June Hölderlin returned to Nürtingen, arriving greatly distressed: the abandonment of his Jena circle of friends, especially Schiller, seemed to have left him too upset to work. At this point he made some visits to Tübingen, where he took hungrily to the philosophical conversations available with friends he made there. The year ended with the offer of a new position as tutor of the children of a rich Frankfurt banker, Gontard.

In January of 1796, twenty-six-year-old Hölderlin assumed his duties in Frankfurt. Soon he was captivated—and inspired—by the intelligence and charm of Gontard's young wife, Suzette, who soon became the "Diotima" of his novel and his poems. (Shortly after their graduation, Hölderlin had gone so far as to secure Hegel a tutoring job with a family of his acquaintance. And while Hölderlin was working for the Gontards, in 1796 the philosopher wrote a 58-line oracular poem, "Eleusis," dedicated to his poet friend and praising his poetic genius and attendant high character.) That summer, the war with France forced Suzette and her children—along with Hölderlin—to flee Frankfurt. In the town of Kessel, where they took refuge, Hölderlin met Wilhelm Heinze, a friend of the Gontards' and author of the novel *Ardinghello*. In 1797, true to his word, back in Jena, Cotta brought out the first volume of *Hyperion* in mid-April.

Now Schiller arranged a meeting between Hölderlin and Goethe, who briefly talked about the young poet's work with him. Echoing Schiller, the elder poet advised Hölderlin to work on "short poems about particular objects of human interest." Pretty much everyone, over the previous year or so, had seemed to agree that the heights of philosophy, where by temperament Hölderlin wanted to dwell, were finally too heady for him and left the young man exhausted, drained, and sickly.

Possibly because volume one of *Hyperion* was now a reality, even as he worked on volume two Hölderlin planned out an ambitious tragedy, *Empedokles*, projected at five acts, on the Greek model, based on the story of the philosopher who, in despair of the world and the uselessness of all knowledge, threw himself into Mount Etna's volcanic cone in Syracuse (Sicily). Wrote Hölderlin of his hero: "He is the sworn enemy of all one-sided existence and thus . . . dissatisfied . . . even in truly pleasant conditions simply because they are particular conditions." Completing one act (with a few small gaps), he got halfway through a second, and amassed endless notes on the rest, but—though there are basically three extant versions, one almost complete—it remained unfinished.

By the end of 1798, however, Gontard had become unhappy over the intensity of the relationship between his young, brilliant wife and his children's tutor. In September, Hölderlin was dismissed. For the next two years, Hölderlin's and Suzette's letters and—very occasional—meetings were carried on in secret. Cotta published *Hyperion*'s second volume in 1799 (the year of Beethoven's first symphony); Hölderlin sent Suzette a copy. In that second volume "Diotima" (who dies in the end) is a major element. The letter he sent Suzette, which accompanied a copy of the book, speaks of a disagreement they'd had over whether "Diotima" should, in the end, die or not. Hölderlin had felt that her death was integral to the novel's tragic structure. Suzette had felt it would truer if she had lived.

A further year of irruptive creativity followed, during which Hölderlin had his last meeting with Suzette. It included the nine eighteen-line stanzas of his elegy "Brod und Wein" ("Bread and Wine"), which he dedicated to Heinze, whom he'd met the year before when Heinze had sheltered Suzette, her children, and Hölderlin in Kessel.

Hölderlin began 1801 with still another tutoring position, this time in Switzerland. There he composed his 156-line free verse poem "Friedensfrier" ("Celebration of Peace"). Although (for unknown reasons) he was let go from his position by mid-April, his employers gave Hölderlin a positive letter of reference. Returning home to Nürtingen, he took a boat across Lake Constance, which he celebrated in his hymn "Heimkumft" ("Homecoming"). Writing from home, in a last letter to Schiller, Hölderlin pleaded for a position as a lecturer in Greek at Jena. Schiller did not reply. A planned edition of his poems fell through.

Up until this time, we have a fairly complete record of Hölderlin's activities and travels. By now he'd published the two volumes of *Hyperion* and some sixty poems in various literary magazines. Here, though, a six-month gap occurs in the record.

Another offer of a tutoring job came, this time in Bordeaux, and on December 10, 1801, Hölderlin took off from his mother's by foot.

He did not reach Bordeaux until the end of January 1802, where he wrote back to his mother:

> I have experienced so much that I can barely speak of it now. For the last few days my journey has passed amidst a beautiful springtime, but just prior to this, on the fearsome snow-covered heights of the Auvergne, in the midst of storms and wilderness, in the icy night with my loaded pistol beside me in my rough bed—there I prayed the finest prayer of my life, and one I shall never forget. I've arrived in one piece—give thanks with me!

This position too lasted only three months, and he made his way back to Germany, probably by way of Paris. During this time, basically Hölderlin was a homeless vagabond. From his own accounts, later, we know that he almost froze to death in the mountains on several occasions. He saw lots of suffering in the war-torn provinces, which tore his soul apart and—perhaps—contributed to a psychotic break.

Only in mid-June do we pick him up again, once he'd arrived in Stuttgart, where he visited a friend (writes his first biographer, Weiblinger): "pale as a corpse, emaciated, with hollow wild eyes, long hair and beard, and dressed like a beggar."

Within days his friend Sinclair took him for a brief visit to his family, back in Nürtingen, where his half-brother Karl found him obviously mad. His conversation was deranged; he broke out into irrational rages and seemed incapable of caring for himself. Then Sinclair returned with Hölderlin to Stuttgart where, on June 22, Sinclair told the poet that Suzette Gontard, his "Diotima," had indeed died—of tuberculosis.

Once more at Nürtingen, Hölderlin was placed under medical care. Now Sinclair took him to Regensburg where Sinclair's employer, the Landgrave of Homburg, informally commissioned Hölderlin to write a poem expressing "true Christian piety," which started the poet to work on what would become his most famous poem, "Patmos." Now Sinclair sent an optimistic letter to Hölderlin's mother, telling of her son's "complete return to mental health." But this was probably optimistic exaggeration. Back in Nürtingen, the poet wrote to his old friend Böhlendorff, the recipient of many of the letters that had gone into the first volume of *Hyperion*:

> It's been a long time since I wrote to you; I've been in France and have seen the mournful, lonely earth, the shepherds of southern France and things of beauty, men and women who have grown up with the fear of confused loyalties and of hunger. The mighty element, the fire from heaven and the tranquility of the people, their life amidst nature, their simplicity and contentment, moved me to no end, and as it is said of heroes, I can well say that Apollo has struck me.

In June of 1803, Schelling met with his old friend, who had once protected him from the taunts and the bullyings of the other boys. Shortly Schelling wrote to Hölderlin's former Stift roommate Hegel:

> The saddest thing I saw during my stay here was Hölderlin. Since his trip to France . . . his spirit is totally shattered. Although he is to a certain extent still able to do some work—translating Greek, for example—he is otherwise totally withdrawn. The sight of him really shook me up: he neglects his appearance to a repulsive degree and although his manner of speaking would seem not to indicate madness, he has taken on the outward demeanor of those in that condition. There are no hopes for recovery if he stays here. I thought of asking you if you could look after him were he to come to Jena, which seems to be his wish.

Hegel was not enthusiastic and, despite his praise in "Eleusis," basically withdrew from the situation. So the idea was dropped.

Hölderlin was indeed well enough to live with a friend, Christian Lauderer, giving private lessons and translating *Oedipus* and *Antigone* from the Greek, which he sent to the publisher Friedrich Wilman that year and which were published in two volumes in 1804.

By now Hölderlin was far less involved with his friends. He was translating Pindar, and during the same time, he revised a number of early poems, "Canticles for Night" (doubtless inspired by the late Novalis, whom he had met briefly at the famous "Romantics" House in Jena, and whose *Hymns to the Night* had recently been published in the *Atheneum*).

One psychoanalytic biographer, Jean Laplanche (in his book *Hölderlin ou la question du père*), felt that the lack of a father in Hölderlin's life was the source of the great absence that Hölderlin was always writing about in his poems, hymns, and fragments (a theme that the philosopher Martin Heidegger would feel deeply in sympathy with): the "God" that is "near / and hard to grasp" in Hölderlin's "Patmos," his most famous poem, and who in so many others is "hiding," "about to arrive," "far off," or "recently departed," but is never *there*, present. This absence, which clears a space for the transcendental to be a human or social contruct—an effect of discourse rather than a substantive thing-in-itself—may be one of the richest images operative throughout the modern era, as disseminated by Nietzsche in the second half of the nineteenth century, by Heidegger during the first half of the twentieth century, and by Derrida during that century's second half. Laplanche suggested as well that the lack of a father may have had something to do with an absence of active sexuality in Hölderlin's life.

In a review article on Laplanche's biography, Michel Foucault takes careful but finally vigorous exception to this idea.

Periods of lucidity now alternated with periods of derangement. Hölderlin became deeply involved with the republican political activists (Sinclair, his friend from Jena, and Blackenstein, who betrayed them to the authorities), and was arrested for treason—getting off only because the court decided he was mad.

During their trial for high treason for involvement in a Jacobin conspiracy against the Elector of Württemberg, before the sentencing Hölderlin "fell into a sort of madness, hurled insults at Sinclair and the Jacobins and cried out to the astonishment of all present: I am through with all Jacobins! Vive le Roi!"

From here comes the theory, still held by some, that Hölderlin's madness was, at least in part, a pretense to escape the authorities; this idea was sparked by another too-optimistic letter by Sinclair to Hölderlin's mother: "Not only me, but some 6–8 other people as well who have made his acquaintance, are convinced that what looks like mental confusion is . . . in fact a calculated act of simulation." Finally, however, there is too much evidence that his mind had really snapped. The physician brought in by the court at this time wrote: "During the course of my visits his condition worsened and his speech became more unintelligible. Once his madness reached the point of a constant, wild agitation and his speech became a jumble of German, Greek, and Latin, one could no longer understand him at all." Before going into exile from Württemberg, Leo von Zeckedorf, one of Sinclair's co-conspirators, visited Hölderlin and left with a number of the poet's poems—"Bread and Wine," "Patmos," "The Rhine," and "Remembrance"—which he later published, in part or in whole, without the poet's knowledge.

A "job" as a librarian (really a sinecure, which also included a small cottage to live in) given Hölderlin by the local Landgrave at his friend Sinclair's request, fell through after a few months, largely because of his—and even more-so Sinclair's—political involvement, but also because of his unstable mental state. In 1806, at thirty-six, Hölderlin was hospitalized at the Autenrieth Clinic, again at Tübingen.

The Landgravine Caroline Hessen-Homberg wrote to her daughter, on the morning of September 11: "Poor Holterline [*sic*] was carried away this morning. . . . He tried desperately to throw himself from the carriage, but the man charged with his care held him back. Holterline believed that he was being abducted . . . and scratched the man with his long fingernails until the man was all bloody." At the clinic the treatment—bleedings, ice-cold baths—was not unlike what was to be inflicted on Antonin Artaud at Rodez, two hundred years later, and might well have killed the poet. A fellow patient actually died of the regimen while Hölderlin was there. But Hölderlin survived.

After seven months of confinement, in 1807 a carpenter, Ernst Zimmer, a great enthusiast of *Hyperion* (though not particularly interested in the poems—one reason Zimmer is often described as "semi-literate"), after visiting Hölderlin at the asylum several times volunteered to take the poet out of the Tübingen hospital, and moved him across town to the stone tower on the Nekar riverside in which Zimmer and his family lived, since the madman was now fairly calm and seemed to have settled into a harmless dementia. In 1806 Zimmer acquired a flute and piano for the poet, two instruments that he had played during the time of his sanity.

Playing on them seemed to calm him even further.

Though doctors had given him "only three years to live," Hölderlin stayed with Zimmer in the upper floor of the stone tower for the next thirty-six years and died at seventy-three. Meanwhile, admirers of his early poetry put out a second edition of *Hyperion* in 1822 (spearheaded by Waiblinger, whose enthusiasm for the poems brought him to visit the poet at this time, and to lead the Hölderlin "revival") and the first volume of Hölderlin's *Selected Poems* in 1826 (the year Beethoven completed the finale of string quartet Op. 130, not long before his death in 1827). Other than an extremely small circle of readers, all major interest in Hölderlin dates from this "revival."

In 1827, Waiblinger published his essay "Friedrich Hölderlin's Life, Poetry, and Madness."

From this swell of attention until his death in 1843, for the last fifteen years of his life Hölderlin was something of a European intellectual curiosity. Many people visited him; some even contributed (minimally) to his upkeep. Frequently they would ask for a poem, and Hölderlin would dash off a "mad" fragment for them, often in exchange for tobacco. These fifty-odd "Scardanelli" poems (named for the person the mad Hölderlin insisted was writing them) were later collected; but, while they have a certain surreal slant, sadly they are not quite mad *enough* to be interesting. The subject of several essays (e.g., "The Essence of Poetry," "Remembrance of the Poet," "Man Dwells Poetically . . .") and three summer-long lecture courses by Martin Heidegger (one course on "Germania" and "The Rhine," another on "Andenken" ["Remembrance"], and still a third on "The Ister," an unfinished hymn by Hölderlin, titled by the editor Norbert von Hellingrath. "Patmos"—to repeat—is often considered his greatest poem. It begins with the famous call to the unrisen sun: *Jetz komme, Feuer! / Begierig sind wir / Zu shauan den Tag* (. . . Now come, fire! / We are eager / To see the day . . .).

More than a hundred students turned out at Tübingin to walk behind his casket with the Zimmer family—with whom he finally lived in their "tower" on the Necker—to the grave site; most, like Zimmer, enthusiasts of the novel.

Hölderlin's work has been the topic of readings by Paul de Man and practically every great European literary theoretician or philosopher. With his novel *Hyperion*, the unfinished play *Empedokles*, and the elegies, hymns, fragments, and translations written between 1790 and his 1806 confinement for madness, today Hölderlin is considered the greatest of the early German romantic poets.

An expanded collection of Hölderlin's poetry was released, three years after his death, in 1846, with a biographical essay by his friend Charles Schwab.

—2003
Philadelphia

NOTE

Much of the information and all of the quotations in this essay come from the excellent chronology in Eric L. Santner, ed. *Friedrich Hölderin: Hyperion and Selected Poems*. The German Library, Volume 22. New York: Continuum, 1990.

Acknowledgments

Many of the essays in this collection were previously published, sometimes in earlier versions.

"More About Writing: The Life of/and Writing" was published in the *New York Review of Science Fiction* (October 1990).

"The *Algol* Interview: A Conversation with Darrell Schweitzer" was published in *Algol* 13 (Summer 1976), 16–22.

"Liner Notes, Anecdotes, and Emails on Theodore Sturgeon": The liner notes originally accompanied the LP recording *Theodore Sturgeon Reads Bianca's Hands / The Hurkle Is a Happy Beast / Britt Svenglund from Godbody* (AWR 3340: Alternate World Recordings, 1977). The emails I exchanged with Noël Sturgeon have not previously been published.

"*Star Wars*: A Consideration of a Great New SF Film" was published in *Cosmos Science Fiction and Fantasy Magazine* (November 1977).

"Samuel Delany, Settling Future Limits: An Interview by Pat Califia" was published in *The Advocate* 332 (December 9, 1982).

"Introduction to the Graphic Novel *Empire*" was originally included in Samuel R. Delany and Howard V. Chaykin's *Empire: A Visual Novel* (Berkley/Windhover, 1978).]

"The Gestation of Genres: Literature, Fiction, Romance, Science Fiction, Fantasy . . ." was published in *Intersections: Fantasy and Science Fiction*, edited by Eric S. Rabkin and George E. Slusser (Southern Illinois University Press, 1987).

"Theodore Sturgeon, *In Memoriam*" was published in *Locus* 294 (July 1985).

"Note on Le Guin: The Kesh in Song and Story": This review of Le Guin's *Always Coming Home* was originally published as "The Kesh in Song and Story" in the *New York Times* (September 29, 1985).

"Eden, Eden, Eden: Genesis 2:4–22" was published in *Chain* 11: *Public Forms*, edited by Jena Osman and Juliana Spahr.

"How Not to Teach Science Fiction: Thoughts on Sturgeon's 'Hurricane Trio'" was published in the *New York Review of Science Fiction* (September 1989).

"Letter to *Science Fiction Eye*: Some Impertinent Rebuttals" was published in *Science Fiction Eye* 1, no. 5 (July 1989).

"An Antiphon" was published in the *New York Review of Science Fiction* (January 1991).

"Atlantis Rose . . . : Some Notes on Hart Crane" was previously published in Delany, *Longer Views: Extended Essays* (Wesleyan University Press, 1996).

"Afterword to Theodore Sturgeon's *Argyll*" was previously published in the chapbook *Argyll* (The Sturgeon Project, 1993).

"Interview: Questions by Felice Picano" was previously published in several versions: in the *Washington Blade* (November 31, 1993); in the *Bay Area Reporter* (February 3, 1994); in the *Publishing Triangle* newsletter (Fall/Winter 1993–94); and in *Mandate* magazine (Fall 1993).

"The *Loft* Interview" was published in 1995 in the newsletter of The Loft Literary Center of Minneapolis, Minnesota.

"Note on Robert Hayden's 'Middle Passage'" has not previously been published.

"Beatitudes" has not previously been published.

"Dialogue with Octavia E. Butler" was previously published in *Vibe*, 1997.

"Racism and Science Fiction" was previously published in the *New York Review of Science Fiction* 120 (August 1998); in the book *Dark Matter: A Century of Speculative Fiction from the African Diaspora*, edited by Sheree R. Thomas (Warner Books, 2000); and in Samuel R. Delany's book *The Atheist in the Attic* (PM Press, 2018).

"Some Queer Notions about Race" has not previously been published.

"*The Star-Pit* Notes" was previously published online at www.pseudopodium.org/repress/TheStarPit/SamuelRDelany-NotesOnTheStarPit.html.

"Introducing Octavia E. Butler" has not previously been published.

"Poetry Project Interview: A Silent Interview" was previously published in *The Poetry Project* newsletter (March 18, 1999); and in the book *About Writing: Seven Essays, Four Letters, and Five Interviews* (Wesleyan University Press, 2006).

"How to Do Well in This Class" appears here in print for the first time. This was often distributed as a photocopy to students as a study aid.

"His Wing, His Claw Beneath the Arc of Day" was previously published in Doreet LeVitte Harten's *Heaven* (Ostfildern, Germany: Hatje Cantz, 1999).

"Student of Desire" was previously published as part of "Born in Flames: The short life and long legacy of David Wojnarowicz" in *POZ* (March 1999), www.poz.com/article/Born-in-Flames-1478-6215

"A Centennial Life from the Roaring Twenties: *The Broken Tower: The Life of Hart Crane* by Paul Mariani" has not previously been published.

"9/11: Echoes" was published in *110 Stories: New York Writes After September 11*, edited by Ulrich Baer (New York University Press, 2002).

"Eleusis: A Note on Friedrich Hölderlin" was published in *Encyclopedia, Vol. II, F–K*, edited by Tisa Bryant, Miranda Mellis, and Kate Schatz (Encyclomedia, 2006).

Index

ABOUT THE AUTHOR

Samuel R. Delany is the author of innovative fiction, essays, and
memoir, including more than twenty-five novels. He has received
four Nebula Awards from the Science Fiction Writers of America,
for *Babel-17*, *The Einstein Intersection*, and two of his short stories. He
received Hugo Awards for the novella "Time Considered as a Helix
of Semi-Precious Stones" and his autobiography *The Motion of Light
in Water*. His most recent SF novel is *Through the Valley of the Nest
of Spiders*. Along with fellowships at numerous institutions, he has
taught at the University of Massachusetts in Amherst, SUNY Buffalo,
and Temple University. His honors include the 1997 Kessler Award
for LGBTQ Studies, the 2007 Stonewall Book Award for his novel
Dark Reflections, and the 2015 Nicolas Guillén Award for Philosophical
Literature, and he is the subject of a 2007 documentary film by
Fred Barney Taylor, *The Polymath*. In 2002, he was inducted into the
Science Fiction Hall of Fame, and in 2016 was inducted into the
New York State Writers Hall of Fame. In 2013, the Science Fiction
Writers of America named Delany a Grand Master of Science Fiction.